BISENTIENT

Patrick O'Connor

First Published in Great Britain by Blackbeard Independent Press 2023.

Hardback ISBN: 978-1-3999-3158-8
Paperback ISBN: 978-1-7391136-1-2
E-book ISBN: 978-1-7391136-0-5

To Vee

1

Mason Plater was an experienced cameraman who had worked on award winning documentaries and TV series. He was rubbing his hands vigorously on his jeans to get feeling back in his frozen fingers. He glanced up to see Molly James, a young production intern heading his way.

"Hey Molly!"

"Hey Mason. I'd rather follow you around than that old bat. I might learn something."

"Beatrice isn't so bad." said Mason Plater, smiling. "Most producers are manic, it's in the job description. Anyway all I do is point a camera, not much to it really. Fancy a cuppa?"

With bitter temperatures hanging on into March there was a long line at the refreshment van. Plater would rather have been filming a motion picture or a television series but work was work. He told himself a documentary on an old loony-bin would do until something better came along.

"What's the schedule look like then?" Plater asked.

Molly looked a little surprised that someone with a decade in the business needed information from her then grinned and said "You're in Crew-1 aren't you?"

Plater nodded and looked over to where lighting engineers were unloading their rigs. He wanted to make sure they steered well clear of his delicate equipment.

"Well you're going to be doing some exterior shots for atmosphere and fillers then you have an interview with Dr someone-or-other who runs the place and then something called the Dead Zone."

Plater turned back to Molly, slightly frowning "The Dead Zone?"

"That's what the staff call it. It's a ward where all the patients are in comas or something. They just lie there and don't do anything."

"Sounds great." said Plater, grabbing a handful of small blue packets. "Sugar?"

The buildings of Lievesham Hall were a curious amalgam of Victorian grandeur and suppressed menace but with modern insertions of sky-lit corridors, unexpected open spaces and an ever-present, if subtle, technology. In some of the older parts, with the tall arched windows and the cool heavy walls, you could almost imagine starched nurses pacing the corridors in their sturdy leather shoes, their footsteps echoing like tourists in a cathedral. Who hasn't heard stories of people locked away in Victorian sanatoriums when they were as sane as the next person. Places where society hid away the freaks and failed humanity of generations, along with the truly sick, the simply confused and those considered too dangerous for prison.

Zeigler Ward was a slightly surreal place. Most

obvious was the neatness. Six beds along each wall, all immaculate. There was a table by each bed displaying a vase of flowers and nothing else. Plater couldn't help wondering if the flowers were there just because they were filming. It certainly wasn't for the benefit of the patients. It was a mixed ward but then that hardly mattered as all the patients were motionless, on their backs, precisely positioned in the middle of the bed. A small touch screen device instead of the old clipboard hung on the wall and recorded aspects of treatment. The chemicals and electronics required to sustain life were discreetly placed beneath the beds and in the side cupboard. After some discussion it had been decided to film around bed number four. The patient in this bed was a very attractive blonde woman. Before filming started patient number four's long hair was brushed and arranged to frame her striking features against the white pillow.

Twenty minutes later it was all over. Some words from Dr Granger about the special problems dealing with patients in such states and then a leading question that allowed him to describe one of his pet theories. It was about potential use of drugs and new brain scanning techniques to identify patients with what the profession termed potential for cognition. In layman's terms some patients in apparent vegetative states might in reality be aware but just unable to communicate. This is sometimes referred to as 'locked in syndrome' and Plater found that idea one of the most disturbing he had ever heard.

All but Plater then left the ward. He was done for the day and took his time detaching the camera from its stand and packing it away lovingly. He began to think about patient number four. She was perhaps in her late thirties, with smooth pale skin. Plater had thought how sad it was that all these people spent their lives unmoving and probably unthinking. Growing older with the seasons but never living their life. Kept alive by a chemical cocktail delivered through a tube.

He couldn't help spending a few moments gazing down at patient number four. As he sighed at the unfairness and turned to grab the trolley he jerked his hand away as if it had been stung. Something had touched his fingers. He looked down at patient number four once more. She was still in the same restful pose. Of course she was. He must have imagined it, or caught his hand on something. He was being ridiculous. The slight breeze from the swing doors at the end of the ward had pushed a wisp of hair across patient number four's cheek. Plater felt an urge to restore her perfection. As he reached for the errant hair, he stopped short. Patient number four had opened her eyes. Their vibrant blue held Plater's gaze in a grip he would later recall as both pleasant and unnerving. Her eyes closed. Plater could feel his heart beating. He glanced around but the ward was as silent and bereft of conscious humanity as when he'd first entered. Looking back down patient number four was as serene as when he'd first seen her. Had he imagined it? No. He looked around again, wondering if he should tell someone. He imagined the conversation and thought better of it. The swing doors opened, and a young nurse came in.

"Oh I thought you were done in here." she said.

"I'm just packing up." said Plater.

The nurse began to collect the vases of flowers from beside the beds. When she saw Plater watching her, she said "These were for your benefit, time to put them back in the common room."

"Yeah, they wouldn't be appreciated in here."

As the nurse headed for the swing doors with two vases Plater said "Excuse me, you'll think I'm mad but, well, this patient, in bed number four, does she ever... move or anything ?"

The nurse put the vases down and joined Plater in looking down at the patient.

"This is Gail." she said. "Gail Hartston. She's been here all the time I have, so that's more than five years and I've never known her to move at all."

"It's just." began Plater. "Well I thought I noticed her eyes open earlier."

"Well Mr...."

"Plater, Mason Plater, but just Mason."

"Mason." said the nurse. "When I was first working nights here I thought I saw her open her eyes once, but Dr Granger assures me that her condition is a very deep coma and that precludes any muscular movement of any kind I'm afraid."

2

Zach Hamilton would rather have been raiding with his Guild in World of Warcraft than scanning the three monitors on his desk. He checked his phone for the time, he didn't own a watch and calculated that he could be back to his flat by 2 a.m. which would give him 30 minutes to shower and zap a microwave meal from the freezer before his Guild attempted the raid. He needed to make it. This raid had been planned for almost a week and he needed some of the gear desperately. Unfortunately the logs he was processing were not the boringly similar type he'd been expecting. Damn it. There was something different here, something he needed to log and process. For a moment he was torn. He could abort the program processing the logs and claim some sort of problem in the morning. Trouble was these results were intriguing and Zach began to imagine what they might mean. His phone juddered on the desk.

"Still on? Tank or DPS?" read the text message. It was from one of his Guild members, who lived in

Manchester, which was unusual as most of the other players that belonged to Zach's Guild were in California or Germany.

Zach quickly stabbed in "meh. Work. PITA!!!" and hit send. The raid would still be there next week. Zach fired up his own workstation console on one of the monitors and searched for a program he'd written to display the log data in a unique way. He paused the log analysis, copied the raw data then restarted the analysis job. With his newly copied data he kicked off his program. A kaleidoscope of coloured arcs appeared in a window on the screen. Zach reached for his coffee as the program juggled the results from the log. After a minute or two the coloured arcs began to settle into a nearly regular pattern. Zach tapped a button to un-mute the speaker and a noise like a herd of cattle trampling over corrugated iron filled the silent laboratory. For some patterns Zach found it easier to watch the curves on the screen but for others the audio representation made it easier to spot what he was looking for. This time he had to admit that neither made any hidden pattern easy to detect. On the third screen Zach began to make notes.

Subject: Herman Zeitmann
  ID: 17490
  Carrier detected. Hopkins-Huang filters used, indicative of 95% activity. Target zones 12, 18 & 77. Recommend Rattinger Analysis. Full demodulation scan against database E19.

Zach cut and pasted three screen captures from the log scan and one from his own program before emailing his report. He called up Herman Zeitmann's data and background file. The photograph showed a man in his mid-30s. The profile said he was a fireman who had been struck by a collapsing roof beam as he'd tried to get people from a burning restaurant in Hamburg. That was seven years ago, and he had been in a coma since that night. Zach's program was still running but had started to create small coloured buttons along the bottom of the screen. He selected one and a new window opened. Each button represented the program's best guess at what the underlying patterns in the log data really meant.

The raw data held brainwave patterns from coma patients, seventeen of them in all, assembled for study from across Europe and the Middle East. Zach's program was based on some pretty wild research that Zach only had a passing knowledge of. A Russian neuroscientist had written for years that he believed that many coma patients were still highly active mentally. He postulated that the trauma that had induced the coma had also induced other changes to brain activity. He claimed to have measured the effects of these changes, by their apparent effect on other comatose patients' measured brain activity. He even claimed to have recorded this effect having moved one of the patients four miles away from the other.

No reputable science journal would touch his work. No other neuroscientist had been known to try and reproduce his results. Even entertaining the notion that telepathy might actually be a reality was sure to kill any funding for research and probably black-ball a scientist permanently. Those restrictions evidently don't apply to

Government scientists, thought Zach. His phone buzzed. "Cracker ur lame wk sux" read the text. Like you'd know, thought Zach, the closest the sender had come to work was a paper round.

Mr Braberson will want to see this, thought Zach, but it needs tidying up. He grabbed another giant coffee and swore at Meek as there was no milk left. It was an unwritten rule that you didn't grab the last of something, coffee, milk, Jolt cola, sugar or filters without getting more. Meek was nowhere to be seen, probably in his basement flat with a soldering iron in his hand. Not happy building and fixing machines all day at work he spent his spare time building wilder creations at home.

Three hours and two more pots of coffee later Zach arched over the back of his chair and stretched. He'd run the full Rattinger Analysis and the demodulation scan against the database. The results were even better than he'd expected. Even allowing for error the correlation was indisputable. Not only had Zeitmann's brain reacted to other patients' episodes of activity but had also been stimulated by the department's ultra-secret Kan transmitter. Zach filed his results both to the database and via email to Edwin Braberson, the Director of the lab. As he left the lab Zach thought he might even get a small bonus after this. He needed to upgrade his Alienware at home, the frame lag on high resolution was annoying him and he still had his eye on a 47" flat screen monitor.

Braberson didn't particularly enjoy reporting to the Home Secretary. It involved going through his

Permanent Secretary, Michael Sangster, a character Braberson felt belonged to a bygone age. Sangster's clipped tones and agonizing attention to protocol seemed to embody the very worst remnants of the Empire. It offended Braberson's meritocratic attitude and somehow devalued his own struggle from the foot of the educational ladder to the same Oxford College that Sangster had gone to without a second thought. As he sat in the soft leather armchair, polished by generations of expensive tailoring, Braberson ran over again in his mind what he would tell the Home Secretary. The report Zach Hamilton had filed the night before was staggering. He had him double checking the scans and analysis today but he knew Hamilton was an excellent technician. The percentage match in activity was striking and many orders of magnitude beyond chance. This had to be what they were looking for, albeit in a rough and still mysterious form. Contact between humans on this level was previously the terrain of science fiction and fantasy.

"Mr Braberson, the Home Secretary will see you now." Michael Sangster said.

Damn, thought Braberson, it seems they even teach you to move silently at Public School.

"This way, sir." continued Sangster.

"Thank you. I know the way."

The Home Secretary's office is not an impressive room bedecked with oil paintings and sumptuous red leather furniture. No huge antique desk as one would find in the Foreign and Commonwealth Office, more Ikea than Chesterfield. Braberson thought the new building looked more like a multi-national's head office than home to one of the three great offices of the British State. James Carver, the Home Secretary motioned Braberson to a modern corner seating area surrounded by pale wooden tables.

"Edwin, good to see you." said Carver.

"And you Home Secretary."

"Some tea please Michael." began Carver. "Or would you prefer coffee?"

"Tea would be fine, thank you."

"So, Edwin, you have some news I understand?"

"Last night one of my technicians analysed data from yesterday and found an almost perfect match. I have him checking the results now, but I wanted to let you know straight away."

"Good, you were right to do so Edwin. Congratulations."

"Assuming there are no errors on the results we'll move to stage 3." said Braberson.

"The subjects." began Carver. "Are they suitable for further work?"

"It seems so, yes. One is a former fireman, excellent physical condition, the other was a housewife, young and healthy. Interestingly they are different nationalities."

"But I thought we expected there to be no issues of language?"

"That's true Home Secretary, but it is always reassuring to have any assumptions confirmed."

"How soon before you'll have any results from Stage 3?"

Braberson paused a moment, they had no experience with Stage 3 tests yet as these were the first subjects to pass Stage 2.

"Hard to say. I wouldn't expect anything usable for at least two weeks."

"Edwin, have you read the protocol for Stage 3?"

"I opened the envelope on the way here Home Secretary."

"Will it be easy to comply with?"

"I have some people in mind. I'll review their clearances, but I don't see any major problems."

"Good. Ah, here's the tea, thank you. Do you take sugar Edwin?"

Almost before the enormous oak door had swung shut with Sangster and Braberson on the outside Carver had taken a small mobile phone from his trouser pocket and pressed a pre-programmed hot key.

"Contact established." said Carver.

"Decoding?" said the male voice on the other end.

"Stage 3 initiating."

The call was disconnected and Carver opened the back of the phone, removed the sim card and cut it into four pieces before burning it in the oversized glass ashtray on his desk. As Home Secretary these past two years he was the keeper of numerous secrets. People had died as a direct result of decisions he had made. Sometimes people that had meant to bring harm or chaos to the UK but sometimes not. He had confidence in the Prime Minister, they had been colleagues for more than twelve years and he trusted his decision making completely. Still, he was starting to feel uncomfortable.

He crossed to a small ante room off one corner of the

main office and entered the combination into the smaller of two safes embedded in the concrete shell of the room. Inside was a small device resembling a pocket calculator. On the keypad he entered a nine-digit number and waited for a moment. The device was communicating over an encrypted link, where to he had no idea. The single line screen on the device showed two sets of four digits. Carver opened the larger of the two safes and removed a flat steel box. He unlocked the box with a key that was hidden inside the bulky house key for his official residence. Using this key disabled the powerful electrical device that would otherwise have fried the sim cards arranged on trays within the box. Each sim card was fixed in a slot that had two four-digit numbers underneath. Selecting the matching card, he closed both safes, placed the sim card in the phone and replaced the phone in his pocket.

Unusually for Carver, he then poured himself a large single malt. Deception was not something he was comfortable with. Keeping secrets in the national interest went with the job but keeping secrets from the Prime Minister, one of his closest friends, and for reasons he only partially agreed with was much harder than he had imagined.

3

The beach seemed to stretch for miles in each direction. Plater's toes felt the moist firm sand at the water's edge and the warm breeze reminded him of days spent in Cornwall as a child. Another figure was on the beach, some way ahead, walking slowly towards him. It was a woman wearing shorts and a shirt, carrying her shoes in one hand. She had long dark hair swept from her face by the gentle breeze. As the woman came closer Plater could make out attractive features on a tanned face, a bright orange bikini top beneath her open shirt. As he wondered if he should try to start a conversation or might be intruding, the woman spoke first.

"Do you come here often?" she said, smiling beneath her designer shades.

Plater was about to answer but then realised the weirdness of his situation. He had absolutely no idea where he was nor how he had come to be there. He realised he should speak.

"I...I'm not sure really."

The woman maintained her smile then turned to gaze

out to sea.

"It's beautiful here at this time of year." she said.

Plater could smell a pleasant perfume mingled with the sea and sand, but he had to concentrate.

"Have you come far?" he asked, wishing he hadn't said something so inane.

The woman turned back to look at Plater and pulled her sunglasses away to reveal dark smiling eyes.

"Please don't be alarmed, it is never easy." said the woman, who stepped a few paces onto the dry sand and sat down, motioning Plater to join her. "Will you sit with me for a while?"

Plater sat down but still had no clue what he was doing. He knew who he was, where he lived, what he did for a living, could remember football scores from last Saturday but had no recollection of coming to the seaside. The nearness of the woman was pleasant.

"You don't remember coming here do you?" asked the woman looking out to sea, her toes digging gently through the sand, dark eyes squeezed against the twinkling reflections from the water.

"No." said Plater.

"It's okay." she began. "What you're going through is quite normal. Well not unusual. I know who you are, I know what you do for a living, and I know where you live."

"But how..."

"I feel as if I've known you for a long time." the woman said.

"Forgive me." began Plater. "But I'm sure I would have remembered."

He could feel the slight twitch by the left corner of his

mouth that was a sure sign of nervousness. He'd had this since he was a child and could normally control it.

"You've been having headaches recently haven't you?" said the woman.

"Yes."

The woman had replaced her sunglasses and was looking out to sea once more.

"Do you remember what you did before the headaches began?" she asked.

"What do you mean?"

"Your work takes you all over the place, do you remember the project you were working on at the time the headaches began? "

Plater thought for a moment.

"I'd just done the Lievesham documentary, the mental hospital, we'd been editing that week."

"Interesting project?" asked the woman.

"Not my usual thing." began Plater. "Bit weird really, unsettling place but how..?"

"You don't remember me do you?"

"I'm sorry we've never met."

"Please, close your eyes for a moment." said the woman and placed her hand gently on Plater's leg.

Plater closed his eyes, feeling he might do anything this woman asked but unsure why.

"Open them."

As Plater opened his eyes again he suddenly became even more confused. The woman sitting next to him was now remarkably like the woman he'd filmed for the Lievesham Hall documentary. The woman from The Dead Zone, Gail Hartston.

"But you can't be..." started Plater leaping to his feet.

"What's going on, what's happening to me? This isn't real..."

The woman stood and looked up at Plater.

"Real is such a difficult word." she began. "My name is Gail and yes I am the woman you filmed that day."

"This is crazy, am I dreaming?"

"Not exactly."

"I must be going mad."

"According to some so-called professionals perhaps but no, you're not mad."

"But you, you changed just then, when we first met you looked different."

"I'm sorry, it's a failing of mine. Vanity you might say. I've never really liked my nose and my eyes look so much better dark don't you think?"

Plater noticed now that despite appearing like patient number four, Gail Hartston, the woman had brown eyes. Gail Hartston had the most vivid blue eyes Plater had ever seen.

"Yes, you can't be Gail Hartston, she has blue eyes." There was a note of triumph in his voice.

"Mason, look closely."

As he looked at the woman her eyes gently faded from brown to the vibrant blue he remembered from that strange afternoon in the Dead Zone.

Plater couldn't speak.

"You are unique." said the woman. "Please, sit, we have much to talk about"

Plater woke up with a headache and it hadn't shown any signs of easing by the time he'd reached Rice-Henway Productions' offices in Isleworth.

"Yes, hello. Is Molly James in this morning?" said Plater to the receptionist.

The glass reception area looked like the overflow from Kew Gardens. Foliage clawed its way up every part of the steel structure. Two large plasma screens looped highlights of the last Rice-Henway production to make networked television, a documentary about illegal immigration.

"I'm sorry sir I can't seem to find a number for Miss...."

"James, Molly James. She's an intern here."

"Oh an intern, one moment." the receptionist pressed a button and waited. "Hello is that Molly James? I have a Mr...."

"Plater, Mason Plater."

"...Plater in reception to see you. Thank you. She'll be right out."

The receptionist returned to surfing the web, the new millenium's nail file.

"Hi Mason, this is a surprise." said Molly, emerging through double glass doors.

"Yeah I wanted to have a chat, actually, do you wanna grab a coffee or something? Is there a canteen here? Or there's a little place nearby if you can get out of school."

"Okay. Yeah there is a place here but it's crap. Lead on."

Plater wasn't really sure why he'd picked Molly, an intern of about 26 he guessed, to tell about this. She'd seemed very friendly as soon as he'd met her and he found her company easy. Mario's coffee shop was well known to be good. It was quiet this morning but that suited Mason, he was embarrassed enough about talking to Molly without risking being overheard by someone.

"Do you remember that job out at the hospital?" said Mason.

"Lievesham Hall?"

"Yes, well ever since then I've been..." he wondered again if he should say anything, but his throbbing head made up his mind. "...I've been having dreams."

"Is that unusual? What sort of dreams?"

"Look this is going to sound weird but I've got to tell someone and well, you were there and you saw..."

"Saw what?"

"The Dead Zone." said Plater. "You saw the woman in the Dead Zone."

"Yeah, what's this got to do with her?"

"She's in the dreams."

"Well you've got good taste I'll give you that, she was a very attractive woman. If I was, you know, that way I could definitely fancy her."

"It's not like that." said Plater. "She talks to me."

Molly chuckled.

"Bad luck." she said.

"No, the dreams aren't like that at all. There's something I didn't tell you, that happened the day we were filming. After you and the others left I stayed a bit, packing up you know. Anyway just as I was leaving I thought that woman opened her eyes."

"Whoa!"

"I thought her hand moved too but I spoke to a nurse and she said that this woman, Gail her name is, had some condition which meant she can't possibly move."

"That's wild." said Molly "So what does this woman do

in your dreams?"

Plater quickly summarised his dream of the beach.

"Sounds like you were pretty taken with this woman. I used to have a recurring dream when I was a kid of someone chasing me, your one sounds a whole lot better."

"But the weird thing is this woman told me, in the dream, that she was actually the woman in the hospital. Told me that she was speaking to me while she was lying in that bed, in that hospital."

"That's crazy, you don't actually think..."

"No, of course not, but I just thought this was some weird thing that would wear off, you know, after a few days. I see this woman every time I fall asleep. I don't always remember what happens too well. There are gaps and things don't match up but she always tells me the same stuff, that she's the woman in the hospital and that I'm special."

"Special? Does she say why?"

"No I don't think so but lately I've not been remembering the dreams too well, I've been so tired I think I'm sleeping pretty deeply but in some ways that's even worse. I want to know what's happening to me and I think if I can find out more about this woman it might help. That's why I came to see you."

"I don't know what I can do." said Molly.

"You've helped me already." said Plater. "You're the first person I've mentioned this to. But I was thinking maybe you could get hold of the research material for the film. Maybe that has some background on that woman or the hospital or something."

"Sure, I've got most of it on my laptop and there's

some hard copy stuff upstairs. I can't really get it now" Molly glanced at her watch. "I've got a pre-production meeting in ten minutes, you live quite close don't you? I can stop by after work if you like?"

Plater wrote his address on the back of his business card.

"I'm sorry to lay this on you like this." he said.

"It's okay, I'm kinda curious to be honest, I'll see you round 6:30."

Plater tried to find a chemist, he was running short of headache tablets.

4

It was closer to 7 p.m. when Molly rang the bell outside Mason Plater's house.

"Sorry I'm late, that woman does go on." said Molly.

"No problem." Plater said and Molly sat on the large, old leather sofa that dominated the sitting room. She opened her laptop on the wooden coffee table and switched it on.

"Would you like a drink of something?" asked Plater. "I haven't got much, there's tea and coffee of course or beer and I might have a bottle of wine somewhere..."

"After the day I've had a beer sounds good. Listen, that old place has quite a history." said Molly while scrolling through a file on her laptop. "It's about four hundred years old and was originally the home of Lord Westcott but then the family seem to have done a bit too much of the in-breeding because some of their descendants around two hundred years ago developed some decidedly eccentric habits."

Plater returned with two beers and sat next to Molly.

"Thanks." she said. "Anyway, the family started to go a

bit bonkers and a couple of generations later the house was left in a will to be turned into a hospital for the mentally disadvantaged. It seems the family spotted the trend and stopped breeding, so the male heirs ran out."

"Anything about the woman?" asked Plater, wondering if he should be having the beer as he was still popping headache pills like Smarties.

"Well, that's where it gets interesting. I couldn't find much about her in the research. The Dead Zone got a mention but probably just because it had a catchy name for use in the program. So, I called the hospital. I pretended we needed a little more info on the woman for the commentary. Anyway, they put me through to the ward, the Dead Zone and the woman I spoke to said she remembered you. Said you'd been quite interested in the patient. Anyway, she told me the woman's name, Gail Hartston, and that we were the second lot of people to be interested in her recently."

"Oh?"

"Yeah, apparently they'd had a visit from some government bod that was asking if hospitals would mind letting some of their patients with particular conditions be part of a new international study."

"What are they studying?" asked Plater.

"They didn't say but they must be either very important or have offered something good because that Granger guy that runs the place apparently told the staff to give them all the help they needed."

"And this woman, Gail, is going to be part of their study?"

"Looks like it, they were especially interested in her and another man as well."

"What government department was it?"

"She didn't say. I'll call her back tomorrow. She said to call back anytime. Do you think this is relevant?"

"I have no idea. Bit of a coincidence though."

"Well have a look through the other stuff, I need the loo."

"Second on the left." Plater said, and started scrolling through the research material. He had no idea what he was looking for, or if there was anything to find. He was starting to feel tired again and not looking forward to going to sleep. His dreams weren't threatening but he still didn't like what he didn't understand.

"Wow, is this Africa?" said Molly after she returned, looking at a framed photograph of Plater beside a lion that hung by his desk in the corner of the sitting room.

"Yes, I tried filming for some nature programs. They were hot a few years ago."

"Don't you do any of that now?"

"Too bloody uncomfortable, you spend weeks waiting for some animal to poke its head out and you end up with about 10 seconds of useful film. Plus it's a young man's game, there are hundreds of specialists nowadays, all over the world."

"Were you married?" asked Molly, seeing a picture of two young boys with a younger looking Plater, on his desk.

"For nine years. Started way too early, was still a kid."

Molly was expecting a little more.

"How old are your boys now?" she asked.

"Mark, he's the taller one, he'll be sixteen in June and Rick was nineteen about a month ago."

Seeing Molly continuing to look at the photo Plater

went on

"They live with their mother. She's married again and lives in San Francisco, with a dentist."

"I'm sorry."

"What for?"

"That things didn't work out, that you're so far from your boys."

"Occupational hazard of being a freelance cameraman. Lois, my ex, probably thought it was cool while she could come to wrap-up parties and meet people whose names she'd heard of, nothing A-list of course but TV people sometimes. Then I hit a dodgy patch, the work dried up and we started arguing. Along comes Victor Samson III with his perfect teeth and houses in Mountain View, Milan and somewhere else, I can't even remember, and that was it."

"Must be hard, not seeing the boys."

"I see them about once, maybe twice a year, but there's always Facebook and I chat to them online a fair bit, Skype, that sort of thing. They even try and get me to play their online games, but I'm no good at them. They're okay, their mum loves them and old Victor seems to look after them too. Just bought Rick a new car for his birthday, worth more than mine."

As Plater turned back to the laptop bright lights began dancing across his vision. The screen was lost behind the twinkling blues and greens and reds and yellows. He suddenly felt quite sick and went to stand up to make for the bathroom. His balance was gone, and he collapsed sideways to the floor, knocking his beer bottle after him.

"Mason!" shrieked Molly, crouching and supporting

his head. "Mason...are you ok? What's wrong?"

"My head...hurts...lights...just need to lie down, I'll be ok in a minute, just need to lie down."

Molly helped Plater onto the sofa and lifted his legs so he could lie along the length of it. She propped his head on a cushion. His eyes stayed closed, his forehead slightly wrinkled and tense.

"I should call a doctor." said Molly.

"No!" said Plater sternly. "I'll be fine in a minute or two, this has happened before"

"Has this just started since the filming?"

"Yes."

"My god."

Molly checked Plater's forehead but he was not feverish. She found a roll of kitchen towels and mopped up the beer as best she could. Plater was silent, although she didn't think he was asleep. Molly checked the refrigerator. As she walked into the sitting room Plater was trying to sit up.

"Take it easy." said Molly, helping him rearrange himself to a sitting position, "Are you feeling better?"

"No lights anymore." he said. "But still a dull ache, but I don't feel like throwing up now."

"That's good. When was the last time you ate something?"

It had been two pieces of toast that morning.

"A while ago." said Plater.

"Okay, you relax there and I'll fix a little snack. Whatever this thing is starving yourself isn't going to help."

"No, it's okay..."

"Just sit tight, it won't be anything great."

An hour, an omelette and two glasses of water later, Plater felt much better.

"Thanks." he said.

"Glad I could help, listen I'd better get going but I'll call the hospital again tomorrow and see if I can find out more about that government thing. I'll call you later, ok? No don't get up I can find my own way out. You need to rest."

As Plater heard the door close his eyelids felt very heavy. Perhaps tonight would be different, perhaps he could sleep without dreaming of Gail Hartston, perhaps he could sleep without dreaming at all.

5

"Good evening Reverend Daniels. Recently critics of your Church have called it a cult and questioned whether your standing for the vacant Senate seat is just a publicity stunt to get more members. What do you have to say to those folks ?"

Erik Nordstrom could still hear the old, battered TV above the general bar buzz and peered at the smiling, clean-cut face that filled the screen. Somehow the three whiskeys and four beers still weren't enough for him to escape the relentlessly pious Reverend Ethan Daniels. Four men at the far end of the bar raised their voices as if arguing. Erik felt he'd have just one more for the road. He had a big day tomorrow and he needed to have his wits.

"....and my Church has never supported any political party, but we feel that the nation is losing its way, from a moral standpoint. Our Founding Fathers were strongly righteous and followed the teachings of the Lord. In these difficult times we seem to have lost sight of that very compass of wisdom, compassion and faith that can navigate us through these dark and dangerous waters...."

Reverend Daniels' increasingly earnest tones were replaced by the glow of floodlights. The Texas Rangers were in the bottom of the seventh inning and cruising at 4-0 against Boston. A cheer erupted from the far end of the bar as they noticed the score.

Erik got another whiskey and pulled a crumpled note from his jeans. He took his phone out and was about to dial the number on the paper. He wanted to tell her that it would be alright. Trouble is he didn't know it would be alright. He put the phone on the bar by his drink.

Kathleen Moran reminded him of his favourite aunt, Karita, who was Swedish, as his mother had been. She would always have a kind word if things were going badly. She could always see the good in people and would always give them the chance to show it. She had a certain social wisdom that many Swedes seem to have. Able to cope with personal and emotional stresses with a stoic inner strength. Kathleen Moran had certainly surprised him. Her family had collapsed around her but still she maintained her humanity and dignity. Erik wanted badly to help this woman.

He scooped the phone off the bar, downed his drink, added another $20 to the small stack on the bar and waved at the barman. In the car park he found his old pickup. He was well over the limit but from the outskirts of Fort Worth to where he lived he'd be lucky to see another living thing, let alone the Highway Patrol. Before he turned the key in the ignition he called Kathleen Moran.

"Hallo."

"Kathleen, it's Erik."

"Hi."

"How is Dawn?" asked Erik.

"Sleeping, I think."

"That's best right now, she needs her rest, these past few days will have taken it out of her."

There was a pause.

"Well, I guess I'll see you in the morning then, around ten?" said Erik.

"Thank you Erik." Kathleen sounded close to tears.

"Now you get some rest too now."

"You're a good man Erik."

"In the morning then, goodnight Kathleen."

Before he started the old Dodge Ram he beat his fist on the dashboard.

The next morning was crystal clear with wide blue skies as Erik pointed the old pickup towards Fort Worth. A little over twenty minutes later he was parking outside a nondescript single-story house in a tired suburb of the city. Three Mexican children were kicking a ball around in the road nearby. Erik pulled open the screen door and knocked. A small Mexican woman answered. Seeing Erik she smiled and he went in. Kathleen Moran was in the kitchen.

"Morning Kathleen." said Erik. "Thank you, Carla."

The Mexican woman disappeared down the hall.

"How are you managing? Do you need anything, you know, food or clothes or?"

"No." said Kathleen. "Carla has been wonderful. Coffee?"

Erik half smiled and nodded. The coffee was a rich

Columbian blend, not the sort to be found in most Texas supermarkets.

"Is Dawn awake?" asked Erik.

"I took her breakfast this morning, about an hour and a half ago. I tried to talk to her but she didn't say anything."

"You didn't go in?"

"No, you said..."

"That's right, it's too dangerous for now."

Kathleen was absently turning her wedding ring round on her finger, her gaze not focused.

"I spoke to Liam yesterday." began Erik. "And he told me that there has been no Police report so far. It's important we keep out of sight though. It's gonna be okay."

He reached across the kitchen table and placed his hand over Kathleen's.

Kathleen looked up and Erik saw tears forming in her eyes. Her hands turned over and grasped Eriks' tight. They stayed that way for what seemed a long time until Erik said:

"I should probably get started."

"Yes, of course." said Kathleen wiping her hand across her eyes and busying herself clearing the coffee cups.

Erik slipped out of the kitchen and opened a door that seemed to be in the outside wall of the house, but actually led to a staircase going down. From the outside it looked like a cupboard had been built out of the side of the house. It had been there two years and the paint was starting to blend with the rest of the house's tired exterior. Paint didn't look good for long in the scorching summers and icy winters of Texas.

The cellar covered almost half the area of the house. It was full height and a dusty single bulb illuminated the bottom of the stairs. There was a small room with a table against one wall and a heavy door built into another. Light in the room was controlled by computer to follow the natural cycles so the room was well lit as it was now mid-morning. As Erik came in the figure on the bed was motionless. He picked a chair from around the table spun it round and straddled it beside the bed.

"Dawn?" he began. "It's Erik. We need to talk. You haven't eaten the breakfast your mother gave you. You need to eat, you've had a difficult few days."

Erik thought he noticed one of Dawn's hands clenched a little tighter but otherwise she didn't move at all.

"Please, can't we talk about this?" said Erik. "We just need to talk this through and then you can get out of here."

The figure on the bed began to uncurl.

"I've got nothing to say to you." said Dawn Moran, sitting up on the bed and sweeping her long auburn hair off her face. "You kidnapped me."

"Actions need to be seen in the proper context, Dawn."

"You grabbed me off the street and drove me off in a van, what's the proper context for that?"

"Your mother and I felt that you weren't able to make your own decisions."

"So you decided to make some for me?"

"Your mother loves you and only wants what's best for you. She felt you were being used. Lied to and made to do things against your will."

Dawn laughed.

"That's rich. So what does my loving mother do? Hires some thugs to kidnap me and keep me prisoner. What's the difference?"

"That's exactly why we need to talk." said Erik, maintaining his calm tone and eye contact. "Why don't you tell me how you came to join the Church of the Reclamation?"

"What's the point?"

"I want to understand. I want to hear from you what the Church is like. Why you left home to join it and why you never contact your mother or father."

"You don't want to understand. It's just another trick. They told me you'd say this stuff. You just want to trick me with more lies. You don't understand what the Church is trying to do."

"Help me then." said Erik, "Help me to understand what the Church is trying to do."

Dawn fell silent. Nothing Erik said could elicit a response. It was as if a switch inside Dawn had been turned off.

"Kathleen?" called Nordstrom, as he closed the door to the underground floor.

"In the front Erik." called Kathleen.

She was sitting on the plain wooden armed sofa cradling a cup of coffee and gazing onto the street through the tired net curtains.

"Dawn's resting now." said Nordstrom. "We made a little progress but it's still early."

He tried to sound positive but didn't think he'd succeeded.

"What's going to happen to Dawn?" asked Kathleen.

"Am I ever going to get my little girl back?"

"It will take time."

"Why?" Kathleen wondered. "Why do these people do this?"

Nordstrom didn't know what to say.

"I really don't know Kathleen." he said "A need for power and to control people. Some actually believe in something. Some are functioning sociopaths or psychopaths."

Kathleen turned to Erik and met his gaze.

"How did you get into all this?" she asked.

Nordstrom considered making something up but decided Kathleen deserved the truth.

"It was by accident. While I was at university, my friend Marco's sister, Laura, had been on holiday in San Francisco with two other friends. Her friends came home but she stayed behind after meeting some people in the city who took her to their community in the Napa Valley. For two months we didn't hear nothin'. Marco planned to go to California and find his sister. I went with him. We had no idea what we'd do if we found her. It didn't take long to get directions to the community. We hired a car and drove out there. It was almost dark when we found the place. There were three men with rifles at the dirt road that led to the community.

"We asked to see Laura but they said that wasn't possible. We asked to speak to the person in charge, but they said he was not available. So, we said we'd be back in the morning.

"We couldn't wait 'til the morning so we circled round, ditched the car and went back on foot. The community was half a dozen shacks round a fenced enclosure that had pigs and chickens. There was a faint engine noise which we guessed was a generator powering some dim lights strung off the shacks.

"One shack was a little bigger than the rest and had more lights; it also had lights on inside, so we headed for that one. Inside we could just make out there seemed to be some sort of meeting. The windows were filthy. Folks sat on the floor and those that couldn't sit stood around them. At one end a small oriental man sat in a chair, slightly raised on a small stage. On either side of him were two men with rifles. The man had to be Kwai Chun Li. He was the leader of this alternative community and according to local newspapers believed that the sins of the world were due to bring about visitation from an intelligent species from space.

"A while before this guy appeared on local television and ended the interview shouting at the presenter and telling her that the aliens were recording all broadcasts from Earth and that her ridiculing of his beliefs would only further convince them that humanity must be cleansed from the planet.

"We heard a vehicle approaching from behind us so we went and hid in the trees. It was the three men from the gate. Instead of going into the meeting they began patrolling outside. After about half an hour they met at the door, kinda hugged each other and went into the meeting. We waited to see if they came out again. After a minute or two the door burst open and someone ran out. Just behind them one of the guards from the gate leveled his rifle and fired twice. The running figure never made it to the tree line.

"We argued about what we should do. Should we get

the sheriff or try something ourselves? We stayed but there was no more shooting. After what seemed like ages but couldn't have been more than five minutes or so we crept up to the window again."

Nordstrom stopped speaking. Kathleen touched his hand.

"Go on." she whispered.

"We saw all the people. They were all piled up. In a sort of pyramid in the middle of the room. There was no-one standing anymore, they were all in the pile. We ran in and tried to find Laura, we was just dragging bodies off the pile and tossing them aside but then we found her. She was about halfway down. I still remember her face. She looked like she was asleep. She was still warm. Marco, he tried mouth to mouth and CPR but it was no good. We didn't know it then but there had been poison in their food that night."

"I'm so sorry." said Kathleen, taking Nordstrom's hand in hers.

"About four weeks later they sent Laura's stuff to her mom and dad, once it ceased being evidence. There was a diary that Laura had kept while she was in the community. She must have hidden it because it would never have been allowed. When I read that I decided. I decided that I had to try and stop this from happening again. They had inquests and such and I went along. The judge said the members had committed suicide, well all except that one poor guy who tried to run."

Nordstrom and Kathleen sat in silence.

6

The smell of the mountainous fresh cut flower arrangement in the Church of the Reclamation's headquarters in Dallas was almost overpowering. Warren Gatts had been waiting for more than half an hour, he consulted his watch for the third time before crossing to the receptionist's desk.

"Miss, I have been waiting for some time now, could you check with Reverend Daniels please? We did have an appointment."

The receptionist, an impeccably dressed woman in her late forties with the air of a headmistress glanced up from her screen and fixed Gatts with a look bordering on contempt.

"Mr. Gatts, I have informed the Reverend that you are waiting. He is running a little late, as I told you when you arrived. You will understand that the Reverend is a very busy man and I'm sure he will be with you as soon as he can. Now if you will take a seat, please."

Returning her gaze to the screen, Gatts was left in no doubt what his next move should be and he retreated to the same seat. He looked again at his watch, although he knew exactly what the time was. He cleared his throat noisily and snatched up the Dallas Morning News that he'd discarded next to him ten minutes before.

Gatts had hardly reached the end of the first article when the large door to his right opened and a conversation spilled into the vestibule.

"Thank you Reverend, we look forward to your visit and you can count on us." said a small man who was almost scurrying out of the office pursued by the unmistakable figure of the Reverend Ethan Daniels, all six feet seven inches of him.

"No, thank you George, the Church is most grateful for your support and I look forward to coming down and sampling some of that fine sweet potato your dear wife makes!"

Gatts was almost physically offended by the naked politicking but nonetheless, thrust aside the newspaper in anticipation.

"Mr. Gatts." said Rev. Daniels, closing the distance to Gatts in two giant strides, "It's good to finally meet you"

Rev. Daniels held out a massive hand and swallowed Gatts' in a vice-like grip. Although his Texas State football days were well behind him his physical power remained. Gatts trailed Daniels back to his paneled office.

"Please, make yourself comfortable. Mary, may we have some coffee please?"

Gatts noted the unwavering politeness, even to his staff, that he had heard about from those he'd interviewed before.

"So, Mr. Gatts, how can I help you?"

After all Gatts' preparation and the pages of notes he still carried in his battered briefcase, being in the same room as the Reverend Daniels was causing some unexpected reticence.

"Well, Reverend Daniels, I'm writing an article about you, now that you're standing for the US Senate seat, and I wanted to just explore why you think you're the right man for the job."

This wasn't the hard-hitting approach to this interview that Gatts had practiced but it was all he could manage for now. Twenty five years as an investigative journalist and this was the big one. He had something, something big, on a prospective US Senator. But he'd have to handle it right. Seated at his imposing dark wood desk Reverend Daniels leaned forwards with his forearms resting on the enormous blotter. The pose and poise could have been taken directly from a State of the Union address or a party political broadcast, even to the point of having the flag of the United States of America in the background.

"All my life, I've tried to follow what my momma used to tell me when I was a kid. 'Ethan,' she'd say, 'Trust in the Lord with all your heart and lean not on your own understanding; in all your ways acknowledge Him, and He will make your paths straight.', Proverbs 3 verses 5 to 6. In my life I've found that following that simple guidance has led me through any adversity. It has shown me that I can help people find their own way and that way leads to the Lord."

"Does that mean that your actions, if elected, will be driven by your faith and not by the will of the people that elected you?" asked Gatts, moving closer to his pregame plan.

"Now Mr Gatts, we both know that many, perhaps most, of the good people of the state of Texas that will vote for me will be voting for me precisely because I will let the Lord be my guide as I prosecute the office of Senator. I think many folks see the people that claim to represent them on TV and feel betrayed. Once some men get power, they forget how they got it and the promises they made."

"Alright, so let's come on to experience, what skills will you bring to public office? You've never run a company or held public office of any kind before, do you think you're up to the job of running a large staff and still being an effective representative of the people?"

Gatts detected the faintest hint of a smile from Rev. Daniels. You may not be smiling in a minute, he thought.

"I may not have run a company or held public office in the past but you are sitting in the home of the Church of the Reclamation. We have a worldwide membership of more than two and a half million spread through forty countries. Now that does require a certain level of leadership and organizational skill and since we are still growing at a rate of more than two hundred thousand new members each year, I would say that this has provided me with some valuable experience. Not only that but the ministries of the Church in foreign lands have given me the opportunity to travel extensively and meet many foreign leaders, who support the work we do in their countries. In many ways, Mr Gatts, I have more relevant experience for helping this country rediscover it's destiny than any corporate executive, self-made man or lifelong politician could call on."

Gatts shifted in his seat. He was about to drop his bombshell and he was totally unsure of how the 280-pound giant sitting opposite him would react. If some of his racier research was to be believed he might find himself cowering before a screaming madman in fear for his life. He was unlikely to get another invitation, so this was his only chance.

"Do you know a man named Darrell Vance?" queried Gatts.

There was just the slightest hint of a pause before the Reverend came back.

"What has that got to do with your article, Mr. Gatts?"

"Darrell Vance is the son of the Republican Senator Rupert Vance. According to my sources Darrell had a problem with controlled substances. Two years ago, he was contacted by members of your Church and was a member for a time."

"I can't see where you're going with this, Mr. Gatts."

"Well, it seems that while he was a member of the Church, his father began to discuss your nomination as a future Republican Candidate for high office with others in the party. Now you will know that Rupert Vance is one of the most respected Republicans of the last forty years and so to have him endorsing you probably ensured your nomination for the Texas seat."

Rev. Daniels turned his palms upwards.

"I would have to agree that Senator Vance has become a close colleague since I've begun to embrace politics. We see eye to eye on most issues. That's no secret."

"No, Reverend, that is no secret. What is less well

known is that while Darrell Vance was a member of the Church the person who supplied him with the controlled substances, one Ignacio Rodriguez, was found shot dead in his home in North Miami Beach. By a strange coincidence, according to police reports, eyewitnesses saw Rodriguez talking to two men the afternoon before he was killed. Further investigation shows that these men were members of the Church of the Reclamation, working for the Miami Beach branch of the Church at the time."

Rev. Daniels' right hand closed into a fist although his demeanor remained calm.

"I'm not aware of any of this." said Rev. Daniels.

"It's also true isn't it that the Church paid for the drug rehabilitation that Darrell underwent in California?"

"That is true, but whenever a member comes to us with problems, we strive to help in any way we possibly can. The evils of drugs are well known but, by the grace of our Lord, we have ways to cure people of this terrible addiction. It was our duty in the name of the Lord to help his fallen son."

"Perhaps so, but if I was to tell you that these very police reports that described your church members associating with Rodriguez the day he died had mysteriously disappeared, then I'd say we have some interesting areas for speculation, wouldn't you agree Reverend?"

Gatts was warming to his task now and could feel the adrenaline kicking in.

"I don't know what you're implying Mr Gatts and I don't see how this can be relevant to your article. I thought you came here to talk to me about my ideas for improving the lives of our citizens in this great country of ours not to try a poor attempt at scurrilous muckraking."

Gatts noticed a new edge to the Reverend's normally mellow tones.

"On the contrary sir, I see it my duty to outline what I see as at best a piece of opportunism and at worst a piece of coldly calculated manipulation of an elected member of the Senate in pursuit of personal advancement. Until Darrell Vance became a member of your Church, he did not have a drug habit. Nor had his father ever even heard of you, let alone believed you to be the reforming force the Republican Party was looking for."

"Ok, Mr Gatts I don't really see any point in continuing this interview."

The huge frame of Reverend Daniels stood up and moved around his desk.

"Isn't it true that you persuaded, duped, forced, somehow got Darrell Vance into the Church, then hooked him on drugs and knew you could use it as a lever to influence his father?"

Reverend Daniels now loomed over Gatts and extended one long arm towards the door.

"Mr Gatts, I think we're done here, if you'd be so kind..."

"Those police reports in Florida. Isn't it true that a member of the Church, Martina Ruiz, was sleeping with the Lieutenant investigating the Rodriguez murder? What she didn't know, or the Lieutenant, was that a Sergeant on the investigation made copies of those reports because he thought something was odd and wanted to follow up in his own time."

A heavy hand landed on Gatts' shoulder.

"Please, Mr. Gatts, I'm sure the police will investigate if there is anything wrong here. I have nothing to hide but I would ask that you not publish unsubstantiated rumour. I think that someone has seen an opportunity to slur my name and that of the Church, that's all. Sadly, the forces of evil are abroad, Mr. Gatts, and we must be ever vigilant to avoid their clutches. Have a safe journey home Mr. Gatts, it was nice to meet you."

No vice-like clasp of the hand, but a powerful arm guided Gatts to the door.

"What about investigating what happened in Miami? Members of your Church implicated in a murder and a conspiracy....how's that going to play with the electorate?"

Gatts found himself addressing the polished surface of the closed door to Reverend Daniels' office. He glanced sideways and noticed the receptionist staring at him. After a moment, she returned to her work. Gatts slowly turned and made his way to the elevator. He switched off the digital recorder in his pocket. Daniels was clever, he'd have to give him that. There was nothing on the recorder, but his body language betrayed him. He knew all about it, thought Gatts, but linking him tangibly to this would take more digging.

The pole dancer had already picked him out as a good tipper. Her energies now focused on the tall slim man with the steel rimmed John Lennon glasses. Instead of dollar bills, he was adding tens to the dancer's thong whenever it was offered within tantalizing reach.

Perhaps he'd go for a private dance, real money to be made with this guy. He moved his hand to his shirt pocket and took out a phone. He left his seat and disappeared. Shit, thought the pole dancer, back to the cheapskates and drunks.

The man stepped out a fire door into a deserted alleyway.

"Yes." he said into the phone.

"We have a problem. I need to see you."

The man with the John Lennon glasses thought Reverend Daniels sounded worried and that made him worried.

7

The room was almost completely featureless. Just the basics- floor, ceiling and the regulation four walls to keep them apart. A table and three chairs in the middle and a single door, which Plater was on the inside of.

No texture to the walls, thought Plater. It looked as if they were perfectly smooth. With nothing to look at, Plater began to wonder how the surfaces were so smooth. Whenever he painted walls at home they never looked as good as this.

The door opened and a woman came in. She was striking, with long dark hair. Plater thought he recognized her but couldn't place where from. She sat on one of the chairs and said:

"Mason, why don't you sit down?"

"I'm sorry, I know we've met but I can't quite remember where?"

Mason sat opposite the woman. Not having a reliable memory for names was a constant annoyance to him.

"We talked about how it would be hard for you to remember in the beginning. I want to try something to help you."

"Okay." said Plater.

The door opened again and a man came in. Small and a little overweight, with bushy blonde hair and bright blue eyes.

"This is Raymond."

"Raymond." said Plater, shaking hands.

Raymond was wearing some sort of rucksack and he helped Plater put one on as well.

"We think what Raymond has in mind will help you to remember Mason. It's very important that you remember, okay?"

Plater wasn't really sure what was going on, but he knew he liked this woman even though her name escaped him.

"Mason, we're going for a little trip now." said Raymond.

"It's very important that you concentrate, can you do that for me?" asked the woman.

"Sure." said Plater as Raymond took his arm and led him to the door, "I'm sorry but what is your name? It'll bug the hell out of me if I don't ask."

Raymond opened the door.

"It's Gail, Gail Hartston."

Raymond suddenly shoved Plater hard through the doorway. The rush of air and the shock of falling caused Plater to cry out. His arms flailed as if trying to grab onto something, his legs thrashing against nothing. The noise of the wind rushing past his ears was overwhelming. He tumbled and spun, then seemed to steady for a moment. As he stared at the ground rushing up to greet him, he could see words written in what must have been huge letters to be readable so high up. As he wondered why someone had written words on the ground like that he woke up.

In less than a second or so, Plater had realized that he was sitting up in bed, was sweating enough that he could taste a drop on his lips and that he had to remember something.

He grabbed his watch off the side table. It was approaching four a.m. He felt an urge to write or draw or something. He leapt off the bed and scrabbled around the bedroom looking for paper and something to write with. Finding nothing, he ended up in the sitting room with an old ballpoint and the back of an A4 envelope. For some time, he drew on the back of the envelope, just adding lines and shapes with quick, comfortable strokes of the pen. When he was done, he looked at it. This had something to do with what he had to remember but it just looked like shapes and lines on paper to Plater. He turned the envelope around to each different angle but still made no sense of it. Angry and frustrated, he threw the pen against the wall and clutched his head. The ache was better, not so ever present as it had been but still there. He took another pill with a handful of water from the kitchen tap. He splashed cold water on his face. Whatever he did, he couldn't shake the belief that he had to remember something and the shapes on the envelope were the key.

8

Zach picked up the letter again and glanced through it. He wasn't sure whether he should do it or not. It sounded like a promotion; it certainly involved more cash but there was something about it that sounded dodgy. Braberson's signature was on the bottom, and it was on official stationery, but this didn't sound like your typical Civil Service project. Mind you the current project was hardly normal. Trying to detect some sort of telepathic communication between humans wasn't what he'd expected to be doing after his Computer Science degree at Cambridge. Especially when he'd signed up for the Government. He thought maybe something in defence doing battlefield simulations or perhaps in some sort of cyber security role.

"You got one too." said Meek, who had wandered up behind Zach without him noticing.

"Jeez! Shouldn't you wear a bell or something...." said Zach, instinctively folding the letter.

"You gonna do it?" asked Meek.

"Dunno." replied Zach.

"Where the hell is Blythburgh?" asked Meek, unfolding his letter from Braberson that he'd been carrying in his rear jeans pocket.

"Suffolk." said Zach.

"Middle of nowhere then." said Meek. "Bet the net access is lousy out there."

"So, you gonna sign up?" asked Zach.

"You kidding? Dunno about you but they're offering me 20% more. I could use the extra cash, there's a circuit board I need from Korea but it's five hundred quid, not counting shipping."

"But it means spending..." Zach looked at the letter again "...eight weeks to start with and then there might be additional periods '...as the work dictates.' Whatever that means. Since Government projects never finish on time we could be stuck out there for months."

"Afraid your little orcs and dwarves won't be able to manage without you?" said Meek, already taking evasive action as Zach reached for his nerf gun. He loosed off a single sponge missile but it flew harmlessly out the office door. Meek was retreating along the corridor to his workshop.

Zach picked up the letter again and looked through it. So Meek was getting 20% more. Zach was promised 30% more and an additional bonus of 15% if the project was completed ahead of time. He grinned and folded the letter into his pocket. Worth a shot. Surely, they had decent broadband in Blythburgh, right?

Zach needn't have worried. The new location just outside Blythburgh was an old radar station that hadn't been used since the 1950s. It held a group of three buildings; one housed the laboratory, one the patients and the other was living quarters for the twenty or so personnel. Zach only recognized three of the others, including Meek. Once he'd been shown his own room, he was quick to plug his laptop into the fast Ethernet connection. Impressive. Apart from being behind the standard UK Government firewall, the detected speed was hovering around 10Gbps, certainly faster than the best public networks. Cool. Zach had no reason to believe that his homegrown software would have any more difficulty slipping out of the firewall onto the internet from here than he'd had in London. He tutted to himself. They should have assigned me to cyber security, he mused. He decided he needed some food and that meant exploring the communal kitchen.

Meek was already monopolizing the four-ring stove; the smells from the three saucepans were mysterious to Zach, but not in a good way.

"What the hell are you making?" asked Zach.

"Something that is healthy, nutritious and organically grown." said Meek, "I wouldn't expect a carnivore such as yourself to appreciate a balanced diet."

"I wouldn't call an obsession with beans and lentils all that balanced." said Zach "Ah, the four major food groups…"

He pulled a meat-laden pizza from the chest freezer and ripped open the box.

"What's your setup like?" inquired Meek "My lab's pretty well stocked."

"It'll do."

"Do you know that guy with the limp?" asked Meek.

"Nah, seen him before though, he came in when we

had that out of band result last August. What's his speciality?"

"That's the thing." said Meek, stopping his incessant stirring and facing Zach, "He specializes in implants."

"Implants?"

"Yeah, he was the guy that put chips in his own body back in the day, remember?"

"You mean before it became standard issue for the spooks?"

"Yeah. Last paper I saw of his he was talking about implanting chips in the brains of high functioning mammals. He claims to have developed memory chips usable in animals."

"Is he the guy that did the rat/maze thing?" inquired Zach.

"Yeah, teach the rat a maze then cut half his brain out so he can't find the food then stick one of his preprogrammed chips in and voila...fatty ratty again."

"Neuro-Enhanced Organisms was the technical term wasn't it? NEO!?" Zach rolled his eyes, "You couldn't make this shit up. Aronson was his name wasn't it? What do you think he's doing here then?"

"That's the thing." said Meek, "I've been assembling circuit diagrams and optimizing them for layering onto a chip. If I remember right what these circuits are doing is imitating some of what Aronson's chip was doing with those rats. But I think they're different."

"In what way?" asked Zach, squeezing his oversized pizza into the undersized microwave.

"I can't tell."

"Is this related to the stuff that Puthoff and Targ were doing, you know, the Stargate stuff?"

"It could be." said Meek, "I think the end goal is that we have chips that augment any natural ability for what they discovered with the Remote Viewing work back in the 70s. This is where some of Aronson's papers might help. He discusses a crossover with Targ and Puthoff's work. He even suggested they collaborate at one point but that doesn't seem to have happened."

"So we check his papers from the database." suggested Zach.

"Obviously, smart ass, except his papers aren't on the database anymore."

The Jolt cola can fizzed as Zach popped the ringpull.

"They must be there, who'd want to remove them?" said Zach.

"Yeah, I don't know. You don't think they're gonna, you know, stick chips in the subjects?"

"Nah, what do think this is, some sort of bad sci-fi movie? Perhaps they want to compare results we're getting from the subs against his circuits?"

"Yeah. I could go with that except for room 7G."

"What's in room 7G?" said Zach.

"A fully equipped 21st century operating theatre, which comfortably exceeds the requirement for onsite First Aid facilities, if you see what I mean."

There was silence in the communal kitchen until the ping from the microwave made them both jump.

9

Plater's mobile rang.

"Hello."

"Mason, it's me, Molly, how's the head?"

"It's a little better actually, I've only taken one pill so far today. Listen can you meet me for lunch, only my dream last night was different and I need to talk to someone about it."

"Sure, where?"

"There's a pub, Hansford Arms, on Gordon Lane."

"I know it, they do a pretty good chilli, 12:30 ok?" said Molly.

Molly was early but Plater was already sitting in an old armchair in the corner of the lounge bar.

"Hi, what would you like?" asked Plater.

"Becks please." said Molly, "What's this?"

She held up an envelope covered in drawings from the table in front of Plater.

"It's what I wanted to talk about." Plater said, as he headed to the bar.

Plater sat down with a second pint, his headache

fading.

"Did you do this?" asked Molly.

"Yes, after I woke up last night, I just felt a need to record it, I don't know why."

Molly was turning the shapes round and round but finally placed it back on the table.

"What's it supposed to be? Any idea?" asked Molly.

"None at all, that's one of the reasons I asked to see you, in case there's something I'm not seeing."

"Not for my fascinating company then?"

"What? Oh yeah, well..."

Molly smiled.

"Kidding. You have to lighten up a bit, this stuff's a bit odd, I know, but there'll be some simple explanation." she said.

She looked down again at the envelope, it was lying at a skewed angle on the sticky table.

"Have you got a pencil?" she said.

"No, but..."

"I thought I saw something then, I want to add some lines, hang on they'll have one behind the bar."

Molly returned with a stubby pencil and began adding lines and curves to the drawing.

"That looks like a 'K' and this one in the corner could be a 'W'. I think they're letters."

She would stop occasionally and turn the envelope round before adding more lines. The shapes seemed to follow a swirling pattern and by turning the paper they almost looked like letters.

"There." she said finally, holding up the envelope.

Although somewhat stylized, the modified drawing now seemed to be words. Not all the letters were clear but there seemed to be three words:

R A ? M O ? D   B A ? T H O ? E ? E W   W A ? B ? R S ? I C
K

"Yes!" said Plater grabbing the envelope and stabbing it with his finger, "Raymond. That name seems familiar...I don't know why but it must be...thanks...but what does it mean?"

"I think it says 'Raymond Bartholomew Walberswick'."

"Hell of a name." said Plater still staring at the design.

"Walberswick is a place in Suffolk." said Molly. "I have an aunt and uncle that lived in Suffolk and I remember seeing it on maps and signposts."

"But what does it mean?" Plater was sounding tense again. He felt he was close to remembering what all this was about, but the answer was slipping through his grasp like sand between the fingers.

"Have you ever been to Walberswick?" said Molly.

"No."

"The name Raymond Bartholomew means nothing?"

"No....although something tells me I should know a Raymond, but I can't think, I'm useless with names."

Plater sighed and sipped his beer, gazing into the distance but desperately wracking his memory for something, anything, that related to 'Raymond Bartholomew Walberswick'.

"Well let's look at it logically." said Molly. "You woke up in the middle of the night and drew this, well, almost this."

"Yes."

"Did you dream while you were asleep this time?"

"Yes, but I don't remember it very well now."

"What do you remember?"

Plater thought for a moment.

"There was a room. A white room. A woman was there."

"Was it Gail Hartston?" said Molly.

"I'm not sure, it might have been. There was someone else. A man."

"Did he have a name?"

"I don't know. He pushed me, and I was falling. Yes, falling...it was noisy...I was just panicking and shouting and spinning..."

Plater paused.

"What?" said Molly.

"On the ground...on the ground...letters, writing, on the ground...that's it....this was on the ground....I had to remember...this is what I had to remember!"

Plater looked triumphant for a moment.

"That's great." said Molly.

"That feels better." said Plater, his shoulders relaxing as he sat back in the chair.

"Now we just have to find Raymond." said Molly.

"What do you mean?" said Plater, "You think he's a real person?"

"Could be, worth a look don't you think? There can't be two 'Raymond Bartholomews' in Walberswick anyway, the place isn't that big if I remember right."

Plater took another gulp of beer.

"Well don't just sit there." said Molly grabbing her jacket, "I'm taking the afternoon off and we're going to Walberswick."

"How far is it?" asked Plater trying to finish his pint

but failing, "How long will it take?"

"No idea, you have anything better to do?"

At Plater's house, they Googled Raymond Bartholomew. They even managed to find what looked like a business address, a book shop, in Walberswick. Within an hour they were in Plater's battered blue Golf negotiating the M25.

It was nearly two hours later that they breached the outskirts of Walberswick on the B1387. It wasn't hard to find the address, The Azeroth Bookshop, The Street, Walberswick. Finding somewhere to ditch the car was a bit trickier. Villages that have such small roads and plenty of summer traffic had cornered the market in yellow paint. Ten minutes later they were at the low door of the Azeroth Bookshop. Plater hesitated.

"Well go on then." said Molly.

As the door opened it sprung a hammer onto an old bell above the doorway. They went down the two small steps into the tiny shop. As if feeling they were intruding, they just looked at each other for a moment. Then a door behind the counter opened and a small blonde-haired man came in.

"Mr Plater, I've been expecting you." he said. "Won't you come through."

The man indicated for them to follow and disappeared again. Plater hesitated and Molly shoved him, mouthing the words 'Go on'.

Plater had to duck slightly to pass through the door behind the counter and found himself in a sort of cross between stock room and sitting room. There was a small, cottage style settee and two small armchairs surrounding a fireplace, most of the limited space was taken by stacks of books.

"Please, won't you sit down." said the man. "Can I get you some tea?"

Plater was still gazing around.

Molly said:

"Yes, please that would be lovely, thank you." She motioned for Plater to sit down.

"Did you have any trouble finding the place?" called the man from the kitchen. "Once you get to the village it's a piece of cake, really, isn't it?"

"Yes." said Plater. "It was no trouble. I'm sorry but do I know you?"

The small man appeared in the doorway to the kitchen.

"Well in a manner of speaking, but perhaps not in the accepted sense." And with a smile he returned to quiet the whistling kettle.

The piles of books that hemmed them in were mostly very old with what would once have been luxurious bindings before the rigors of time, sunlight and centuries of use had taken their toll.

"Here we are." announced the man, placing a tray on the tiny table by the fireplace. "I'll pour but please help yourself to sugar and milk."

He carefully poured three cups of tea in flowery cups and saucers before settling back in one of the armchairs.

"My name is Raymond." said the man. "But then you know that. In fact we have met before Mr Plater. Last night in fact. Although you may not recall very well."

Molly looked from Bartholomew to Plater, wondering what he would say.

"Forgive me." Raymond went on. "I'm being unreasonable. What you are experiencing is both profound and as far as we know, unique. I imagine you've been having some rather unusual dreams lately. Am I right?"

"You could say that." said Plater.

"And these have caused you some concern. That is only to be expected. But you have found me and that means we have taken our first step on what may be a long and difficult road."

"So what does this mean? Why am I here?" said Plater, replacing his cup on the table and leaning forwards. The tightness across his brows returning.

"I know you want to know everything, Mr. Plater, but we think it is better if we take things slowly and at a pace we're all comfortable with. You have had a difficult few days so let me describe what we would recommend from here."

Bartholomew turned and opened a wooden box next to his chair. He removed a soft leather-bound book and placed it on the table.

"The first stage in your training is to have improved recollection of your dreams. This book is to become your constant companion. In it you are to record, immediately upon waking, whatever you can remember of your dreams. This is very important as there will come a time when we can move to the next stage in your development, and we must be sure that you are ready."

"Development? Training? What are you on about? I've been having weird dreams and somehow your name was in one and here you are talking as if you knew this all along. Who are you, Mr. Bartholomew? What is happening to me?"

"It is quite possible, Mr. Plater, that you are what one might call a new breed, a true New Age man, if you like. You have an innate ability to project. By that I mean that when you dream you travel to a different world and can interact with it. Take your dream from last night. The one that brought you here. I don't imagine you can remember it very well, but you remembered enough to find me. I'm sorry about the falling, we felt that something dramatic was needed to bring you to wakefulness quickly in the hope that what remained of your dream could be better recalled. It seems to have worked."

"But how do you know what I dreamed last night?"

"Because I was with you, Mr. Plater, I was in your dream. I was the one that caused you to fall, don't you remember?"

For a moment, Plater was unable to speak.

"You. You're the little man with the rucksack...." said Plater.

"I think the proper name is parachute, but yes."

"But how is that possible?" asked Molly, "How can you be in the same dream? I've known people to have similar dreams but not the same dream and have conversations in them."

"Actually, Miss er..." began Bartholomew.

"Molly, just Molly." said Molly.

"Molly, certain people have had shared dream experiences for millennia. From man's earliest recollections of dreams, he has wondered if, when one sleeps, one travels to mysterious places to live out these dreams. Modern man has experimented with various forms of what are called 'altered states of consciousness'. Mankind has always had a hunch that there is more going on than he can sense or feel in his waking moments. It turns out that while these artificial attempts may one day find the key, the easiest path to altered consciousness is through a medium we all as humans are forced to share - sleep."

Bartholomew paused to sip some tea and the only sound was the significant tick of the lacquered clock on the mantelpiece.

"Sleep is a time when the incessant interruptions of wakefulness are removed." he continued. "The brain may turn its attention to matters other than those of daily life. Of course, perceptive men from the past have sensed this need to remove external temptations and in extreme cases have left society for solitude."

"Do you mean yogis, monks, nuns and that sort of thing?" said Plater.

"You are right." said Bartholomew. "In most cases from history those who felt there may be something else were looking for religious enlightenment. That is because this was how such things were described in society and over time this search for enlightenment became synonymous with religion. In fact, there need be no such connection."

"Are you telling me I've had some sort of religious experience?" said Plater.

"No, quite the reverse. I'm saying that it is quite likely that those in history that have claimed to have had religious experiences were probably having an experience similar to yours."

"I'm confused." said Molly, "What do Mason's dreams indicate?"

"It's quite simple, on one level. Your dreams show you have not only an innate ability to enter this alternative reality, if you like, but also to communicate and remember your interactions when you return to our reality. This is rare in, shall we say, normal people. Very rare indeed without intensive training."

"So, I'm in some other world when I sleep, is that what you're saying? What is in that other world? I'm still asleep in my bed. I don't travel anywhere."

"It is best to think of it that way." continued Bartholomew, "I'm afraid that none of us really understand the science behind this phenomenon. As you learn more about us you will understand, I hope, why that is."

"You keep mentioning 'us' Mr. Bartholomew." said Molly. "Who's 'us'?"

"When I said that Mr. Plater was probably unique, I meant that he is the first person we know of that seems to have an innate ability to enter this altered consciousness without training. There are others that have this ability but they pay a heavy price for it. More tea?"

Bartholomew leaned forwards and picked up the heavy teapot.

"Er, yes, thank you." said Plater, easing himself back into his seat. "Please, go on."

"Yes please." said Molly, as Bartholomew glanced at her.

Bartholomew carefully poured their teas and sipped his own.

"It was a very happy coincidence, Mr. Plater, that you took the job at Lievesham Hall. Your chance encounter with Miss Hartston was most helpful. I can't explain why, we just don't understand these things, but since she had some effect on you that day she was in your mind when you went to sleep that night. Somehow, and again, I apologise for not having a cleaner explanation, this helped you to 'find' her in this alternative reality."

"You were attracted to her." said Molly.

"Exactly." said Bartholomew "My point is that people in Miss Hartston's unfortunate condition seem to find access to this other reality very easy. It is a blessing really as it affords them the opportunity to live in something like the manner in which we do here in the physical world."

"So, let me see if I'm getting this." said Plater. "You're saying that I'm some sort of freak that slips into this 'other world' when I sleep now, just because I saw that woman in the hospital? That's insane."

"I'm saying that we, as humans, seem to have vast areas of our brains that we know little of. Most of our actions in our daily lives, up to 80% I believe, are actually handled by our 'unconscious' or 'subconscious' minds rather than our conscious. You have a genetic ability that was unknown to you before you ran across Miss Hartston. The fact you were apparently thinking about her as you slept has enabled your mind to bridge the gap to this alternative reality. As much as any other learning skill works in the brain the more it is used the easier it becomes. Now that you have found the way it will be hard to lose it so you must learn to control it."

"Mason can learn how to turn this on and off?" asked

Molly.

"Oh yes." said Bartholomew.

"If it's all the same to you I think just learning how to turn it off will be fine." said Plater.

"Perhaps, but I think once you have heard the rest of my explanation you may change your mind. Your life may depend on it." said Bartholomew. "Would you like some biscuits?"

Neither Molly nor Plater took up Bartholomew's offer, so he took one of the digestives for himself and took a crumbly bite.

"How were you able to be in my dream?" asked Plater. "I thought you said I was 'unique'?"

"When I was younger, I was a student of the occult Mr Plater. The books you see around you are partly the remnants of my personal collection. I was young and open to new ideas; I was curious about life; why are we here? What is our purpose?"

Bartholomew looked behind his chair and picked a leather-bound book from one pile.

"'The Book of Sacred Magic of Abramelin the Mage'." he said, riffling the beautifully bound book lovingly. "This is a signed first edition, you know, of the MacGregor Mathers translation from the Aramaic. If you were to sell this now it would fetch upwards of £20,000 to a collector. But as I read more, I also joined some like-minded people in a society called the Golden Dawn."

"I've heard of that." said Molly. "Wasn't Aleister Crowley a member?"

"Who?" asked Plater.

"Aleister Crowley." said Bartholomew. "Was something

of a distraction. He was more famous for his lifestyle than any contribution to knowledge or interpretation of ancient writings."

"Yeah, he was into sex and magic wasn't he? And drugs?" wondered Molly.

"Indeed." said Bartholomew. "He also was searching for that altered state that he believed would enable contact with a higher plane. He sought it through the ecstatic state of congress and the use of hallucinogenic drugs. However, his claimed successes in his writings are hard to verify and it is commonly felt he enjoyed the search for enlightenment rather too much, if you see what I mean."

"I'm still not sure what all of this has to do with me." said Plater. "I just want these dreams to stop and to get back to my life."

"I fear." began Bartholomew. "That your life will never get back to 'normal', whatever that meant to you. If you will let me complete my story, perhaps you will understand."

He paused and Molly glanced at Plater, who nodded to Bartholomew.

"On joining the Golden Dawn, I was taught the basics of ritual magic and various skills that should help me on my path to enlightenment as prescribed in such books as this. One of the main skills is known as Astral Projection, which we might understand as a sort of 'directed dreaming'. At the start of one's training the goal is to remember dreams, by writing anything that is remembered in a book, such as I have given you. This must be done immediately on waking as consciousness wipes our memories of dreams like a teacher dusting a blackboard.

"Then, as that skill in remembering improves, the next step is to fall asleep thinking of something and being able to dream about that idea. It could be a football match or a trip to the seaside. Once that can be accomplished the next step is the most powerful. You agree to meet others in your dream and exchange information known only to you. This way you will know that a successful meeting has taken place. Beyond that lies treading the path to enlightenment and there, I'm afraid the occultists wander off into flights of fantasy. I myself parted company with the Golden Dawn some years ago."

"Okay, now just supposing I believe this stuff about controlling dreams and meeting people and all that, which I'm not saying I do, why can't I just make it stop and leave all this stuff to people like you, who obviously have some interest in it?" said Plater.

Bartholomew took a noticeably deeper breath.

"That, Mr. Plater, is going to take more explaining than I can accomplish myself. Suffice to say your obvious talent, which we believe to be God given, or nature, if you prefer, is of such potential value to human society that we must try everything to encourage you. Using your skill will save countless lives, Mr. Plater, perhaps the entire future of humanity on this planet."

The drive back to London for Molly and Plater was composed of long silences broken by occasional exchanges. They were both trying to rationalize all that they had heard from Raymond Bartholomew.

"The guy's as mad as a hatter." said Plater as they

headed South on the A12.

"He seemed pretty sane to me." said Molly. "Don't forget we're only out here because of what he apparently showed you in a dream."

"Do you have the envelope that he gave us?" asked Plater.

Molly reached into the back seat, retrieved her soft leather shoulder bag and rummaged in it.

"Yeah." she said holding up an envelope with the word 'Wednesday' written in fountain pen in a flowing almost Dickensian script.

"Do you think we should open it?" asked Molly turning the envelope in her hand and holding it to the light.

"Bartholomew seemed keen we shouldn't." said Plater. "Although if it has instructions in I can't see why we shouldn't know now."

"Shall I?"

"No, let's give the old coot a chance. Listen, since you've been such a help these past few days can I buy you dinner when we get back?"

"Ok, on one condition." said Molly.

"What's that?"

"That we don't talk about this stuff."

"Deal." said Plater, as he indicated to join the M25.

10

Zach burped loudly after his third cola and woke his laptop from hibernation. He glanced round his room but of course he was alone. Since he was about to do something that might not only get him fired but also possibly imprisoned, he couldn't help himself. He signed into the Department network and opened the research library. Entering 'Aronson' in the search box, he hit enter and waited for the search to run. Within about 3-5 seconds, a list began appearing of papers authored or co-authored by 'Aronson'. He was able to eliminate most of the first page of results from the wrong Aronson, but he hadn't expected there to be three. As the results mounted up, he cancelled that search and refined it to 'Aronson P.'. The P was for Paul. This time the search took a little longer to find the first match but then only listed 5 papers. The most recent of these was dated two years ago. Zach was sure he'd only read about Aronson's latest announcement on the net about six months ago.

He knew there had been more recent papers than

this because Meek had mentioned them. The work was a bit off-the-wall which had attracted Meek, but he'd said he hadn't the time then to analyse them too much. As far as he could remember, this was the first time Zach had heard of data being removed from the Department Research database. Over the five years since he'd joined, he had only known the data store to grow in size, with ever more sophisticated search facilities and data mining tools.

He tried a couple of variations on Aronson's name, like using two As, but these came up empty. There seemed no logical reason to remove Aronson's papers from the database. Only people with high level clearance had access to that area in the database anyway. Zach went to his rucksack and from one of the numerous zipped pouches on the outside, he took a USB stick. Once inserted in his laptop, a small box appeared asking for the time. Instead of the time, Zach typed in a long string of characters including letters, numbers, symbols and even key combinations that have no associated printable character. Once the 16th character had been input the box evaporated, and a new window appeared. Zach was now able to access all log files kept of activity on the Departmental system, including the Research Database. He entered details of what he wanted to look for and then clicked the button marked 'Go'. Within a second, a red button lit up that had 'Tidy-Up' written on it. Zach hit it immediately. He'd executed a long string of actions, which themselves would have shown up in the very logs he was looking for, so it was key to execute them in the smallest possible time slot and then to remove traces of them immediately. Opening the file 'results.txt', he saw that the Aronson papers had been deleted the same day he'd submitted his report to Braberson about the 95% match between subjects. Even the log kept certain details encrypted, like the identifiers for the person or machine that performed the actions. So, Zach now needed to cut and paste the garbled string of junk that hid the name into his decrypting suite. It took about four minutes before the second guess by the program for the decoded string of letters flashed 'BRABERSON'.

He switched to another virtual screen on his laptop and executed his suite of programs that established his path to the internet. Until the Government changed their standard router/firewall manufacturer or they discovered his 0-day exploit, he'd be able to silently slip out to the internet whenever he wanted and without leaving a trace. Sure, he could have sold his discovery on one of the 'exploit marketplaces' on the net, where hackers sold their discoveries for cash, to anti-virus manufacturers, those whose software was exploited or even those with more sinister intent, but this beauty was more valuable to him than a few thousand US dollars.

The familiar Google screen appeared, and he began looking for references to Aronson's work in the rambling vastness of the net. After more than half an hour he'd only managed to find references to work from about two years ago. There were some articles in Scientific American, New York Times, some blog posts about his inserting chips into his own body, but they were even older. He then tried cross referencing against academic papers relating to Targ and Puthoff's work on

Remote Viewing as well as papers resulting from the work done in the former Soviet Union. Nothing pointing to anything by Aronson more recently than two years ago.

Zach poured himself a coffee and gazed out of the window. Not that the view was too great. His room overlooked a courtyard at the back of the building which held dustbins and two unmarked vans. The view beyond was of some trees and densely filled bushes. With the landscape of Suffolk being largely flat he reckoned that these three quite large buildings would be invisible from the surrounding countryside.

Returning to his laptop he placed questions on 5 forums that discussed advances in neuroscience and related disciplines. These were under an online-only identity and since he always used Tor when at work, this would hide the real source of his surfing, the IP address that could be traced to his physical location. The questions were about Aronson's more recent work. Unless he was very lucky, he'd have to wait for the timezones to unwind to get any answers. He undid his internet escape tunnel and hibernated his laptop again.

As he finally killed the light and tried to get to sleep, he couldn't help wondering why someone in Braberson's position was manually deleting stuff from the database. He needed to get hold of those Aronson papers somehow, so Meek could tell him what this was all about.

On the ground floor of the laboratory building Angela Crawford was in a flap. This was her first 'special project' for the Department and she'd only been in post a few months. She'd been hoping for a quiet night shift while she got used to the strange surroundings but no such luck. The red alarm on her screen meant she would have to call the Director. She'd never even seen the Director let alone spoken to him. She wished she could just hit 'clear' and remove the alarm, but she knew it was logged in at least three places within the system (actually it was five but only select administrators knew that). Now she couldn't even find the Director's mobile number. If she couldn't find it this could be her shortest assignment in her short professional career. Finally, she found a laminated card in the pocket of the administration pack she'd been given when she started. The Director's three contact numbers were there. She selected the mobile and dialed.

"Braberson."

"Good evening, sir, sorry to bother you but this is Security at Stage 3 Control. I have a red alarm on my screen."

She paused while she scrolled the screen to find the alarm reference details.

"Well, what does it say?" snapped Braberson

"It's a search argument reference to a listed identifier, sir."

"Which listed identifier?"

"Aronson, sir."

"By whom?"

"Hamilton, sir, Zach Hamilton."

"Thank you." said Braberson.

"Would you like..." began the security guard, but the line was already dead.

* * *

Of the many duties expected of a government minister, drinks receptions were not among James Carver's favourites. He wasn't averse to a drink, but he always found the need to indulge in pleasantries with strangers difficult. This particular early evening gathering comprised mainly of executives from British and European armaments manufacturers. He had met most of them before and hadn't hit it off with the French contingent at all, nor the Scandinavians; in fact Sir Richard Thorncroft of the British company Falcon had been the only one he'd hoped to speak with again.

Falcon developed unmanned aerial vehicles (UAVs) and remote-controlled robots similar to those first used to such effect in Iraq and Afghanistan by the Americans. As Carver glanced around the room, he saw several senior MoD officials deep in conversation with Falcon staff. Indeed the French looked somewhat put out but were drowning their sorrows in some rather decent champagne and switching their attentions to two of the personal assistants from the Scandinavian delegation, two striking Nordic blondes.

As he pondered whether he should have a second glass of champagne, the mobile phone in his trouser pocket vibrated. Carver placed his empty glass on a passing waiter's tray and moved swiftly but politely through the guests until he left the reception, turned left and went through the next door along the corridor. He pulled out the phone and saw a text message on the screen. It was a sequence of digits. As he touched the numeric keys of the phone to mirror the numeric text he'd received, a complex sequence of communications began between his phone and that of the sender. Once the two devices had established a secure channel, which took about five seconds, a message in English appeared on Carver's phone:

'Phase 2 data confirmed. Phase 3 data required soonest. Raw data via Bluenet every 12 hours. Attempt simulation. Move to physical immediately.'

Carver re-read the message then touched the red square in the lower left corner of his touch screen phone. The message vanished. No trace of it remained, not even for the latest in digital forensics to find.

He didn't like it. Things were moving too fast in his opinion. Simulation was one thing but moving into physical now was too much. He absently rolled the phone over and over in his hand, his fingers brushing its smooth surfaces while he considered his options. To do anything other than what he'd been told would have inevitable consequences. Some he knew or could anticipate, such as being removed from his job, but others, probably worse, he couldn't know.

The door opened quickly and Michael Sangster glanced inside.

"Home Secretary." he said. "The French are insisting on some time with you sir. I think you should give them perhaps ten minutes or so…"

"Yes, yes of course." said Carver. "Please make sure they have drinks and I'll be there in a moment."

"Of course sir." said Sangster almost bowing as he closed the door.

Carver pressed a speed dial on his phone and waited. He had no choice but to do as instructed.

* * *

Zach was very nervous. He felt like a naughty schoolboy waiting outside the Headmaster's office. Actually, he was sat outside Braberson's office in the Stage 3 Control Centre. He wasn't a very good liar and knew that if Braberson asked any awkward questions he'd give something away.

"Zach, good of you to wait, do come in." said Braberson in a suspiciously welcoming tone. Zach had an image of a fly taking tentative steps towards the centre of a spider web.

"Take a seat." said Braberson and picked up a three-page document stapled at one corner. "I wanted to ask you about something Zach."

Zach could feel blood rising to his cheeks and he hoped he wasn't looking too guilty. If his nocturnal excursions through the Top Secret network had been detected, he could be looking at a prison term but a far more worrying period with the Security Services before that.

"I have a report here from our security people." Braberson peered at Zach over the document, then went back to reading it. "You seem to have taken a sudden interest in an area of research outside your normal duties."

"Sir?" said Zach, not wishing to confirm anything until he knew what they knew.

"You performed searches of the restricted database last night looking for work by Paul Aronson. Would you mind telling me why?"

Braberson placed the document carefully on his desk and looked directly at Zach.

"I remembered seeing something by Aronson a while

back. Something about implants, and I wanted to check if his chip program might be usable in our work, sir."

There was a short pause and Zach knew his complexion must be reddening, he just hoped it was slight.

"What was your conclusion?" said Braberson.

Zach had to think quickly, he must be sure to keep Meek out of it and not reveal anything he may have learned through his illegal excursions to the internet.

"Well, it was a bit odd actually because I had expected to find a more recent paper by Dr Aronson but I must have been mistaken." said Zach.

"Not entirely." said Braberson. " There was a newer paper by Aronson on the system but some flaws were discovered in it and it was withdrawn for closer scrutiny. We can't have misleading data doing the rounds, now can we?"

Braberson was looking relaxed and moved the document to one side.

"How are you finding the accommodation?" he asked. "Room comfortable?"

"Yes, pretty good really." replied Zach, now totally off balance. He'd expected a grilling. The apparent ease with which Braberson had covered the incident made Zach uneasy.

"Excellent." went on Braberson. "If progress continues as it has so far, we may be able to shorten our stay here and get back home ahead of schedule."

"Oh, good." said Zach.

"If you speak to Williams he will provide you with the programming for the Aronson chip."

"Er great, thank you, sir." said Zach.

Braberson had begun punching a number into the phone on his desk. When he noticed that Zach hadn't moved he covered the mouth piece and said:

"Anything else Zach?"

Zach suddenly realized their interview was over and hurriedly left. Something was still worrying him about why he'd been let off so lightly. He should have completed an online request to access the data on Aronson's papers as they were outside his authorized access areas. This was a significant security breach and yet Braberson had treated it as a minor indiscretion. Offering to let Zach see the programming was an unexpected bonus, but he knew he'd now need to provide a report comparing the functionality as it related to his own area, just to maintain the lie.

11

Kathleen Moran busied herself washing some dishes and tidying the small kitchen. Time was her greatest enemy. Nordstrom had strongly advised that she stay indoors, at least for the first two weeks as he feared that the Church of the Reclamation would be looking for both her and her daughter. Nordstrom was sure that the Church knew of some of the safe houses the Cult Recovery Network, or CRN, used in Texas but this one was a recent addition, so he felt it was indeed safe.

Nordstrom had been waiting for a blood analysis of the sample he'd drawn when Dawn was first lifted. It was not unusual these days to find cult members being fed a cocktail of synthetic drugs to manage their behaviour. Nordstrom didn't think that Dawn was drugged but he needed to be sure.

Kathleen Moran saw the huge Dodge pickup as it turned into the street. Even in the wide suburban Fort Worth streets, the truck was a monster. It lurched up the driveway and stopped a few feet from the kitchen window.

"Hi Kathleen." said Nordstrom and kissed Kathleen Moran on her cheek.

"Hi Erik, coffee?"

"No, I want to get straight on with Dawn if I can. How is she today?"

"Quiet, I tried to talk to her when I took her food, but she was just lying on the bed."

"You didn't go in?" said Nordstrom.

"No, I just passed it through the slot. You said…"

"That's right, until we know more about her state of mind it's important that we limit contact, for everyone's safety."

Nordstrom headed down to the basement, carefully emptied his pockets and removed his watch. As he opened the door, he caught movement from inside. Dawn made a sharp movement of her hand against her arm. When the door swung wider, he saw the blood. It was a standing rule that nothing breakable was to enter the room. Erik saw the remnants of a broken pottery mug on the floor, it was the mug Dawn had made at school, her mother had shown it to him while they'd talked about Dawn's early years. Kathleen must have given Dawn a drink in it by mistake. The blood was coming from Dawn's wrists and as she rolled onto her back it could be seen squirting more than a foot into the air as it pumped from her. Erik ripped his t-shirt from his body and wrapped it frantically round the thrashing girl's wrist. She was clawing at him with her other hand, bitten fingernails raking his face. Erik began shouting for Kathleen to call 911. She appeared at the doorway and needed Erik to shout at her again to call the emergency services before she caught herself and ran back upstairs.

Dawn now lay quietly on the bed, smiling up at Erik. They both knew why she had done this. They both knew she had waited until Erik came in so that he could help her. She was fortunate that he acted so quickly. Now she would have to go to a hospital and once there, she could call her friends at the Church and they would come and get her. This also meant her mother and this deprogrammer would be arrested for kidnapping her and holding her against her will.

12

Her skin was smooth under his hand. The dip of her waist and the climb to the crest of her hip as she lay on her side, facing away from him. Not wanting to disturb her, Plater rolled onto his back but, too excited to sleep, propped himself on his hands behind his head. He realized he was smiling. He was happy, really happy, for the first time in a very long time.

She was much younger than him but that didn't seem to matter to either of them. He was feeling more like a man than he had for more than five years. In his newfound peace, he closed his eyes, and when he opened them, his heart missed a beat. Reflected in the mirrored door on the opposite wall of the bedroom was a figure. It was wearing a hood, but Plater soon realized it must be standing close to the window to one side of the bed. Without a second thought, he rolled off the bed and faced the intruder. Plater was naked and the intruder had their back to him. Plater reached forwards but the figure spun round to face him. It was wearing a cowled robe and the face was completely hidden. In its hand was a slim, black object that looked like an artist's paintbrush. Before Plater realized what it was, he felt a sudden jolt in his chest which knocked him over backwards.

Plater woke with a start. At first, he had no idea where he was. It was barely light outside, just a faint brightness around the edges of the blinds at his window. He reached for his watch on the bedside table. 06:55.

Then he remembered the intruder, but almost before he'd glanced to where he'd seen him, he realized it had been a dream. His mouth was dry but his neck was damp with sweat. He flopped back to the pillow and stared at the ceiling. Damnit. The disappointment was tangible. He glanced over but the other side of his king-sized bed was unoccupied. Just as he was about to roll out and head for the shower, he remembered the book. He found the page for today and started to write.

Although he'd only been writing his recollections down for a week or so he'd already got to the stage where he hardly saw the need. For him, there was now a new problem. He was beginning to have difficulty in separating reality from dreams in his memories but also occasionally during his experiences. He was so convinced that an intruder had been in his bedroom that after his shower, he'd examined the area where he'd seen the figure for physical evidence. Of course, Plater found nothing. He sat on the side of the bed with his head in his hands for a few minutes. He'd thought that he was getting a handle on this thing but just as he began to feel he had control, it was slipping away.

He finished dressing and, before going downstairs,

looked in on Molly. She'd stopped in after work to check on his progress with recording his dreams. They'd talked about how much they believed all that Raymond Bartholomew had told them. In fact, by the time they stopped it was into the early hours so it seemed natural that she stayed. He could make out her sleeping form from the door.

Two fried eggs began sizzling in a small pan while the toaster worked on two slices of bread; the coffee machine spluttered and dripped. Then Plater remembered it was Wednesday. He hurried into the sitting room and scooped up the envelope from the mantelpiece. He paused, wondering if he should wait until Molly got up then decided he couldn't. He ripped open the thick, old-fashioned envelope and pulled out the sheet of high-quality writing paper. Written in the same flowing hand and distinctive purple ink was:

Mason,

If you have done as we agreed you should be ready to take your next step towards fulfilling your potential.

Tonight, before retiring, you must try to memorize the following information:

Mr Black had Blue shoes, Mrs White had Red shoes, Mr Green had Yellow shoes and Mrs Brown had Orange shoes.

It is very important that you memorize this exactly. We will be waiting.

* * *

With very best wishes,
   Raymond

Plater read the letter a second time. It seemed like nonsense. He read the sentence over a few times, then put the letter aside. What was the chance that he was actually going mad? Why hadn't this special ability been noticed before, if he had such a thing? Why now? The woman, Gail, why couldn't the crew have chosen someone else? None of this would have happened then. Plater's biggest decision today would have been whether he needed to go grocery shopping rather than contemplating a meeting in some other world or dimension. Thoughts began racing through his mind. Thoughts of his sons, his work and Molly asleep upstairs. His life so far. He suddenly saw in a wider context of his house, then his street then London then the UK then spiraling out like Google Maps until he flashed on the view of Earth from space.

"Is there enough for two?" asked Molly, piling her tousled hair onto her head before letting it fall again. She padded into the kitchen barefoot and wearing one of Plater's shirts.

"I'll put some more on." said Plater.

She sat at the table and Plater poured her some coffee.

"Thanks." she said "Hey, it's Wednesday, have you looked at the note?"

"Here." said Plater passing the letter to Molly. "God knows what it means, looks like nonsense to me."

Molly seemed to be reading the letter more than

once.

"I see what you mean." she said. "Well you've got about 12 hours to memorize it."

"Are you going to work?" asked Plater.

"What time is it?"

The clock on the wall read 07:45.

"I'd better put in an appearance this morning." said Molly. "We're bidding for a corporate multimedia contract and there's a possible comedy series for Channel Five. Meetings until about one. We could meet for lunch?"

"Yeah."

"I'll test you on your homework." said Molly, with a smile.

13

The phone calls had started the evening of his interview with Rev. Ethan Daniels. Calm but assertive in the beginning. But by the next afternoon, after speaking to his source in Miami on the phone, they became more threatening. Still nothing that would alarm a court, but the thinly disguised menace was unmistakable to an old stager like Warren Gatts. In his twenties he'd been threatened by any number of unscrupulous businessmen, con men and small-time local gangsters, and he'd taken it as a badge of honour. If he was rattling their cages enough for them to come after him, he must be doing something right.

Now in his late forties his attitude had changed. The fires of right and the desire to bring some of these shadowy figures out into the light still burned within him, but he had a kid to support from his failed marriage. She needed help paying doctor bills since she'd been hit by a drunk driver twelve years before and his insurance ran out long ago. His ex-wife never let him forget why she left him. His work meant more to him than his family.

Sitting in his cramped office surrounded by old files and an unhealthy amount of dust, he thought she might have been right. He opened a drawer and took out the photograph that used to stand on his desk, before the encroaching papers left no room. His wife and daughter, she would have been about ten, were posing outside Disney World. That had been a good holiday, one of the best. But he got little credit from his ex-wife for that either. Just because he was investigating staff conditions within the Disney leisure empire and spent a couple of afternoons poking around. What she hadn't understood was that they couldn't have afforded that holiday if he hadn't been on expenses and spent his advance for the article.

He slid the photograph back into the drawer and put new batteries in his mini recorder. He grabbed his battered shoulder bag and was driving into the parking area of the Fort Worth Sheriff's offices within twenty-five minutes.

"But I called yesterday and spoke to Ralph." said Gatts to the disinterested Deputy who continued reading some yellow forms.

"Listen Deputy...." Gatts craned to read the badge on the Deputy's shirt. "...Mallory, I spoke to Ralph...Sheriff Benjamin yesterday and he said I could speak with the suspect at 3 p.m. and it's 3.05. Why don't you give him a call?"

The Deputy glanced up at Gatts then back to the forms.

"Sheriff Benjamin is not here right now, sir. There is no record of your visit in the diary."

Gatts was about to say something he shouldn't when the swing doors admitted the sturdy figure of Sheriff Ralph Benjamin.

"Warren." said the Sheriff in a gruff greeting. "You here to see that boy?"

"Yeah." said Gatts.

"Deputy, would you show Mr. Gatts here into interview room 3 and bring him the abduction suspect please?"

Gatts thought he kept the smile under wraps, but the Deputy wasn't impressed. Still young and thinking that everything should be done by the book. A couple more years dealing with the detritus of Fort Worth might loosen him up a bit.

Interview Room 3 had a table and four chairs. One either side of the table and two against a wall along with a small reinforced glass porthole in the heavy door and recessed neon lights. Gatts prepared the recorder as he waited for the suspect. He didn't bother with the niceties of asking if he could tape the interview. No point, the interviewee might say no.

Erik Nordstrom came in in handcuffs, trailed by a deputy.

"Sit." said the deputy and Nordstrom slumped into a chair by the table. His cuffs thudded onto the heavy wooden tabletop.

"I'll be right outside so don't cause no trouble, y'hear?"

Nordstrom shot the deputy an almost quizzical look. He had the air of someone slightly bewildered to be in his situation.

"Mr. Nordstrom my name is Gatts, Warren Gatts."

Gatts offered his hand then realized the awkwardness and withdrew it. "I'm glad to have this chance to speak with you, Mr. Nordstrom..."

"Erik."

"...Erik, because I am investigating incidents that are associated with the Church of the Reclamation myself."

"What incidents?" said Nordstrom.

"I can't say at the moment. I'm afraid, but I understand that you have had dealings with the Church before?"

Erik looked at Gatts and wondered why he didn't just come out with whatever it was he wanted to know.

"If you mean have I tried to help people that have fallen for their bullshit then yeah, so what? Look where it's got me."

"I wonder if you'd mind looking at some photographs I have here." Gatts laid out nine photographs of people, six men and three women. They were clearly surveillance pictures.

Nordstrom looked at them.

"Have you seen any of these people before?" asked Gatts.

Nordstrom picked up one of the pictures of a man.

"Yeah, this guy."

"Where did you see him?"

"Before we picked up Dawn, we spent three weeks watching the CoR's Dallas properties. This guy was a regular visitor. "

"Do you know his name?"

"'Fraid not." said Nordstrom replacing the photograph amongst the others.

"You haven't seen any of the others?"

"Nope."

"While you were watching the Church's offices, did you by any chance keep a log of people coming and going? Did you write anything down?"

"We're not the FBI, Mr. Gatts, we don't have stakeout teams, we're just some private citizens trying to save some kids that have taken a wrong turn."

"Yes, of course." said Gatts. "Can you tell me what first got you interested in the Church of the Reclamation?"

Nordstrom thought for a moment.

"I guess it was six years ago we first heard of it. There are folks that tell us about stuff they've seen on the in'ernet and there was this kid, a girl, whose brother had upped and left home to join some Church. She wrote on the in'ernet that she'd tried writing to her brother but he replied at first, then nothin'. She used to speak to him by phone sometimes then one day she called and was told he'd moved to another location. They wouldn't tell her where."

Gatts noticed a tired wariness in Nordstrom's eyes.

"So, what happened?" asked Gatts.

"One of our folks that spends time on the in'ernet sent her an e-mail and she came in to talk to us. It was obvious this Church was nothin' but a cult setup, being used to take money off these poor misguided kids. We agreed to help."

"But what could you do?"

"Nothin' at first, we just watched and found the girl's brother out at some Church property in Louisiana. They were working at a Church sponsored refuge for the homeless, handing out food and spiritual guidance. One of our guys went along, pretended to be homeless, got talking to the boy, Michael I think his name was. Anyhow, Michael tried to help our guy and they would talk most days. Turned out Michael wasn't so sure about the Church anymore. He'd seen and heard about some stuff he didn't like but they made sure he had no time to do much more than work and sleep."

Nordstrom bowed his head.

"Our guy, Sam was his name, he managed to persuade Michael that he should leave the Church, just walk away. So they arranged to meet one afternoon behind this warehouse between the Church headquarters and the homeless refuge. Michael was just going to leave, that day, with Sam."

Nordstrom stopped.

"What happened?" asked Gatts.

"Well, the official report said that a retaining wall of the old warehouse collapsed on them. Buried them. When they dug 'em out they were a mess. Couldn't hardly tell 'em apart, except for their clothes."

"You don't think it was an accident?"

Nordstrom looked up at Gatts.

"We had a second postmortem done on Sam. They found small puncture wounds in his neck. Like from a needle, a syringe."

"What about the other boy, er, Michael?"

"We couldn't check with him, his family had him cremated."

"What was your man injected with?" asked Gatts.

"There were traces of some muscle relaxant, like vets use for horses and such. Seems folks like to use them during sex too. So, they said that this didn't prove anything and that it was just an accident, like the judge had said before."

Gatts sat in silence. The more he discovered about the Church of the Reclamation, the more he thought he could be getting too old for this.

"Oh yeah." said Nordstrom. "That guy."

"Who?"

"The one in your pictures, the one with those little round glasses, he was at the hearing when the judge ruled it an accident."

14

Plater spent the first two hours after Molly rushed to catch a train for work busying himself around the house. He was like a domestic whirlwind, cleaning, tidying and loading the washing machine. By around 10:30, he stopped and his thoughts turned to his boys. He determined to call them that evening; it must have been about three weeks since he'd last spoken to them. He'd had an occasional email, but he needed to see them.

He poured a cup of aging coffee and flopped on the giant sofa, pushing off his shoes. As he sat, looking up at the ceiling, he thought he could hear voices, only they weren't from the street outside. Murmurings as if those speaking were just too far away to be understood. He began to think of his boys and remembered teaching Ricky to drop-kick a rugby ball. Ricky was seven and the rugby ball had seemed huge in his tiny hands.

"It keeps moving dad!" said Ricky in frustration. "Watch."

The boy dropped the ball and it fell at an angle and as

the point touched the ground it veered off to the left, just as Ricky's right leg swung and caught only air. He scowled at his father as the ball wobbled to a stop by his feet.

"Do you remember how we decided to do this, Ricky?" said Plater. "Hold the ball like this, in front of you, then drop it straight and as soon as you let go try to kick it, okay?"

The boy retrieved the ball almost reluctantly and prepared another attempt. He held the ball out in front, his tongue creeping out one side of his mouth in concentration. As he dropped it his foot came through and caught the ball cleanly. It went almost straight up into the air about twelve feet while Ricky had lost his balance and fell flat on his back. Plater lunged forwards to catch the ball to stop it dropping on Ricky. As he took the catch, he shuddered. Instead of the international rugby ball he was holding a human head which by its discoloured appearance was from a body that had been dead for some time.

He had fallen asleep. Somehow, he knew this. He turned around and he could see nothing but grass, extending off in all directions as far as he could see. His son, Ricky, was no longer there nor the human head. Plater stood gazing round at vast open fields beneath a wide blue sky. He caught some movement in the distance, but the movement seemed all around, at the very limit of his vision. Then gradually he could see. It was trees. Coming closer to him, from all directions, there were hundreds, no thousands, perhaps tens of thousands of trees. All shapes and sizes and they were closing in around him. There was no noise. It was an almost audible silence, where the mind substitutes sounds to fill the absence, like a faint whine or whistle as if an amplifier is on with no music. It seemed as if the trees were closing in faster and faster the nearer they were. Plater found himself covering his head, closing his eyes and bracing for an impact as the huge trees rushed at him from every angle.

When he opened his eyes again, he was in a forest. The trees had settled into a dense wood. He could barely see ten yards in any direction as the foliage closed between the trunks.

"You do not belong here." said a male voice.

Plater jumped. He couldn't see anyone in the dark undergrowth nor tell from which direction the voice had come.

"You do not belong here." the voice repeated, slightly louder this time.

"Who are you?" called Plater looking around him for any sign of movement.

Suddenly, Plater could make out movement, but it seemed as if the very forest floor was alive. The carpet of fallen leaves rustled and shook. The climbing vines that encircled most of the trees seemed to shift and uncoil, their leafy tendrils snaking from the trunks of the trees towards Plater. He recoiled but the tentacles were coming from all sides. He felt the first one brush his arm and flailed madly to escape, but others covered his feet and began to wrap themselves round his legs and work higher to his chest and wrapping around each wrist, they held his arms out from his body allowing other strands to complete the cocoon of his torso. As the coils tightened, he was finding it hard to breathe. They began to wind around his face and he heard the voice again.

"You do not belong here."

This time, the voice seemed to be inside his head and it was the last thing he heard as the creepers closed over his eyes and the tightening grip around his chest forced the breath from him.

The rhythm was unmistakable...tap tap tap, sets of three beats separated by a pause. Plater felt as if he was floating but all around him was darkness. He had no sensations of touch or heat. He couldn't even feel his limbs. Tap tap tap the rhythm began again. All at once sparkling lights began exploding across his vision. In the same instant he could feel his arms and legs, his head, his pulse and heard the familiar tap tap tap. The sparkling lights coalesced to an image of his sitting room and his brain slotted into consciousness like an open drawer being closed.

Tap tap tap.

Plater pulled himself wearily from the sofa and answered the door. It was Molly.

"You took your time." she began cheerily, until she saw his tired appearance. "Are you okay? Has something happened?"

Plater just turned and retreated to the sofa, sighing heavily as he sat back down.

"Mason, are you OK? You look shattered."

Molly cast aside her coat and bag to join Plater on the sofa.

"I've just been sleeping." said Plater through pinched eyelids. "It was a bit weird this time."

"Well, I'm listening." said Molly. "Do you want anything? Something to drink?"

"Water...please."

"Was the woman in your dream this time?" said Molly fetching some water.

"No, I was..."

"What?"

"I was going to say I was alone but I don't think I was."

"What do you mean?" asked Molly.

"There was some sort of presence. I was in this forest and then the trees...well the trees attacked me."

"You're kidding" said Molly.

"Creepers wrapped around me from all over and just crushed me."

"That's scary, what did you do?"

"There was nothing I could do, I just remember the breath being crushed out of me, I thought I was going to die."

"This is getting too weird." said Molly, touching Plater's arm as it lay between them on the sofa. "I think you should see someone."

"What do you mean?" said Plater. "Like a shrink?"

"Well, you look terrible and if that was just from your dream that means this isn't harmless anymore."

"I have to meet up with Bartholomew tonight."

"You're going through with this?" asked Molly.

"It's the best chance to get a handle on it. When I was in the forest there was a voice."

"A voice? What did it say?"

"It told me I wasn't meant to be there. I didn't belong there, something like that."

"And then the trees tried to kill you…"

Plater looked at Molly.

"I have to meet Bartholomew." he said.

Molly looked unconvinced and just squeezed his arm gently.

"Look, as it stands, I'm afraid to sleep now." said Plater. "If I can follow through with Bartholomew maybe that'll help. It's all I can think of to do right now."

"Okay." said Molly. "But in the meantime, why don't you take a shower and change, we need to get out of here for a few hours, there's a decent Indian not far from here, an ex-boyfriend took me there ages ago. My treat…"

There was no talk of dreams and other worlds at the Light of India. Just a preponderance of red on the walls, some Indian lager and surprisingly good food. Molly took the lead and told Plater about her childhood in Devon, her secondary school days, her failed sporting efforts, bar a medal for swimming at fifteen and her comical first steps at dating. They were both laughing when the waiter asked if they needed the bill. It was 11:30 p.m.

With the thought of what might be ahead they walked back to Plater's in virtual silence. Molly pushed her arm through Plater's and walked closely by his side.

"There's no choice is there?" she asked, her head leaning against his shoulder.

"No." he said.

"I want to stay with you."

"There's no need.." began Plater.

"I want to." said Molly.

They finished the walk in silence. Plater made a

herbal tea from supplies Molly had brought and they drank it quietly. Sitting like patients in a dentist's waiting room, the clock edged towards 12:30.

"Okay." said Plater. "Let's do it."

He disappeared into the bathroom.

Molly stood up and stretched.

"I'm done." said Plater heading for his bedroom.

"I want to be with you." said Molly, "I'll just watch you to make sure you're okay. If you're in distress, I can wake you up."

Plater wasn't sure if that would be a good thing or not, but he was very grateful to not be facing this alone. His attraction to Molly only served to confuse his feelings.

"Well, there's a chair in my room but it won't be very comfortable."

"You've got a double bed, haven't you?" asked Molly.

"Yes, but..."

"Fine, you sleep one side and I'll just lie on the other side."

Plater could feel colour heading to his face.

"Are you sure...?" began Plater.

"You are a perfect gentleman Mason, now hush and get into bed."

How Plater wished for other circumstances when he might hear Molly say those words. But he was being stupid. He lay down and pulled the cover over himself. Molly lay on top of the cover, next to him, fully clothed.

"Goodnight." she said.

Plater said nothing.

After about twenty minutes Molly thought Plater's breathing was slower and shallower. She couldn't see but was pretty sure Plater was asleep.

15

The air conditioning wasn't coping well. Warren Gatts' office was in an old building in Downtown Fort Worth. He took the second to last bottle of Coke from the small fridge in the corner and popped the top off with a practiced swipe against the corner of his desk. The bottle top bounced along the floor joining several more between two piles of paper. He kept replaying the phone call over in his mind. "I have evidence against the Rev. Ethan Daniels and I want you to tell the world the truth." the caller had said. The voice had been male and had sounded very calm. He'd gone on to say that the subject was too dangerous to discuss over the phone and that they had to meet. The caller had said he was afraid of what the Church might do if they found out.

There was something he didn't like about the call though. He'd not heard from Rudi in Miami since speaking to Rev. Daniels; his sister had said he'd gone on vacation. That didn't chime as Rudi, apart from being devoted to his sister, who had a muscle-wasting condition that kept her housebound, just didn't do vacations. He used to say he lived in the best place he could imagine, so why would he want to go someplace else?

As he drained the last drops from the Coke bottle, he made up his mind. He had to go. He had to take the chance that this man, whoever he was, had something that could be used to stop Rev. Daniels. Even with the evidence from Miami, it was all circumstantial and couldn't conclusively implicate Daniels. It would hardly take a slick New York attorney more than a morning to utterly dismantle any case and introduce so many elements of doubt that no jury would convict.

Gatts planted the Coke bottle firmly on a spare patch of desk and picked up his recorder. He attached the small extension microphone and slipped the recorder and wire beneath his shirt. With practiced ease, he attached it so that the folds of the loose-fitting shirt hid the device from all but a pat-down. He took his old aviator shades from the shelf and made for the door.

The location the caller had picked for their meeting was only three streets away but the change in atmosphere was noticeable. As with many mid-Western cities across America, the Downtown area lived cheek by jowl with low rent housing and light industrial areas. East Madison Street was just such a street. Narrow by comparison to the four-lane main road Gatts' office stood on, East Madison was home to a personal storage warehouse, two auto workshops, a small, dusty pawn shop and an empty lot that was surrounded on all sides by wooden panels. It was by this empty lot that Gatts was to meet the caller. He had no idea what the man looked like. The caller had said he would recognize

Gatts and just to be there on time.

Gatts checked his watch, 11:26. There was no foot traffic at all on the sidewalks. A few cars and pickups moved sedately past. As Gatts approached the empty lot, he noticed a makeshift door in the wooden screens. The door was slightly open. He looked up and down the street again but saw nobody on foot. He gently pushed the door and it swung unevenly open on its makeshift hinges. Stepping through he found himself in a large open area strewn with the last remains of whatever building had stood there before. There was a temporary prefabricated cabin on concrete posts in one corner. By what looked like large double doors, beside the cabin stood a dusty green van bearing the construction company's logo. He was sure this was where the caller had said to be and he was right on time.

The door of the cabin opened and a man wearing a bright yellow hard hat emerged. He began to walk towards Gatts. As he got within a few yards he said:

"Mr Gatts, thanks for comin'." and held out his hand.

They shook hands and Gatts noticed a rather cool feel to the man's skin which was surprising in the heat. He thought he recognized something about him too, but the hard hat cast a deep shadow over the man's face. The man seemed very relaxed. Gatts was more accustomed to meeting contacts that were skittish and uncertain if they should go through with it.

"We can talk inside." said the man. "Out of the sun."

Gatts followed the man across the lot. As the approached the hut the man stood aside.

"Please." he indicated for Gatts to go first. There was

an instant of hesitation as Gatts wondered why this man seemed so calm but he had to follow-up and see what this man had on the Church.

As Gatts put his foot on the bottom of the three steps up to the doorway he felt a sharp pain in his neck, like an insect's sting. His hand brushed something metal as it retreated. Looking to his right he saw the man holding something shiny. By this time the edges of his vision were blurring and even before he crumpled to the hard baked dirt, he was unconscious.

As Gatts opened his eyes his first sensation was nausea. He went to cover his mouth but his hands were bound to the wooden arm rests of the chair he sat in. The initial wave of sickness passed and Gatts took a couple of deep, slow breaths, raising his head from his chest as his vision cleared. His head lolled to one side as he tried to hold it steady, the shapes in the room settling as his muscles woke up.

"Mr. Gatts, welcome back." said the man, who was seated a few feet away in a chair just like the one that held Gatts.

"What do you want?" asked Gatts. "Why are you doing this? Are you with them?"

The man smiled and sipped from a glass of water before replacing it on a small table beside him.

"Now let's not get off on the wrong foot here Mr. Gatts." he said. "I just need to ask you a few questions and this will all be over."

Gatts' head tipped backwards but he caught it and faced the man again.

"Why did you have to drug me, kidnap me? Why not

just ask your damn questions?"

"Well you see, it's human nature." said the man, taking off his round spectacles for a moment and squeezing the bridge of his nose. "If I would've asked you these questions back there when we met, there's a dollar would get ya ten that you wouldn't have answered me. Oh, maybe you'd've told me somethin' but it would probably have been a lie and I think we need to build our relationship on trust, Mr. Gatts. I think that's so important don't you?"

"What are you talking about? Who are you?"

"My name is Clayton, Mr. Gatts, Wallace Clayton, and we have a problem, you and I."

"What problem?"

"Well, it's like this, you went to see a friend of mine just recently and made all sorts of threats and I'm a God-fearin' man, Mr. Gatts, and I just don't like that sort of behaviour."

"You mean Daniels? You work for Ethan Daniels?"

"Well in a manner of speaking yes, but the Reverend is a friend of mine. He found me when I was in need of guidance and he saved me, Mr. Gatts. I don't have much in the way of worldly possessions as you might say, so I repay Rev. Daniels with my service."

"That man is evil." said Gatts, fixing Clayton with his unsteady gaze.

"Now you have no right to be saying such things!" yelled Clayton, getting to his feet and leaning his hands on Gatts' arms and bringing his face close. "It is you that are doing the Devil's work Mr. Gatts!"

As he spoke Gatts could feel the fine spray of spittle on his face and smell Clayton's odour of sweat and coffee. Clayton pushed himself upright and paced the room.

"You made threats and accusations against the Reverend and I need you to tell me who spouted these blasphemous untruths to you."

"What makes you think I would tell you anything?" said Gatts, less cocksure than he was twenty years ago but with all the firmness he could muster.

"Well, Mr. Gatts, life is full of choices. Choices and negotiation. I'd like to offer you a choice and then, perhaps, we can negotiate a little. How does that sound?" Clayton's manner was calm once more.

"Just let me go." said Gatts. "The police'll be looking for me and they know I was investigating the Church and Rev. Daniels, how's that gonna look you keeping me against my will?"

Gatts was fully conscious now and starting to understand his situation more clearly. He could feel the blood pumping in his temple and his mouth was dry.

"Well now." said Clayton. "We both know the police have no idea you're investigating the Church, why you even told that fat Sheriff you wanted to talk to that low life Nordstrom for the kidnapping angle."

Gatts couldn't see how Clayton could know that. Then he noticed Clayton's left hand. The little finger was curled in tightly to the palm, unnaturally so, and on the ring finger was a large ring, like a signet ring. It looked familiar and Gatts tried to remember where he'd seen one before.

"So, let's get back to choices Mr. Gatts. I want to offer you the chance to save your ex-wife and daughter's lives. Now you'd want to do that if you could now, wouldn't you Mr. Gatts?"

Gatts remembered where he'd seen the ring, on the Deputy's finger at the Sheriff's office the day he went to talk to Nordstrom.

"What?" said Gatts, not wanting to believe what he heard.

"It's a simple choice. You tell me the names of the people you spoke to in Miami and your ex-wife can continue to spend your divorce settlement and your daughter will be able to celebrate her High School Prom. Now I call that a very fair offer Mr. Gatts."

Gatts felt as if a huge hole was opening in his stomach, and he could feel the warmth spread across his lap as he urinated uncontrollably.

"But if you kill me, what's the point in killing my wife and daughter? What will that achieve?" he said in an unsteady voice.

"Retribution." said Clayton. "Just as Jesus died to save us from our sins so your sins will be paid for by your family, unless you give me the names."

Gatts closed his eyes and could feel all the muscles in his face tighten and contort. His finger-nails dug into the wooden arms, some tearing against the wood as he clenched both fists in helpless rage.

"Help me....!!" Gatts screamed, with all the voice his dry throat could provide "Help me!"

Clayton stood in front of him.

"There's no-one to hear you Mr. Gatts. Now come along we have business to conclude, tell me the names of the sinners you spoke to in Miami and we can bring your suffering to an end."

It wasn't as he'd imagined. Gatts had imagined, or

maybe hoped, that he'd end his days in bed with his daughter there to hold his hand. Certainly not in some dingy room God knew where, with a quasi-religious psychopath. In the midst of this madness, Gatts had to stifle a laugh. His whole body began to heave as he started to laugh then cry as waves of chaotic emotions fought for control.

He knew he would tell this madman what he wanted to know. What good was bravery now? He'd been dead from the moment he threatened the Rev. Ethan Daniels, but not his daughter, she had her life to live. He'd never give her away at her wedding now, or even see her graduate college. Never see any grandchildren. He hadn't expected this. He knew he'd upset Daniels but he expected a press campaign, maybe drag up his past battles with alcohol, try and ruin his reputation so no-one would listen. But not this.

"Alright." said Gatts quietly. "I'll tell you. My daughter will be safe?"

"Of course, Mr Gatts, God's retribution will be visited on the sinners. I'm listenin'."

16

"Welcome!" said Bartholomew taking Plater's arm and guiding him forwards.

"Am I doing it?" said Plater.

"Indeed you are, Mr. Plater." said Bartholomew cheerfully.

Plater was surprised to find himself in what seemed to be a hotel reception area with marble flooring. Rich reds, golds and greens shone from the thick carpet and the waiter moving past had a vibrant white jacket that dazzled him.

"Where are we?" he asked.

"As this is our first proper meeting here we thought tea at the Ritz might make you feel less...awkward." Bartholomew chose his words carefully.

They swept through double doors and ahead, Plater could see a striking woman in a beautifully tailored suit. She had long legs that unwound as she stood to greet them.

"Mason." she said, extending a slender hand.

"This is Gail." said Bartholomew. "You have met but

you may not recall."

Plater caught himself thinking that he ought to remember such a beautiful woman, then remembered that this was the woman from the mental hospital and all at once, realized he was thinking, remembering and yet dreaming. As a result, he stood while the others took their seats.

"I'm sorry." he said, quickly sitting. "This is still a bit..."

"Difficult I should imagine." said Gail. "But we are very impressed, you seem to have learned your lessons well so far."

"So far?" queried Plater.

"There is much still to do." said Bartholomew. "This is but the beginning."

"Of a great adventure." added Gail, smiling.

"This is so normal." said Plater looking about him and seeing just other people sat enjoying tea while waiters moved silently amongst them.

"It does seem so, doesn't it?" asked Gail. "However things are not necessarily as they seem. If you'll forgive us, we tried to make your first proper visit as safe and unthreatening as possible."

She smiled again but Plater felt different this time.

"Perhaps a brief demonstration?" suggested Bartholomew.

"Yes." said Gail. "Now Mason, please don't be alarmed, but could you close your eyes for a moment, please?"

Plater closed his eyes. Almost immediately, he felt a breeze on his face and then what might have been rain on his cheek. Then the room seemed to tip to one side, and he grabbed for the arms of his chair and opened his eyes. He was sitting on the deck of a ship. It was an old, wooden, square-rigged ship and all around him were what seemed like extras from a pirate film. Men of various nationalities, but all sharing rugged, weather-beaten complexions moving about their duties hardly noticing him. It was a fine day, the sun was high in the sky, but a stiff breeze brought spray across the deck as the ship bowed into the waves.

"Ahoy there! Mr. Plater, would you join us please?"

The voice rose above the noise of the ship and crew. It was Bartholomew. He was standing on the sterncastle by the large wheel.

Plater got unsteadily to his feet and swayed along the deck and up the narrow stairs to join Bartholomew.

"How did you...?" he began.

"This is nothing." said Bartholomew. "But come below, we have a stiff South Westerly and the rigging sings rather loudly!"

With that, Bartholomew disappeared through the small door down into the stern. He bounced off the walls of the cramped corridor and pushed open a narrow door at the end.

"Mid-shipman Plater, Captain!" Bartholomew announced and stood aside so Plater could see Gail Hartston dressed in period clothing, with a loose white shirt and britches, one polished boot propped on the small table and leaning back in a chair. Her long dark hair was more like a mane around her pale face, but the dark eyes were fixed on Plater.

"Sit!" she said. "We don't have as much time as we hoped Mason."

Plater sat on a small wooden chair and waited. The whole room creaking in rhythm with the rising and falling of the waves.

"Your ability to join us here in this world is special." said Gail. "But with that comes a special responsibility. We need your help Mason. The whole world needs your help." Gail made a sweeping gesture with one arm and Plater couldn't help but remember films he'd seen as a kid like the Crimson Pirate. Images swam before his eyes for a moment before he settled back to the cabin.

"Having some trouble staying with us I see." said Bartholomew. "It is to be expected. For now Mr Plater, please try to concentrate on what Gail has to say."

"Yes, don't be alarmed but try to stay with us if you can. We need your help. You know that I am rather useless in your world."

Plater nodded.

"In this world Mason, I live my life. This is a world with few limits, some of which we know about but we are still explorers ourselves."

"Why do you need my help?" said Plater, catching the table for support as the ship lurched to starboard.

"A long time ago, perhaps millennia, your world, the physical world, came under attack. But not a direct attack. We think it may have taken centuries for humanity to even notice."

Plater looked puzzled. He also felt a little uneasy in his stomach, probably due to the pitching ship. As a result his mind wandered to tablets, doctors, a cruise he once took when he was a boy. The room shimmered then he fixed back on Gail and the room was restored.

"We believe a subtle enemy is trying to destroy humanity." said Gail. "Although we can't be certain we believe an entity is trying to influence events here on

Earth."

"For what reason?" asked Plater.

"Their only goal seems to be chaos and destruction." said Gail. "Do you remember the words that Raymond asked you to remember?"

For a moment, Plater's mind went blank. He started to lose the small cabin again but focused on the face of Gail Hartston and managed to hold onto it. An image of the letter popped into his head, and he tried to read the words from it.

"Yes." he said. "Yes, I do! Mr Black had Blue shoes, Mrs White had Red shoes, Mr Green had Yellow shoes and Mrs Brown had Orange shoes. "

Plater looked expectantly at Gail and she smiled again.

"Excellent Mason!" she said. "Now you must read this."

She passed him a parchment scroll which he unrolled. On it was a diagram which he didn't understand and some words, apparently annotations to the diagram.

"What is it?" asked Plater.

"We don't know." said Bartholomew. "But we need to get this information into the real world to find out."

"So you want me to remember this?" asked Plater. "But it's so complicated, I'll never be able to do it."

"You may surprise yourself." said Gail. "A byproduct of the ability to interact with this world is that images of location become more vivid. Did you think the colours in the hotel were rather intense?"

"Yes, now that you say it, I did think..."

"What we hope is that you will be able to remember the full details of your time here, including the design on this paper." said Gail.

"But what about this entity, is this something it has done? Where is it? Who do I tell about this?"

"For now, Mason." said Gail. "You should return with this information and see if you can retrieve it. We'll be seeing a lot of you from now on. Any time you sleep, it is likely you will jump across to our world. It will be hard to stop yourself. You must try not to be alarmed; we will try to protect you from harm, although I must tell you that this world is not without its risks."

"I know." said Plater.

"You know?" repeated Bartholomew. "How?"

Plater recounted the experience he'd had in the forest.

"It knows." said Gail.

"What do you mean?" asked Plater.

"We had hoped to hide you for a while." said Bartholomew. "Until you felt comfortable with all this."

Plater looked from Gail to Bartholomew.

"Was that this entity?" he asked.

"Probably." said Gail. "Although it may have been its followers."

"Followers?"

"People, like us, humans, working on behalf of this entity."

"In the real world?" said Plater. "So this entity can affect people in the physical world?"

"Yes, that's how it is able to engineer chaos." said Gail. "We don't know precisely how and we hardly know who, but we know they are out there, affecting humanity."

"Why does it want that?" said Plater.

"We don't know." said Batholomew.

"What do you know?"

"We must be careful not to overtax you while you are still a novice." said Bartholomew, looking over to Gail. "Perhaps we should leave more explanations for another time. Please take another look at the diagram Mr. Plater."

"But why can't you memorize the diagram?" said Plater to Bartholomew. "You can enter this world but still operate in the physical one."

"It is hard to explain fully." began Bartholomew. "But we think it is a problem that most have when they cross worlds. They can remember aspects of their time here but not always fine details. For example, the simple words we asked you to remember prove virtually impossible for almost every person that can cross the barrier."

Plater spread the parchment across the table and carefully followed all the lines, read all the arrowed comments and then stood back to see it as a whole.

"I don't know what else I can do?" he said at last.

Gail stood up and came round to Plater's side. She held out her arms.

"Until the next time Mason." she said stepping forwards and leaning up to kiss him on the cheek, one hand gently stroking his neck.

"Good luck." said Bartholomew, holding out a puffy hand for Plater to clasp.

"How do I..." said Plater.

"Of course." said Bartholomew. "A very important lesson I completely forgot about, how to return to the real world. There are many ways, and I'm sure you have experienced a number already. The most comfortable is to picture the location from which you came. Fill your mind with this image and you should wake up. Please, try it now."

Plater closed his eyes, then immediately wondered if that was really necessary. He tried to picture his bedroom, tired paintwork, overflowing linen basket and all. For a split second, it seemed he was looking down on his bedroom, as if he was on the ceiling. He could see Molly lying on the bed beside a body that must be his. Just as he began to wish he was lying with her, he felt an unpleasant sensation as if he couldn't breathe. Instinctively he gasped for air and woke up with a start.

His sudden arrival shook Molly awake too; she leaned over him until he could feel her warmth and smell her perfume.

"Mason, are you okay? What time is it? I must have dozed off...what happened?" she asked.

Plater took a long, slow breath and exhaled.

"It's a long story." he began. "You're not going to believe it."

17

Molly could barely concentrate on work with thoughts of other worlds and some creeping evil. It was barely credible, and she surely would have laughed. As Mason described his dream or trip, she hardly knew what to call it anymore, had it not been for Bartholomew. Plater hadn't even known where Walberswick was and knew nothing of the strange little shopkeeper before his earlier dream.

On her computer screen was the website for Bartholomew's bookshop. Nothing fancy but had links to his fairly extensive inventory of bizarre sounding titles, many of which dated back to the 1600s or even earlier. Molly followed some of the links and saw strange images, mostly taken from illustrations in the books themselves. Unearthly creatures, witches with their familiars, lots of portraits of old bearded scholars that had spent a lifetime delving into the arcane.

The sound of the telephone made her jump.

"Yes." she said.

"I have a call for you from Lievesham Hall." said the

receptionist then there was a click and Molly heard the voice of the nurse she'd talked with a week before.

"Miss James?" said the nurse.

"Molly, yes."

"It's about the patient you were interested in, Gail Hartston." said the nurse.

"Go on." said Molly, turning away from the open plan office and trying to speak more softly.

It was a short call, no more than a minute and a half and as soon as Molly hung up she was collecting her bag and making for the door.

"I've just got to check a source for the Radovic exposé, it might run into the evening, I'll be on the mobile." she said to the assistant producer as she shoved through the swing door to the reception.

Before she'd reached the road she had her mobile in her hand and was dialling Plater.

"Hello." he said.

"It's Gail." said Molly. "She's going to be moved, she's going to be part of that trial or experiment or whatever the hell it is."

After a moment Plater said "I don't like it, whatever treatment they're going to do it might change her."

"You mean affect her ability to join this other world?"

"Yes. I thought this government thing was happening later?" asked Plater.

"Been brought forward." said Molly as she jogged across the road waving and smiling at a driver that had to brake to avoid her.

Plater was silent.

"What can we do?" wondered Molly.

"I don't know." replied Plater. "Are you at work?"

"I was, I'm on my way round to you now."

By the time Molly was knocking on the door, Plater was turning the latch to let her in.

"The more I think about it the more I think we should help her." he said.

"How?"

"Stop her being part of this experiment."

"But we can't just roll up and say you know this woman in another world and you think experimenting on her would be bad, can we?"

"The nurse you spoke to, she seemed to like Gail, right?"

"Yes, she said that she always felt calm and peaceful when she was caring for Gail. Whether it was changing her feed tubes or bathing her, she said she felt some sort of connection. Do you think..."

"What?"

"Do you think Gail Hartston affects other people, even people that aren't like you?"

"God knows." said Plater. "But we need to get her out of there before some government white coat starts dosing her with drugs or giving her electric shocks or whatever they have in mind."

"So, what do we do?"

"When are they coming for her?"

"Sometime tomorrow she said, that Granger guy was saying after 10:00am and they would get the man too."

"Okay, call your nurse back and see if she's on shift tonight." said Plater sitting down in front of his laptop in the corner of the room and calling up Google.

"What are you doing?" asked Molly.

"I think it's time Gail Hartston had a change of

scenery." said Plater, typing furiously.

As it began to get dark several hours later Molly and Plater got into his car and set off towards Lievesham Hall.

"Are you sure we should be doing this?" asked Molly.

"No, but this woman has no life in our world but is so alive in the other. These government types have no idea, she'll be just another test subject to them, a number in a spreadsheet."

Plater had to try very hard to obey traffic laws on the way to Lievesham Hall. Even though he hardly knew Gail Hartston, he felt as if he needed to be her guardian in the physical world. With no living family there was nobody else to care what happened to her. Nobody to ensure that she didn't become the equivalent of a lab rat.

As he pulled into the car park at the hospital he paused and scanned the building. He'd remembered from the filming that there was a door close to the Dead Zone ward, as he'd wheeled his camera equipment out that way. Eventually, he spotted it and slowly edged his car as close to the door as he dared.

Molly and Plater walked into the entrance and straight past the single nurse stationed at what was the reception by day.

"Excuse me." said the nurse as they almost disappeared round a corner into a long corridor. "Can I help you?"

"Hi." said Molly. "We're here to see Nurse Hawkins, I'm a friend of hers, we were passing and she said it would be alright just to pop in to say hi."

"It's not really allowed." said the nurse. "This is a secure facility."

"Can't we just stay for a few minutes? We live miles away and I hardly get to see Laura. We won't disturb her or anything."

"Well okay." said the nurse. "But just a few minutes now."

Molly smiled.

"Thank you." she winked and guided Plater towards the Dead Zone.

As they hurried down the long corridor Plater was studying the walls and ceiling trying to locate the security cameras so they could try to offer the least identifiable angle as they passed. Molly had long hair so was at an advantage. Plater even resorted to turning and walking backwards past one of the cameras, pretending to be talking to Molly.

They needn't have worried about being seen, not in real time anyway, the guard on shift to monitor the cameras was on his hourly rounds manually checking fire doors and emergency exits.

As they rounded the last corner before the Dead Zone, they almost bumped into the security guard. Plater saw him, shaking the catch on an emergency exit about twenty yards away. He pulled Molly back round the corner and put a finger to his lips. He mouthed the word 'guard' and Molly looked nervously back the way they had come. If she was having second thoughts, she managed to hide it. Plater peered carefully around the corner again and then jerked back pushing Molly back along the corridor until they came level with a door marked Linen. It wasn't locked and once inside Plater pulled the door closed. In the darkness they stood close; the linen store was barely able to fit two people between the shelves of sheets and blankets. As he strained to hear the guard approaching Plater realized he liked being this close to Molly. He felt embarrassed and cross with himself, entertaining such thoughts at a time like this. Molly's hands clasped his arms and her head nestled against his chest. As they both breathed carefully, they could hear the guard move past the door, on his way towards the Reception area. Plater tried to see though the crack of the door and watched the guard turn out of sight.

"That was close." he said as they stepped back into the light.

The last fifty yards of the twisting corridor to the Dead Zone made them feel they were leaving one world and entering another. There were fewer lights on and they both felt a drop in temperature. As they rounded the final turn, they could see Nurse Laura Hawkins sat at a small table with a single lamp. The rest of the ward was in darkness. As they entered, she stood.

"You must be quick." said Nurse Hawkins in a low whisper. "Michael, the guard, he watches the cameras but he'll be a few minutes yet."

The nurse set off into the gloom of the ward and stopped next to bed number four.

"Where will you take her?" she asked.

"Best you don't know, eh?" said Plater. "But somewhere she'll be cared for, don't worry."

The nurse walked further into the shadows but quickly returned with a wheelchair, which she drew alongside the bed. Plater and Nurse Hawkins carefully slid Gail Hartston's warm and pliant body into the chair. Gail's head sank to her chest and her hands lay where they were placed in her lap. Just as Plater began to push the wheel chair forwards, Gail's body began to pitch forwards. Plater caught her and slipping off his belt he looped it under her arms, across her chest and round the handles of the wheelchair.

Molly was near the doorway glancing nervously up the corridor and straining to catch any approaching sound. She gestured with a thumbs up and a beckoning wave. Plater wheeled the chair quickly out into the corridor and turned towards the emergency exit door that had been open on the day he'd filmed there. He hoped there was no alarm on it. Suddenly, he realized, stopped and went back to the Nurse who was standing at the entrance to the ward.

"What will you say?" said Plater.

"Don't worry." said Nurse Hawkins. "It'll be at least another six hours before shift change and the nurse coming on is a lazy cow. She won't do a bed check right away, it'll be ages."

"But when they do find out she's gone?"

"I'll swear blind she was there when I started and plead ignorance. They don't have cameras in this section so they won't see you leave. Go on, you don't want to risk Michael getting curious and seeing you drive off."

Plater smiled briefly and rejoined Molly, maneuvering the wheelchair up to the exit. No alarm. He nodded at Molly and she pushed the door open being careful not to let the pushbar make too much noise.

Cool air rushed in and Plater could see his car about

twenty yards away across the grass. Molly tried to get the door shut again as best she could, but it hung slightly ajar. It was much harder work pushing the chair across the grass and a couple of times the smaller wheels caught, nearly pitching Gail Hartston clean out of it. By the time they'd reached the car, Plater was breathing heavily, partly from his exertions and partly from the tension. Molly opened the rear door and they struggled to feed Gail's dead weight onto the back seat. Just as they stood up having tucked her feet inside floodlights suddenly illuminated the grounds. In that instant they both felt a shiver of fear.

"Get in!" said Plater.

They both scrabbled for the door handles and fell into the car. They could see the main entrance and could make out a running figure. It had to be the security guard and he was heading their way. Plater fumbled for the key and the car started first try. Over-revving in panic he went for reverse and the car shot backwards. It mounted a grassy bank and jolted to a stop. Plater flung it into first and lumps of torn turf and mud sprayed from the back wheels as they struggled for grip on the damp grass. Once the tyres held, the car lurched to the right and away from the main building. Plater checked the mirror and could see the guard slowing down as he realized he wouldn't catch them. He saw him stop and bend forwards, his hands at his waist catching his breath. The next thing he noticed was that Molly had a vice-like grip on his arm. She was twisted around in her seat looking backwards too. Relieved to see their pursuer give up the chase. Plater steered the car in crazy arcs across the sloping lawns of Lievesham

Hall as he circled towards the exit. As the car bumped and lurched, Gail Hartston rocked and slid around the back seat, her body assuming unnatural shapes. Once the car settled back onto the road Plater glanced across at Molly.

"You okay?" he asked, adrenalin still pumping madly.

"Yeah." said Molly. "We just kidnapped someone."

Plater glanced across again, holding Molly's gaze for an instant before remembering to drive.

"Yes, yes we did, didn't we?" he said and then started to laugh.

"Do you think they really believed that story about the foreclosure notice?" said Molly as she busied herself making coffee in Plater's kitchen.

"I think so, but they're in business don't forget, they almost bit my hand off." said Plater.

Gail Hartston was now a resident of Holworth Hospital, a small country house clinic that specialized in long term care. They had seemed perfectly happy about the emergency relocation, due to the imminent closure of this other institution. Plater had been deliberately vague on details.

"What if they hear about what we did on the news?"

"I'm not sure too much fuss will be made on the news." said Plater. "I don't think either Dr Granger or the Government will want too much attention drawn to them over something like this."

Molly wanted reassurance she wouldn't be woken at 5 a.m. by police with a warrant for kidnapping but it wasn't happening.

"But kidnapping is a serious crime Mason." she said

passing him coffee and joined him on the sofa. "They can't just let it go."

"I can't think that way." said Plater. "Not now, I need Gail to help me to understand what's going on with me. She's proof that I'm not going mad."

"So, what now?" asked Molly tucking one leg under her and facing Plater.

"Damn." said Plater. "The diagram."

He put his cup down and grabbed a legal pad and pen from the table. Poised with the pen above the paper his eyes lost focus as he tried to put himself back in the creaking cabin of the old ship.

"I can't make it out." he said. "Damnit!"

Plater cast the pad onto the coffee table and thumped his knee with a fist.

"This is ridiculous." he said. "I can't do what they want me to do, but I can't avoid them. Whenever I sleep, I can't help falling into their world. But if I can't do what they want what good is it? What'll I become? Some paranoid schizo who can't tell dreams from reality?"

Plater's hand was still tightly clenched. Molly put her coffee down and reached over. Her arm slid round him and guided his head to her shoulder.

"It's going to be okay." she began, not sure if she believed that or not. "I'll help you. You just need more practice and you'll be able to control this, this gift you have."

They sat in silence as the first fingers of light from the new day began clawing at the curtains.

18

Dr. Granger's receptionist barely had time to read 'HM Government' on the small identity card before the holder, a tall man in a dark jacket, had pulled it from her view and was placing it back in an inside pocket.

"We'll see ourselves in, thank you." said the man.

Then he and a shorter man in a leather jacket, crossed to Dr. Granger's office door and entered without knocking. The receptionist's startled complaints were lost as the men closed the office door behind them.

"Who are you?" said Granger, getting to his feet.

"I believe you're expecting us, Dr. Granger." said the taller man.

Granger seemed to be anticipating more of an explanation, but the two men just waited.

"Your colleagues have gone." began Granger. "They left more than an hour ago, I'm sure I can't answer any more questions."

"We're attached to the Home Office sir, you're expecting to release two patients to our custody." said the tall man.

"Yes, yes of course, I'm sorry, I thought you were more police. I have the files right here." Granger began to walk his fingers through a pile of files on his desk.

"What were the police doing here?" asked the tall man.

Granger pulled two manila folders from the pile.

"Yes, well it's a bit awkward actually. Will you sit down?" he said.

"No, Dr. Granger, we really need to press on."

"It's just that, well, we had an incident here last night, involving one of the patients you've come to collect actually." said Granger, starting to sound nervous.

"What sort of incident?"

"The woman, Hartston, was removed from the clinic." said Granger, holding out the two files for the tall man to take.

"By whom?" said the tall man, making no attempt to accept the files.

"I don't know." began Granger, slowly letting his arm holding the folders sag, until he placed the files back on his desk. "Two people turned up here pretending to visit one of our nurses and the receptionist let them go through. Then it seems they took Hartston from her bed, out through a fire exit and into a car."

Granger could see this news was not well received.

"Our security guard gave chase." he added.

"What do the police know?" asked the tall man.

"That's the thing." said Granger. "The CCTV shows nothing, not inside or the ones in the grounds and when they drove off, they cut across the grass and the cameras operate closer to the buildings."

The taller man glanced at the shorter one, who turned and left the room.

"Did the guard get the number of the car?" said the tall man.

Granger looked pained.

"It was too dark." he said.

"Well, that isn't very good now is it, Dr Granger?" began the tall man. "I understood that this was a secure facility. My superiors will no doubt be in contact. In the meantime, we'll collect the man."

Granger selected the man's file from his desk and this time, the tall man took it. The door opened and the shorter man came back in. He spoke softly to the taller man as he passed him. Granger couldn't hear what was said.

"We understood that neither patient had any family?" said the tall man.

"That's right." said Granger.

"Had the woman been visited by anyone recently?" said the tall man.

"No, she'd been here for three years and never had a visitor in all that time."

"I don't think you'll be hearing from the police again on this matter Dr Granger, it wouldn't look good for the clinic. But perhaps a review of security might be warranted?"

Granger seemed a little surprised.

"Yes." he said. "Yes, we'll certainly be tightening things up around here, you can count on that."

Neither visitor looked impressed and waited in silence. After a moment Granger realized he should escort them to collect the male patient.

19

The heavy curtains moved easily on the steel rods and within seconds, the outside world seemed very far away. Huge church candles flickered in dark metal holders, some shaped like fantastic creatures with coiled tails and bat-like wings.

Two figures busied themselves at a strong wooden table draped with a red cloth. They arranged items from an old metal box carefully in a line. First, a black bowl about the size of half a grapefruit, then a dagger with jewels embedded in the handle.

"You must tell me." said one of the figures, the smaller of the two. "I deserve to know."

The other figure, taller and with an air of command, stopped his arranging of two pieces of parchment bearing circular designs. He stood to his full height, which was a good half a foot taller than the other.

"Grobus, you are nothing but the shit to be scraped from his feet. You deserve nothing!" The words stung the shorter man and he continued his work, shoulders rounded.

The taller man, known as Oculus, turned and left through a wide door in the far wall, leaving Grobus to his task. Grobus was not his real name but a magical one. It was customary in the Order to adopt a magical name.

Once finished laying out the items on the table, the hunched figure collected a bucket and mop that stood by the door and began cleaning the shiny black floor. A pattern was etched in the stone tiles that created a double circle more than ten feet in diameter. The inner circle was about a foot inside the outer and in the space between the two were inscribed symbols. At four places around the circle the cardinal points of the compass were picked out. Once finished with the mopping, Grobus placed metal stands at these four points.

Grobus glanced at his watch; two hours to go. Two hours should be enough time for the remaining tasks he had to complete. Preparation was so important. Even he knew that. He resented the words Oculus had used. He was not a Master but neither was he a Novice. Seven years he had studied. He had performed every task set for him by Oculus and the other High Grades of the Order. He had never complained, since he had taken his own magical name of Grobus, as all initiates must. Had he not given up most of his non-magical life to better serve the Order? A wife and daughter he now hardly heard from being but a part of what he had surrendered in his pursuit of power. Not earthly power, but real power, over the souls of men. Now he only wanted to know what the significance of his vision had been. Ever since he had described it, Oculus and those of the higher degrees had urged him for more detail but he told them all he could remember. He needed to know if his visions might in some small way advance the Order's quest for The Book. Being of such lowly rank, he was only aware of The Book by deliberately oblique references dropped in his presence by those of higher rank. He thought it was at times deliberate, to remind him of his ignorance. But he knew from his own reading and study of the old texts that a book existed that held the words of beings from the very highest planes. Words of power and words of the old language that few understood. He knew that the members of the High Order did not have The Book. They knew of it and sought it but, Grobus believed, they had so far only managed to discover pieces. Others sought this knowledge. Others less worthy. The Order was engaged in a struggle and a race. Grobus wanted with all his being to be a part of that struggle.

He had performed his daily exercises, meditating and visiting the lower houses, the levels of the astral plane that befitted his station. He dutifully recorded his experiences and described them to his mentor, Frater Iratus. It seemed he had seen something unusual. Something of significance. But no one would tell him what it was. His vision seemed to have been important enough that today's ritual would involve all the High Order. They'd seemed worried when he'd seen them leaving a closed meeting the day before.

As he returned to his room Grobus wondered, not for the first time, what could have been the significance of his experience. Often hard to construct from fragments of memory, this time he had strong feelings of having flown across water, great expanses of water, and finding a ship. He'd felt drawn to the ship and looked down on it to see many figures moving around. One caught his eye. A man that seemed to exude a glow, an aura of some kind. One minute red, one minute turquoise, then white, then green. He was with a woman whose form he had come across before. Oculus had described to him a woman, a powerful demon, from the third house, who was beautiful to behold but strong. A shape shifter and devoted to the light. Oculus had been so filled with energy when he first noticed this being that he had drawn images of her and painted the most wild and vibrant pictures for days afterwards. Each time featuring this female with long dark hair, striking eyes and pleasing form. Each time he had painted with vigour and anger and completed the imagery with stakes piercing the woman or fire consuming her. Sometimes wolves snapping at her form or snakes coiling around her. Oculus would never answer Grobus' questions about this woman, only to warn him that she was powerful and to be careful in his travels in the astral dimension. If he ever saw this creature, he was to say so, at once. Grobus assumed that this was the reason for the ritual tonight, that he'd seen this woman but perhaps it was because of the glowing man with her, perhaps this was what it was about.

20

As Zach hit the send key, he wasn't totally convinced. It wasn't until Meek appeared at his workstation about ten minutes later that he realized it had probably worked.

"So, what's with the rabbit?" asked Meek

Zach had sent a message to Meek containing an animation of a white rabbit that bounded across the screen before disappearing down a hole. He also asked a work-related question as he knew full well that all communication was monitored.

"Just wondered if you were still curious." said Zach.

"About?"

"Room 7G." said Zach, unable to stop himself from glancing around despite knowing only he and Meek were in the small lab.

"Yeah?" said Meek. "Curious like a moth and a flame."

"So, you'd be okay with us being part of some Frankenstein experiment, where they're sticking god knows what into totally innocent people?"

"More like vegetables." said Meek. "The subs are all

beyond the help of medical science man, they can't stay alive without tech."

"So that makes it okay in your book does it? Sawing off the top of someone's skull and hooking their brains up to some box of bits that is going to try and figure out what the poor bastard's thinking?"

"Look, we don't know what they're going to do right? So far, they've measured activity, that's all. Number three and number five show signs of unique communication. That's big stuff man. It's natural to want to locate the source of this communication."

"Fine, but do they need to slice and dice to do that? No. There's something else going on here. They're in a hurry. The results I sent to Braberson last month, that probably started this whole show off, should have taken months, maybe years, to process and understand. Why are we here getting ready to carve chunks out of people's brains to replace them with your circuit boards?"

Meek fell silent. He knew what Zach said was basically correct.

"You thinking what I'm thinking?" asked Meek at last.

"They've seen those results before?" said Zach

"Yeah, but where? When?"

"Dunno, but I want to see room 7G."

"What for?" said Meek. "It's just an operating theatre."

"No, it's more than that. I've seen people in and out of there all week. They have a network node in there, which I have a discreet trace on."

Meek sucked air between his teeth.

"That's dodgy man." he said. "You're good with the standard setup but how do you know this doesn't have better sec?"

"You leave that side to me." said Zach. "But I need you to check the hardware."

"You're going in there?" Meek raised his eyebrows.

"Tonight." said Zach. "According to the schedule tomorrow 7G is blanked from 1000hrs to 2200hrs."

"You think...?"

"Yeah, someone's getting upgraded."

Meek was quiet again, fiddling nervously with his Swiss Army knife that hung from his belt on a chain.

"I'm not sure..." he said at last.

"C'mon." said Zach. "We'll be in and out before those dozy drones on the cameras have finished watching Britain's Got Talent."

"Yeah." said Meek. "But I don't like it."

"So, you're good to go?"

Meek nodded and turned out of the room.

Although they shared the kitchen at dinner time they hardly spoke, Meek preparing a complicated meal while Zach heated a microwave dinner. They ate at the table and spoke briefly about a recurring error in one of Meek's circuits. More for the benefit of anyone that may have been listening or watching than anything else. As Zach closed the dishwasher door after depositing his plate he said:

"Ten minutes?"

Meek just nodded.

Ten minutes later they stood at the end of the corridor that contained Room 7G.

"You sure about this?" asked Meek.

Zach looked at his friend then clapped him on the arm and headed off towards the door to 7G. Once outside, Zach pulled a small box from his pocket that was attached by a ribbon cable to a plastic card. The card was credit card sized, similar to the access cards used throughout the buildings. He paused briefly then swiped the card down the slot by the door to 7G. To their combined relief no alarms sounded and the small box in Zach's hand sprang to life. It had five small LEDs attached to the brushed steel case, four were red and one green. As they stood watching the first two red lights came on. Meek glanced nervously around but the corridor was quiet. The third, then fourth red lights flickered on. Zach shifted the box to his other hand and wiped his empty hand on his jeans. They both stared intently at the final light. It flickered on. Zach immediately swiped the card a second time and a metallic clunk signaled they were in.

They both carried LED torches and left the lights off. Splitting up, they examined different sides of the room. Dominated by a large, hydraulic operating table and ceiling mounted light array there were equipment trollies and sink units as you'd expect to find in any operating theatre. Zach was drawn to some cupboards on one wall, but they held only medical supplies, many of which he recognized.

Meek found a computer on a small workstation trolley in one corner and waved for Zach to investigate. Meek pressed on and found a shelving system that held electronic components, leads, circuit boards and surgical-grade tools. Most components, he quickly realized, were for the laboratory experiments, being far too big and cumbersome to consider implanting. Then he found two cool boxes. He lifted the first onto the bench and opened it. Inside he found three compartments, each containing a small black chip with forty gold connectors protruding from it. The chip was about the size of a pound coin and of similar thickness. There was a seven digit number written on the casing of the chip. Meek grabbed his mobile phone and recorded the number. He did the same with the other two chips. It seemed to him that two of the chips were from a similar series but the third was different. Only the serial numbers would reveal what the chips contained.

The other cool box had one chip in, the other two slots were empty. Meek recorded the number and replaced it carefully. He looked over to where Zach was sitting in front of the computer screen. He was typing faster than anyone he'd ever seen. Meek could see a video opening on the screen. After a few seconds, a figure in front of the camera moved and it was possible to see a patient on the operating table. Meek couldn't believe what he was seeing. The figure on the operating table had had the top of his head removed, exposing what seemed to be about two thirds to three quarters of the surface area of his brain. As figures moved and crossed in front of the camera Meek could still make out that something of the order of 70-100 fine wires trailed from a slim beige box on a trolley and attached to various points on the exposed brain.

"That's a G750." said Zach.

"Prototype for the chip." agreed Meek.

As they watched, the camera was suddenly adjusted to focus on a bank of monitors to one side. Zach could tell immediately what each displayed.

"Alpha readings, vital signs and that looks like Kan signals." said Zach pointing to each display on the screen.

"Right." agreed Meek, although he knew little of this side of things.

As they watched another trolley came into view with a much larger beige box on it. One of the technicians bent over it and then looked across at the monitor bank. The Kan display began to show violent activity, massive wave amplitudes and an irregular pattern.

"That's incredible." muttered Zach. "That's better than 98%. That's sub 9, he didn't even register in the top 10 subjects on his own. I've got to see the programming for that box."

Meek looked round, although they were making no noise he was getting very nervous. Even the drones they employed for security were supposed to make periodic checks.

"Come on." he hissed. "Let's get out of here."

Zach held his hand up and from the other produced a small USB device that he slotted into the workstation. In one corner of the screen a small box opened; in it a unicyclist cycled back and forth across the little box until a progress bar completed. Zach pulled out the USB stick and shutdown the workstation. He smiled at Meek and was about to say: "See, no worries." when they heard footsteps outside the door.

In blind panic, they searched the room for somewhere to hide. Everything was against a wall but the operating table. Meek lunged for a cupboard to one side of the door and flattened himself as best he could alongside the cupboard. Zach dropped to the floor behind the operating table.

The security guard was whistling some inane yet familiar jingle from a TV ad. He swiped his card and opened the door. Meek tried to make himself even slimmer than he already was and held his breath. Zach listened intently and squeezed as close as he could to the heavy metal base of the hydraulic table.

The guard took two steps into the room, shone his torch around and went to leave, then stopped. He bent and picked up a small plastic figure that he'd trodden on as he turned to leave. He shone his torch on it for a moment, then scanned the room again, then put the figure in his pocket and left.

Zach and Meek were too scared to move for at least a minute, although it seemed far longer to both of them.

"He picked something off the floor." said Meek. "What was it?"

Zach shrugged and motioned for them to leave.

As they waited for the filter coffee maker to work in the shared kitchen Zach checked his pocket.

"Shit!" he said.

"Shit what?" said Meek.

Zach held up the USB stick he'd used in 7G.

"What?" said Meek.

"Ermintrude." said Zach. "It must have come off in there."

Meek just stared.

"A figure, Ermintrude, you know, the cow in Magic Roundabout, it was on my keyring, the one I had the USB stick on..."

"Shit!" said Meek.

"Shit!" said Zach.

"Shit!" said Meek.

"Wait." said Zach. "It's nothing, I mean no-one knows about it, I've had this in my rucksack since we got here. It's fine."

"Never hear of DNA?" said Meek.

"You're kidding?" said Zach. "DNA tests on a plastic cow?"

"Well it's not like they don't have the kit and the expertise?"

Zach looked serious for a moment, then said:

"Did you see the guard take it?"

"Yeah."

"Did he just pick it up?" said Zach.

"Gotcha." said Meek. "God they're thick."

"Cheap and cheerful, all the Government can afford. There's probably more of his DNA on old Ermintrude than mine by now."

Zach afforded himself a relieved grin.

"They'll still know someone was in there." said Meek. "Someone with odd habits."

Zach looked at him.

"How many people do you know that would have a keyring with a minor character from Magic Roundabout on it?" asked Meek.

Zach knew it was a mistake, but still didn't think it would lead directly back to him. They drank their coffee in virtual silence.

21

Memories of the previous night's ritual were still fresh in Grobus' mind as he assiduously recorded everything in his magical journal. He hoped that he would be allowed to progress to the next level in the order soon as he had diligently observed all the required tasks. He had learned the five rituals associated with that level. He had memorised all the associations and alignments relevant to the region of the astral plane explored at this level. He knew Oculus didn't like him, but it was not a decision for Oculus alone. It was by agreement of the High Order to allow a member to prove their knowledge and skills and advance to a higher rank.

Grobus finished his writing and slid the journal into his backpack. The woman creature from Oculus' paintings filled his mind. She was indeed beautiful. It did seem that Oculus had become obsessed with her. He spoke of little else and it now seemed to Grobus that the High Order itself was focused on this creature. What did they hope to learn from her? And this new person, Plater, what did he have to do with their work? Oculus had seemed insistent, saying:

"Find out all you can about Mason Plater."

Perhaps he and the woman creature were connected in some way.

As the clock pushed past 1900 Grobus collected his uniform and ID card before catching the bus four stops to the thirty-two floor bank building where he worked as a cleaner. Within ten minutes he was switching on the floor cleaning machine and settling his headphones to listen to recordings he had made of the plant, gemstone and mineral associations he needed to memorise for rituals at the next level in the order. Grobus felt he did some of his best work at night.

Days passed and then a week with nothing mentioned on either the television, the internet or in the papers about the events at Lievesham Hall. Molly and Plater had dropped into a routine. Most nights Molly stayed with Plater and watched him as he slept until she too dozed. Most days Plater would wake with half remembered images of Roman buildings, the old ship or being surrounded by skyscrapers in some mega city. Each time he woke he reached for the pad and tried to draw more fragments of the image. In his dreams the image appeared on a flag flying on a building, the scroll in the ship's cabin or as graffiti on a wall. Each time he returned to normality he carefully recalled both his experiences and more details of the design to write down.

Molly would hug him as he woke then slip away to grab breakfast before heading off to work. Plater found that his dream-filled sleep often left him less than refreshed and one morning, listening to some Brahms in his living room he fell deeply asleep. This time he slept, without dreaming, for more than five hours and he later realised that he'd slept for about as long as the classical music playlist would have lasted on his phone.

The next day he tried the same idea, listening to the music on his large sofa and once more drifted into a deep and rejuvenating sleep. He excitedly told Molly about this when she staggered in after work, laden with shopping from the Tesco Express.

"That's great." she said, as she packed the food into the cupboards "You were starting to look a bit..."

"Not any more." said Plater, suddenly crossing behind Molly and squeezing her sides as she bent to a low cupboard. She squealed and twisted in his arms. For a moment they looked at each other, she giggling from being tickled and he laughing in the relief that they both felt. Her hands came to rest on his shoulders , then slid towards his face. Cupping his cheeks she moved to kiss him. What began as a sensitive, tender brushing of lips suddenly became a coming together.

Molly felt the edge of the kitchen table and under Plater's weight lay back onto it. Plater swept tins and packets right and left from under her before pulling at the waistband of her jeans. Buttons popped from his shirt as Molly ripped it open sinking her teeth playfully into his bare chest. In their urgency, they almost toppled from the table before switching positions so Plater lay on the table with Molly sitting astride him. As they pushed and pulled in abandoned rhythm Plater looked up at Molly. Her tousled hair framed her face and with the light behind it seemed for a moment...just a fleeting glimpse Plater would try to recall later, as if the woman grinding above him, synchronising her gyrations to the thrusting of his hips was Gail Hartston. In the instant that he saw this he hesitated, his head began to swim, he saw a beach, the dark-haired woman, the one who became Gail Hartston while he watched. Then he felt the real world again, felt the gripping of knees by his sides and saw again the woman above him. Young, beautiful, eyes closed, lips parted and now completely naked. Plater thought Molly had never looked so beautiful.

22

Only the most dedicated members of the Church of the Reclamation ever visited Redemption. Some church members even thought the existence of Redemption might be a myth. A myth that encouraged to get them to work even harder in the hope that one day they may get the opportunity to go there.

Victor Sanchez had never given much thought to where Redemption might actually be. Where it was didn't seem as important as what it represented. It represented the pinnacle of learning for the CoR. It was where the writings of their leader, Rev. Ethan Daniels were housed along with many ancient texts central to the CoR's teachings. Sanchez knew that they were closely guarded because they contained knowledge that mankind was not yet ready for. Even at the level he had attained within the church, he knew that much. From the time Rev. Daniels had travelled in the Holy Lands he had been working tirelessly to prepare humanity for what he had discovered there. His books were but an introduction. Something of use to the common man or woman struggling with modern life while yearning for a more spiritual one. The small holdall that Sanchez carried with a few clothes for his stay also held the first two volumes of Rev. Daniels teachings.

That Redemption was a secret place seemed right. Sanchez had been told that the world was not yet ready to learn the truth that had been imparted to Rev. Daniels. Sanchez was a little surprised at being blindfolded as soon as he had boarded the minibus from his home. It was several hours and two changes of transport, including a small airplane, before the blindfold was removed.

"Welcome." said a smartly dressed young woman as the new arrivals collected their luggage from the rear of the bus.

"I will take you to the accommodation zone and then the first briefing will be in twenty minutes." she said, heading off immediately through double doors and down a well-lit corridor.

Approximately seventeen minutes later, the new arrivals entered an auditorium to find around a hundred others already seated. They were shown to places on one side and greeted warmly as they found seats. Victor Sanchez thought of Maria and wished she could have been with him to share the experience. While the image of his partner was still in his mind, everyone around him suddenly stood and began applauding. As Sanchez stood he saw Rev. Ethan Daniels striding towards a lectern at the front.

"Friends." began Rev. Daniels extending his arms in welcome. "Welcome. Welcome to those who call Redemption home and welcome to those for whom this is their first visit. To earn a place here is truly special. You are the soul of the Church my friends. Your sacrifice, your labour, your energy, your faith has made this Church what it is today."

The audience, seemingly without prompting, burst again into applause.

"You know that we do good work on every continent and work tirelessly to spread the true teachings of our Lord. But there is a work so important, so critical for the safe deliverance of our humanity from evil that we must pursue it in secret. The forces of evil are everywhere. They wish to bring chaos and death when we labour for order and life and deliverance from this evil."

There was yet more applause and some whooping and whistling.

"I have news friends. You one hundred have been chosen. You are to be the vanguard of the new order. You will be the first to witness the true teachings of our Lord as revealed to me when I journeyed to the cradle of humanity on Earth. These teachings may shock you, they may cause you fear but do not be afraid. Our Lord will watch over us in our endeavours and protect us from those that would do us harm. Be uplifted, be humbled, be awed by his power and glory, my friends, for he is coming."

There was more whooping and shouting with some members of the audience visibly emotional and some standing and applauding wildly. Rev. Daniels paused, then held one hand up to calm his flock.

"As you know, friends, Redemption is first and foremost a place of learning and study. All of you have completed lengthy studies within the Church but here is where your true learning begins. We have been charged with preparing the way for our Lord to once again visit us on this Earth. But friends I am here to tell you that wishing for him to come, leading a blameless life, preaching to others of his glory, that will not be enough. Here at Redemption, we are building the means by which our Lord will once again walk among us and you, the chosen one hundred, you friends are the instruments that will make this happen."

Rev. Daniels flung his arms wide again and the inevitable ovation began. Many of the audience had tears streaming down their faces and all clapped loudly and enthusiastically as the Rev. Daniels stood down from the lectern and moved to shake hands with those near the front. Within a few minutes, he had left the auditorium and three men stood in a line on the small stage. One of them said:

"Friends, we now have to divide you into your teams for the coming work. I will hand you over to Mr Chambers who has your assignments."

For the next half an hour all members of the audience were allocated team leaders and individual numbers. They each received a welcome pack and were instructed to read parts of it before beginning work early the following morning. All were then marshalled away to eat dinner together before being instructed to return to their rooms and sleep. Their first working day began at 0500 hours.

"Good morning." said Grobus to the woman behind the reception counter. "My name is Rufus, Rufus Henry. I'm sorry to bother you like this. I believe a man called Mason Plater has done some work for your company recently?"

The woman stopped typing.

"Plater, you said?"

"That's right, Mason Plater." said Grobus. The receptionist clicked her mouse a couple of times and read from the screen.

"Yes, he worked for us recently." she said, now looking at the short man.

"Do you happen to have any contact information for him?" he asked. "I'm an old friend from years ago and I heard he'd done some work here, you know the grapevine, but I lost touch a while back, a phone number or address or something?"

"It's against company policy to give out any personal information I'm afraid."

Grobus smiled and revealed a gold tooth on one side of an otherwise perfect anatomical set.

"Well perhaps if you were to turn your screen around slightly while you gave me directions to somewhere I could get some coffee we might get over this problem without anyone breaking any rules."

The receptionist wasn't sure why she'd done it, but she stood up and as she did so she rotated her flat screen just enough that the small man could read an address. Then the receptionist explained in distinct tones how to reach the High Street and where she thought the best coffee was served. As she sat down again, she really couldn't think why she'd done that. It wasn't as if she'd even found the small man attractive. She shuddered. In fact, something about him was distinctly unattractive and it hadn't only been his stature. She told herself off and pulled the screen back to its proper place, hitting cancel to remove the screen with Mason Plater's photograph, address and phone number.

Grobus walked briskly back to his car, an unassuming dark blue Skoda.

23

Zach woke with a bad headache. His mouth was dry and his tongue seemed too big. Managing to reach his phone he saw it was 10:23 a.m.. A couple of drowsy button pushes told him it was Tuesday. But that couldn't be right. Pulling himself up to a sitting position, he stared dumbly at the phone and absently scooped his hair off his face. It can't be Tuesday, he thought, because yesterday was Friday.

Standing slightly awkwardly and swaying a little he reached for the small table across the room. There was a can of cola on it that he thought might have some left. It was warm and flat but crucially it was wet. Zach's mouth seemed to reconstitute, and his tongue felt as if it belonged.

Standing up was harder than he thought and he sat on the side of the bed again. His headache seemed to be at the back of his head and not above the eyes. Zach remembered having no more than one or two headaches ever but always across his eyes. Probably as a result of all-night gaming sessions and prodigious amounts of high caffeine drinks. This was different though and he felt around the back of his head up towards where the spine supports the skull.

He pulled his hand away and looked at it. Then felt again. Putting his phone down he felt with both hands. There was no mistaking that he had, what felt like, one or more stitches over a small wound.

Zach was confused. He went into his tiny bathroom and tried to turn himself and see in the small shaving mirror. It wasn't doing his headache any good to be twisting and contorting like this and without being able to see, he gave up and went back to sit on the bed. Getting up made him feel a bit queasy and his headache got slightly worse too. He sat quietly, wondering how it could be Tuesday. Then his phone made a sound like a robot cow mooing, and he picked it up. It was a text message from Meek.

"You awake?" it read.

Zach slowly replied "yes" but managed to mistype two letters before he sent it. He looked at his hands quizzically. Zach was usually a two-handed, two thumbed blur with a texting speed faster than a touch typist. He was feeling very thirsty again.

After the most perfunctory of knocks, his door opened and Meek slid in, closing the door like a burglar. Before Zach could form any words Meek said:

"How you feeling?"

Zach was going to say something about having a headache and being very thirsty and why was it Tuesday but before he could begin Meek continued.

"I've been scared shitless since you went missing." he said. "What happened?"

Zach was feeling really thirsty again and when he went to speak, he had to clear his throat twice before any words would come out.

"I don't know what you mean. I just woke up and I've got a bit of a headache and I'm really thirsty."

"You don't remember being ill then?" said Meek. "It was after dinner on Friday. You had some plastic lasagna or something and before we'd even got through coffee you were puking up."

"Don't remember that." said Zach. "Could you get me a glass of water."

He reached towards the empty tumbler laying on the bedside table. Meek took it and filled it from the bathroom. Zach downed it in one.

"That's nice." he announced, licking his lips. "Could I?"

He held out the glass and Meek got a refill. Another healthy gulp and Zach continued.

"I don't remember anything like that. Certainly not puking. I feel like shit now."

"Must've been something pretty nasty in the food cos you've been laid up for days."

"Days? Is it Tuesday?" asked Zach.

"Yeah, and somethin's been going on in 7G." said Meek. "Security through the roof and even a VIP."

"What do you mean?"

"Saturday night, probably just before midnight this convoy turns up, you know big Merc and a couple of 4x4s. One or maybe two knobs and their minders, went right to 7G, stayed about two hours then left."

"What were they doing?" wondered Zach.

"How the hell should I know, nearest I could get was corridor 3 and that was only to get to the kitchen.

Someone even followed me in to see what I was doing. Saw them leave out the window."

"So, I've been ill for like three days?" said Zach looking down at his knees. "That's weird, I mean I've never been out for days."

"Braberson said you'd got food poisoning and it was pretty bad. You've been in the clinic until today."

Zach's head throbbed again.

"Can you see what's happened to my head...here?" he asked pointing to what felt like the stitches. Meek looked.

"Ouch." said Meek "I guess you did that when you collapsed. Braberson said you'd hurt yourself. Looks like a neat job though."

"That makes me feel much better." said Zach sarcastically.

"You well enough for some news?" said Meek crossing to the door, opening it and checking nobody was in the corridor before gently closing it again. Zach just nodded for him to go on.

"I've been doing some investigation on those chips we found." continued Meek. "It's pretty wild."

Meek paused as if wondering how to continue.

"Well, what is it?" said Zach urgently and then wished he hadn't as a heavy throbbing began in the back of his head.

"I found not only circuit diagrams but test results. This is gonna sound crazy but they're visualizing the signals. It's amazing."

"So, what can they see?" he said. "It's got to be just noise or patterns, like the Kan displays."

"That's the point." said Meek, his body seeming to be

alive with energy "The test videos show images, proper images, of a boat and a house."

For a few moments there was silence, the words seeming to hang in the air like the finishing note of a piece of music.

"You mean?" began Zach.

"Yeah." said Meek. "They've translated a human's thoughts."

"Can't be." said Zach.

"No doubt about it, I've seen the test images. They're the ones the walkie-talkies look at before they try to transmit to the veggies."

Meek's colourful terms for the experimental subjects usually annoyed Zach but this time he didn't seem to notice.

"You're sure these results were from the comatose subs?"

"Absolutely." said Meek. "Looks like they've hit the jackpot."

24

Carver didn't really feel at home in his ministerial 'grace and favour' property in Central London. The beautiful five story townhouse was sandwiched between others owned by the Government. On one side the interior was mainly smaller apartments for key staff. On the other side a permanent security presence monitored not only the Home Secretary's residence but the other six ministerial properties in the area.

The surveillance in the ministerial house was discreet but nonetheless present. Ollie Stamp, a former MI5 officer who had been one of the 'Watchmen' while in the Service, had shown Carver where the cameras and listening devices were. Stamp was now employed by a private security company that was often used on Government sponsored projects within the UK. Carver had met him years earlier, before he knew he worked for the Security Services. They'd shared a passion for fencing and found themselves well matched. Whenever Stamp was in London, he would always see if Carver could spare an hour or so at the exclusive Baldwin Club to cross swords.

None of the obvious places in the house, like any of the five bathrooms or the three toilets, provided haven from the listeners. Only a quirk of architecture provided a coveted dead zone where two people, at a squeeze, or an individual with a special phone, might hold a private conversation. It was halfway up the flight of stairs between the second and third floors, at the back of the house. An incongruous alcove sat on the half landing as the wide staircase headed upwards. Carver had hung an oil painting that showed a wood nymph whispering in the ear of a sleeping woman under a sprawling oak tree. It had been painted by a moderately famous Italian artist in the eighteenth century and presented to HM Government many years earlier. The notion of secret communication behind the cupped hand of the wood nymph appealed to Carver's sense of humour.

He nestled into the small alcove and drew out the mobile phone from his pocket. The speed dial took a few seconds to negotiate the secure connection then Carver heard it ring once.

"Yes." said a man's voice.

"Stage 3 is operational but I don't like it." said Carver, constantly surveying the staircase.

"It is vital that we progress. The results so far have been very good. Better than we could have hoped."

"But the chips are untested in humans, I mean conscious humans. We have no idea if there will be side effects. There are so many people involved now, so many opportunities for a leak." said Carver.

"Do you have cause for concern?" asked the voice.

Carver knew he should mention what Braberson had

told him about the technician but chose not to.

"No." he said. "But we risk..." he seemed to grapple for the right word. "...damaging our best subjects."

"There is little time. The entity grows stronger. All indications point to multiple coordinated activities. We must know what is happening. You understand what is at stake."

Carver could not speak for a moment. He thought he knew what was at stake. Then at other times he felt as if in a dream or a form of madness. No-one should have to live such a double life. The pressures of perhaps the most difficult and thankless role in British politics and this. The unfathomable weight of responsibility for the fate of...what? The country? The West? Civilisation? Humanity?

"Yes." he said finally, his voice less steady, less authoritative than normal.

"When can you visit?" said the voice, at once lighter in tone and even warm.

"I don't know." said Carver.

"You must make it soon. Before the summit in Washington. It will help you relax."

The concept of relaxation had become alien to Carver during his time in office.

"I will." said Carver. "Thank you."

Before he'd even properly registered the hand appearing round the bannister from the floor below Carver had killed the call and begun casually descending the staircase.

"Sir." said Mrs. Fennell, the housekeeper, smiling warmly as they passed on the wide stairs. Carver's smile was strained and he had no doubt that Mrs.

Fennell had noticed.

God truly seemed to work in mysterious ways, at least that's how it seemed to Victor Sanchez as he studied a complex wiring diagram. Having served in the military for seven years and trained as an electronic and electrical engineer, he could hardly have imagined that one day his occasionally classified training would be of such vital importance in his spiritual fulfilment. Dawn Moran was busy soldering tiny connections on a custom circuit board using an industrial magnifier to view the intricate trails on the silicate.

Victor had immediately felt a connection with Dawn. They had inevitably fallen into conversation during a lunch break. Victor felt that Dawn wanted to talk about something. Eventually Dawn described how she had joined the Church after feeling lonely and having issues at school. She touched on her faltering relationship with her mother, made worse when her father had left. It seemed to Victor that Dawn had joined the Church to escape from something rather than because she had been drawn to it for any spiritual reasons. When Dawn explained that she had been kidnapped by her mother Victor was outwardly shocked, but inwardly felt sympathy for her mother. Dawn seemed like a confused young woman. She seemed to Victor to be looking for something to believe in, somewhere to feel she belonged and for some purpose in life. The more she spoke the less Victor felt it was really spiritual enlightenment she was seeking.

After only a couple of days, it was clear that Dawn had a real talent for the detailed assembly work on the integrated circuit boards. She was able to place and solder the tiny components with great precision and at almost twice the speed of anyone else that had tried.

As he and Dawn walked along the corridors to the canteen after their shift Victor studied again the various labs and workshops they passed. In some, large sheet metal work was underway while in others detailed laboratory work on a microscopic scale took place. Whatever they were building was drawing on man's knowledge from many branches of science and technology. It was also, according to the lectures they received every other evening, under the guiding hand of a power beyond that of mortal man. They were fulfilling prophecies made in some of the earliest writings of man. Writings that had come into the CoR's possession through careful excavations and explorations in the Holy Lands and through the special efforts of Rev. Ethan Daniels. Their efforts were being guided, they were told, by the hand of the Lord himself, through the Rev. Daniels. They would be the means by which the Lord would descend from the Heavens to once more save his Earthly flock from the gathering evil.

25

"It's a nice day for a drive." said Plater.

Molly was pushing clothes into the washing machine in the kitchen.

"I thought you wanted a quiet weekend, just the two of us?" said Molly.

"I do." said Plater. "But I have to talk to Bartholomew."

Molly appeared at the kitchen doorway.

"Has something happened?" she asked. "About the drawing?"

"I think so, but I can't be sure." said Plater.

He had a dozen or so sheets of yellow paper arranged on the coffee table in front of him. As he studied them, he reached and twisted one through ninety degrees. In his mind they formed parts of the larger design he'd been shown. Over the past few nights, he'd tried to focus on smaller pieces of the picture as trying to recall the details from the entire design in one step had proved impossible.

Molly squeezed beside Plater on the sofa. "So, what is it?"

"I don't know exactly." he said. "I thought at first it was a map, I thought these lines were roads or railway lines or rivers or something."

Plater paused and scanned the pages once more then reached for one on the far side of the table. He turned it in his hands and pointed to features of his drawing.

"See this bit?" he said. "I thought this represented a church, you see the cross there?"

"Yeah." said Molly.

"But then I saw this part a couple of nights ago."

He took another page and pointed to two triangular shapes with jagged lines and circles close together.

"These reminded me of school." he said. "But I couldn't think why."

Molly looked at the page, then at Plater and shrugged.

"Why school?" she said.

"Physics." said Plater.

"I'm not with you at all." said Molly.

"These are symbols used to describe electrical circuits" said Plater "Look, this triangular one here is the symbol for a transistor. See, I looked it up on the net, and this is a resistor, but I knew that, and this is something called a thyristor. But it's only this page and this one that seem to have those symbols. The others don't have them so I need to talk to Bartholomew in case this is significant."

"Can't you call him?" said Molly. "It'll take at least a couple of hours to get to him."

"I thought we might make a day of it." said Plater. "A walk on the beach, clear our heads of this mess for a while?"

Molly jumped up and made for the kitchen.

"Okay, we've got some average red and I can chuck some salad and cold meat together, how about a picnic?"

Plater was behind Molly now, as she closed the fridge door with lettuce and cold chicken in her hands. He slid his arms round her and nuzzled her neck.

"Sun, sea and ….." Plater let his sentence hang in the air.

"Salad!" said Molly, twisting free and scooping up the bread knife from the counter. She jabbed it towards Plater "Why don't you do something useful like filling the car up with petrol?"

Forty-five minutes later they were on the road to Suffolk, loud dance music from Molly's phone filling the car and her hand resting absently on Plater's thigh as he negotiated the Saturday morning traffic. The sun was indeed shining and the few clouds never threatened to hide it. On the back seat was a battered brown folder that held the drawings. About three cars behind them as they indicated to join the A12 from the M25 was a dark blue Skoda.

26

Victor had confessed to Dawn at breakfast to feeling nervous about the tests. He still felt uneasy about the circuits he'd been working on. The piece of the device he and Dawn had constructed had been removed from their workshop the previous evening and now formed a small part of the overall machine that sat in the middle of the main hall. It was evident that the main hall was the only room with a high enough ceiling to accommodate the assembled project, which stood centrally, climbing more than thirty feet towards the rough-hewn ceiling.

Victor and Dawn stood in a group of technicians lined up down one side of the hall to witness the first test of the device. A low hum pervaded the hall from the enormous refrigeration units that stood at each end and trailed thick pipes to the base of the machine. A large digital display on one wall counted down showing two minutes and twenty-three seconds.

Vapour spilled and sank in the air from the three tall cylinders around a weblike mesh of struts and cables that surrounded a central core that was gradually beginning to glow a faint blue green colour. Victor had no idea what any part of this gigantic construction did except his own, and even his own had mysteries. He just knew he had built it according to the precise plans he had been given. All his own preliminary tests of each minor component had worked as expected and he had no reason to believe his piece of this group test would fail.

He had expected others to be present for this test, at least Ralston, his disagreeable supervisor; then he would see that Victor's work was perfect. Ralston was witnessing the test, but from the safety of the main control room buried fifty metres further inside the mountain. Rev. Daniels also watched with interest on the wide screens in the control centre.

"Pressure within bounds, increase plasma density." said an earnest young man glancing between two computer screens that showed eight constantly updating tables of figures and two coloured diagrams that glowed blue.

"Second Stage initiated." boomed a speaker in the main hall.

A new sound joined the soft hum of the coolers, a high-pitched tone that seemed to be slowly sinking in pitch. One of the women technicians put her hands to her ears but then slowly withdrew them as the sound became more comfortable for human ears.

In the centre of the device whatever lay in the mesh now seemed a more purple colour and Victor felt a faint vibration in his chest. It was something like he'd felt before, as a boy, when he'd been to one of the nightclubs in Mexico city and stood too near one of the huge speakers. The centre of the machine now began to glow brighter and was becoming a richer purple. Dawn and Victor both took a small step back from the rumbling machine.

In the control room, Rev. Daniels rubbed his hands together absently, perhaps nervously as he watched the vapour clouds grow around the machine, masking off some of the deep purple radiance from its core.

"Test 1 limit in 10....9..." a technician counted down to test termination, watching the numbers dance across his screens.

In the main hall, one of the refrigeration engineers noticed what looked like a small leak from one of the cooling cylinders. He pulled on a protective helmet and stepped over the low rope that circled the device about fifteen feet from its base. He needed to get closer to see if the leak was at risk of rupturing as a spillage of supercooled fluid would be dangerous to both the machine and potentially the audience behind the rope.

"Field is at 60% and holding." recited another technician in the control room.

"Who's that?" said another voice pointing at the big screens. "He's getting too close..."

The sound in the main hall was sinking further in pitch and Victor's chest was starting to feel uncomfortable. It had never been like this in the nightclub. He felt a strange pressure on his chest and realised he was concentrating on breathing. It was becoming an effort. He sensed rather than saw others around him also wondering what was happening. He could feel Dawn's grip tighten on his hand.

"Stop!" screamed one of the technicians in the main control room, as the cooling engineer got within six feet of the base of the leaking cooling cylinder.

Victor now held his chest with his free hand and began to bend forwards. As he did so he caught sight of the cooling engineer in his distinctive blue helmet. In his discomfort, Victor wasn't sure what he was seeing; he couldn't believe it. He clutched his chest in real pain and forced himself to breathe in. The figure of the cooling engineer seemed to quiver. When Victor thought about it later, he would remember it as if he was watching TV on his uncle Pepe's early satellite receiver. The picture would often break up and reform and this is what Victor thought he saw happen to the cooling engineer. One minute he was there, then his body seemed to break up into a fuzzy interference pattern before coming back, then blurring again. Victor's last memory before he blacked out was of a scream. Oddly, the scream seemed to break up too.

In the control room, nobody spoke. Technicians typed furiously and the screens of the computers jumped from figures to diagrams to figures. Rev. Daniels was replaying what he had seen in his mind.

"Hallelujah brothers!" he announced. Nobody seemed to notice as the technicians typed and the supervisors watched over their shoulders in baffled helplessness.

"Hallelujah!" yelled Rev. Daniels and now those in the room turned towards him, "Our Lord has taken his loyal servant. We have witnessed a miracle. How I wish it was I, now, looking into the face of His Majesty. This is a wonder."

The faces of the others in the small control room

were sidelit by the glowing screens. Some seemed torn between making sure the machine was now safe and listening to the bellowed words of their leader.

"We are blessed!" went on Rev. Daniels. "Not since the days of the very earliest scriptures has our Lord manifest his power on Earth in such a way. He is coming my brothers, he is coming and we must be ready to greet his magnificent arrival."

Rev. Daniels, who had raised his gaze to the ceiling now lowered it to scan the faces of the others. His large hands slowly came together in the symbol of prayer.

"We must spread the word. Brothers and sisters, we must spread the word of what we have witnessed today. We have all seen the power of our Lord, we have all seen one of us lifted to join Him in his glory. Finish your work here, then join your brethren, rejoice in what has been bestowed upon us this day. Then redouble your efforts for you see now that this is our Lord's work, he is watching us in our labours and he is pleased....yes he is most pleased."

Ralston stood up and was about to speak. He wanted to say that what they had witnessed seemed to be a catastrophic malfunction in the containment of some form of energy produced inside the device. His head kept telling him this was true. His heart wanted this to be the work of the Lord. They had followed the build specifications precisely and this energy was not familiar to him, despite his background in nuclear technology. The little alarm bells got louder in the back of his head.

Rev. Daniels seemed to feel the doubts, seemed to recognise the body language and stood before Ralston. He reached out a massive hand and clasped the man's shoulder.

"Brother." he whispered. "I feel your doubt. Open your heart and see this for what it really was. You know what is right."

The Reverend's eyes held the man's for a few moments. Rev. Daniels could feel the tension releasing from Ralston's shoulders. Inside Ralston's head the nagging alarm bell became silent.

Rev. Daniels sat in silence in the dark. He was afraid but his fear gave him strength. If he could have seen his skin, he would have expected it to be glistening. It felt cool to him, the cooling sweat tingling and collecting in the creases by his nose and at the corners of his mouth. He could feel his heart rate slowing, his breathing was gradually becoming deeper and quieter. He raised the cut glass tumbler to his lips and heard the ice tinkle before he felt the whiskey touch his lips. They always used to use the phrase 'God-fearing man' to describe someone devout and obedient to the Almighty. Rev. Daniels thought they ought to use that phrase today. After what he had witnessed an hour ago it never seemed more right. The unseen hand of the Lord had reached down and plucked, there seemed no other word for it, plucked one of his servants from this earthly realm. It was a miracle.

The whiskey warmed his throat as it slid down. He set the glass on a small table and sank back into the soft leather chair. He closed his eyes although not needing to in the subterranean dark. This was truly the Lord's work. After today there could be no doubt. He wanted to laugh. To cry out and proclaim to all those unbelievers what he now knew, what he had always known. That the Lord was powerful and that he would return. His visions had been powerful and persuasive. Right from his time in the Holy Land when they had really begun. At times, he hadn't been sure if he'd been awake or asleep, so vivid were his experiences. He had felt compelled to write his story and to persuade others of the need to prepare for the coming of the Lord. He'd never written anything before but in the few weeks it took him to commit his revelations to paper, he had produced a book that would sell close to a million copies in its first year. It had seemed the most natural thing in the world for him to start a church based on his visions. He had to tell as many people as he could of the wonders he had witnessed. The Lord had guided him as he took his first stumbling steps. Surely, he had helped Rev. Daniels and the CoR to reach so many people and to become the fastest growing religious organisation in the world. Rev. Daniels needed no further convincing, he was sure he was doing the Lord's work and he would finish it, if it was the last thing he did.

Forty metres away, through the solid rock, sat Victor. He was hunched over on his small bed, rubbing his thumb over the crucifix on a silver chain that his wife had given him on their wedding day. He did this when he was troubled and the small cross was smooth and shiny from thirty years of worries.

Victor had tried to understand what he had seen. The cooling engineer, Ralph or Randolph or something like that, Victor couldn't remember, had been there, then he'd gone. Gone like someone had flipped a switch and turned his life out like a light. Victor felt bad that he hadn't been able to remember the man's name. There'd been a stunned silence at first, then gradually concern, and eventually near panic as word spread. An announcement over the address system instructed everyone to return to their quarters. Nobody knew what to say. The uniformed security men had shepherded the technicians into the corridor and the heavy main doors to the hall had swung shut. Some had peered through the closing doors still unable to believe that a human being that had been in that room with them had suddenly vanished in plain view of anyone that cared to look.

Victor had walked Dawn back to her room in virtual silence. The look they exchanged at the door was one of confusion and uncertainty. Victor had seen the worried look in Dawn's eyes and said:

"Best get some rest, I'll come by on my way to breakfast, as usual."

His smile was genuine, but Dawn saw the slight shake of his lips and the way Victor wouldn't hold her gaze but stepped away and made off down the corridor.

Rubbing the cross was soothing Victor, as it had many times before, like when his mother had passed. He wanted to believe that he had witnessed a miracle. He wished he could be with his wife and his children. He wanted nothing so much as to be back in his steady life at home. Returning from work and hearing his wife in the kitchen or the garden. Calling out to her and wanting to hear how her day had been.

There were mixed emotions inside Victor. He squeezed his eyes shut but still saw the face of the engineer as he disappeared. Still heard his fractured cry. The look in his eyes had not been one of amazement. His muscles had been taut, wrenched tight by nature's instinct. The sound from his lips had not been a cry of joy. Not an outpouring of ecstasy at beholding the wonder and majesty of his creator and Lord. It had been a scream of primeval terror.

27

Carver's visit to a former Home Secretary's country house in the run-up to a major intelligence conference in Washington hardly registered in the tabloid press. Sir Alastair Kenwright was well known in the local area for his parties. Having been privately wealthy before spending twenty-five years as a Member of Parliament, which included four separate Ministerial posts, he had always enjoyed entertaining. The guest lists at his gatherings were never public but also never without people of real significance. Not necessarily those that made headlines in the media, but more likely those that had more discreet power and influence, in both business and politics.

Carver had arrived quietly the previous evening, very late, after a prolonged but vital debate on social policy that required full Government attendance for a close vote. Kenwright was there to greet his friend but on seeing the drawn and tired face, insisted Carver retire and they'd catch up the next day.

After a light breakfast around seven Carver sought

out the former Home Secretary and found him finalising details of the coming dinner with his chef.

"Jim, good morning." said Kenwright. "So, you'll check again about the pheasant?" he said to the retreating figure of the chef, who held up a hand as he disappeared through an archway towards the kitchens.

"You can't rely on anyone these days." went on Kenwright as he guided Carver through to his study. "I had a little dinner last month and ordered 30 pheasant from this chap, bugger me if he only sent 18, I mean what good's that on the day before the blasted dinner. I told Henry he should find another supplier, but he insists this chap's the best."

They emerged from a narrow paneled corridor into a high-ceilinged, airy room with tall windows. The natural light made the colours leap from the ancient tapestries on the walls and the sumptuous Chinese carpets on the floor.

"Sleep well?" asked Kenwright as he motioned Carver to sit on one of the two Chesterfield sofas that faced each other across an inlaid Indian coffee table.

"I always do in this house." said Carver.

"The country air." said Kenwright. "Good to get out of the city. Too easy to get submerged in all that Whitehall nonsense. Oh, sorry, would you like anything? Tea, coffee?"

Kenwright got up and pressed a small button by the fireplace.

"Coffee would be good." said Carver.

They exchanged pleasantries for a few minutes until Jeffries, the housekeeper had deposited a coffee pot and two cups on the table between them. As Carver sat back with his black coffee he sighed.

"I'm not happy with moving to Phase 3 without more testing." he said.

Kenwright paused before answering.

"Jim, do you remember the undertaking you gave in this very room when we first met?"

Carver stirred his coffee and watched the swirling eddies subside.

"Yes." he said.

"We took on a duty." said Kenwright. "A duty to spare nothing in our efforts to understand and resist."

"But we don't even know what we're fighting here." said Carver. "Decades, centuries of wondering, of theories, of experiments, of secret meetings, diaries, documents. Christ we're a conspiracy theorist's wet dream. We're what the Illuminati would aspire to be, and what do we have to hold on to? What do we really know? Millions, maybe billions spent scrambling to confront what? Something we can't describe and daren't try to."

Kenwright sipped his coffee and carefully slid the cup onto the table.

"I know it can be difficult Jim. When I was first approached, I thought they were mad. An alien intelligence trying to interfere in society and using mind control? I laughed in their faces. It sounded more like some bad Cold War thriller from the sixties. The Manchurian Candidate meets Flash Gordon. I know how it sounds when you're told. But then I saw the work being done. I read the documents, as you have by now."

"They can be read in more than one way." said Carver. "We're placing an interpretation on their words that could be completely wrong."

"If you mean the Capetown Conjecture 2002?"

Carver nodded, Kenwright continued.

"That idea has been analysed by the finest minds we have. All available evidence suggests it's correct."

"Forgive me, but we're being asked to believe that essentially all mainstream religions have been somehow subverted by this thing? My wife's family is Catholic."

"I need hardly remind someone with your knowledge of history that the vast majority of wars are instigated or influenced by religion." said Kenwright. "Today's major religions are still making headlines for reasons you would not associate with pious living and care for their fellow man. Take 'the troubles' in Ireland, yes they are based in rejection of imperialism but that has morphed into a straight tension between religions. Passed down from generation to generation until few recognise anything beyond an 'us' vs. 'them' struggle. Subtle adjustments are all that is required to instigate mayhem. The muslim faith purports to be one of peace and in its roots it is, but a slight change in interpretation of words which are supposed to come directly from God and we have ruthless killing from a small following that are certain they are doing God's will. The Catholics meanwhile have managed to amass resources that dwarf many countries while operating outside any laws. They have tolerated priests with peccadilloes that are totally unacceptable in mainstream society, let alone a supposedly Godly calling. They supported the Nazi Party up to and including the Second World War and continued celebrating Hitler's birthday until the war ended. Their history is chequered at best, with much of it likely locked away in the Vatican Archives, never to see the light of day."

Carver put down his cup and stretched backwards, looking up at the elegant plasterwork across the ceiling.

"I can certainly see why there is such a need for secrecy." said Carver. "These ideas are dangerous. In fact exposing ideas like this could bring about precisely the chaos we're trying to prevent. Who's to say we're not part of the problem and not the solution?"

"But the evidence is there." maintained Kenwright, holding Carver in a steady gaze.

"What evidence?" asked Carver, now leaning forwards. "What evidence do we really have?"

"You read the Swallows paper?"

"Yes."

"Before that it was all based on the ideas of fringe research, writings of eccentric scholars and wild connections across time and recorded history. There was nothing that could possibly link these apparent human aberrations through time. We're fortunate that the Americans became quite so paranoid about Soviet and Korean mind control efforts. If the CIA hadn't sponsored some of their more radical research, and especially the Stargate Project, we would not have that evidence."

"Stargate?" said Carver. "Was that the LSD experiment?"

"No, you're thinking of MK Ultra, Stargate was the Remote Viewing. It was subject 79 and the shared subconscious experience. It was the final piece of the jigsaw. A way that information could pass between individuals in a completely new and at that time undetectable fashion."

"But these guys were flakes, they claimed to be able to travel to distant parts of the world and see what was happening."

"And they were so successful that one of them was awarded the Legion of Merit by a grateful US Government for determining, quote, '150 essential elements of information unavailable by any other means', unquote. The work of Targ and Puthoff is undeniable, although the CIA managed to deny it several times, especially to Congress. We know they carried on that work even after lying that they had stopped. As far as we know, it continues to this day. Evidence for outside interference is pretty compelling. The Thompson paper even suggests there could be a parallel 'society' on a plane of consciousness we're only beginning to detect."

"You mean the wacky experiments that Braberson and his team are engaged in?"

Kenwright nodded.

"But the evidence for that is inference and opinion." said Carver. "We have no way of knowing that this isn't something the Chinese have developed."

"All indications are that governments have given up on so-called parapsychological research. Even the Russians suspended funding after the wall came down. Our agents in mainland China have never even heard a rumour of anything remotely connected with research in this area. The Chinese have more pressing issues to concentrate on. Anyway, James, I don't need to lecture you on the incomplete nature of intelligence gathering.

We, rather you, and others, make decisions almost every day based on incomplete knowledge gathered bit by bit via subterfuge, deceit and lies. You look at the information and make a judgement call, assess the risks and the consequences, then act. No difference here."

Carver sat back in silence for a moment.

"I don't like keeping this from Andrew either. Why wasn't he approached too? Surely he could be of use to the cause?" he said.

Kenwright smiled.

"Andrew Ridgewell is a good man. So far, a good Prime Minister too, but he has enough to handle as it is. You know we only recruit those of real value because of their position or special skills and occasionally money. The role of Home Secretary can be a thankless one, I can still remember, but you are afforded certain privileges when it comes to keeping activities secret within the UK. Your help so far has been invaluable and I'm sure when the results come in from Phase 3 we'll be sitting here toasting another major breakthrough."

Kenwright looked at Carver and could read the conflicted expression.

"You'll have time to meet with our American friends while you're in Washington?" asked Kenwright.

"There's an official dinner on the second evening, I'll decline with a slight gastric condition."

"Excellent." said Kenwright. "More coffee?"

28

Bartholomew locked the shop door behind Molly and Plater before switching round the sign to show 'Closed'. Plater spread his drawings across the counter in the shop and started to explain what he thought some of the symbols might mean.

"What do you think." said Plater finally.

"I think I'd like to get a second opinion." said Bartholomew. "Can I keep these for now?"

"Of course." said Plater.

"What are you going to do with them?" asked Molly.

"I have a friend who might be able to tell if Mason's interpretation is correct." said Bartholomew. "He was at college with me, works for the Government these days, something in research, no idea what but I'm sure he could offer an opinion. Would you like some tea?"

"We planned to have a picnic actually." said Molly.

"It seems you have picked a good day for it. " said Bartholomew. "There is a lovely sheltered spot on the beach just there."

He pointed to a large local map on the wall.

"You could even walk from here." he said.

"Do you know that man?" asked Molly, who was looking out through the shop window across the road at a small man. The man was trying to look as if he was waiting for a bus but kept staring directly at the small bookshop.

Bartholomew crossed to the window.

"No." he said. "And I think you might like to leave by the back door."

"Why?" said Plater, now also looking at the little man.

"Look at his left hand." said Bartholomew.

All three peered across the quiet road at the small man by the deserted bus stop. He was looking up the road as if expecting a bus and his hands hung by his sides.

"I don't see anything." said Molly.

"Look at the little finger of his left hand." said Bartholomew. "Do you see how it is curled up into the palm?"

"Yeah, so what?" said Plater.

"Why don't you try to do that?" said Bartholomew.

Both Molly and Plater looked down at their left hands and tried to curl just their little finger tightly into their palms. Neither managed it.

"Can't seem to do it." said Plater at last.

"Why is it important?" said Molly, who was trying to push her finger into the right shape with her other hand.

"We think that people with that unusual feature are under the influence of the Others, people such as that appear in paintings through the centuries and even in Egyptian tombs. It's as if the Others can affect some people but this aberration in muscle control is always present."

"So that little guy is under their control?" wondered Plater. "But what's he doing here? How did he know about you?"

"He may have followed you." began Bartholomew. "I've lived here for twelve years and never seen one of them here in the village. I'm not dangerous to them in the same way that you must be, my connections between the other realm and reality are not strong like yours. I am average in the other realm and less than average in reality, I'm afraid."

"Do you think he might do anything? To us I mean?" asked Molly.

"I'm not sure." said Bartholomew. "He could just be following you to see what connections you make or to work out what threat, if any, you pose."

"So you think he's just following us and checking what we do and who we meet?" said Plater. "Well that means he now knows about you."

"I don't understand." began Molly. "He doesn't look like a zombie or anything, what does he think he's doing?"

Plater took two photographs of Grobus on his mobile phone.

"Maybe we can find out who he is." said Plater.

"It's creepy." said Molly.

"I don't think you have anything to fear Molly, whatever the Others want it will be to do with Mason."

"That doesn't make me feel much better." said Molly.

"Please." said Bartholomew "Let me show you out the back."

* * *

It had been two days since Zach woke up, but he still felt a dull ache at the back of his head. He seemed incapable of taking on any liquids without almost immediately needing to pee and when he accidentally caught sight of some of his other body waste, it had been a disturbingly yellow colour. Dr Hunt had reassured him that this was to be expected and that he should only need to be on the medication for another few days.

The lack of sleep tended to encourage Zach to try coffee to perk him up, but that only caused trips to the toilet and on his way back from his third visit of the morning, he stopped at the door to Meek's lab.

"Not again." said Meek, without looking up from the microscope he was peering down. "Your bladder is officially the smallest in the world."

"So where is it?" said Zach.

"Voila." said Meek, crossing to a cupboard and taking out a small aluminium box and setting it on the bench in front of Zach.

Zach picked it up but there wasn't much to see. It had two sockets on one end and a single set of data pins at the other.

"You reckon this can intercept the signals from the Aronson chip?" asked Zach.

"Yes." said Meek. "It's only a prototype and there are some minor bugs."

"Bugs?" said Zach.

"The frequencies of the Aronson chip cause interference during signal processing and I haven't dampened the resulting feedback. I can filter it out on my test-rig."

"Show me." said Zach, handing the small box back to Meek.

For about five minutes Meek busied himself on the test bench on the far side of his lab. He connected the small box between his computer rack and two beige boxes on trollies that were similar to the ones they had seen in the operating theatre, room 7G.

"So this little beauty can capture the near-field variations of the Aronson chips and the remnants of code I've been able to scavenge can represent some of what the chips themselves are processing. Look, this was from subject 3 yesterday..."

Meek hit a key on the computer keyboard and the display showed a grainy and highly coloured image of a sailing boat.

"Basically, I'm taking the raw emissions, isolating the relevant module, meaning filtering out the power circuits and input/output stuff so I just get the beans..."

Meek hit another key and the display closed.

"I've got an actual Aronson chip mounted in the test rig here and it's setup to cycle through its test settings. Watch the display, you'll see that I'm able to decode the test sequence exactly, a bit like having the encryption key to a code....see..."

Meek flicked a switch to activate the test rig containing the Aronson chip.

Zach suddenly saw streaking, bright lights before his eyes. He closed his lids but the lightshow continued. A tone sounded in his ears, or at least he thought it did, but he covered his ears with his hands and the sounds were just as loud and distracting. He could feel his balance going and what he could see of Meek's lab beyond the bright lightshow tilted and swayed. The noises in his ears seemed right inside his head and not very pleasant at that. Zach was desperately trying to stop the room from moving but everything he tried seemed to make little difference. A shape seemed to be forming through the kaleidoscope of colours and fractured shapes before his eyes. It was Meek's face, but it was frayed around the edges, no not frayed, blocky. Meek's face looked like a bad satellite signal on TV. As abruptly as the sounds and lights started, they stopped, the room settled and Meek's face in front of his was smooth and clear.

"You okay?" asked Meek. "What happened?"

"Dunno." said Zach. "I got dizzy and got a sort of buzzing in my ears."

Meek's expression changed. He quickly dismantled the test rig and stuffed the small aluminium box in the pocket of his jeans. He rearranged the test rig to reflect one of his earlier test runs then pressed the button again on the red box in his drawer.

"Coffee." said Meek.

"What about the demo?" said Zach.

"It wasn't a question." said Meek and guided Zach into the corridor, towards the communal kitchen.

Meek loaded the coffee machine and switched it on.

"I felt a bit weird just now." said Zach. "I missed the show I think."

Zach was sitting at the table and absently twisting his neck and squeezing his eyes shut and open again.

"We...errr...well you actually." began Meek. "Have a problem"

Zach was only too aware that he had a problem, his headache was back and if anything, worse than the last time.

"What do you mean?" he asked.

Meek sat at the table and leaned across it to whisper.

"Don't move or say anything." began Meek, glancing for emphasis to his left in the direction of the security camera. "But your reaction just now, in the lab, suggests that you have a STZ3798-2 connected to your cortex."

Zach's eyes registered something in the realm of shock and horror. He sat upright and Meek could see the tension. Zach's eyes began to dart around the room as if they needed to keep busy as his brain took in what Meek had said. Without really thinking Zach's right hand crept slowly to the back of his head and he gently explored the healing wound just inside the hairline.

"Bastards." he thought. "The fucking bastards."

29

"So, there's a parallel society there, with, like, a Government?" said Molly.

Plater was looking thoughtful and couldn't seem to settle. He stood by his living room window as if expecting to see someone or something.

"I told you." he said. "There's an entire city, there must be millions there."

"All dreaming." said Molly.

"Or sick."

"What time is he coming?" asked Molly.

"I don't know, but he'll come." said Plater.

"He knows what that thing is?" asked Molly.

"He took it to someone, someone in a Government lab, a scientist. They think they know what it is."

There was a sound from the kitchen, a tapping. Bartholomew was outside the back door.

"What are you doing?" said Plater as he slipped the bolt and let Bartholomew in.

"I'm terribly sorry." said Bartholomew, who was brushing his suit trousers with his hands. "I thought it wise to arrive discreetly, one never knows who may be watching. I'm afraid I may have damaged your wild rose."

"What?" said Plater before realising Bartholomew had clambered over the fence and tangled with the rambling wild rose bush that squatted in the back corner of Plater's city garden.

"Who might be watching?" said Molly as Plater and Bartholomew appeared in the living room.

"The same people that followed you to my shop." said Bartholomew. "We don't know who they are or what they want so I think it best to take precautions until we know."

"Tea? Or something stronger?" asked Molly, realising that Plater seemed in no mood to be a good host.

"A whiskey would be admirable Molly, thank you." said Bartholomew smiling. "I thought my days of climbing fences were long gone."

Bartholomew took a decent slug from the two fingers of single malt Molly had poured.

"I can tell you." began Bartholomew. "What my friend at the Ministry has deduced from the diagram you brought out. He's a physicist actually. He believes that the diagram you drew is part of the construction plan for a most interesting piece of equipment. It seems there are theories about such machines, but the technology just isn't there to construct a viable device."

"What's it for?" asked Molly.

Bartholomew paused a moment and looked at Plater and Molly in turn.

"Well it's a bit strange really." he said. "It seems these are instructions for building a machine that can distort spacetime."

Bartholomew looked again from Plater to Molly and back again.

"You're going to have to explain." said Plater.

"Well, I'll do my best but this isn't my field." said Bartholomew. "According to Brian, my friend, it is theoretically possible to distort space and time. I know it sounds ridiculous, but it seems scientists have known of this possibility since the days of Einstein. Indeed some believe it will be the way we can one day visit other planets without taking many lifetimes to reach them."

The expressions on Plater and Molly's faces told Bartholomew he needed more explanation.

"But what would a machine like this do exactly?" asked Molly.

"Well nobody really knows." said Bartholomew. "They are really the province of science fiction. Brian saw elements in the diagram that would need to be present in such a theoretical device."

"Okay, so why is this such a big deal?" asked Plater. "If it's not even possible to make one of these things what were details doing in the Realm?"

Bartholomew took another healthy dose of whiskey.

"Those plans were taken from the Others, this much you were told. There was a considerable sacrifice made to obtain them. There were" Bartholomew paused. "...casualties."

"Casualties?" said Molly.

"Fourteen people were lost to bring that information to safety." said Bartholomew.

"What do you mean?" asked Plater.

"In the Realm we mounted an operation. We knew that the Others were planning something important. Our watchers reported lots of activity in the Valley. It's the area of the Realm where the Others congregate. It is a largely empty place that appears to us to contain many objects associated with the less savoury aspects of humanity."

"I'm sorry Raymond." said Plater. "But this isn't making much sense."

"It can be hard to accept." said Bartholomew. "But we watch the Others all the time and it was said that much activity was being put to creating something very important. They were busy compiling a book. They believed that these were mystical writings handed down to them from the gods. They believed that once they had compiled the book they could decipher it and learn secrets known only to the gods."

"This sounds crazy." said Molly.

"Yes, but we believe the information was supposed to be carried into the real world for use by their agents. We believe that they intend to build this device."

Bartholomew drained his glass. Plater and Molly said nothing.

"So we were able to steal a large part of one of the copies." said Bartholomew.

"Copies?" Plater questioned.

"Yes, the Others were writing their dictation from the gods as received by more than one of their number. Competing Prophets, one might say. We were able to get hold of some of the pages from one version, but at a great cost. Our watchers were discovered. We're not sure how, perhaps someone from the city gave them up.

But fourteen of them were lost."

"Do you mean dead?" asked Molly.

"We have no easy way of knowing." said Bartholomew. "Only a handful of those we have lost have ever returned. We have not seen anything of the fourteen."

"But could that happen to Mason?" said Molly. "Could he be 'lost'?"

"It is always possible." said Bartholomew. "We know much but understand little. We are locked in conflict and in conflict there are always casualties."

"Why?" said Plater. "What is this machine supposed to be for? What do they hope to achieve?"

Bartholomew took a deep breath and continued.

"As you were told this is a struggle with a force that we believe is not of our world. An alien force able to interact with humans via the Realm and other ways too in some cases. We are forced to accept the possibility that this force represents a physical race of beings."

"You mean..." began Molly. "Like ETs ? Like the Greys?"

"What are Greys?" asked Plater.

"That's what they call the sorts of aliens with big heads and big eyes that people report being abducted by." said Molly. "I read about it on the net, these people said they'd been taken up to alien spaceships and had experiments done on them and stuff."

Bartholomew shook his head slightly.

"Those poor people seem to have problems of an earthly nature rather than unearthly." he said. "But yes, we do mean actual beings from another place in the universe. We believe that by using their influence to cause people in the real world to build this device they hope to use it somehow for their own ends."

"That's quite a story." began Plater. "But what good would this 'spacetime distorter' be to these things?"

"The most likely possibility is also the most terrible." said Bartholomew. "If this device works it is possible that these creatures might be able to use it to create some sort of bridge, or shortcut if you prefer, to enable them to reach our world faster."

"My god." said Molly.

Plater turned and gazed out of the window into the street.

"What do we have to go on?" said Plater.

"Well." said Bartholomew. "It seems some of the components of this device are unusual and Brian was able to find out that a single company in America had recently bought virtually all the necessary items. Funny thing is it's a company called 'Meadowland inc.', ostensibly a property holding company."

"Who owns it?" asked Plater.

"Well that's the really odd thing." said Bartholomew. "It's owned by some quasi-religious cult that calls themselves The Church of the Reclamation. They own huge amounts of property across the US and use this company to control it. It seems they are very wealthy and have more than a million members worldwide."

"So what do we do?" said Plater. "Can't we alert the authorities or something?"

"I hardly think that would be well received. How would we explain our knowledge of this enterprise and why we regard a crackpot cult's attempts to build a machine most scientists believe is science fiction, should be of concern ?"

"Well what then?" asked Molly. "Should we join this Church, see if we can find out what's going on from the inside?"

"I'm not sure you'd be safe." said Bartholomew. "If one is to believe the press The Church of the Reclamation is not, it seems, a typical religious organisation."

Molly got up and crossed to the table, flipped open Plater's laptop and switched it on.

"Time to find out about this lot." she announced.

30

Carver's stay in Washington had not gone well so far. He had received a call from the Security Services, MI5, while in-flight informing him of a suspected terrorist attack in London. When he arrived in the US, his first meeting had been with an angry Secretary of State who had complained that the same Security Services had failed to show the necessary politeness and inform the CIA in London, as had been agreed in previous versions of the meetings Carver was in Washington to attend. He sometimes wondered if the so-called 'special relationship' had ever really existed. Things worked well when information flowed from the UK to the US, but he doubted the appropriate levels of information flowed in the other direction.

He was only too happy to cry off the official dinner on his second night. He was of course deeply apologetic and politely declined the State Department's offer of medical assistance to help ameliorate his gastric distress.

So it was that at 21:00 he left his hotel through the

service area and got into a car rented by Glade Industries. It was waiting for him and driven by a short hispanic man with ornate tattoos on each forearm, wearing a Redskins baseball cap. After a fifteen-minute drive the car pulled into an underground car park.

"Mr. Carver." said a man in his mid-thirties, extending his hand and smiling broadly. "My name is Franklin, Conrad Franklin. Please, come this way."

Carver followed Franklin along a short dark corridor to a lift. Franklin inserted a key and the lift began to move. There were no floor indicators at all and after a few moments the doors opened directly onto a large room that was neat and luxurious like an expensive hotel suite.

A man and woman sat talking on a sofa. As the lift doors opened they broke their conversation and turned towards Carver.

"Mr. James Carver." said the woman. "I'm so glad you could find the time to join us, I understand the schedule is tight this visit?"

Carver noticed the lift doors close on Franklin, obviously a discussion above his station.

"You must be Mrs Cantrell, I've heard a lot about you." said Carver. "There have been developments on our side."

"Please, just call me Faith." said Cantrell "I have heard of the developments, yes. This is Professor John Straker from Illinois."

The men shook hands and exchanged pleasantries before all three relaxed into the deep cushions of the cream sofas.

"So, am I correct in thinking that you have subjects

already at Stage 3 over there?" said Cantrell.

"We have just begun Stage 3, yes, and we have two subjects that have shown synchronized activity to 98% and better." said Carver. "I have asked Braberson to send a results package by the secure channel."

"98% is truly remarkable." said Straker. "Are they implanted?"

"Yes, the second implant was inserted just before I left England."

"No side-effects? Rejection of the implants?" said Straker.

"Rejection is being managed and so far no adverse reaction at all." said Carver.

"That really is exciting news James." said Cantrell. "We have some news of our own, but it isn't as encouraging as yours, John..."

Straker seemed to take a deeper than normal breath before he spoke.

"One of our people in the Department of Defense reports that a peculiar event was detected five days ago. An event that might suggest we have a local problem."

Straker paused as if unsure how to continue.

"Go on." said Carver.

"A military survey team, from the Corps of Engineers, was measuring seismic activity in Northern California and one afternoon their measuring equipment went off the scale. Now they've been expecting the 'big one' in California for years now but the odd thing about their measurements was that the disturbance they saw was not geological in origin. According to their instruments there was the equivalent of a quake at more than 9 on the Richter scale but it was located in the Rockies and apparently almost at the surface."

"Forgive me professor but I'm not sure I understand the significance of what you're telling me." said Carver.

"I'm sorry." said Straker. "What I'm saying is that we believe there was a release of energy, somewhere in the Rocky Mountains that caused seismic detectors hundreds of miles away to flatline. This was definitely not a natural phenomenon Mr. Carver, er... James."

"What could it have been?" said Carver.

"That's just it." said Cantrell. "We don't know of any technology that could have caused this event. It also lasted for a matter of seconds and appears not to have caused damage."

Carver looked back to Professor Straker.

"What do you mean?" asked Carver. "What happened here?"

"It's early days but we think this may have been caused by the operation of a device we thought beyond current science." said Straker. "From the time man first ventured into space it has been a dream to explore distant worlds and galaxies. But every schoolboy knows that the sheer distances involved to even our nearest neighbour solar system would required decades to travel by any means we know of today. But every schoolboy has also watched Star Trek and any number of other sci-fi films where inter-stellar travel is possible. They call it 'warp drive' at least in Star Trek, in other films it gets other names but the concept is the same."

Straker paused but nobody spoke, so he continued.

"The classic way to explain this idea is to imagine the universe is like this sheet of paper, a two-dimensional representation of our three dimensions." Straker took up a pad that lay on the coffee table, he drew two 'x's on the paper about twelve centimetres apart.

"Let's say we're here." he indicated one of the crosses. "And the place we want to visit is here." He indicated the other cross. "If we travelled in a conventional manner the shortest route would be a straight line like so." he drew a line on the paper to join the crosses. "But let's suppose that this represents interstellar distances, thousands of light years, it would be impossible to make the trip."

"I still don't see where this is going." said Carver.

"What if we cheat, like on Star Trek." said Straker, tearing the sheet from the pad and curling it up so that the two crosses almost touched. "What if there was a way to bend space like this so that we could make the distance we'd have to travel smaller?"

"But this is impossible surely?" said Carver. "And what does it have to do with your event?"

"Theoretically this is possible." said Straker. "But impossible to do in practice, or so we believe. The reason the event measured last week is of interest to us is that it represents a release of energy of the same order of magnitude required to permit bending, warping if you will, of the fabric of spacetime. There is a better than even chance, James, that someone, somewhere, within these United States has developed the technology to warp space."

"But that's crazy." said Carver. "There must be some other explanation."

He looked from Straker to Cantrell and back.

"We have a theory of our own." said Cantrell. "We

adhere to the theory that the entity represents an alien intelligence, a species from a distant planet. We've theorised about why they have any interest in us and why they seem to want to interfere in human affairs. You know that the dominant theory is survival as the entity's home may be in some sort of existential crisis. You've read the same papers as us no doubt. We also believe that they are able to influence individuals here on Earth. Well what if they're getting people here to help them build one end of a bridge to allow them to travel to Earth from wherever the hell they come from?"

Carver's immediate reaction was to laugh, he had only rudimentary scientific training but had read enough popular science speculation to know that these concepts were real enough. But to believe this idea needed aliens that could control humans to the point of persuading them to build some machine, and presumably a highly complex device. Surely this was an endeavour for a government not some band of drones being directed from space.

"So have you traced the source of this event." said Carver.

"Unfortunately, the detection of the disturbance represents many reflections and distortions of the original release of energy. The geological instruments are detecting indirect evidence of the distortion. The disturbance didn't last long enough for precise location. We can only say it came from somewhere within an area of approximately three thousand square miles, most of which is thinly populated, mountainous or heavily forested." said Straker.

"Wouldn't this sort of machine need a lot of power?" asked Carver.

"According to the theory more power than is generated for the entire continent of North America in a year." said Straker.

"We need to get a closer look at the source." said Cantrell. "James, do you have some people that could do that? If something were to go wrong, we need some deniability and I think your guys have particular expertise in this sort of thing."

Cantrell was implying the ex-SAS men that were available to Carver, and had performed well in a previous mission, would be best to investigate the mysterious energy burst in the mountains. Carver also thought this but wanted to check with them himself before committing them.

"I'll speak to my team, but the final decision must rest with them, from an operational standpoint." he said. Cantrell nodded.

There was silence until Carver said:

"Is there anything to drink?"

The four walls of Zach's small, but comfortable room seemed closer together as he curled in a ball in his bed. They say knowledge is power but although he knew about the implant in his head Zach now felt powerless. Sure, he knew that his department was engaged in experiments on unwilling (and unwitting) human subjects. He knew the basis of the technology being used but what good had it done him? He and Meek had bumbled around gathering information but how long had they known? How long had Braberson been watching them?

The time edged past 3 a.m. although Zach was totally unaware. He just knew he had to get out. Get out of this claustrophobic atmosphere of Frankenstein experiments and secret comings and goings. Briefly the letter inviting staff to take part in this special project flashed before his eyes. He'd been interested in the money; he couldn't deny it. He should have smelt a rat. When did public servants earn that kind of wedge for a few weeks work? He'd give anything to wind back time and respectfully decline the chance to spend six weeks in the Suffolk countryside.

Each time he thought about the technical aspects of the implant he was dragged back to his situation. Why had he been implanted? What could Braberson hope to gain from involving him? Zach wasn't anything out of the ordinary, as he'd done the screening tests, like everyone working here had done. But he had only barely outscored Meek, and they had both been far behind one of the security guards, who exhibited quite unusual brain activity. Nothing they could use in the project, but it seemed to shatter the myth that security guards had very little going on in their heads. Zach hoped that Braberson intended the implant mainly as a tracker. Braberson obviously knew that Zach had been poking around, perhaps he just wanted to keep a tighter rein. But why one of the new chips then? One of the older, standard variety would have done. Meek was sure it was not a standard implant; they didn't react to his device at all.

It didn't make sense. If the implant had been a standard device Zach thought he'd actually have been relieved. Working on secret projects came with restrictions, he'd known that. Of course, it also came with interesting stuff to work on. He could almost understand Braberson wanting to keep him around for his technical skills but know he wasn't stepping over the line and compromising the security of the project. Having one of the new implants didn't fit with that and Braberson's motives were obscure. It was the not knowing about the full range of the implant's function that haunted Zach.

For the umpteenth time Zach came to the conclusion that his only course of action was to get out. He needed to get beyond the range of the transceiver and recover something of his privacy and freedom. He knew this was madness, to abscond from a secret scientific installation with little prospect of remaining at liberty in surveillance Britain for long. Somehow, as the night crept by in his lonely corner of Suffolk, the idea seemed less and less crazy.

31

Grobus took criticism poorly. Perhaps a psychologist might have made something of his upbringing in trying to explain this. His father had been authoritarian, while his mother, a kinder, more spiritual soul, had been a mistreated casualty in her marriage. Oculus often reminded Grobus of his father in his utter disdain and constant harping criticisms, even when none might be warranted. Just because he had lost the man Plater in Suffolk, Oculus wanted punishment from the High Order. Hadn't he, Grobus, resumed watching Plater later when he returned to his house? This finding of fault angered him.

Oculus had made it seem some sort of privilege that Grobus be included in the astral confrontation planned at the direction of Aziel. To confront the man and by this means approach the woman creature. It was necessary to catch her off guard for she was more powerful. So it was that they hatched their plan to take the man Plater and force the woman creature to do their bidding.

Grobus was torn. He was pleased that he was included in this most important work of the Order. But he understood some of the dangers they faced. To confront a creature such as this on the astral plane and to attempt to restrain or destroy them was to risk everything.

The quiet of night was only broken by a distant police siren which quickly faded. Plater lay curled into Molly's backside and both slept soundly. While Molly dreamt of nothing Plater wandered the streets of the city in the Realm becoming more familiar with its extraordinary blend of architectures and marveling at its virtual normality. Gail had explained that for most people he would meet in the Realm they were just dreaming and less than fifty percent were actually aware. Of that number, Gail thought fewer than half were people like her, living their lives in the Realm while their physical body remained all but inert in the physical world. The others were a strange mix of people whose quest for some meaning to life, of a spiritual kind, had led them through one means or another to unlock areas of their unconscious. It was hard to be sure, but Gail believed that these people did not perceive the Realm, its inhabitants and the events that took place there in the same way that others did. She thought that the spiritual or religious framework that they had used to gain entry had somehow overlaid their interactions in the Realm putting all events they experienced in the Realm in the context of their belief system. Gail thought this was an interference of the conscious mind over the unconscious, forcing a logical and acceptable interpretation of their experiences.

It was the clarity with which Plater separated his time in the Realm with his time in the physical world that was so unique. For him the blurring of the two was no more than everyone has experienced when waking from a vivid dream and being unsure of one's surroundings for perhaps a minute or two, until full wakefulness is achieved. Then to be able to recall in detail the events from the Realm and place them in context in the physical world was very special indeed.

Plater's musings were interrupted when he saw Bartholomew.

"Mason." said Bartholomew. "There's something I must show you."

"I wanted to talk to Gail, do you know where I can find her?" said Plater.

"Later." said Bartholomew, taking Plater's arm. "Please come with me."

Bartholomew steered Plater around several corners, winding deep into what resembled an Italian town, with cobbled streets and many small alleyways beside shuttered windows.

"What's this about?" asked Plater.

"Come, we have little time." said Bartholomew, finally stopping by a faded wooden door. He knocked twice and then glanced both ways. The door opened and Bartholomew bundled Plater through it.

"Steady on..." began Plater as he lurched forwards under Bartholomew's urgings.

Before he could regain his balance he was struck by something hard to the side of his head and the room spun into blackness.

As he opened his eyes Plater immediately felt pressure on his body. He was not lying down but rather leaning backwards at a slight angle. From the gloom in front of him he could see four figures standing in a huddle talking. Then he made out more, perhaps ten in all. Each was dressed oddly. One had the regalia of an American Indian Chief while another looked like an Egyptian Pharoah. Others appeared as soldiers and priests. Plater closed his eyes again but opening them revealed the same strange tableau.

One of the figures noticed Plater was awake and soon they all formed rough semi-circle around him but keeping at a distance of several yards. Plater realised he was fixed to some sort of board and looking down he saw straps, chains and ropes coiling around his outstretched limbs and held to the board with what seemed to be large iron nails.

"What the hell is going on?" said Plater "Who are you? Why are you doing this?"

He looked at Bartholomew but then noticed that it didn't seem to be Bartholomew at all. Before his eyes the face of Bartholomew faded to one of harder, more angular features. One of the number, a male figure dressed as an ancient Egyptian stepped forward and shouted:

"Be silent!"

Plater's surprise at the vehemence of the command was shortlived.

"Get me off here! Don't you know who I am?" said Plater.

"Yes, we know who you are." said the Egyptian, his blue eyes burning through the slits in his ornate headdress. "You are the servant of the woman creature Memoth, you will be the means of her destruction!"

At this the others in the group shouted and waved their arms, gesturing towards Plater.

"You're off your trolley, I have no idea who this 'Memoth' is but I'm nobody's servant, now cut me loose."

"You will be silent." said the Egyptian. "The vessel!"

A smaller figure, dressed as a monk, emerged from the group holding a golden cup, encrusted with brightly coloured stones. He presented it to the Egyptian and withdrew, head bowed. The Egyptian approached Plater and then with a flourish drew a long, slender knife.

"What the fuck?" said Plater.

The Egyptian carefully drew the razor-sharp blade down Plater's right forearm, which was held aloft by his bindings. A stream of blood soon ran down his arm and dripped from his elbow. The Egyptian caught the run off in the cup and after a moment or two held it aloft to more shouts from the others.

"Jesus!" shouted Plater. "You're fucking mad"

"It is time." announced the Egyptian and the room became brighter as flaming torches on the walls sprang to life. What Plater could now see only added to his confusion. He was fixed to a round wooden slab but on the floor was drawn an intricate design of concentric circles, triangles and other geometric shapes Plater had long since forgotten the names of. As he watched the group joined hands, solemnly, in a circle around the Egyptian and began to mumble words he couldn't make out. Periodically they would raise their joined hands as one and the Egyptian would hold up the cup containing

Plater's blood.

With the weirdness of the scene Plater couldn't help but wish he could wake up and be back at home in bed with Molly. Gail's warning popped back into his head. She and Bartholomew had both insisted that he must never wake up to get out of a difficult situation, one where he felt threatened. It was something about hardwired defence mechanisms in the brain and that if he were to wake out of danger he could suffer serious mental loss in the real world. It didn't sound like something Plater wanted to risk. Instead, he tried to bring a picture of Gail Hartston into his mind, perhaps he could communicate with her and get help.

There was a crashing sound behind Plater and the group looked towards the source of the noise. Their faces showed fear and their circle broke up. The Egyptian shouted:

"No! Hold your places! We are almost there..."

His words had no effect and Plater noticed from behind him a sudden piercing sound that seemed to get louder and louder until he couldn't hear anything, just a profound silence. His captors were all kneeling, heads in hands and contorted expressions on their faces. Even the Egyptian had sunk to the ground, the golden cup cast aside and its contents running onto the stone floor.

Figures appeared from behind Plater, too many to count, and the kneeling kidnappers were dragged away. Faintly he thought he heard a voice, then a face appeared close to his. It was Gail. A look of concern was quickly replaced by a smile. Plater saw her lips move but still heard nothing. As he spoke to say he couldn't hear she pressed a finger to his lips. Suddenly Plater felt a wave of exhaustion and could not stop his eyes from closing.

32

As the first faint traces of the new day reached up over the trees, Zach had all but completed his plan. Despite all they had risked together he felt he couldn't involve Meek in what he had decided to do. After all it was he not Meek that had been detected snooping on the databases, he not Meek that had apparently sneaked into room 7G, and carelessly left evidence behind. For all Zach knew Meek was not even on the security services radar except for being an obvious 'known associate'. No, he couldn't let Meek risk getting deeper into trouble. The same Meek who had panicked on receiving a letter from HMRC about a tax error in the princely sum of £119 that ended up having been a mistake by his HM Government paymasters anyway. Meek liked to follow rules, he never questioned figures of authority, even privately most of the time. Zach knew that if he tried to involve his friend Meek might suffer real mental anguish, to go against a lifetime of conformity. Instead, he left a note, disguised within some notes he and Meek had been working with for the circuit board design. Zach hoped Meek would find it, in fact he was banking on the fact that Meek would retreat into work to cope with the sudden disappearance of his friend.

The reality of disappearing now occupied Zach. He assumed that his implant was being constantly monitored, for position if nothing else. He couldn't simply interfere with it somehow or attempt to shield the transmissions without alerting the watchers. So, he had to be patient. It was still far too early to start moving around the labs, Zach and Meek were known to be night-birds but definitely not early-birds, so that would also arouse too much interest. So, Zach fired up his laptop and employed his stealth bridge to the internet and entered the World of Warcraft. He had things to do that could only be done in the online world of wizards and warriors.

Hours pass quickly in the vast online gaming universe and so it was that Zach noticed it was now a reasonable time to venture to the kitchen for breakfast. Meek, he assumed, rightly, was still asleep, having worked until well past midnight. The kitchen was empty. Zach fried two eggs and three rashers of bacon and made a pot of colombian coffee strong enough to raise the dead. He was sure there would be someone paying attention to the monitors today, perhaps even someone tasked only with watching him. He tried very hard not to turn and smile at the security camera or offer the universal modern American hand gesture.

The bacon and eggs tasted good, and the caffeine soon coursed around his body fortifying the alertness he already had from his predicament. Dishes and pans dumped in the sink as usual he stopped back at his room briefly to brush his teeth, the normal routine, before heading to his lab. The one thing different this morning was that he took his rucksack with him.

It proved very hard to concentrate on his tasks or even to perform a passable impression of working normally for the camera. He was constantly replaying his plan and looking for the hole, the little wrinkle that could derail the whole thing. Meek assumed his level of concentration and general moroseness was just normal behaviour when working an especially tricky problem. Unusually perceptive for Meek.

"So." began Meek, talking in a low voice as Zach tried to ignore him. "What are you going to do about...you know."

Zach continued studying his screen.

"Not much I can do right now." he said. "Next move could be down to them."

"I heard there's another visitor due today." said Meek.

This caused Zach to stop and look up.

"Who? What time?" he said.

"Dunno." said Meek.

"Think." snapped Zach. "It's important."

"Easy." said Meek. "I'm not the enemy here."

"Yeah." said Zach. "Bit jumpy. Sorry. But who's coming?"

"Sounded like the same sort of visit as when you were out of it. I heard one of the security drones mention it as I was walking here this morning."

"Time...did they mention a time?" asked Zach.

"Don't think...no, it must be around three, because one of them said he'd probably miss some stupid program on TV, some game show I think."

Zach was quiet, his mind was busy. As the silence lengthened Meek realised the conversation was over and wandered back up the corridor to run more tests.

Finally, the wall clock reached 10:45 and Zach calmly, he hoped, got up and made his way to the kitchen. Neddleton was making his normal coffee. You could set your watch by most of Neddleton's habits. A mid-fifties hardware engineer with long, now mostly grey, hair in a ponytail. Zach moved past the door hoping Neddleton wouldn't see him, the last thing he wanted was to discuss the finer points of component placement within integrated circuits and minimizing the power curve. Zach speeded up as he realised Neddleton hadn't seen him. He reached the workshop where Neddleton lived and found his jacket. Neddleton loved military-style clothing and his jacket was typical. Zach's heart was beating noticeably faster as he fumbled each pocket for what he was after. A metallic click told him he'd found it. He slipped the keys into his pocket and tried to arrange the combat jacket as he'd found it before scurrying back to his lab. The cameras in Neddleton's workshop, oddly, had not been working for about a week. It seemed that the lab had a rodent problem and the little beggars had chewed through the cables. Odd they'd only chewed the camera cables or at least it would have been odd if someone hadn't been placing food in the only cavity reachable by humans. The one used to perform maintenance on the camera systems and the central wiring junction. Neddleton didn't much like being watched either. Zach and Meek had just been impressed by the simplicity of Neddleton's solution.

Meek stopped by at noon to see if Zach wanted to eat.

"Nah." said Zach. "I'm right into something, maybe I'll grab something later."

"Shit food and irregular eating habits." said Meek as he disappeared down the corridor "You'll die young."

Today was Thursday and right on time the white and red delivery van from Simpson's Caterers approached the security checkpoint. By now this was a formality and the barrier was already rising as the driver handed over the paperwork to the soldier. Instead of following procedure the other soldier was lifting the barrier rather than training his Hechler & Koch automatic weapon on the cab of the van.

At first the high revving engine noise startled both soldiers. Their heads turned instinctively towards the source of the din. The high-powered motor bike was already within fifteen yards of them and accelerating. The first soldier dropped the paperwork and tried to grab his gun, that had slipped casually round his back and he couldn't easily get it into position. The other soldier tried to reverse the upward motion of the barrier but the black and silver 1200cc bike ripped up the gravel as it bore down on the first soldier. Before the first soldier could command his weapon, his own survival instinct took over and he dived clear of the marauding bike, which whipped past him in a shower of small stones.

He glimpsed the rider and realised it was someone off the base. One of the smart-arse technicians. He recognised the red rucksack. As he rolled to his feet, he loosed off three rounds after the fast-disappearing bike but it didn't seem to impede its progress. Within four seconds it had passed out of sight down the long single-track road.

Adrenalin was pumping through Zach as he heard the crack crack crack of the Heckler and Koch. No pain, no thumps like an electric shock, they'd missed. The road was hardly ideal for escape on two wheels and Zach's heightened awareness was needed to avoid catastrophe from large portions of tree limbs or potholes that formed traps for the careless biker. He daren't reduce speed as he didn't know if he would be pursued but country lanes are unnerving for someone used to city streets. Not least someone that had not ridden a bike this powerful, nor any bike at all for three years. Zach's body was a ball of tension, his knees gripped the bike as if his life depended on it, and perhaps it did. He swerved but failed to avoid a low hanging tree branch which hammered hard on his helmet and almost caused him to lose it. As he grappled to bring the bike straight, he glimpsed a dark shape ahead. It almost filled the carriageway, which was barely wider than a single vehicle. The gap closed blindingly fast and just as Zach thought impact inevitable, he bent the bike to the right and the dark shape shifted left. As he tore past, he felt something brush his foot and he realised it had been the side of the car. Before he had time to accept his lucky escape another large vehicle rounded the next bend. Another dark saloon car but this time the driver had more time and mounted the verge to let Zach scream past. No more vehicles obstructed his noisy progress.

Inside the second vehicle, James Carver followed the screaming bike until it shot out of sight. He turned back

to face forwards and pressed a speed dial on his phone.
"We need to talk." he said.

33

"At least you remembered the golden rule." said Gail Hartson.

Plater felt strangely at home in the familiar surroundings of the Captain's cabin aboard the old sailing ship. He was relieved to learn that it had not actually been Bartholomew that had led him to the ambush but someone appearing as him.

"But what did they hope to achieve?" he asked.

"I don't know." said Gail. "Perhaps they wanted to damage you somehow, so you couldn't bridge between worlds so easily. They clearly see you as a threat."

"And you think they are somehow linked to that little guy that has been following me?" he asked.

Gail crossed and stood behind Plater, who was gazing out the window at the horizon. He could sense her presence and seemed to smell the same perfume as when they'd first met on the beach.

"From their dress I think they are occultists in the real world." she said. "To them the Realm is the astral world, written about for centuries and described with the distillation of mystics' interpretations of what they found here. They dressed that way because it fits with their belief system. I couldn't tell you who they thought they were, but Bartholomew has many books on the subject I believe."

"How do you know all that?" asked Plater.

"We don't." said Gail. "It is just the best idea to fit what we see. But it seems they have you in their sights so you must take care both here and in the real world. Your home, is it safe?"

"What? Er, yes, what do you mean safe?"

"This is new territory for us." said Gail. "Those of us most closely involved in the struggle have little to fear in the real world, we are anonymous. But you are known to them, in that world and this. We don't know what they'll do but you could be in danger. Basically, they can solve their problem in either world."

Gail's words settled into Plater's mind and he realised for the first time that he could no longer separate the two worlds. He'd been happy so far to feel safe in the physical world, at his house with the tired wallpaper and familiar sounds and smells. The Realm was a new and, he had to admit, exciting development, but he'd been confident that if he felt he couldn't deal with it any more he could retreat to the familiarity of reality.

That confidence was now gone.

"So what do I do?" he said.

"You should be careful when you sleep." began Gail. "Is there someone that can be in your home at night?"

Plater had not grasped it at first but now saw that it wasn't only him that was affected.

"Yes, but I can't involve others if.."

"You must." insisted Gail. "The enterprise we are set on is vital."

Plater knew there would be no problem having someone with him while he slept but involving Molly with the real threat of danger disturbed him. Gail could see the conflict in his eyes. Slowly she brought her hand to his face and moved her lips to plant a delicate kiss on his cheek. A moment later she pulled back then turned away and crossed the cabin.

"You are very important Mason. Important to me and to the Realm." she said, her back still towards him.

Plater wanted to speak but no words came out, his mind had begun to dart in many directions at once. He was certainly attracted to Gail, from the first time he'd seen her. To discover a real person behind the doll-like coma patient confused his emotions even more. Then he saw Molly, sat in his bedroom, beside his sleeping body and he slipped back into the real world.

34

As a citizen of the most surveilled society on the planet Zach had little doubt that someone, somewhere, would eventually spot him. Anonymity he knew belonged to most people simply by virtue of them not being of interest to those watching. Once you became the focus of attention for any one of a number of government sponsored agencies, you'd effectively crossed a line. Now anonymity, in almost any form, was lost indefinitely. Any and all information held on databases in your name could be accessed, stored and mined. The use of mobile phones, credit cards, travel cards indeed any of modern society's conveniences would trigger alerts on the screens of the watchers.

To disappear in modern Britain involves a knowledge of the techniques used to track you and an ability to survive without technology. So it was that Zach had zig-zagged across the Suffolk countryside, first heading South on the A12 but then discreetly turning off and heading first West and then North. Always keeping to the pitch-black country roads, except when he needed petrol. When paid for, in cash, he stuck once more to the dark lanes as he meandered towards a small village about five miles southeast of Spalding, Lincolnshire. He reflected with some satisfaction that he had probably passed no more than two CCTV cameras for the entire journey, both in the petrol station, and he had blocked a direct view to either of those as well. He was sure that the initial assumption would be that he'd return to London. It is a persistent belief that to vanish it is better in a crowd. Zach thought that rather than being a needle in the first haystack they'd look in, he'd choose a different haystack.

It was daylight by the time he coasted to a stop about eighty yards from a pair of stone cottages. As he watched, there was no movement, no traffic along the quiet road nor comings or goings from either house. At just before 9am Zach pulled slowly up to the side of the first cottage and rocked the huge bike onto its stand next to a large mature apple tree. He checked visibility once more and satisfied himself that the vehicle would be obscured from satellites and all but the lowest of low-flying craft; ducking under the low porch he knocked on the door.

After the third knock the door opened.

"Zach?" said the small elderly woman. "Is it you?"

"Yes Aunt Dorothy, it's me."

"What you doing way out here then?" she asked, then as if remembering quickly added "Don't stand out there boy, come in!"

Zach followed as the little woman headed off down the narrow hallway.

"Bless me." she muttered. "How long is it since I saw

you? Got to be...got to be...it's about six years isn't it?"

"Probably nearer seven." said Zach.

"Cup of tea?" said Aunt Dorothy scooping the kettle from the kitchen stove and sticking it under the tap.

"That'd be great Aunt, thanks." said Zach. "How's Barney?"

"He's been dead these past three years, accident."

"Oh I'm sorry to hear that, how did it happen?"

"Silly old bugger." said Aunt Dorothy. "What was he doing riding horses at his age, I told him that chestnut mare would do for him one day, barely saddle broken that one. Sit."

Zach sat at the small kitchen table and Aunt Dorothy busied herself rinsing a large brown teapot that had already seen much use. She'd been up and about since first light and was rarely far from her last cup of tea.

"You in some sort of trouble then?" said Aunt Dorothy. "Can't imagine what else'd bring you all the way out here."

Zach was momentarily disarmed by the candor but always knew where he stood with Aunt Dorothy, a trait he had always liked in older people.

"Sort of." he began. "It's a bit complicated but I thought I could do with getting away from it for a while, just for a couple of days, if that's okay? I wouldn't be any trouble."

Dorothy turned from the sink.

"Dah! It's no trouble boy. You're always welcome here. Don't see nearly enough of you as it is. And don't you start on about me visiting you in London. When you get to be as old as me you get to be the one who's visited, right?"

"Yes Aunt." said Zach, grinning.

"Alright then. And you don't need to be calling me 'Aunt', look at you, you're a grown man. Well let's get this tea in the pot then we'll see about sorting out the back room, of course there's been nobody in there for a while, bed's not aired."

For the first time since he'd got up the previous morning Zach felt he could relax. Just for a while, just until he could think and plan what to do next. He was fairly sure they wouldn't find him here. When he was little his family had introduced numerous men and women as 'Aunts' and 'Uncles', but it wasn't until he grew up that he realised most of them weren't related at all. Dorothy had been friends with his grandmother, they'd served as Land Girls together in the second world war. As a kid Zach always enjoyed visiting Dorothy as she used to live on the Norfolk coast and Zach would take her dog Ragtime for long walks through the dunes. For a few years he would spend at least three weeks of his summer holidays there. He couldn't remember Dorothy's husband, Bill. He was often away as a trawlerman and Zach hardly saw him. He died in a huge storm, far off in the North Sea in the eighties. He'd been only a few months from retiring. A picture of Bill when he was a young man stood proudly on the Welsh dresser beside the tea caddy.

"Well, I've opened the window to blow out the cobwebs." announced Dorothy as she came back into the kitchen and poured the tea. Placing two cups and saucers between them on the table, she sat down.

"Right, what have you done?" she asked.

35

Plater had long since gone to bed and Molly sat illuminated by the laptop's glow still following strands of research on the Church of the Reclamation. She hadn't expected there to be quite so much information to get through.

Recent items mentioning the Church all seemed to revolve around its founder's political aspirations and his run at the Texas Senate seat. Most sources had the Reverend Ethan Daniels a solid five points ahead and with only a matter of days to go until the elections, he seemed a hot favourite. There seemed to be a wave of reaction against what was perceived to be a general loosening of moral values across the US and groups approaching from a faith perspective were much in vogue.

Conscious of the need to use multiple sources Molly had searched websites, known public databases, newspaper archives and finally social networking sources. This last batch included the obvious sites such as Facebook, Instagram, Reddit and Twitter. In this arena much of the information on CoR involved personal stories of finding happiness and fulfillment performing the Lord's work. This was set against some harrowing stories by family members and ex-CoR faithful of abuse within the Church, intolerable emotional pressure and even physical intimidation. Molly found attempts by the new and traditional media to pick up on some of these tabloid-style stories but for each attempt there had been a swift legal response that had silenced the story, usually before it had been widely released to media channels.

One journalist seemed to be getting close to the CoR, certainly according to the blogs of one or two anti-CoR activists. Warren Gatts had been a noted investigative journalist in the 90s and seemed to have come out of retirement to run the rule over the CoR. It was on the third page of her search for CoR references alongside Warren Gatts' name that she came across the reports of his death.

"What the hell are you doing still up?" said a blinking Plater from the doorway.

"Research." said Molly. "And I've just found something odd."

"Hold it for a minute, I have to go." said Plater as he headed for the bathroom. His eyes were acclimatised when he returned and slumped onto the sofa. "What have you got?" he said.

"Well the CoR..." began Molly.

"CoR?" said Plater.

"Church of the Reclamation." said Molly. "The CoR is the fourteenth largest real estate owner in the entire United States and has four million registered members worldwide. But there have been rumblings about it being a cult. Each time a paper or TV station has run stories like that they've been sued and settled out of court. In each case they've never run any negative stories on the CoR again."

"Sounds like Scientology." said Plater sleepily.

"Yeah, only worse." said Molly. "There was this guy called Gatts, a journalist. He was pretty famous back in the day, managed to do some exposés on big corporations in the US, remember the Elliott & Buller case? The waste disposal company that took billions from half a dozen states for ethical disposal of their waste, then they found it was being sunk in the Gulf of Mexico? That was Gatts. Anyway, he's dead, but in unusual circumstances according to a couple of blogs I've found. Seems he was tracking some link between the CoR, its leader Rev. Daniels and a scandal involving the incumbent Senator of Texas's son. Something to do with drugs."

"Where's this going?" asked Plater, who had closed his eyes and was resting his head back onto the soft pillows of the sofa.

"Well, the point is that Gatts interviewed Rev. Daniels and less than two weeks later he turns up dead. Apparent drug overdose but the man had no history of substance abuse, except a slightly unhealthy liking for booze."

"What does this have to do with the Church?"

"Maybe nothing but also, according to this blog, a guy that had supposedly been Gatts' snitch about the Church also died, also of drugs. Mind you he had a history of abuse at one time. In fact the Church supposedly saved him. But the odd thing about Gatts was that although he died of an overdose and was found in his office in downtown Fort Worth he had three broken fingers and a cracked rib."

"You found this stuff on a blog? How do we know it's true? Whose blog is it?"

"It's well thought of, in the cult information scene, written by the mother of a member of CoR actually....hang on the name's here somewhere...yeah, Kathleen Moran. I sent her an email a while back just checking some facts. Haven't heard anything yet." Molly checked her watch. "It's evening in Texas now so I might get a reply soon."

"Well maybe you could help me out now." said Plater. "I need a warm, soft body to hold, it helps me sleep."

Molly smiled and pulled the laptop closed. She could get the email in the morning.

Carver felt the vibration in his pocket as it stirred him from thought. The detailed presentation being made by the Director of the CIA about current initiatives being taken in Pakistan was of considerable interest but highly technical. This was a closed session with only five people present and was already the fourth such meeting since he'd arrived at the State Department at 7:30 that morning. It was now nearly 4 p.m. and with only a brief pause for lunch it had been an intense day. He hoped he had seemed casual as he shifted position to be able to retrieve the phone and glance at the screen while still remaining attentive.

'Coyote in play' was the brief message. Carver hit the 'back' button which had the effect of forensically removing all traces of the message from the phone's internals. For some the idea that one could sit within the inner security circle of the most powerful nation on Earth while simultaneously covertly operating a high-risk mission within their territory would prove irresistibly exciting. For Carver he felt the need to drink some water and wished the air conditioning could do more.

36

Kathleen Moran was no longer newsworthy in Fort Worth. For the three weeks of her trial for the kidnapping and imprisonment of her daughter pictures of her were rarely off the front page. Since the last day of the trial, she hadn't seen Erik Nordstrom. He had told her when they had embarked on their plan to rescue Dawn from the Church of the Reclamation that if they should ever be picked up by the police, they were to deny knowledge of each other. Since the cults had begun to use narcotics to accelerate the indoctrination process on new recruits it had become progressively easier to avoid implication in kidnapping or false imprisonment.

Indeed, when Dawn harmed herself and was taken to hospital, she was unaware that she was first taken to another location. The ambulance which eventually arrived would record where she had been collected from, which was another house some blocks away from the safe house. Records would show that the house had been rented to Kathleen Moran. Further records showed that Erik Nordstrom had been working at the property on the day of the incident and had helped staunch the bleeding from Dawn's wounds until help arrived. However, the Church of the Reclamation knew of Erik Nordstrom and within forty-eight hours of the incident he was arrested after a tip off and the conspiracy theorists went into overdrive.

When traces of not only cocaine but hallucinogenics were found in Dawn's blood, the Church began seeding stories that Nordstrom and Kathleen Moran were lovers and used to routinely entrap young men and women, using Dawn as bait, for wild drug-enhanced orgies and worse. Before the trial had even been scheduled a TV crew from the tabloid show Scandal had made a half-hour expose on the couple. The program featured lurid recollections from supposed former acquaintances, school friends and even one girl, speaking with her voice distorted and blacked out on screen, who claimed to have attended orgies at Kathleen Moran's house.

Once the cold light of day intruded during the actual court proceedings it soon became clear that the prosecution, even with the covert assistance of the CoR's legal team, could not supply any evidence to support the kidnap claim. Nor the false imprisonment charge. Such was the background level of narcotics and evidence of heavy usage in Dawn Moran that the jury found it reasonable that much of her evidence could be discounted, or at least diluted. Ultimately, it took less than three hours for the jury to return Not Guilty verdicts on all counts. Dawn Moran was referred for psychiatric examination and the judge advised her to seek a treatment program.

Dawn had seemed impassive throughout the trial, sitting amongst a group never numbering less than five from the CoR. For the first few days she had hardly seemed to notice the proceedings but by the end she seemed fully aware. Hardly a glance was exchanged between her and her mother, which visibly pained Kathleen Moran more than Dawn.

For Erik, this was the third time in his career as a rescuer of cult members that he had found himself in the dock. On no occasion had he been convicted but he had been concerned that this might be the first. It had been hard for him to sit each day in the sweltering courtroom and not look at Kathleen Moran. Not offer the support that he knew she needed. Never before had he appreciated the sound planning and preparation that is always so important when going up against cults as well financed as the CoR. When the verdicts were announced he barely held back from punching the chair but instead assumed his air of passive confusion at the whole experience that he had adopted from the outset.

Kathleen had returned to Seattle after the trial and found that although some of her neighbours had been dragged into the maelstrom by the media the story had not really caught there. This was a relief for Kathleen, who was able to drop back into her life and savour normality.

As she pushed open her front door and carried two bulging brown grocery bags into the hall, she could hear the phone in the kitchen ringing. She managed to slide the two bags onto the marble topped counter and grab the phone before it stopped.

"Kathleen?" said a familiar voice.

"Erik, where are you?" she asked.

"Having a break." said Erik Nordstrom. "You okay?"

"I don't know." said Kathleen. "I'm not sure what ok is anymore, should you be calling me?"

"We're old news." said Erik in his comforting drawl. "Anything from Dawn?"

"No." said Kathleen.

"This isn't the end."

Kathleen's eyes were drawn to a photo above the sink. Happier times when she and her ex-husband had taken Dawn to Disney World in Florida. The slightly surreal image depicted the three of them and a swollen-headed Mickey Mouse.

"When things cool down, we'll start again." continued Erik. "They'll have moved her but we'll find her."

"Yes." said Kathleen. "Thank you Erik."

The words were like a needle piercing Erik's skin. He felt a mixture of anger and compassion as he imagined the lonely figure of Kathleen Moran standing in a family home that no longer contained a family. Surrounded by reminders of what she had lost.

"Kathleen, we will find her again. Don't give up. As soon as I hear anything I'll call you."

"Thank you Erik."

Kathleen Moran brewed some fresh coffee and opened her laptop at the kitchen table. She had found that writing about her feelings online as someone that has lost a loved one to a fringe religion seemed to help. She had received many warm emails both from others in her position and ex-members of cults who recognised the pain and tragedy.

As she opened her blog site, she noticed that she had six new messages. She took a sip of her coffee and opened the first.

37

Zach decided a walk might do him good. It was still rather early for him to be up and about, but he'd risen with the sun and already been served a sizeable breakfast by his Aunt before grabbing his rucksack and heading into Finbridge village. As he walked, he remembered that he'd always loved his Aunt's breakfasts when he'd spent those summers here. It was easier to get out of bed somehow in the country. Zach always slept with his window open anyway but, in the country, the early morning cacophony of birdsong seemed to remind him that a teeming life was already at work on a new day. Zach had settled on 'girl trouble' to explain his sudden appearance. His story of a highly strung girlfriend that had begun stalking him when he'd ended their relationship seemed to raise hardly a question. A few days away from 'that London' was just what he needed, his Aunt had confided.

Despite being a community of only just over two hundred, Finbridge still retained a tiny Public Library. Managed by the increasingly frail Mrs Florence Perkins, who had seemed a much more imposing figure in Zach's memory, it also boasted the only known internet connection in the entire village. Probably the only one for a few miles in any direction as well. Somehow, the relentless advances in technology seemed to have been lost on this little hamlet. But with an aging population and no likelihood of new lifeblood, it would probably cease to trouble the statisticians within thirty years.

Mrs. Perkins didn't recognise Zach but was certainly put a little off balance by such a young customer. She showed Zach the ancient PC that stood on an old school desk in the corner of the single room. The good news for Zach was that the PC, although old, (it had come from the nearby Police Station in Dunstead when they upgraded) was not so old that it wouldn't suit his needs. He thanked Mrs. Perkins and settled to his task, hoping his presence wouldn't mean that the librarian would watch his every move. After ten minutes of harmless surfing Mrs Perkins had lost interest in her only customer and was once more engaged in crocheting, her aging fingers still nimble enough to move too fast for the eye to follow precisely what she was doing.

When Zach was sure she was distracted, he leaned forwards and plugged a USB stick into one of the sockets at the back of the base unit. This particular stick contained a variety of World of Warcraft client versions, some dating back to its very early days. He selected one and installed it. After a few attempts he finally managed to get it working and connected to the online game. In the online gaming world and especially surrounding such epic games as World of Warcraft, which can consume truly huge amounts of time, enterprising people had begun offering a service to effectively 'play for you'. In this way businesses emerged, especially in parts of the world where labour is cheap, such as China and parts of India, that would run your character (on your game account) and greatly increase your wealth in the game and your status. All this for a modest investment of realworld cash. This was considered cheating by the game makers and so they did, and do, all they can to prevent and discourage such activities. Anyone caught using 'gold farmers' or 'power levelers' for cash in World of Warcraft risk having their account removed. Zach, who would never use such techniques himself, had experimented in using some of these services. But his only reason was to blog about them, criticise them and eventually put them out of business. To do his research, he had created a number of additional game accounts, which were not traceable to him in the real world. Some of the businesses he had ratted on were run by Chinese organised crime and he had no wish to make himself known to them.

These old accounts would come in handy now. Being on the run would mean your spending of money and moving around would be monitored. But if one was on the radar of the Security Services, this introduced a whole new level of sophistication and intrusiveness in the pursuit. Zach knew they would have on file details of his interests, friends and since this is the twenty-first century, extensive details of his activities on the internet. They would know about World of Warcraft and they would know that it afforded a means to communicate in a slightly unorthodox manner with 'known associates', via its in-game chat feature. Zach was hoping that they would not know about his alternate identities from his fake accounts.

38

Zach was no expert in the field of secret messages. His scheme used the in-game ability to send items to other characters via the postal system. Zach had devised a cipher that used the number of items, the names of the items themselves and even the titles of the messages to pass simple information.

To pass complex information usually involved a number of swaps of items and messages but this was not uncommon in the game so unlikely to draw attention. Still this was a laborious business and Zach was glad he had kept his word lists on his smartphone. He'd listed common words with their coded equivalent and used this to send his first messages. His friends were not online so he'd have to check back for any response, and he hoped they would recognise the post for what it was. He was confident they would, as if they didn't know the character name, they would soon decide the items sent seemed odd and he trusted them to do the rest.

It had been three days since his escape, but nothing

had been mentioned on any media as far as he could tell. Of course, he knew that he would be sought. He knew things that his masters would not like in the public domain. Mrs. Perkins now greeted him with a warm smile and even offered him a cup of tea on his third visit.

He hoped Meek had found his note. He wondered if security had become even tighter as a result of his flight. He wondered if his friends and family had noticed the inevitable surveillance that would now have descended on them. He wondered if any other subjects had been implanted. He wondered what the range of the devices, like the one in his head, could be. He wasn't an expert on this stuff and although he knew he was pretty safe where he was, he knew he would have to visit civilisation eventually.

As he ambled back to his Aunt's cottage Zach tried to plan his next move. His Aunt was happy to have him stay but he knew he couldn't impose much longer. Anyway, he needed to sort out the mess he was in. He wanted to get the implant out of his head. He wanted to stop others being experimented on but had no idea how. He felt guilty for being involved with something like this. He missed being able to bounce his thoughts off Meek.

Zach was asleep by the time his first message was received. The player reading the post thought it odd at first, not recognising the character name of the sender. Then she picked up a pen and jotted down some letters on a scrap of paper. The player logged out of her character and logged in as another and sure enough she had post waiting. She wrote more on her paper before logging out again and entering the game with a third character. There was a third post and a fourth. The player now had letters written on four pieces of paper and she rearranged them into the correct order. The message appeared as gibberish until you knew two additional pieces of information. The long sequence of letters was an internet domain name and the initial characters of the first words of each message were "f", "t" and "p". The last message began "not" which meant to ignore that part of the code. So, the letters were 'ftp' which represented the 'file transfer protocol', a means of moving data around that predated the world wide web.

It had been more than a year since Angie had seen this code. She knew who must have written it but had no idea why he had decided to reactivate this laborious means of communication now. She had Zach's mobile number and he had hers; it would have been an awful lot easier to just call. She knew he worked on secret stuff, which she thought was kinda cool. She lifted the lid on her Macbook Pro and fired up a ftp client program. She carefully entered the string of characters and hit enter. A login prompt appeared asking for a username. Often ftp is used for letting just about anyone download files so one old convention is to use the name 'anonymous' for a username and then your email address as the password. Angie tried this but it failed. She glanced back at the four pieces of paper but there was no other information in the messages. She thought for a moment then tried the name of her favourite character "Apollonia". The name was accepted and now a password was required. Angie tried her character name again, although she didn't expect that to work. She tried to think of what word Zach would have known she would think of. Suddenly she began to feel hot and could feel herself blushing. He hadn't chosen... She typed in the word "Heaven17" and the screen welcomed her with "You are in a maze of twisty little passages, all alike". Angie almost laughed out loud. Heaven17 had been the place that Zach had taken Angie when they had their first date. It had been an awkward affair during which neither of them felt comfortable but neither wanted to be anywhere else. The evening ended with their first kiss, but neither were ready for relationships and university at opposite ends of the country cooled things off.

The welcome screen was a homage to the first popular adventure game on a computer. In this first adventure game, using only words, as computers were simple things back then, the writers used wordplay to construct puzzles and impart information in a slightly oblique fashion that certainly appealed to early geeks.

Angie entered "take message" on the screen. In this first-generation game only certain commands could be understood by the machine and they were always two-word commands (go east, take axe etc.). The words "Don't understand" appeared on the screen. Okay she thought, that was a bit obvious. She tried a few other common combinations of two words but no luck. There was probably a timer on the retrieval of whatever information Zach was pointing her to so she knew she had to hurry. She smiled as she typed the next guess, "take m3$$@g3" as it used the kind of phoney 'leet-speak' mixture of letters and numbers that were supposed to look like letters that Zach had always hated. The screen cleared and a directory listing appeared with seven files in it. Angie immediately started downloading them. However bad the trouble Zach was in at least he still had his sense of humour it seemed. She'd been right about the timer and digits began counting down in the top left corner of the download window. It looked like the counter had started at 300 and it had reached 112 by the time the files began to download.

Within two and a half minutes Angie had all the files, had disconnected from the site and was reading the first file's contents. Her act of disconnecting from the site caused the copies of the files on the server to be erased. As she read in the weak glow of the screen her expression changed and the happy, almost excited mood she had been in at getting a message from Zach became darker and she began turning a pen over in her left hand, something she tended to do when she was anxious.

39

Plater felt tired as he got off the bus and walked towards his road. It was as he felt for his keys in his jacket pocket that he noticed the man standing on the corner of the cul-de-sac almost opposite his house. It was dusk and the oddly flat light made it hard to pick out his features but he was sure it was the same man who'd followed them to Suffolk. He had a short, thick-set torso and short, slightly spikey hair. Plater would normally cross the road now to approach his house, but he kept heading for the short man. As he got within thirty yards the man turned slightly and even in the dusk, Plater could make out the tattoo on the man's neck. It was him. Plater walked faster.

"Hey!" he called.

The short man immediately set off running down the cul-de-sac. Plater went after him. The road ended in a wider circular area for cars to turn around. Next to the house on each side there was an alleyway and the short man disappeared down one without breaking stride. Plater was closer to him now but still ten yards short. A clattering sound greeted Plater as he rounded the house to see the man clambering over a fence that was just too high for him to manage easily. Plater saw his chance and launched himself. He crashed against the wall but clutched the man's left leg tight. For a moment his weight dragged down before the man's grip gave way and they fell together to the floor. As they scrambled to get to their feet Plater clawed at the man's back. He thought he heard a metallic click and got a handful of the man's coat, hauling him round to face him. The man's eyes were frightened, his pupils seemed lost in a sea of white. Plater felt a sharp pain in his side and without thinking relaxed his grip and sought out the pain with both hands. His jacket was wet. The short man staggered backwards, and Plater saw the glistening blade with the dark smear. The short man suddenly rushed forwards, shoving Plater and heading back out of the alley and round the corner. Plater wanted to follow but his body seemed preoccupied and wouldn't obey. The pain from the damp patch in his side was growing. He started to walk and as he left the alley, saw the little man get in a car which hurriedly snaked off.

Plater was certain that this had been the same man as in Suffolk. Why were they watching him? Why was he so important to these people. Plater now hoped Molly would be in his house. He could think later.

Molly had tried to get Plater to go to A&E but in truth the wound did seem minor. She would tease Plater later that his love handles had saved him, but humour wasn't coming easily now.

"And you're sure it was him?" asked Molly.

"Same tattoo." said Plater smoothing the tape that

Molly had gently applied across the gauze bandage to hold it in place.

"You said he seemed scared?"

"He looked terrified. And he was muttering something as he left but I couldn't make it out. It didn't sound like words."

Plater went to stand up but winced as he bent forwards.

"I'd sit still for a while if I were you, what do you want?"

"Whiskey." said Plater slumping back into the sofa slowly.

"You know it's funny." said Molly. "But I think something big might just be happening."

"What do you mean?" Plater frowned, taking the glass from Molly and taking a decent gulp.

"The Church of the Reclamation, it seems their leader, a Rev. Daniels, has not only got a seat in the US Senate but now they think he'll declare to run for President."

"I'm not following."

"Well, it's a bit of a coincidence isn't it? We're interested in the CoR because of what you're doing on the other side." Molly tipped her head sideways. "And here's their leader hitting the headlines and moving into a position of power."

"You think that's connected?" said Plater.

"Something's going on Mason. This guy's come out of nowhere and suddenly people are talking about him being the next US President."

"Any country that elects Donald Trump is capable of anything."

"I got a reply from that woman in the States. The one

who blogs about the CoR. She sounds really nice. Her daughter is still with them, but she hasn't given up. These people are dangerous. Some of the other entries on her blog, there are stories about people just going missing or turning up dead in another state. The CoR has gone from being a small church in a single state to worldwide in just eight years. They have a larger net worth than most Fortune 100 companies."

"How?" asked Plater.

"Officially they have received donations from around the world and invested in real estate and companies that promote the church's work. Unofficially there are rumours that they deal in drugs through some church properties in Miami."

Plater grunted, then grimaced and reached for his bandage.

"I always thought there wasn't a lot of difference between organised religion and organised crime." he said.

"According to my research organised crime doesn't pay as well."

"Okay, so we now know a lot more about this CoR, but how do we use this knowledge?"

"Well according to Bartholomew's friend, the company that bought all the stuff took delivery in a town in Colorado, called Gunnison."

"I'm no clearer on what we do next." said Plater

"We follow where the trail leads." said Molly. " To Gunnison. So we go there. I've always had an urge to discover the meaning of life, maybe the Church of the Reclamation can be my guide."

40

"Okay, showtime in, four, three, two, one...."

The floor manager dropped his arm and The Mitch Hancock Show theme tune gave way to the measured tones of the brightly lit and heavily made-up Mitch Hancock, seated on the low dais across from the Rev. Ethan Daniels, who made the furniture look a size too small.

"Good evening. At a time when our Government seems to have tried everything to recover America's moral authority in the world, I'm joined by a man who says he can do just that. A newcomer to politics, but not a new name to many of you, he has just become a Senator and many predict he will soon announce that he intends to run as an independent in the next election for the President of the United States. He is, of course, the Rev. Ethan Daniels."

A practised smile broke across Rev. Daniels' face.

"Welcome to Washington Rev. Daniels." said Hancock.

"Thank you." said Rev. Daniels. "This is my first visit to the Capital."

"Well, it will soon be your second home."

Hancock glanced at his prepared questions in his lap.

"Some people have questioned whether you were a good choice for the Senate, with your lack of experience in politics. What do you have to say to those critics?"

"Well Mr. Hancock." began the Reverend in is measured, mellow Texan tones. "I think many of the people of this great country have grown tired of politics. They tell me when I speak to them that they wish they could be represented by someone that thought like they did. That knew their hopes and fears. Understood the struggles of their lives better. What they see are slick operators in Italian suits more interested in their latest soundbite than representing the ordinary working man and woman that sent them here."

"How do you plan to be different from our current crop of representatives?"

"I have no axe to grind, Mr. Hancock. I have no need of earthly wealth and power so I'm not subject to the same temptations that haunt our nation's leaders. I won't be negotiating my seat on some bank's board of directors in return for favourable tax rule changes. I won't be advocating aggression against another state simply to increase the weapons sales of a company I may work for in a few years' time. For too long, our government has been subject to market forces, Mr. Hancock. Like lobbyists that wine and dine your Congressman on the tab of some pharmaceutical company that needs his vote to avoid strict controls on embryonic stem-cell research. For too long, our politicians have assumed the people don't understand what happens up here. I think they're mistaken. I think the working men and women of America know only too well how much of their tax is wasted. They want to recover control, Mr. Hancock; they want to be proud to call themselves Americans again."

"It has been mentioned already that you might even enter the race for the Whitehouse as an independent candidate, is that true?"

"I am guided in all I undertake by my conscience and the Lord. What I see on my television on the news appalls me. American soldiers across the world engaged in conflict. Our own sons and daughters giving their lives, but for what? When people in other countries, in Africa, in Asia and the Middle East see these images what do they see? They see the most powerful military nation on earth set against farmers, carpenters and teachers that just want to run their own country. How would we feel if some other country's soldiers were mounting roadblocks on Pennsylvania Avenue? No, it's time to bring our young men and women home. We have some problems of our own to deal with. We have people living on the street because they can't find a job. We have fat-cat bankers on Wall Street causing the world's markets to all but collapse and yet they suffer not at all. Not for them the pain and despair of losing their home because they can't meet their mortgage payments. I say it's time America got back to the values that made this country what it is - freedom, fairness, the love of a good day's work for a good day's pay and an allegiance to God and country that supersedes allegiance to the dollar."

Before the director could indicate he wanted to go to commercials several of the crew on the floor began to clap and cheer. The microphones picked it up and for a few seconds the Mitch Hancock Show resembled the Jerry Springer Show in its audience participation.

As the heavy black SUV slipped out of the underground parking at CBC Studios, Rev. Daniels drank from a water bottle and listened as his assistant chattered excitedly while reading from a small laptop.

"Early indications show that could be a season-high audience sir. The website for the show has collapsed with all the discussion going on. Clark just texted to say he thinks Carlson is planning some sort of statement as a direct result of your appearance."

Rev. Daniels gazed at the Downtown Washington lights and smiled. Ronald Carlson, a centrist Democrat, was the bookies' favourite to ride into the Whitehouse on a tide of right-wing Christian support. This was but the opening shot in what would surely be a long and personal campaign. Carlson was known for his aggressive tactics and for being no respecter of reputation or rules. That would make Rev. Daniels eventual victory more satisfying. He wished he could have seen Carlson's face as he'd laid out plans that went even further than his rivals'. He knew to expect retaliation but also knew he kept his own trump card. Rev. Daniels would first try to outmatch his opponent on strength of personality and policies but if that should prove ineffective, he knew he had a winning hand. He idly thumbed through the menus on his smartphone and opened a photograph. It showed a young woman of about 22 in a very low-cut dress. She held a champagne glass in her hand as she leaned on the balcony railing of a penthouse apartment in New

York. Behind the girl Ronald Carlson could clearly be seen, gripping her hips, trousers round his ankles, as he climaxed inside his $2,000 friend.

41

Grobus rarely had cause to consider himself lucky. From the time he had fallen from a swing as a child and smashed both front teeth out, to the time he went on his first date and got so drunk he ended up urinating on his partner as passions rose. His career, such as it was after his divorce, served only to permit him money to rent a small room in the house of a family friend. But at least his cleaning duties meant shift work, leaving him time to pursue his unusual interests. Still, he was undoubtedly lucky. Although sent only to observe the man Plater, who associates with the woman creature on the astral plane and must therefore be a powerful magician, Grobus was able to return with some of the mage's blood.

Until that part of the story the fact that Grobus had been spotted would have brought chastisement from those in authority. At the mention of the acquisition of not only something connected to the mage but something so personal, thoughts of punishment were forgotten.

Work on the ritual began immediately. A lock of hair, some fingernail clippings these were tokens enough for powerful restraining or attack spells against a person. To have some of their blood, that most personal of fluids, opened up new avenues of attack. Something to which those of higher rank than Grobus now bent their wills.

They were grateful to him, except Oculus whose eyes betrayed his continuing contempt. Grateful enough to begin his transition to the grade of Philosophus, still in the first tier but only one step from the portal to the second tier. Grobus had never felt so happy. He wrote in his magical diary that he hoped this might be a significant step towards becoming enlightened about The Book.

Plater, Molly and Bartholomew sat around the table in Georgio's seeming to study their menus but their minds were far away in thought. When the young waitress came over and asked if they needed more time, they looked at each other and all nodded.

"It sounds a crazy idea." said Plater as the waitress retreated.

"How else do we find out what they're doing with those components?" asked Molly.

There was a moments pause.

"It will of course be difficult." began Bartholomew. "But I don't see a better way."

"Why can't I join this bunch of weirdos?" said Plater.

Molly grinned.

"Two reasons off the top of my head." she began. "One, you don't seem the spiritual seeker type and two you have enough other stuff to be doing. I'll be fine, I'm not like any other innocent being suckered in by their claptrap. I'll play my part that's all."

"Molly is right." said Bartholomew. "You don't fit the profile of a typical disciple. I think the linguine pescatore is supposed to be very good here."

As they ate and worked their way through a second bottle of wine Molly said:

"I mentioned on email that we might go to America and Kathleen wants to help."

"Is that the woman with the blog?" asked Plater. "How can she help?"

"I understand she knows a lot about this cult." said Bartholomew. "You'll need details of how they recruit and what makes a good candidate for acceptance."

"Yeah, I said we'd be in touch if we decide to do it." said Molly.

"So we're agreed then?" began Bartholomew.

They both looked at Plater, who had just taken a large mouthful of pasta. He paused then shrugged.

"Something for the trip." said Bartholomew, placing an envelope on the table by Plater's hand.

As he swallowed Plater slid his finger across the top of the envelope and peered inside.

"Jesus! How much is in here?" he said.

"Twenty thousand dollars." said Bartholomew. "One never knows when unexpected expenses may arise. It never hurts to be prepared."

He smiled at Molly and raised his glass.

"Remember, we're never far away..." said Bartholomew.

They touched glasses over the table, Plater more

reluctantly. He slid the bulky envelope into his jacket.

Despite almost getting caught, Grobus was back at his post, watching. He was much more discreet now. He had found a spot some distance away from Plater's house that afforded direct line of sight to the door. Fortunately, he was also able to remain in his car and still see whenever someone came or went. It was tedious work. Grobus would stare at the door and front window for minutes at a time without looking away for fear he might miss something. He feared failure and the punishment that would surely come.

Oculus had boasted of the power they now had to get close to the man whose blood he, Grobus, had won for them. Oculus claimed they had performed the Ritual of the Third Eye, using the blood and that now, they, the members of the High Order, could see what the man saw, through the hidden 'Third Eye'. Why then did Grobus have to sit in the cold when the council could spy on this man in a much more intimate fashion? Oculus told him it was because the ritual was lengthy, and the effect was short so someone must still watch him.

Grobus wanted to go home, to get some sleep; it had now been five days since he had slept properly. Each time he had thought to catch a few hours rest his dreams had disturbed him. His astral form had visited familiar places but often there seemed to be figures watching him. Figures like those that had attacked him and the High Order when they had captured the man. These figures did nothing except watch him. He recalled their bright eyes vividly and shuddered. It might just have been the cold. Nonetheless his eyes felt very heavy and as the car's windows slowly fogged Grobus drifted into sleep.

A car passing within inches of his woke him at around 6am. Commuting in London, especially by car, was an early-bird's game. Grobus was startled and immediately checked Plater's door. The curtains were still closed at the window. Grobus felt relieved. As he fumbled in the back seat for his flask, he caught sight of the curtains opening. Before he could unscrew the flask's lid the door opened and Plater and Molly appeared, wheeling small cases behind them. They got into Plater's car and pulled away. Grobus quickly ducked down until they'd passed before hurriedly turning and following them.

Oculus studied the automatic writing he had scribed while performing the Ritual of the Third Eye. Although the ritual permitted images to be seen in the Waters of Urz, consecrated water in a wide bowl that served in many rituals of second sight and clairvoyance, the wording of the Third Eye ceremony also encouraged automatic writing by the one initiating it. The pen had moved urgently in Oculus' hand but as he now tried to read the writing, it was not clear in its meaning. Such was often the case when a force from the astral world is given control. Sweeping strokes of the pen mixed with jerky, sudden moves left a puzzling script. Oculus thought he saw a name in the jumble of malformed letters and words: 'Gail' and later another word seemed clear: 'Holworth'. Oculus assumed that these words were on one of the papers that the man Plater had been looking at while the Third Eye connection was made. He resumed his study of the script. Somewhere in the whirls and jagged lines lay important information, of that he was sure. He must wait no less than one rotation of the Earth before attempting the Ritual of the Third Eye again.

Using a satnav on a scooter was not easy. When Angie had entered the coordinates that Zach had included in one of the files she'd downloaded she saw that it was in Norfolk. That's a long way from Romford and Angie was starting to shift in the seat to relieve the growing discomfort. At least now she was on the same screen as her destination, although from her smartphone satnav app it didn't look as if there was even a road where the coordinates pointed.

It was well into the afternoon as she coasted to a stop and planted both feet on the ground, stretching her legs gratefully. About fifty yards ahead there were two cottages leaning against one another beside some trees. These were the only buildings in view, so she assumed this was where Zach had directed her. She slowly approached and saw a large motorbike under a tree next to the first cottage. She knew Zach liked bikes but last time she'd seen him, he hadn't got one. She rocked the scooter onto its stand and knocked on the first door. An elderly lady opened the door and before Angie could say anything she called:

"Zach, you have a visitor. Do come in dear, it's getting chilly, that East wind gets its coldness from Russia you know."

Angie followed Aunt Dorothy into the kitchen as Zach came down the narrow stairs.

He remembered Angie as a bit plain. She was great company and knew more about World of Warcraft than Zach would ever know. She'd always had short hair and wore rather shapeless sweatshirts and jeans but the new Angie had long wavy dark hair and although still in jeans Zach's eyes were drawn to the previously unnoticed curves the jeans clung to. Once she slipped off her coat Zach knew he was staring but had trouble lifting his eyes from her t-shirt. It wasn't the mathematical joke written in script across the front he was admiring.

"Hi Angie."

"Hi Zach."

There was an awkward moment before they leaned towards each other and hugged delicately.

"I'll put the kettle on." said Aunt Dorothy. "You two sit down through there and I'll be two minutes."

42

The BA8403 touched down in Denver in the early evening. Although the pilot made an almost perfect landing, it stirred Plater from his sleep. Molly had completed the landing cards and Plater was still only half awake as they cleared immigration.

"Are you Molly?" asked a woman's voice.

Molly turned and saw an attractive woman, in her forties she assumed, in a sweatshirt and jeans.

"Yes...but..."

"I'm Kathleen." said the woman. "And this must be Mason."

"Yes, this is a surprise." began Molly. "What are you doing here?"

Kathleen Moran shook hands with Plater, who still seemed disconnected from his surroundings as he didn't show any surprise.

"It's been a long trip can I buy you a coffee and we can talk?" said Kathleen.

Molly hesitated but only because she was still wrestling with why Kathleen Moran was in Denver.

"Sure." said Molly.

"I'd like you to meet my good friend." said Kathleen turning. As she did a tall man approached, as if waiting his turn. "This is Erik Nordstrom, he knows why you're here and we'd both like to help if we can."

The coffee was strong but good and Plater was now firmly in the present.

"Why would you want to get involved in what we're doing?" he asked.

Kathleen and Erik exchanged a glance.

"We each have our own reasons." said Erik. "But neither of us wants Rev. Daniels to go any further in his political career and if we can expose wrong doing by him or his Church we'll stop him dead."

Molly was gradually adjusting to the heavy Texas drawl of Erik's speech.

"But you don't really know why we're interested in the CoR do you?" she said.

Plater stopped mid mouthful. He wasn't sure they should explain too much to these strangers. Apart from the unbelievable nature of their reasons for traveling so far he knew nothing of these people. He only knew that Molly had exchanged some emails with this Kathleen about the CoR.

"We just want to help." said Kathleen. "We know that you don't like the Church and you have evidence that they are involved in something. We have a long-standing issue with the Church and are more than happy to help anyone that goes against them."

"You've come over a thousand miles to help us without knowing why we're here?" asked Plater.

"I know that you have a beef with the CoR." began

Erik. "Kathleen lost her daughter to them and between us we can't rest until we've got her back. Anything we can do to hurt the Church is extra information for us and a feeling we're doing something positive, until we can find Kathleen's daughter and get her away from these people. You're in their world now and you might just need all the help you can get."

Plater felt sincerity in his words and steady gaze.

Erik and Kathleen had a rental car and after depositing Molly and Plater at their hotel they agreed to meet for dinner in an hour.

The managed efficiency of Redemption had been disturbed by the bizarre events involving the disappearance of the engineer. It took a full twenty-four hours before everyone believed what most had seen for themselves. Victor Sanchez was almost in a state of shock. He was a devout, gentle and principled man. He'd asked several times of his superiors what had happened. At first, he was simply told to get on with his work and that it had nothing to do with him. When he persisted, he was taken to one of the windowless offices and told that the engineer had not in fact disappeared but had been carried aloft by the Lord as a demonstration that their hard work was almost complete. The bridge they were building was almost ready and soon they would be able to use it to join the Lord in his heavens.

It was after he had asked a fourth time when the work would be complete that he was taken aside and told to report to a room he'd never heard of.

"It's in section 3, turn right after the main stores

entrance and take the elevator to Level T."

Victor began to walk then turned.

"But there isn't a Level T?" he said.

"Level T." repeated the officer and turned away before Victor could speak.

Victor was surprised to see that the elevator beyond the stores in Section 3 did have a Level T marked. He was sure none of the other elevators showed it. He pressed the button and waited. He felt the floor move down, slowly and after 15 or 20 seconds it gently stopped. The doors opened and he immediately saw two large, uniformed men carrying automatic weapons. Victor stepped out of the elevator and one of the men scanned his ID card with a handheld device.

"Okay Mr. Sanchez, you're expected in the library, straight ahead, second door to your left."

Victor was relieved to see both men's grips loosen on their weapons. He walked in the direction they'd indicated, it was the main corridor leading away from the elevator, although smaller passages led left and right. The second door to his left did indeed bear a plate with 'Library' on it. Victor wasn't prepared for what he found inside. It was a huge room with giant computer screens filling two walls and a row of people at terminals in front of them. The rest of the room was made up of a row of bookshelves to one side and a number of large tables down the centre. The tables were covered with large sheets that seemed to be diagrams, similar to the small versions he had worked from when building his part of the power supply. But there were dozens of such diagrams on these tables and Victor guessed about a dozen people in three groups were looking at them.

"You must be Victor, I'm Chance." said a young woman of about thirty, holding her hand out.

Victor shook her hand.

"Yes." he said. "What is this place?"

"This is the Library." Chance said, leading Victor towards the bank of computer screens. They stopped behind two people busily working on terminals. Victor gazed at the screens trying to work out what he was seeing.

"You've been with us some time, haven't you Victor?"

"In the Church? Yes, a long time."

"You know the story of the Gift?"

"Of course, everyone in the Church knows...so is this...is this the Gift?" Victor asked, now studying the screens with even more intensity than before.

"This is part of it yes." said Chance. "The Rev. Daniels is still receiving divine guidance and despite his years of devotion and the recording of the Gift there is still more coming."

"We were told that Rev. Daniels received the Gift during his time in the Holy Land." began Victor.

"Only part of the story Victor." said Chance. "The revelation that Rev. Daniels experienced then was just the beginning. The beginning of a great work. It was what caused him to create the Church, and later to build Redemption."

Victor was trying desperately to follow what was scrolling rapidly across the giant screens, but he wanted to ask questions.

"But what is all this?" he said.

Chance took Victor's hand and squeezed it gently.

"We have deciphered the contents of the Gift." she began. "It has taken some of the brightest minds in the Church ten years, but we now know the purpose of the knowledge passed to Rev. Daniels."

Victor was desperate for Chance to tell him, with a hint of apprehension at being invited in to such a secret. Chance was clearly emotional and squeezed Victor's hand again while taking a deep breath.

"It's the Tower of Babel!" exclaimed Chance.

Victor couldn't process what he'd heard.

"I don't understand." he said.

"Don't you see?" said Chance excitedly. "The Lord has passed information to Rev. Daniels and now we know that he is asking us to build a Tower of Babel, so we can reach our Lord."

"But that's..."

"It's as the bible says, the Lord destroyed man's first attempt to build a means of joining him in his heavens and divided mankind by language so that they should not be able to recreate their device..."

"But that was a simple tower!" said Victor.

"Yes, but Rev. Daniels has discovered that this was all the Lord's will. Mankind has now reached a point where we can once again reach out and so he is helping us bring together people who speak different languages. People that speak the language of numbers, the language of physics, the language of electricity, the language of computers, the language of chemistry, all the languages we need to once again build the Tower of Babel and reach our Lord in his heavens."

Victor watched as the numbers and words cascaded by on the giant screens. This was all too much to take in.

He suddenly realised he was squeezing Chance's hand quite firmly.

"It's truly wonderful, isn't it?" said Chance. "Because of your excellent work we want you to help us to understand more of the ways in which we must combine these essences together. It's all here..."

Chance turned and swept her arm in an arc indicating the rest of the Library.

"We are very close to completing the device, but some connections are still hidden from us. With your knowledge we hope we can make those connections."

"Why is this a secret?" asked Victor.

"It was thought that if everyone coming to Redemption knew what they were building they would find it difficult to devote themselves to the intricate work required for each piece of the device. They would be too excited at the thought of what our labour will bring. Rev. Daniels thought it best to keep it a secret to most people until the day when we can all join our Lord and truly experience the Second Coming."

Victor felt a confusing mix of emotions. As a devout man he had always managed to keep his religion as a mostly internal experience. He went to Church and so to some extent he shared his religious experiences, but he always felt closest to the Lord when in solitary prayer. He was struggling with the idea that mankind was actually on the verge of building a machine, with human science, that could deliver them to their Lord.

"Can you feel the love of the Lord, Victor?" said Chance. "By his grace and by selecting Rev. Daniels to receive his word we will all find redemption through our labours in his name. Will you help?"

Despite the whisps of doubt somewhere in his consciousness, Victor found himself swamped by the real idea that this could work. Perhaps this was what his life had really been for. His wayward youth and hard passage to adulthood before he found the Church and eventually was brought here. He wanted to believe.

"Yes." he said.

43

Zach had no idea what time it had been when he'd finally fallen asleep. Aunt Dorothy's old settee was not as comfortable to lay on as it had been to sit on. Decades of use had created an undulating series of lumps in the cushions that didn't fit with Zach's spine at all. Angie was asleep upstairs in the small back bedroom Zach had been using. He wondered if she had fallen asleep easily after he'd described what had happened. He thought she looked at him differently after he'd told her about the implant. For someone who spent her life immersed in ancient history, the idea that evidently an arm of the British Government was prepared to insert an experimental device into an unwitting employee was profoundly disturbing. Fortunately, Aunt Dorothy had prepared one of her famous bedtime drinks of sweet, milky Horlicks laced with a fine single malt. With luck, Angie was sleeping like a baby.

As drowsiness finally clawed at Zach and tried to draw him towards unconsciousness, images of Angie,

Meek, the lab in Suffolk and his insane lunge for freedom, with the sounds of gunfire, swarmed before his eyes. It seemed he blinked but it was now light. He was standing upright. A young woman walked past and smiled, tilting her eyes downwards just as she disappeared behind him. Almost involuntarily Zach also looked down and found, he was naked. His hands closed over his groin and he bent slightly forwards.

The touch of the hand on his shoulder startled him and he spun around, almost forgetting his nakedness and moving his hands, which quickly resumed their covering duty.

"Please don't be alarmed." said the woman who had walked past him. "You are among friends."

She smiled and Zach's first thought was that she looked as if she belonged on a magazine cover. Flawless skin and radiant eyes.

"Where am I?" he asked and immediately wished he'd thought of something less lame.

"All in good time." said the woman. "What clothes were you wearing yesterday?"

Zach looked at her blankly.

"Yesterday, before you went to sleep, what did you have on?"

"Just jeans and a t-shirt with..." he began.

"There, that's better isn't it?" said the woman, glancing down again.

Zach again followed her gaze and saw he was now dressed as he had been the day before.

"But..." Zach's words jammed trying to get out of his mouth.

"Would you like a drink?" said the woman.

With all the thoughts wrestling for position in Zach's head, he didn't reply at first and when he did he realised he was standing in a pub. It wasn't The White Hart, but the woman was with him. She was holding a pint and something in a smaller glass.

"There're some seats in the corner." she said over the general hubbub.

As they sat down Zach took a long drink from the pint glass; it was his favourite bitter. He was impressed on two levels, first because it wasn't served in many places and also that this stranger knew what he liked.

"I'm sure you have many questions." said the woman. "My name is Diana." She held out her hand. "But first I'd like to run through a few things and when I'm done, if there are more questions I'll do my best to answer them ok?"

Zach was starting to think he was either dreaming or going mad. As the woman talked his vision of the crowded bar seemed to digitize or appear blocky like a bad satellite TV signal. It lasted only moments and Zach felt the side of his head.

"Yeah, okay, go ahead." said Zach, and he took another long drink. It tasted good, best pint he could remember.

The sun was barely visible as two rented cars, one a 4x4 the other a modest saloon, left Denver on Highway-285 and began the 250-mile drive to Gunnison. Mason and Molly were in the saloon car while Erik drove the 4x4 as Kathleen slept soundly in the armchair-like front passenger seat. Conversation was sporadic as Molly and Mason went over the plans they had agreed on over dinner the night before.

Mason was still uneasy about Molly being the bait but had to accept that she fitted the profile of a typical CoR recruit better than any of the others. As the single-track highway wound through mile after mile of forest, he occasionally had to tell himself to grip the wheel less tightly. The CoR would hardly expect anything strange about a couple touring and having some relationship issues, brought to the fore by the long hours on the road. Their ranks were filled with people avoiding something, with those for whom real life held just too many problems. People who didn't know they were searching for something until the CoR recruiter told them.

After three hours on the road, they pulled in to fill the cars with petrol and ate at the ramshackle diner that consisted of four tables crammed in one half of the shack that seemed to be the only building for miles. They went over the plan once again and agreed on the finer points of arriving separately and checked their instructions for communicating if, as expected, the CoR found some excuse to relieve Molly of her mobile phone. Erik ran through a number of options and Plater began to think that he was glad this guy had decided to help. While Plater and Erik went to fill the cars with fuel, Kathleen held up a small photograph for Molly. A young girl's face, in a typical school yearbook pose, with flowing hair and a ready smile.

"This is Dawn, my daughter." said Kathleen.

Molly took the photo and studied it.

"She's very pretty."

"She'll be twenty-five next Thanksgiving." said

Kathleen.

"How long..."

"Five years, it's been five years." said Kathleen. "She never even finished college. She always said she wanted to be a vet. She loved all animals but especially dogs and horses. She loved to ride. She seemed to be a part of the horse."

Molly had no experience of parenthood but reasoned that Kathleen's situation must seem to some extent like those that have missing children. Like the ones that used to smile out from the sides of milk cartons across the US. Disappearing just like that and the parents hoping at first, then praying and eventually, as time wears on, existing in some terrible limbo. Not knowing if they still have a child to worry about or one to grieve over. Kathleen was pretty sure Dawn was still alive, at least she had been six months prior. Did that make her one of the luckier ones? wondered Molly.

They got back on the road and made good time to the outskirts of Gunnison. Erik and Kathleen pulled off to the side of the road about ten miles before, to leave a decent gap in their arrival times. As they passed the Welcome to Gunnison sign on Highway-50, Molly noticed the population was signed as 5,854. That was probably more than she had expected for such a speck on the state map.

Plater and Molly performed what they hoped would look like the typical circling and cruising of people new in town and potentially lost. In doing so they managed to locate the offices of the trading company owned by the CoR central to the tiny business district close to the Gunnison County Airport. It was slightly harder to find the Church building itself, but they eventually did, some two miles away. They also found the motel they'd selected off the internet and checked in.

Plater texted Bartholomew to let him know they had arrived and immediately realised how unnecessary that was since he would be seeing him in the realm within a couple of hours.

As Plater and Molly strolled away from their room to find a place to eat the rented 4x4 swung into the campground just to the North of the city and Erik began to erect the tent. Kathleen started a fire in the nearby firepit. A cool breeze nudged the trees about fifty yards away. Kathleen went to her rucksack and pulled on a sweatshirt.

44

Zach was sweating badly when he woke up. At first, his vision wouldn't clear properly. Aunt Dorothy's sitting room emerged from the darkness but then broke apart into a digital blur and he was in a strange place. Not the pub he remembered, but a darker place, with tall trees and a humming that seemed to be coming from inside his head. Then blocky blurring again, more glimpses of Aunt Dorothy's, then the pub, then the sitting room again. Zach covered his eyes with his hand, but the image was there as if he were looking right through his hand. He rubbed both eyes hard and blinked repeatedly, then tightly closed his eyes. He was relieved to not be able to see anything. As he slowly opened them, Aunt Dorothy's sitting room welcomed him with its tired wallpaper. Zach was half sitting up and he slumped back down, gratefully looking up at the ceiling.

In fact, he was still lying on the settee when Aunt Dorothy swept into the kitchen and began busying herself with cups of tea and breakfast. By the time Angie had come downstairs Zach was dressed and sat at the table with his second strong cup of tea. He was still replaying the weird dream he'd just had and seemed distant.

"That flash new bike of yours is certainly causing a bit of a stir." said Angie looking out of the kitchen window.

It took a moment but Zach suddenly jumped up and crossed to the window. Two young lads were admiring the huge bike and one was carefully sitting astride it as it sat on the stand. Zach flipped open the back door and ran towards the boys, shouting:

"Hey, what are you doing?"

The two boys, whose combined age was probably less than Zach's looked startled and made off in a hurry. The one who'd been astride the bike caught his shin as he dismounted and limped away, still quickly enough. On no account did Zach want any attention drawn while he was resting at Aunt Dorothy's. He had no plan, no next move yet, he needed time to think. It seemed suddenly very bright outside and a sharp pain stabbed behind his eyes. For a moment he felt dizzy but then the pain stopped. It was probably just fatigue, thought Zach. He'd not been sleeping well, even before he broke out of the lab. As he trudged back to the cottage the sizzling of fried bacon and sausages made him think that a good breakfast might help. But he needed a plan, and fast.

The two boys were in the nearby woods now, cutting across the neighbouring farm to their houses. Ryan James was spitting on his hand then rubbing it over the gouge on his shin from the footrest. It hurt like hell but at least he had a picture of him sitting on the bike. As soon as he got home, he'd upload it to Facebook. He was sure most of his friends had never seen a bike like that in real life never mind sat on one.

The act of young Ryan James uploading the picture to Facebook effectively started a countdown. Within less than an hour of Zach bursting through the gates of the lab in Suffolk the underlying security level within the UK had been ratcheted up to Level 2. This was the highest that Braberson and Carver dare raise the level without drawing unwanted attention to their project. But even at this level, a number of resources were switched to specific activities to monitor, measure and observe. Of these resources was one of a pair of supercomputers at GCHQ in Cheltenham. This machine was really many thousands of machines all working in parallel. Custom built for the purpose. The purpose of selecting potentially important information from the vast tides of data washing around on the internet and through other telecommunications media.

Unfortunately for Zach, this computer was now running the latest version of Mycroft. Mycroft was the title bestowed on GCHQ's program suite for data collection and analysis. This was an obvious jibe at the Holmes program developed by the Home Office for collating data on crimes, Mycroft being Sherlock's smarter brother. This machine learning program sifted data from all email and social networking sites. With the addition of the latest image recognition software, Mycroft would eventually notice something. A picture uploaded to Facebook seemed to have a 79.5% chance of depicting a vehicle listed as missing and would flag the photo for human analysis. Events with a greater than 75% relevance as determined by Mycroft had to be examined by a human analyst within two hours, although most were checked within minutes. The registration plate of the bike was clearly visible in the picture, with only one character obscured.

45

Plater woke with a lurch into consciousness. It was disorienting and despite this becoming more common as he shifted between the realm and the physical world, he had not developed any strategies to cope better with it. He could feel most of his muscles were tensed and one leg was about to cramp which made him haul himself up so he could squeeze his thigh and try to prevent the uncontrolled tightening.

Molly wasn't in bed; Plater was not so distracted that he didn't notice that. As he wrestled control of his muscles he wondered if the realisation of what she was about to do had panicked her. Today she was to attempt to contact the CoR. It still seemed a high risk plan to Plater but there was no arguing with Molly. Her logic was sound, but Plater still didn't want her to do it.

As he sat on the side of the bed waiting for the last vestiges of tension to ebb from his body the door opened and Molly came in.

"Finally." she said. "It's a lovely day outside."

"Where have you been?" asked Plater.

"Just walking." replied Molly, standing at the window of their first floor room and looking out at the street below. Gunnison life was starting, and a couple of pickup trucks passed each other in opposite directions. She could see three pedestrians and a delivery van outside the general stores opposite.

Plater showered and they ran over the plan once more.

"Okay?" asked Plater.

"Okay." said Molly, Plater thought he heard uncertainty in her voice but it was too late to change now.

They walked the half block to Rosie's Diner and slid into a booth around 07:36 and ordered coffee. Their waitress, Becky, seemed to be the only person serving and there was one other customer, an older man with a bushy beard and tatty baseball cap on the other leg of the L-shaped diner. They'd seen two people from the CoR office visit Rosie's each morning they'd been in Gunnison. One was a tall skinny boy of no more than late teens and the other was an older woman, perhaps in her late thirties.

The plan, which seemed to Plater to come right out of a low budget film, was for them to stage a loud argument, for Plater to storm out and leave Molly, visibly upset, behind. Members of organisations like the CoR were trained to recognise potential new recruits and new recruits usually had emotional problems. Erik had been very confident that this would work; he had seen it or heard firsthand stories of how people were recruited so many times.

Right on cue the skinny boy and the woman came

into Rosie's. They liked to sit by the window that was on Main Street, so they ended up sitting two booths from where Plater and Molly had deliberately chosen to eat. After waiting long enough for the other two to order and receive their breakfasts Molly and Plater began their charade. They'd rehearsed a few lines and things to 'disagree' on and occasionally they were sure to raise their voices but not too much. Molly, who was facing the other two could see when the woman began to take notice. Molly touched Plater's hand as a signal. They could now move to the next stage. After one particularly venomous exchange Plater stormed off to the Men's Room which allowed the woman to see clearly that Molly was crying. When he came back Plater tossed two $20 bills rather theatrically onto the table and walked out. Molly sat hunched, with her head bowed, sobbing. Becky came by and asked if she wanted more coffee and Molly nodded.

It was a little over five minutes, Plater reckoned, from his position back in their room, binoculars in hand, until he saw the woman approach Molly. They exchanged a few words and the woman sat down in Molly's booth. They talked for a few minutes and then the woman beckoned the skinny boy to join them. They talked some more and before Plater knew it, an hour had passed. Eventually the three of them got up and left Rosie's. They headed West and turned down a sidestreet in the direction of the CoR's offices. So far so good. Just as they disappeared from Plater's sight his phone chirped. A text message from Molly with just the number '1'. This was at the suggestion of Erik, who recommended using a very simple code in case the cult took Molly's phone, which they would almost certainly do at some stage, depending on how quickly they managed to convince her to stay. The number '1' just meant that everything was ok, but also confirmed that Molly still had her phone. If asked she could deny knowledge of the message and claim it had been sent accidentally.

Plater was pleased that the plan seemed to be working but the reality of Molly being out of his reach and with what he believed to be murdering pseudo-religious fanatics hit home. He texted Erik the news. The next part of the plan depended on Molly.

46

Zach had never considered himself particularly lucky. As he pushed Angie's scooter up the slight incline towards the centre of the village and Brian's Autos to get a puncture repaired, he didn't consider it lucky at all. Brian explained that it would take at least two hours to fix as he was backed up with other work. Zach glanced around a cluttered but quiet workshop but decided not to argue.

To fill time, they visited the library, where Angie was fascinated that Zach could actually connect to the internet, let alone to the World of Warcraft online game from the antique computer he'd been using there. Zach checked some messages and quickly scanned a few news sites to make sure nothing was being mentioned about the events in Suffolk. By this time the local pub, the Plough, had opened for lunch so they decided to stop off and ended up discussing old friends which distracted them, at least superficially, for an hour or so.

On returning to Brian's Autos they found the scooter with its wheel still off and it was probably only their actual arrival that triggered activity on it. Eventually, it took another half an hour before they wheeled the scooter to the kerbside and rode back towards the cottage.

Zach was just beginning to enjoy holding Angie's waist as they weaved through the lanes when his senses flashed a warning to him. They were approaching a triangular grass island that is a common sight in East Anglia where lanes meet when Zach noticed a man standing casually on the triangle. He was wearing a suit and looked distinctly out of place. Zach tapped Angie vigorously on the shoulder and indicated she should slow down. Eventually she stopped about 200 yards from the man on the verge. Zach jumped off the scooter and dodged close to the hedge, pushing himself into it to reduce his profile.

Angie pulled off her helmet.

"What's wrong?" she asked.

"That man, up ahead, on the grass island, he's Security Services." said Zach.

Angie looked back towards the man and Zach called:

"Don't stare! Pretend you have a problem on the scooter or something then turn around, I'll meet you back up the road about 100 metres. The road bends so we'll be out of sight."

Angie couldn't help looking at the man on the grass again. Zach was right, he did look odd, just standing there in the middle of the country, dressed as if he worked in a bank. She wheeled the scooter around in the narrow lane and replaced her helmet. She slowly moved off and caught sight of Zach running bent over in the ditch between the lane's tarmac and the hedge.

When he thought it was safe, Zach waved and Angie stopped allowing him to get back on.

"Just ride!" shouted Zach. "I'll direct you."

On this occasion the event spotted by Mycroft had been checked by an analyst within ten minutes of it being logged; there were extra analysts on shift for the elevated security level. Braberson had been informed, as per protocol. He however had not followed protocol, which would have dictated that he inform local police and liaise with them to investigate. Instead, it was Braberson's own security team that made the dash across the Anglian countryside but apart from the bike, which was clearly the vehicle Zach had escaped on, there was no sign he had been there. No personal items in the cottage. Aunt Dorothy omitted to mention that her nephew had been with a young woman when he'd left the cottage that morning. She also seemed to have no idea where he might have been going.

"You should go home." said Zach.

He was looking down at the formica table of the booth and toying with a slim unopened packet of sugar. Angie was warming her hands around her mug of chocolate in silence. They were the only two customers in the tiny cafe.

"I should never have contacted you; they probably know all about it and now you're involved too..." Zach's sentence trailed off.

"It's okay." said Angie. "What do we do now?"

"We? No, no, you have to go home."

"But you said they probably know I'm involved now, so won't they be waiting for me? Besides they can't be allowed to get away with what they've done to you. We need to tell the papers or something. What about Facebook? Twitter?"

Zach placed the sugar pack carefully in the bowl with the others and looked at Angie.

"All social media traffic is examined by the Cheltenham spooks; they'll have flagged our IDs immediately and any newly created ones as well. We'd never be able to upload."

"What about somewhere to stay?" asked Angie.

"London." pronounced Zach.

"That's mad." said Angie. "Isn't it? I mean they have cameras all over and shouldn't we try to get as far away from these people as we can?"

"People have hidden in cities for centuries." Zach was smiling as if he was happy to have formed a plan. "Plus, I know a bit about their tech, maybe a bit more than they'd like." He winked and slid out of the booth.

They took the country roads towards London and managed to find two petrol stations with no apparent cameras. The first was too busy but the second seemed ok. The scooter was probably running on fumes by then. It was dark as the buildings reared up around them and swallowed them into the boiling, growling, swarming metropolis.

Angie hadn't wanted to sell her scooter. It was like her first child; she'd saved so hard to get it and had even waited six weeks for the particular shade of purple, but they needed some funds. By the time the paperwork, or online change of ownership had been processed, they'd have vanished into the smoke.

Angie noticed that Zach kept referring to what looked like a smartphone but wasn't. It could have been a hand-held GPS but had some added features.

"This way." said Zach and turned down a quiet street that seemed to go nowhere.

"Where are we going?" asked Angie.

"Like you said, London is full of cameras right? Well Meek and I didn't like that so we built a little box that maps the known locations of all security cameras, look.."

The handheld screen showed a familiar small map of where they were but had four pulsing red dots on the main road that ran almost parallel with the street they were on.

"Okay, but how do you know it's right? They add cameras all the time."

"Same way the spooks know, they have a database, accessible online. But they monitor accesses so we can't use that one, so Meek and I use their backups. The data's a day old but hey, that's a chance we'll have to take. We use a basic shell account in the US to bounce it back via an old server at an estate agent's that I did some work for years ago. They'll have to make some leaps to pick up that trail. The hand-held piggy-backs on BT's network."

"You mean the BT Infinity thing where everyone gives up part of their bandwidth to passersby?" said Angie.

"Yeah."

"Epic!" she said.

They laughed at the beauty of being able to move around in London and be confident of avoiding CCTV.

After walking for twenty minutes, they turned back towards the main road. On the corner of the street was a small mini-cab office. They got a cab to Wembley. As they passed by the stadium, with its landmark arch glowing, Zach showed Angie his CCTV map. There were twelve dots on the screen but seven of them had yellow 'X's across them.

"That means they're down." he said.

"Why so many?"

"Seems the locals here don't like being watched so much."

Zach grinned.

"It's been this way for at least two years." he went on. "Meek and I noticed it after a while, we agreed it'd be a good place to lie low."

The cab dropped them off and Zach set off walking.

"Now where?" asked Angie.

"Just a precaution, we have a bit of a walk."

"So, was I the only one?" asked Angie.

Zach looked puzzled.

"Was I the only one that saw your messages?" she went on.

"No." said Zach. "Rick replied as well but he's kinda 'offside' when it comes to actual help. He's in California."

"Really? I didn't know. Stuck with me then."

They exchanged a look of sardonic humour and Zach rolled his eyes. Angie elbowed him playfully.

About a mile and a half away was a bed and breakfast. Angie couldn't remember a time she'd been so pleased to get her shoes off. Zach went back out and returned with an Indian takeaway, which they ate quickly, with the window of their room open to try and hide the spicy smells. There was only one bed, but they were both too tired to worry and fell asleep, back-to-back with the twitching neon glow from the kebab shop opposite painting shadow pictures on the flowery wallpaper.

47

Molly was surprised that she had been accepted so easily by the CoR. Erik had explained it, more than once, but it still seemed a little odd that the older woman, whose name was Ellen, had so readily taken Molly into the CoR's offices. They had talked for a while, over more coffee, about the problems with men. Molly played up her part and insisted she couldn't rejoin her 'husband', and Ellen offered her a place to stay. Molly insisted she should pay for the room, but Ellen struck a deal instead. If Molly would help at the CoR offices for a while that would be enough.

A day passed, then another, with Molly doing various odd jobs around the CoR offices. It was a two-story building with a large yard out the back. Only around half a dozen people seemed to work there and over the two days Molly met each of them. She found herself doing everything from photocopying flyers to painting a new section of fence in the yard. To this point nothing seemed unusual to Molly. The others seemed just like anyone else, coming to work and seeming to get on well together. Molly had been sleeping in a room in another building on the edge of town that resembled a warehouse. The large ground floor area was virtually empty and two temporary rooms on concrete posts nestled in one corner. Each room had two single beds, but Molly seemed to be the only person using them.

Each day Molly sent a text with the number '1' which was a simple sign that all was well. Erik had explained the stages of being enrolled in the church and if or when Molly recognised them she would send texts accordingly.

On the third day, a man arrived in a more impressive looking car than the average Gunnison vehicle. He spoke for a time with Ellen, who seemed to be the person in charge. About an hour after he arrived the skinny teen that had been with Ellen in the diner, called Gary, asked Molly to go to the office. Inside were Ellen and the man.

"Molly, I'd like you to meet Mr Robertson, he'd just like to have a talk with you if that's okay?" said Ellen.

The man extended his hand and Molly shook it gently.

"Sure." said Molly.

"Ellen tells me that you have had a bit of an unscheduled turn in your vacation?" said Robertson. "I'm very grateful that you have been helping us in our work here."

"The least I could do after you've shown such kindness to welcome me." said Molly, hoping she wasn't overplaying her gratitude.

"What do you know of our Church? About the work that it does?"

"Not too much." said Molly. "I saw Rev. Daniels on TV

a few nights ago but he was being interviewed on a political show."

"Well, the Church is involved in a huge number of humanitarian projects throughout the world and Rev. Daniels believes that we can help even more people by uniting our country."

"He sounds like a wonderful man."

"Ellen tells me that you studied Biomechanics in college?" said Robertson.

"Yes." said Molly. "I had a school friend who lost an arm and I wanted to help people with damaged limbs or amputees."

"That's very interesting." said Robertson. "And a most admirable ambition. If you still hold that ideal, we may be able to offer you the chance to achieve it through the Church."

Molly was a little taken aback by this as it had not been part of the plan.

"I had no idea the Church was involved in helping victims of limb-loss." said Molly.

Robertson glanced at Ellen. "The Church tries to help society in any way it can Molly. Skills such as yours will help us to help even more."

"Do you work with a hospital near here?" asked Molly.

Robertson looked slightly unsettled. "We have our own facility not far from here. It is engaged in vital and complex work. I happen to know that your area of expertise would be highly prized. Now if you'll forgive me, I must get to my next appointment."

"I don't know what to say." she said.

Robertson smiled and extended his hand once again.

"Leave it with me and I will come back with an offer tomorrow."

Molly shook his hand again and was shown out of the office and back to her work of sorting clothing donations. She sent a text message from the toilet with a '2', signifying that she was to be invited into the Church.

The data had made its way in encrypted form to James Carver's secure laptop. The two ex-SAS men had been dropped close to the source of the energy event in the Colorado mountains. They spent two days observing the location and their report made startling reading. Only the backlight from the screen illuminated Carver's face as he tried to process the details. The hotel suite was dark and silent with the lights of Washington, DC carpeting the night outside.

Carver reached for the smaller, silver mobile phone beside the laptop. He pressed a speed dial number and it was answered on the second ring.

"Mr. Carver." said Faith Cantrell. "Have you seen the report?"

"Yes." said Carver. "And please, just James."

"James, it seems we have a potentially bigger problem than we thought."

"What does the Company know about this Church of the Reclamation?" said Carver.

"I have a colleague checking that right now, but as you might expect there are so many groups looking to leverage charity status that religious organisations grow like weeds and even the CIA struggles to keep an eye on all of them."

"Surely a group that owns a huge underground ex-military site must be on someone's radar?"

"Sure." said Cantrell. "But our laws on guns and our geography tend to make setting up something like this pretty damn easy."

"How do we proceed?"

"We'll see what the CIA knows of this church and the FBI, hell maybe even ATF as well. We need to tread carefully. We don't need Uncle Sam tramping all over this or, how do you say...the cat will be well and truly out of the bag."

Carver sometimes found his double lives interfered, one with the other. In his role as a government minister, he had at his disposal certain tools for situations like this. Acting in his role as a member of this parallel organisation he was not yet at home with what his toolbox actually contained.

"Is there something I can do?" he asked.

"For now, James, just be reachable. If we need to move against this 'church' we may call upon some more of your resources. Let's learn what we can and convene a conference in say four hours?"

"Okay."

The conversation was over and Carver resumed his scanning of the report. The sheer volume of supplies going into the mountain base hinted at a significant workforce. Grainy pictures of the device from bodycams implied the men had been able to enter the facility. The pictures meant nothing to Carver but he forwarded them to a special server on the dark web. This server was monitored automatically and notified relevant people as files were uploaded to it. Technicians around the world were already receiving notification to download and analyse the contents. As he closed the lid of the laptop to try and grab a few hours of sleep, he realised that the report did not state whether the two men who uploaded the data were successfully exfiltrated.

48

As soon as Molly seemed to have been accepted by the church, Plater left Gunnison. He maintained the facade of an annoyed partner for the benefit of the hotel staff, who all despised him for seeming to leave his partner to fend for herself in their sleepy town.

He drove out of Gunnison and joined Kathleen and Erik at their makeshift camp.

"Is this really going to work?" asked Plater.

"By the looks of these text messages it seems so." replied Erik, finishing his coffee and tipping the dregs out onto the ground.

Kathleen was sat quietly apart from the men thinking about the huge risks Molly was taking. She was ashamed to admit she was also hoping that somehow this might bring her some news of Dawn.

"Why have they let Molly keep her phone? I thought you said they took away all that stuff?" asked Plater.

"If they take her into the Church then they will take everything." said Erik. "But she's on a kind of probation right now. While they check her out, as much as they can."

"It's only been a few days but how do you stand the waiting?" said Plater.

"I'd say you get used to it." began Erik. "But you don't. Fact is we made a plan and seems like it's working, far as we know. That's a pretty sassy woman and I reckon she'll be just fine, long as she sticks to the plan."

"So, you said it could take weeks to be accepted, right?"

"Uh-huh, whatever you think of 'em, they're not stupid."

"And you're going to stay out here waiting?" said Plater.

"Uh-huh, that's the game. You have somewhere you need to be?"

"No, but it just seems like we're wasting time."

Plater fell silent, scanning the featureless landscape, the warm sun causing him to half close his eyes from the glare. He knew Erik was right. Molly knew what she was doing and from what he'd seen of her in the short time he'd known her, she did have a calm and confident way about her. As the sun rose higher the temperature climbed even more. Plater was tempted to close his eyes and rest but resisted, being unwilling to drop into the realm. Preferring to wait until he had more energy and his thoughts were not so troubled.

Molly lay awake gazing into the starry night through the dirty window of her sparse room. She was wondering what the CoR could want with someone with biomechanics expertise. She had stuck to Erik's instructions to volunteer little information about herself unless asked directly. She had played the part of someone pre-occupied with her failed relationship but was always enthusiastic in any task given to her. She was also surprised that she still had her phone, but the reception was patchy at best. If her degree in biomechanics was going to be helpful, she thought she'd better try to recall some of the key elements. Like most students she'd already forgotten quite a bit of what she'd studied just three years ago.

"Heads up." called Erik, looking down at his phone. "Text from Molly, she's on the move, let's get packed up."

The two tents were collapsed and crammed back into the 4x4 in less than ten minutes. Kathleen had her laptop, tethered to her mobile, showing a pulsing red dot that was Molly's phone. It had already started to move. The 4x4 joined the road and within five minutes they were following the red dot at a distance of about a mile. They seemed to be heading for the mountains.

Rev. Daniels sipped a strong black coffee as his limousine turned into the private airfield. It drove straight to the side of the runway and when the driver opened the door, Rev. Daniels got out and crossed in four giant strides to the door of the private jet.

"Good morning, sir." said a young woman as Rev. Daniels squeezed his bulk into one of the armchairs in the spacious cabin. "Can I get you anything before we takeoff?"

"No darlin', I'm good."

Within minutes, the jet was taxiing to the end of the runway and following clearance began to accelerate.

Rev. Daniels pulled out his phone and scrolled through his messages. Most were sycophantic congratulations from minor party members or donors to his campaign, but there was one from Wallace Clayton.

'Uninvited visitors' was all it said. Rev. Daniels hit a speed dial on his phone.

"Yeah?" said Clayton.

"What happened?" said Rev. Daniels.

"Coupla guys, ex-military, caught sneaking around. Didn't have much to say for themselves. Don't think it's Uncle Sam."

Rev. Daniels paused briefly. With his mind pre-occupied with his campaign and the next rally he first assumed this was related to the intrusion. Maybe rivals trying to find dirt they could use on the campaign trail. But then he reasoned that since he was very careful about visiting Redemption and always had been, he doubted anyone could link him to the place. This meant someone had either detected the first test of the machine or was taking more than a healthy interest in the Church.

"I need to know who sent them"

"Okay. And after?" said Clayton.

"Loose ends." said Rev. Daniels closing the call.

49

Grobus consulted his satnav as he approached a quiet junction in the heart of Buckinghamshire. The screen indicated he should go left and within three hundred yards he would reach his destination. The Holworth private hospital and long-term care facility stood in its own grounds of around five acres. It was a former rectory that had been expanded over the years with several outbuildings added, including a stable block which had been converted to accommodate the hospital's long-term patients.

The effectiveness of the Third Eye ritual had been impressive. Oculus had been able to see clearly the invoice from the Holworth private hospital as Mason had opened his mail. He had managed to capture most of the address, certainly enough for the satnav to get a fix.

The Skoda looked somewhat out of place amongst the Mercedes and Audis of the doctors and well-heeled visitors. Grobus straightened his tie as he approached the reception desk.

"Good afternoon." he began. "I believe you have a patient here by the name of Gail Hartston?"

The receptionist, a local lady in her early fifties, appraised Grobus for just long enough before answering to detect the slightest hint of discomfort in his manner.

"And you are?" she said.

"Rufus Henry, madam, I am solicitor for Mr. Mason Plater." Grobus handed an embossed business card to the receptionist. "He wishes me to check from time to time on the patient, Ms. Hartston."

Grobus hoped he had sounded authoritative enough but the look from the receptionist betrayed some doubt.

"It's normal to register intended visitors." she said, typing on her keyboard to bring up the visitor list. "Your name is not on it I'm afraid."

"This must be an oversight on Mr. Plater's part. I assure you he has instructed me to check on Ms. Hartston's condition and keep him informed."

"I'll need to check with Mr. Plater, if you'd like to take a seat in the waiting area, I'll call him now."

"That won't be possible I'm afraid as Mr. Plater is away on business. If you could just see your way to allowing me to see Ms. Hartston I can be on my way. I'm sure Mr. Plater will sort this administrative issue when he returns."

The receptionist was not happy. Protocols and procedures were central to the efficient running of the hospital and this was most irregular. She didn't like this odd-looking little man either. She couldn't put her finger on it but there was something about him that made her uneasy. She looked again at the business card.

"One moment" she said at last. She picked up the phone and dialed a four-digit extension. "Miss Watson? I have a gentleman in reception wishing to see Ms. Hartston...Yes...No he's not registered but says he is Mr. Plater's solicitor....No he's away travelling...Yes, very well, thank you Miss Watson."

Placing the phone down, the receptionist passed a form and pen across to Grobus and asked him to fill it in and someone would collect him shortly. Grobus completed the form with completely fictitious details and was soon met by another woman, of similar age to the receptionist but dressed as a nurse.

"Mr...Henry." said the nurse, reading from the form Grobus had completed. "Please follow me. This is not the way we usually do things here. Our clients require complete privacy and discretion."

"I do apologise." said Grobus. "I understand that this is a recent arrangement and was quite sudden, so I hope you'll forgive our lack of preparation?"

The nurse glanced at Grobus and forced a brief smile as she pushed open the door to the long-term patients' area. There were only three beds in the room, two with older gentlemen and one with Gail Hartston. The nurse stopped at the foot of the bed and picked up the charts to check that the morning's tasks had been properly performed and signed off. Satisfied, she took a couple of steps back and Grobus approached the side of the bed. He looked down and immediately recognised the features of the powerful astral creature he had seen. Her hair was a different colour but this was definitely her. He could barely contain his excitement. To have found an earthly body for such an astral being could enable the OND to influence, control, even defeat this creature.

A rhythmic beeping came from the nurse's pocket.

"I'm afraid you will need to leave now." she said to Grobus.

"Yes, of course." replied Grobus. "I just need to take a picture and record the treatment status for Mr. Plater, two minutes? I know my way back."

The nurse considered for a second or two but the insistent beeping made up her mind.

"Very well, but please don't take too long."

The nurse left the ward and even before the door had swung shut Grobus had a small pair of scissors in his hand and was cutting a lock of Gail Hartston's hair.

50

The comforting creaking of the old ship masked the pause in conversation. Plater was peering through the small, salt encrusted windows to the stern while Gail and Bartholomew sat silently in the tilting cabin.

"How do you know it is more than normal activity?" asked Plater.

"It seems to be related to The Book." said Bartholomew. "Our spies tell us that much progress has been made and that there is excitement amongst the higher functioning beings in the Valley. Something important is happening and that surely means something in the real world."

"Most of the higher functioning are involved in religion or other esoteric lives in the real world." said Gail, for Plater's benefit. "Their 'lifestyle', or training for some, provides them the ability, like us, to try and make sense of the realm. They are active in both worlds and likely pursuing goals associated with their double lives in each place. So, when they are active and apparently focused on a joint project that is probably going to affect something in the physical world."

"Do we think it is associated with the CoR?" queried Plater.

"This is our working hypothesis." began Bartholomew. "As you know the CoR has grown quickly and now possesses considerable resource. Its leader is charismatic and becoming more powerful in the political system of the major military superpower. The inferences seem clear while the implications are most concerning."

"Can we do something in the realm to slow down what's happening in the physical world?" asked Plater.

"Perhaps." said Gail. "But events in the physical world may be too far along to make a difference, we just don't know."

"This is why Molly's information could be vital." said Bartholomew. "If she can discover what the CoR are using all their resources for perhaps we can alert authorities or somehow interfere with their plans, maybe even in both the realm and physical worlds."

"That's a lot to expect." began Plater. "Molly's no spy, expecting her to discover this secret project....they're ruthless, they could just kill her. We should never have let her go. There's got to be a better way."

"Molly is brave." said Gail. "She is our best hope. When we have tried to involve the authorities in the past it has always been with mixed success. We obviously cannot explain the truth as we would be unlikely to be believed and our opportunity for action would be lost. So, we have tried to persuade them with misinformation or deception, but it has rarely prevented the actions of the Others in the physical world. We must hope that Molly can fill in the blanks for us."

"Can we try to get more information from the realm?" asked Plater. "I could go to the Valley, see what I can find out there?"

"You are not ready to visit the Valley." said Bartholomew. "You would need to maintain a certain 'representation' of yourself to properly blend in. We have not covered that in your training so far. Without those skills you would not pass for one of the Others and be identified almost at once."

"There has to be something we can do; we can't just sit here." said Plater.

"The second phone suggested by your friend..." began Bartholomew.

"Erik." said Plater.

"Erik." continued Bartholomew. "...Has proved an excellent idea. At least we have potential communication with Molly from the CoR location in the mountains."

Plater resumed his gaze out to sea. A stiffening breeze from the SE was causing a few small whitecaps on the waves near the horizon. Perhaps a storm was coming.

51

Molly was impressed with the efficiency and secrecy of her journey to Redemption. Blindfolded all the way she had had her mobile phone confiscated as a 'security precaution' and told she would get it back once they were settled at their destination. Fortunately, the CoR's security had not extended to a cavity search, for which Molly was grateful on several counts. Not least because it meant they had not discovered her miniature mobile, wrapped in a prophylactic and hidden from the normal pat down.

When the doors to the blacked-out minibus finally opened she was escorted with three others and given a cut-down version of the welcome speech. This was not delivered by Rev. Daniels as he was not at Redemption but on the presidential campaign trail at a rally in Idaho.

After the short introduction Molly was approached by a man with a clipboard and clipped speech to match.

"My name is Chambers and I'm the supervisor for the work team you have been assigned to."

Omitting pleasantries was part of Chambers' unique

charm and he continued:

"Follow me." Chambers set off down a corridor and Molly glanced behind but followed. "You are in Team 5 and I'll take you to one of your team and they can explain further. I understand you are an expert in biomechanics and the effects of magnetic fields on the human body?"

"Er, yes, I have a Masters in biomechanics." said Molly, although this was the first mention of magnetic fields.

"Good." said Chambers, who had stopped outside a door and was jotting something on his clipboard. He knocked sharply on the door. It was opened by a man who looked to Molly to be South American.

"This is Victor Sanchez, he will be your Team Leader and explain the work in more detail. Dinner is in two hours and your first shift is in the morning at 0530, any questions?"

Molly had more questions than she felt Chambers would be prepared to answer.

"No." she said and smiled at Victor.

"Very well." said Chambers over his shoulder as he set off briskly the way they had come.

"Come in." said Victor and Molly stepped into what was very much like a college room. There was a single bed, table and chair, handbasin and cupboard, which might have served as a wardrobe.

Realising that Chambers had not thought it necessary to introduce her Molly decided to do it herself.

"I'm Molly." she said, offering her hand, which Victor grasped warmly.

"Pleased to meet you Molly." he said. "Did Chambers give you anything?"

"Just this." said Molly showing Victor a small purple card.

"Ah, you are in room 713, which is two doors that way." said Victor pointing. "It seems we're to be neighbours."

"Okay." said Molly. "I don't know my way around at all is there a map or something?"

"There are maps on the walls, but I can show you the important things." said Victor. "So perhaps you'd like to rest a little before dinner. I will come and knock for you and show you the way."

"Thank you Victor." said Molly and smiled warmly as she stepped back into the corridor and found room 713. The purple card slotted into an electronic lock and revealed a room exactly similar to Victor's. Molly lay on the bed and stared at the rough, rocky ceiling. The feel of the mobile phone inside her was strangely comforting although she knew she would need to get outside to have any hope of it working. The difficulties of her situation were just starting to become apparent.

52

"But it isn't me they're after." said Angie. "Not me that is all over their databases and their surveillance systems, it's you."

Zach was checking their newly acquired burner mobiles and ensuring each had the other's number on speed dial.

"That's true but there may be some link between us." began Zach. "One that I haven't anticipated, not remembered. It only takes one thing, one old email address or login creds that can be associated."

"We need some help." said Angie. "Let me call CJ, she still lives in that old warehouse near Thamesmead. We could lay low there for a while and we can use their net connection, maybe we can find out more of what's going on."

Zach knew that CJ was an old friend of Angie's. She hated her full name of 'China Jade McManus' and just went by CJ. She lived an alternative lifestyle, sharing an old warehouse with five others who also didn't seem to have a place in mainstream society. CJ made a living almost exclusively online, paid in cryptocurrencies and performed a variety of security and web-related tasks for businesses. She never met the client in person and was only ever referred by word of mouth from other, presumably satisfied, clients. Zach had never met her and only heard of her through Angie. He was unsure about involving anyone else but keen to have access to a likely untraceable net connection.

"Okay." said Zach finally. "But we need absolute OpSec, who are the people she shares with?"

"They all have reasons to be anonymous." said Angie. "Or CJ wouldn't be with them."

"Fine."

Zach unplugged the phones, tossed one to Angie and pocketed the other, rolling up the cables and pushing them into his backpack. They quickly scanned the room and removed everything they had brought into it, including their rubbish. It was an hour before their checkout time and they half smiled at a disinterested woman who was vacuuming the hall as they left.

Two hours of detours to minimise camera exposure and identify any physical tail saw them eventually arrive at a bare metal door with old and peeling grey paint. Zach noticed the mounting and recognised it was a high security steel door and frame. This would be the sort of door found on properly outfitted drug dealer's houses, resistant to Police battering rams and the SAS's favoured entry technique of shooting out the hinges with a shotgun. Angie dialled a number on her phone. Zach looked up and down the sidestreet but there was nobody.

"Okay." said Angie.

Seconds later the door opened and a short figure beckoned them into the shadowy passage. They went up two flights of stairs littered with beer cans, some newspaper, and on one half landing a square of chickenwire fencing, just propped against the wall. Zach saw, once they found some light from a window, that the small figure leading the way was a girl, probably late teens or twenties, with jeans, highly polished DMs and a t-shirt with zips and chains that seemed to belong to the punk era. On the second landing, they went out of the stairwell and along a dark corridor only lit by the dirty windows at each end of it. Just as Zach was wondering exactly what they were getting into their guide stopped outside a door and knocked.

"Yeah, it's okay." came a voice from inside and they went in.

The room made a sharp contrast with the corridor. It was bright, with windows on three sides and white walls. Along one wall were six large screens, three of which were on. On the wall with the door there was a double bed and two huge sofas. Sat near the opposite wall, at a long workbench, apparently soldering some electronics was a tall, slim woman in well-worn leather trousers, trainers and a bright yellow waistcoat. As Zach and Angie stepped in and their guide stepped out, closing the door, the woman swiveled round.

"Angie!" she said and quickly crossed the room to hug Angie.

"This is Zach." said Angie.

Zach smiled quickly and shrugged out of his backpack.

"Nice setup." he said, taking in the computer

equipment arranged on a professional rack system in one corner and the array of tools and instruments along the workbench. "I've got a friend who'd be impressed by this." he added, thinking of Meek as he indicated the bench.

"Yeah." said CJ. "Zach, Angie tells me you have some privacy issues just now?"

Zach paused, not sure how much he felt comfortable sharing with CJ for the moment. CJ seemed to sense his reluctance and quickly said:

"Are you hungry ? There's beer and stuff in the fridge, maybe even some cold pizza."

"Thanks, we're.." began Angie and then saw Zach head for the fridge. He grabbed a beer and a slice of cold pepperoni pizza before joining CJ and Angie on the sofas.

"So what's the deal?" asked CJ.

"I..er..work...well   worked   I   guess,   for   the Government." said Zach. "Classified stuff, you know."

"I'm cleared to eSC." said CJ. "So I understand the game."

"'eSC'?" said Angie, looking puzzled.

"Extended Security Clearance." said Zach. "Gives access to 'SECRET' stuff and, under supervision, even 'TOP SECRET'."

CJ nodded. "But something made you leave in a hurry."

Zach paused again. He really wasn't sure he should explain too much. He was already in deep but the fewer people who knew the better for them. Angie jumped in:

"Just tell CJ what you've told me. She may even know of this project. She does do Government work sometimes."

Angie glanced at CJ and CJ nodded.

"Okay, you'll think this is crazy but our Government seems to be picking up some of the research into remote viewing, neuro-enhanced organisms and non-verbal communication using neuro-stimulation that was done by the Russians in the 50s and 60s, and the Americans later on."

Zach looked at CJ for any signs that she thought he was a raving lunatic.

"Go on," said CJ, "Is this related to MilkChurn in any way?"

"In a way, yes," said Zach, a little surprised, as he hadn't heard that project mentioned for two years. It had been a precursor to the current work. Old experiments into psychokinesis were repeated with more modern measurement technologies in the hope of detecting subtle changes in brain function. While in progress MilkChurn had TOP SECRET classification but that was reduced when no tangible results were forthcoming. It showed that CJ did have an eSC clearance.

"Some progress has been made since MilkChurn." he said. "But the results took us off into new areas. Towards direct brain-computer connection and possibilities of decoding thoughts."

He paused, again expecting some reaction, perhaps a smile.

"Using Aronson's work?" said CJ.

"Yes, exactly." said Zach, surprised.

"Pretty wild stuff." said CJ. "Implants as well?"

"Yeah, that's part of my problem." began Zach as he

turned on the sofa and parted the hair over his neck to show CJ the neat 4cm scar.

"You agreed to that?" she asked.

"No."

"Shit, that's a big hole, what the hell is in there?" asked CJ.

"I think it's a new experimental chip, connected directly to the paths into the brain stem. I have some tech details on my laptop but they don't mean much to me. I'm more a software guy."

"They can probably detect your movements with the right gear." began CJ. "But you're okay here, this place is one big Faraday Cage; can't be too careful y'know?"

Zach was relieved, not being detected by a random accidental signal from the device in his head or the detectors that were certainly looking for him might allow him to get some proper sleep.

"If you wanna show me the details I can see if we can knock something up to jam the signals or block them somehow?" said CJ.

Zach fired up his laptop. Although still wary he was starting to like CJ.

53

Molly slept badly in her windowless room and had just slipped back to sleep when Victor knocked to go to breakfast.

The dining hall was noisy, metal furniture on a hard floor and the chatter of perhaps seventy people.

"We'll be working on some supercooled electromagnets today." said Victor. "Did I see that you're a biologist?"

"Biomechanics really." said Molly, feeling better as she devoured a large plate of scrambled egg.

Dawn Moran approached the pair cautiously until Victor noticed.

"Good morning." he said. "Molly James this is Dawn Moran."

Molly got up and offered her hand to Dawn, who slid her tray onto the table before shaking the hand and joining them. Molly tried not to stare at Dawn and hoped she had managed not to make it obvious.

"Molly arrived last night." began Victor. "She'll be in our team."

"Welcome." said Dawn with a warm smile.

Molly tried to focus on her breakfast. She had cut her hair differently to the picture Kathleen had shown her. Molly wondered if she might be able to do something to help reunite mother and daughter but she had no idea how. Twenty minutes later Molly and Victor were in the main hall, circling a huge machine. It had been partially dismantled after the first test but still loomed impressively.

"What is this?" asked Molly, unable to recognise much in the tangle of wires and glistening pipes.

"We don't really know." came Victor's slightly muffled answer. He was under a portion of piping removing a black metal box with a spanner. "It's based on revelations that Rev. Daniels had on his journey of enlightenment in the wilderness."

Back in the workshop that Victor and Dawn shared Victor began connecting up the black box in a large rig that had arrived in a cage on wheels. The majority of the equipment was to reduce the temperature within the centre of the apparatus to as close to -273 degrees Kelvin, or absolute zero, as possible. The experiments they were to undertake related to the effects of high strength magnetic fields on human tissue. Molly asked Victor why this was necessary.

"I don't know." he replied, wondering if it had anything to do with the unfortunate engineer's disappearance three weeks ago.

"The human body isn't really suited to strong magnetic or electric fields." said Molly, helping Victor as best she could by passing him tools as he inserted the black box into the apparatus "They can be very dangerous, with unpredictable effects for some."

Victor hesitated, then continued tightening the fastenings of the box.

"There was an accident." he said. "When the big machine was tested."

"What happened?" asked Molly.

Victor stopped tightening and described what had happened to the engineer as best he could. He also told Molly what Rev. Daniels had said afterwards, about the engineer being accepted into the Lord's paradise and being the first to make that ecstatic journey which they all aspired to make one day.

Molly listened with growing anxiety. If she was here because of her knowledge of the human body and how it might be affected by strong magnetic fields, she wondered if that may have been the fate of the engineer. In extremely strong magnetic fields, the molecules of the body would elongate and the water within could be ripped out, as it is slightly magnetic. As Victor finished his story, smiled awkwardly and returned to his work, Molly realised she had to get to the surface and tell somebody.

54

Braberson toyed with his mobile, turning it over and over in his hand while he looked blankly at the opposite wall of his office. It had surprised him when Zach had absconded from the Suffolk lab. Braberson assumed that Zach had discovered the implant and this had made him want to run. On reflection, perhaps that had been unnecessary. Zach's scores in the tests to find suitable test subjects had been unremarkable, as had almost all the staff. However, the effects of the STZ3798-2 chip had been so far beyond projections that it had been decided to test it on subjects outside the original specifications. If it proved as effective as simulations predicted, then it could work for anyone. This would revolutionise clandestine operations. It would change everything.

Braberson's desk comms device bleeped and flashed.
"Yes."
"Dr Robinson is here."
"Send him in."
A slightly built, greying man slipped into Braberson's

office and hesitated near the door.

"Dr Robinson, please, come in and take a seat." said Braberson, indicating one of the chairs facing his desk. Dr Robinson sat, a pensive look on his face.

"I know this is a little unusual." began Braberson, reaching for a manilla folder and opening it in front of him. "I spoke to Mr Andrews and said that I wanted to borrow you for a while, I hope that's alright ?"

"Er, yes of course." said Dr Robinson, adjusting his position in the chair awkwardly "I'm not sure how I can help?"

"I see you have been taking an interest in instantaneous energy production?" continued Braberson, reading from a page in the folder "That's a little tangential to your normal field isn't it?"

Dr Robinson looked visibly uncomfortable.

"I was just checking some technical details. A friend showed me some technical drawings of an unusual device and I wanted to check if my suspicions were correct."

"A friend?" asked Braberson looking up from the page.

"An old University friend actually, not a scientist himself, on the arts side."

"How did this 'friend' come to possess this diagram?"

"He didn't say." said Dr Robinson, feeling himself starting to blush a little. "Is there a problem?"

"More of an interest really." said Braberson looking up again from the folder and smiling "Would you have contact details for your friend? We'd like to see where this diagram came from, it might be an important find and we wouldn't want it to get lost."

"Right, yes, of course." said Dr Robinson, visibly relieved. He knew of Braberson by reputation. Always the one to manage projects on the very fringes of accepted science. Not someone to mess with by all accounts. Dr Robinson gladly sent Braberson the contact details from his phone for a Raymond Bartholomew of Walberswick, Suffolk, an antiquarian book dealer and esotericist. As he left Braberson's office he wondered if he should call or text Raymond to let him know that others were becoming interested. He decided against it as he didn't want to get involved.

"I'm sorry, sir, but that device won't work in here." said the tall young man standing rather stiffly by the door.

Raymond Bartholomew was trying to make a call from his mobile phone, but the young man was right, there was no signal inside the windowless room. He was sitting one side of a table, with two chairs on the opposite side, the only other furniture.

"How much longer am I going to be kept here?" asked Bartholomew, summoning as much authority as he could in the circumstances.

"Just stay calm sir, would you like a drink ? Tea? Coffee? Some water?"

Bartholomew did need a drink as his mouth was very dry. He reckoned it had been about two hours since this apparently charming young man and his partner had entered Bartholomew's shop. They had made it pretty clear that Bartholomew had no choice but to accompany them. They had Home Office identification. He had been taken at some speed through the Suffolk countryside to a place he didn't know that looked like a small holding but for the absence of farm machinery and what looked like an electricity substation in the grounds.

"A cup of tea would be nice." said Bartholomew.

The young man opened the door to reveal his partner on the outside. He whispered a few words then closed the door, resuming his silent vigil.

"You still haven't told me why I'm here." began Bartholomew. "What is all this about?"

"All in good time sir, there'll be someone coming to speak to you shortly."

Just as he said that the door opened and a well-groomed man in a dark suit and a woman carrying a laptop came in and sat down opposite Bartholomew. The woman smiled and opened the laptop.

"Good afternoon Mr Bartholomew." said the man, sitting opposite him. "My name is Braberson, I work for the Home Office."

"Good afternoon." said Bartholomew briskly. "Are you going to explain why I was taken from my home just now?"

"I'm sure Mr Wilson was the epitome of charm and politeness." said Braberson glancing round at the young man by the door. "In any case you weren't taken from your home, you were simply asked to come for a chat."

"Do you know this man?" said the woman, turning the laptop round so Bartholomew could see the face of Dr Bruce Robinson, his longtime friend from University.

"Yes, that's Bruce Robinson. We both attended St Andrews. What is this about? Has something happened to Bruce?"

"Oh no, nothing like that." said Braberson. "We

understand that you showed Dr Robinson a schematic of a device? Asked his opinion on what it might be used for?"

"Yes." said Bartholomew, rapidly weighing up how much he should say.

"Excellent." said Braberson. "It turns out that this diagram has some very interesting features so we were hoping you could tell us where you got it."

Bartholomew was panicking.

"Well." began Bartholomew, but no sensible explanation came to his mind.

"Come now Mr Bartholomew, it's a simple enough question." said Braberson, fixing Bartholomew with an appraising stare.

Moments seemed like minutes to Bartholomew but try as he might he could not conjure anything that might sound plausible. In the end he thought it best to try and sound like a well-meaning fantasist and hope they sent him home.

"It's a difficult thing to describe." he began. "It may sound ridiculous, fantastical even."

Bartholomew looked down at his hands on the table. He clasped them together and then unclasped, placing them palm downwards. Braberson and the woman were almost leaning forward in anticipation.

Almost an hour later and with a second cup of tea in front of him Bartholomew completed his edited version of the truth about how the schematic had come into his possession. He had left out any mention of Gail and had not mentioned Plater by name. He would have been surprised to learn that much of what he tried to describe, such as the existence of an alternate reality in which people could communicate, did not shock his audience. The most shocking aspects to Braberson were the apparent existence of several people with this ability and the prospect of others who were in conflict. Could this be proof that other countries were also experimenting, similar to the work in Suffolk? The innovations in the schematic suggested a foreign state with considerable resources and highly skilled scientists. According to one throwaway remark when the schematic was analysed by Home Office scientists there was more than one Nobel Prize wrapped up in the multi-page diagram.

55

"Do we ever go outside?" asked Molly as she helped Victor carry the black box he had been testing back to the trolley.

"No." said Victor, scooping wires onto the trolley and pushing it back towards his workshop "Between working and eating there isn't much time."

"Don't people get a bit antsy being shut away down here?"

Victor thought about his wife, for the first time in a few days and the children playing in the garden of their home.

"Yes, I suppose some will." he said, still with the image in his mind. "But our work is almost done, we have the combined test tomorrow and if all is within acceptable limits we may get some time for ourselves."

"So, they're going to fire the whole thing up tomorrow? Like when the engineer disappeared?"

Victor hesitated, the sounds from that day echoing briefly in his head.

"Yes, there have been some safety improvements and

the power supply has been considerably smoothed I understand."

Molly helped Victor unload the black box in his workshop.

"Is the test first thing tomorrow?" she asked.

"Yes, straight after breakfast." replied Victor. "Giving us the rest of the shift to analyse the results."

Molly smiled and nodded then returned to her room. The shift was over and there was about half an hour before dinner. She knew she had to find a signal and get a message to Plater, Erik and Kathleen. She slipped out of her room and walked the fifty yards or so to the toilet block. Inside a cubicle she extracted the phone and peeled off the prophylactic sleeve. She powered it on and was relieved to see it still worked and had 99% battery. She had paid careful attention to all the maps placed around the complex and noticed some large pipes which Victor had explained were part of the air intake and circulation system. Surely, she reasoned, these pipes must have access to the outside. She had seen one such large pipe in a small recess at the corner of a corridor that led away from the main hall, where the device squatted. From the toilet block she managed to reach the recess without meeting anyone else. Everyone was in their rooms having a brief rest before dinner. The pipe terminated close to the floor, turned at a right angle and capped with a grill. Placing her hand on the grill Molly could feel cool air being pushed out. She glanced around, walked back a few paces and checked around the corner, but there was no-one.

She unclipped three of the four retaining clips on the grill, lifted it and ducked inside the pipe, closing the grill as best she could after her. The diameter was about eighty centimetres and the ribs where sections of the pipe were joined provided good hand and footholds as she began to climb. At what she guessed was ceiling height the pipe branched three ways, left, right and upwards at a slight angle. Molly chose the pipe that went up and was able to make faster progress. A few minutes later Molly came to the end of the pipe and found a small room on one side of which a huge fan rotated languidly behind another grill. The fan must have been more than three metres across with three wide blades casting shadows on the walls. Light was coming in from behind the blades and as Molly peered through the grill she could see that the opening angled up through some roughhewn rock to blue sky. She pulled out the phone but there was no signal. The grill in front of the fan had a latch on one side, Molly unlatched it and pulled but the grill didn't move. She pulled harder and there was a slight rubbing noise but little movement. She lay on the floor and braced her feet on the rocky wall and clasping the grill with both hands heaved backwards as hard as she could, pushing with her legs. Amid loud squeaking and grinding the grill moved, enough to allow Molly to get behind it.

The fan slowly turned, drawing air from the outside and pushing it towards the pipes. Molly felt the breeze ruffling her hair. She stared at the mechanism as it tumbled. She could do it. She counted as each blade passed her, if she timed it just right she could rush through the gap between the blades. The blades were heavy, steel construction and if she got the timing wrong, she could be picked up and tossed aside. She had to get to where she could send the message. Molly picked a single blade of the three and watched it circle. The rhythm settled in her head. She clenched her fists, rocking gently back and forth, picking up the rhythm of the fan. She lurched forwards and dived as the blade passed in front of her. She felt a stabbing pain in her left ankle as the next blade caught it as she sailed through the gap. There was a small gash but more graze than cut and Molly began to climb the sloping tunnel to the light.

The tunnel opened onto a small ledge and the view was breathtaking. Rocky valleys and jagged outcrops spread out below. Molly grabbed the phone and saw a single bar on the signal strength. It had been agreed that the best way to communicate was by message as this would not require a great signal. Molly had already prepared a long message which she hurriedly copied to the messaging app and hit send. There was a tense few moments as the phone struggled to send the lengthy text but the reassuring 'sent' indicator appeared and a tone sounded. She hadn't mentioned that she had met Dawn. She didn't want to build up Kathleen's hopes until she'd had a chance to talk more with Dawn. She didn't know if she'd be able to help with getting her out or whether by letting Dawn know that she knew her mother Dawn might tell the Church and Molly would be in worse trouble. She had to focus on the original goal. Now it was up to Mason.

56

Sentinel did not appear on Raymond Bartholomew's mobile phone as an installed app. This was Sentinel's principal selling point. Once installed, it monitored all activities. It had been installed as a result of Bartholomew viewing his emails on his mobile, something he did daily as most of his book sales now happened online. Such was the sophistication of the Sentinel code that it only required Bartholomew to open his email app and not specifically the rogue email from a Mr. Jones enquiring as to the availability of a particular book. The Sentinel code then inserted itself into the depths of the phone's operating system. The only way to detect the presence of Sentinel was a forensic examination of the device, beyond the skills of Bartholomew.

Call records, text messages and contact details along with copies of emails, cached passwords for email, online banking and other websites were all soon in the possession of Braberson's security team. Within a few minutes Braberson had profiles of Mason Plater, Molly

James, Raymond Bartholomew, Erik Nordstrom and Kathleen Moran jostling for screen space on his laptop. Within half an hour Braberson had called the Home Secretary on his secure mobile and brought him up to speed on these new developments.

A group of people working independently had managed to make the connection between the Church of the Reclamation and the seismic event detected on the mainland United States before any intelligence organisations. This same group of people were also connected to activities around non-verbal communication over extended distances, similar to what Braberson's project was investigating. This appeared to change the game significantly. James Carver insisted on a meeting with Braberson at the Suffolk facility. Braberson checked his watch, it was 0407 hours and Carver would be arriving any minute. Gate security had been alerted so hopefully none of them would be asleep as the motorcade arrived.

Plater lay back onto his bedroll. The camping conditions in the mountains near Redemption were not as comfortable as those outside Gunnison. The 4x4 was hidden behind some boulders with branches and a camouflage net trying to make it invisible from above. Rather than erect tents which would be more visible they were using bivvy bags, effectively solo tents that had a very low profile.

Plater was very worried about Molly; his imagination was doing him no favours by conjuring up any number of ways in which her deception might be noticed. He knew that he needed to go over some things with

Bartholomew and Gail, but he was finding it hard to slip into sleep and cross over. Since his life had taken this weird turn, this was the first time he could remember finding it hard to drop into sleep and take up his other life. The frustration he was feeling only made it less likely that he could sleep.

He tried to recall what Bartholomew had said to him about controlling his access to and from the Realm.

"In the same way that you are able to return from the Realm through a conscious technique, the visualisation of your surroundings in the physical world, so you can develop ways to enter the Realm without needing to rely on falling asleep." Bartholomew had explained. "You will need to practice, as to move directly from consciousness to the Realm is an advanced skill that hardly anyone has mastered. Some occultists and religious explorers are able to enter what seems to be a trance state and transition that way. How many of them do this is not well understood and almost certainly involves a lot of irrelevant mysticism and extraneous ritual. Technically, it should be possible to fix your thoughts on a location within the Realm that you know well and transition in a similar way to when you return the physical."

Plater had tried this technique, but it had only worked once. He had chosen the cabin aboard the pirate ship to be his target and worked hard to set in his memory all the details he could of that room. Only once did he directly enter the cabin from an apparent state of wakefulness. At other times, he either didn't enter the Realm at all or found himself on the deck of the ship or even in the water, with no idea where he was or why he was there. He had been so panicked by the experience that he had immediately woken again and returned to the physical world. On one occasion he had been so disturbed he had vomited.

He had to get to the Realm. With his head poking out of the end of the sleeping bag he could see the stars in the cool night sky. At the periphery of his vision, he caught the flash of a shooting star against the inky blackness. As he had been taught Plater closed his eyes and focused on relaxing each part of his body in turn. Beginning from his feet and moving up his body. As he began to focus on his chest and breathing he also pictured the cabin of the pirate ship. His breathing slowed. As the muscles of his face loosened, he felt the familiar lurch and found himself in the creaking confines of the old wooden ship.

He had only stood by the stern windows for a few moments when he heard Bartholomew's voice.

"I'm glad I have found you." said Bartholomew, as he swung the cabin door closed behind him. "There have been...developments."

"You mean with Molly?" asked Plater facing Bartholomew.

"No, but it seems there are others interested in what the Church of the Reclamation are doing."

"Who?"

"The British Government." said Bartholomew. "I was their guest for a while and they know about the device. They must have detected my friend investigating the drawing you memorised. They seemed very interested, very interested indeed."

"Do they know about the stuff in the mountains?"

asked Plater. "What did you tell them?"

Bartholomew explained how he had handled the interview with the man from the Home Office. He explained that he'd played the part of an eccentric pseudo-occultist in the hope they would dismiss him as irrelevant, a nutcase.

"It would sound wild." said Plater. "I certainly had trouble with the idea to start with."

Bartholomew was thoughtful.

"As I recall they didn't seem so surprised by what I was saying." he said at last. "Almost as if they knew about at least some of it."

Plater stared at Bartholomew for a few moments.

"Do you think that's possible? That somehow the Government knows about the Realm, about the Others?" he said.

"We have no evidence of that." said Bartholomew.

"Wait, could that have been why they wanted Gail for some experimental program?" said Plater.

"Under the guise of trying to treat her condition? Could be I suppose. They may have people that can transition like you."

"Well that's good right?" began Plater. "I mean it must be better if a wider number of people know what's happening, surely?"

"It depends how a Government would want to handle this. I'm reminded of the situation with UFOs or UAPs as they seem to be known nowadays. In that situation the Government had evidence of phenomena they couldn't understand but were afraid to publicise it for fear of appearing either ignorant or weak, or perhaps to avoid panic or civil unrest with the implications. This situation seems to have parallels. We may find that Government involvement will make effective action against the Others harder."

"Do you know where Gail is?" asked Plater. "I think we need to work out how we handle this."

"Gail likes to spend time by the lake near the centre of the city. There's a Greek style building, reminiscent of the Parthenon, we may find her there." said Bartholomew.

Gail Hartston was sitting at a table of a cafe in a small, cobbled square less than a hundred yards from the temple building. She smiled as she saw Bartholomew and Plater approach.

"Do we have any news from Molly?" she asked.

"Molly is safe as far as we know." said Plater. "But you need to hear what Bartholomew has to say"

Gail looked across at Bartholomew who began to tell the story of his last twenty-four hours and the new players in the game. As Bartholomew came to the end of his explanation Gail placed a hand to her forehead and pinched the bridge of her nose, closing her eyes.

"Are you okay?" asked Plater.

"Yes." said Gail. "I have been feeling a little tired these past few days, perhaps something has changed in my meds?"

"You don't look great, I'll check if anything is different." said Plater.

"So we believe that this could be why you were selected for that experimental treatment." said Bartholomew. "Perhaps the Government has access to others that can do what Mason can."

"That would help us if they could." said Gail, her eyes still closed.

"We should be careful." said Bartholomew. "At least until we know their motives. I didn't mention either you or Mason by name so you both have some freedoms for the moment."

57

"That has to be it." said Carver, studying the details on Braberson's laptop.

"Yes." said Braberson. "An almost exact match of expected output and the disturbance measured in the US."

"This is incredible, who can be doing this? The Americans?"

"Early indications suggest not sir." Braberson opened another window on his laptop "This is a purchase record from a US Government auction from ten years ago. It shows the site being purchased by a front company. The company appears to be fronting a religious organisation called the Church of the Reclamation. Led by a Rev. Daniels, the one in the Presidential race."

Carver was silent. He read through the auction details on the screen and then scrolled to a window describing the Church and another showing a biography of Rev. Daniels. After a minute or so he pushed himself up from the desk.

"What the hell does a Church want with a device like this?" he asked. "How did they develop this technology when the finest minds we have thought it impossible? This makes no sense."

Braberson paused for a moment, considering whether he would sound insane for what he was about to suggest.

"We spoke to a person who also had possession of plans for this device." he began. "He had a rather fantastic story about how it came into his hands."

Carver looked intently at Braberson.

"Well, go on." he snapped.

"The man was a dealer in antiquarian books, the occult, ancient religions that sort of thing. He claims that there are individuals that can operate in some sort of parallel world. He claims that it was in this parallel world that this information was found. He also claims that there is an intelligence operating in that world that means us harm and is using people that can enter this parallel world to do its bidding in the real world. He claims that the intelligence wanted this machine built but he doesn't know why."

There was a silence.

"This is incredible." Carver said at last. "If this is true then, well all that we have been doing, all the speculation about a hostile intelligence from outside our world could be true. I never really believed..." his voice trailed away.

"We now have precise coordinates for the location of the device." said Braberson. "I have redirected the Horus-7 satellite and we now have constant real-time images and data from the area."

"Good, have you contacted our cousins yet?"

"A secure channel call is scheduled in..." Braberson checked his watch. "...three minutes, with Mrs Cantrell."

"Good, what about this person you spoke to, where is he now?"

"We have him under close surveillance and Sentinel is installed on his mobile device and all other devices he has access to. He is currently at his residence in Suffolk."

Braberson busied himself setting up his end of the encrypted channel and exactly on time the crest of the United States was replaced by the furrowed expression of Faith Cantrell, sat in a panelled room, somewhere in Washington.

"James." she said.

"Faith." said Carver. "This is Edwin Braberson, he's heading up the experiments our end."

"Mr. Braberson, doing fine work from what I hear." said Cantrell. "So what is this news that couldn't wait?"

Carver summarised what Braberson had told him about the device and its connections outside their organisation.

"What do we know of these other folks you mentioned?" inquired Cantrell.

"We have full surveillance on the bookseller, so we'll soon have a better picture." said Carver.

"What if we need to take direct action to neutralise this device?" asked Cantrell.

"That could be difficult." began Carver. "We don't have access to unlimited manpower or hardware. Since they're holed up in one of your ex-military bases I presume any assault would be somewhat challenging?"

Cantrell held her hand up and the screen flipped back to the national emblem of the United States Government. Carver breathed out and turned away from the screen. Within seconds Cantrell was back.

"Sorry about that." she said. "Just needed to check. There might be a way to resolve our problem."

"Am I going to like it?" said Carver.

"I'm not sure anyone will like it." said Cantrell. "There are eleven separate intakes for air hidden from aerial view. Based on our data from your Special Operations guys we also know that this CoR did not think to install air filtration units. They just suck in air from the outside and pump it straight round the base."

"You're thinking we get in that way?" asked Carver.

"No." said Cantrell. "Nerve gas."

"Nerve gas?" exclaimed Carver. "You mean kill them all?"

"That may be our only reasonable chance of success." said Cantrell.

Braberson looked from the face of his boss to the stern face of the woman on the screen. Nobody spoke.

58

Zach was lying on a metal table with a rolled towel under his head. As he glanced to his left, he could see CJ busying herself with her laptop connected to an open case with electronics inside. Zach could see some green and red lights inside the box and multi-coloured wires looped and threaded between circuit boards and makeshift connectors. He looked back at the ceiling and wondered again whether this was a good idea. CJ had suggested that she could try to find the frequency at which the implant was activated and that by knowing this she could build either a jammer or a shield specifically for that frequency. This should enable Zach to move freely without fear of being tracked or having the device activated without his knowledge. Zach still didn't understand the purpose of the implant and was reluctant to find out but he understood the sense of being able to block the device so he agreed to let CJ try.

"I have a program that will gradually work through all frequencies." said CJ without looking round at Zach. "The whole run should take no more than fifteen minutes. You have the safe switch right?"

Zach could feel the tubular device in his left hand which had a button on top. He rested his thumb gently on it. If pressed it would immediately stop the test and shut off the frequency generator.

"Yep, ready." said Zach, not entirely sure he was ready but just wanted it over.

"Alright we're starting low, in three two one, now." CJ touched a key on her keyboard and the program started to run.

Zach felt nothing and time seemed to slow down as he studied the ceiling of the warehouse in minute detail. He had no idea what to expect when the correct frequency was applied. He glanced over at CJ but she was watching the output from her program and Zach could see lines of text scrolling slowly up the laptop screen.

He couldn't be sure, but he thought the area on his neck near the site of the implant was getting warm. He didn't dare reach up to touch it and tried very hard to remain calm. It was then that he started to fall. He thrust out his arms for balance or to grab a handhold to stop himself but his hands grasped empty space. Then he realised he was standing up. He didn't recall getting off the table. He reached up to his neck but his skin was cool to the touch. He looked down and was puzzled as he seemed to be barefoot but he was sure he'd been wearing his trainers. A breeze brushed his cheeks and he saw he was outside. In a city street. Two people were coming towards him, they were talking and walked straight past him. He turned and watched them recede and saw what looked like a giant pyramid in the distance, and something that reminded him of the leaning tower of Pisa to his left. He could feel unease welling up. He had no idea where he was or how he'd got there. Unease was rapidly becoming unrestrained panic. Then he felt a hand on his arm.

"Can I help you?" said the owner of the hand, an older man with bushy red hair and a concerned expression "Are you lost?"

Zach looked blankly at the man for a moment then said "I'm sorry, I don't know where I am. What is this place?"

"You're in the city." said the man. "Is this your first time visiting us? It can be a little confusing at first."

Something in Zach's memory pushed to the front.

"Is The Drowning Swan near here?" asked Zach.

"Yes, it's not far. Down there, take the third on the right, then left at the fountain, about a hundred yards down, you can't miss it."

The old man smiled and began to walk on past Zach.

"Thanks." said Zach and headed off in the direction the old man had pointed.

Zach noticed that the architecture of the buildings was a real mixture. There were ornate stone constructions that looked classical European sitting next to ultra-modern steel and glass buildings that could have come from Far Eastern mega cities or Gulf States. Just from the buildings it wasn't possible for Zach to tell where he was but then he came to The Drowning Swan and found a pub that could have featured in a Dickens novel. It was almost leaning out onto the street and didn't seem to have a straight or perpendicular wall at all. He stepped through the narrow doorway and immediately remembered where he'd seen it before.

"Zach!" a voice called out from the depths of the crowded bar.

Zach looked towards the voice and recognised the woman he had met in this same pub before.

"I thought it was you." said the woman squeezing through the crowd. Seeing Zach pause the woman continued "It's Diana, do you remember? We met here once before."

"Yes, of course, Diana." said Zach trying to remember something of their previous meeting.

"I'm pleased you came back." said Diana "Do you remember what we talked about last time?"

"I'm not sure." said Zach. "Something about this place but I can't quite remember."

"That's not surprising." said Diana. "But you've found your way back here so that's a start."

59

Molly was finding it hard to sleep properly and was at breakfast early. She was sitting by herself when Dawn sat down opposite.

"Hey." said Dawn.

"Morning." said Molly.

"We didn't get a chance to get acquainted." said Dawn. "Are you British?"

"Yes." said Molly. "I'm kinda here by accident."

Molly gave a very quick version of how she had come to be at Redemption.

"What an asshole." said Dawn. "You're better off without him."

"Yeah." said Molly. "So how did you come to be here?"

Dawn paused for a second or two before continuing.

"I had a kinda falling out with my mom." she began. "She had my life planned out for me you know? Work hard at school, go to college, meet some nice man and have kids."

Molly looked at Dawn but was still chewing her scrambled egg.

"I just thought there should be something more." said Dawn, her voice trailing away as if overtaken by a memory. "My dad left us too so my mom was working all the time. I didn't want to end up like her I guess."

Dawn was toying with a pancake without showing any signs of eating it.

"Your mum sounds like she was doing her best." said Molly.

"I guess she was." said Dawn. "But I saw Rev. Daniels on TV one night and he was talking about how the Church was doing all this positive stuff, like building schools in Africa and helping drug addicts in the US and it just seemed like I'd be doing something good."

Molly finished her eggs and sipped her coffee.

"So, is the Church all you hoped it would be?" asked Molly.

Dawn looked up and seemed surprised and suddenly wary. After a second her expression softened again and she returned to forking her pancake.

"I guess it is." she began. "But things are different now."

"Different?" queried Molly.

"When I first joined it was fun. There were about eight of us, mostly women, that joined about the same time. We worked together and it was great, you know? We were like a team. Then it all changed."

Molly waited expectantly for Dawn to continue.

"One day they just split us up." went on Dawn. "We all went to different locations, Susan even got sent to Germany."

"Susan was your friend?" asked Molly.

"Yes, she was real funny." said Dawn, rather wistfully.

"I don't even get letters from her now."

"I guess good works are needed everywhere." said Molly.

"It was all different after that." Dawn continued. "The work got much harder. There was no time for anything. Just work, eat, sleep. We were all exhausted. Then one day they came round and offered us this big chance to do something special. To 'make a real difference' they said. I'd never even heard of this place."

"Redemption?" injected Molly.

"Yeah. I hadn't read Rev. Daniels' books by then. Only read the first one even now. This place is weird."

"Were you at the last test?" Molly asked.

"Yes." said Dawn. "It was pretty scary, that poor man."

"Victor told me." said Molly. "Do you have any idea what that machine is for?"

"Uh-uh, they don't tell us that stuff. Although Rev. Daniels did say we would all ascend to see the Lord, maybe that's how we'll do it?"

"It's a bit secretive, isn't it?" said Molly. "Why don't they tell us what the project is?"

Dawn paused then said:

"There was something odd the other day." she began. "I was coming back from dinner and I saw that Clayton guy and two of the guards. They had these two men in kinda army clothes. They had 'em tied up and it looked like one of them had cut his head."

"What were they doing with them?" asked Molly.

"They took 'em to one of the storerooms over by the main entrance."

"You say they were tied up?"

"Yeah, they had those plastic strap things round their

wrists." said Dawn.

"So you think they broke in or something?" asked Molly.

"Guess so." said Dawn. "But that's not the worst part."

"Go on."

"The day after I saw 'em I had to get a box of those anti-static gloves from the store room." Dawn stopped and looked sideways as if seeing if someone might be listening. "I think they've done something to those men."

"What do you mean?" said Molly, not liking the thoughts that were forcing their way into her head.

"Well they were tied up in that room, on two chairs, but they weren't moving. They were just sat there like they were asleep. I mean I got the gloves and got out of there. That Clayton guy gives me the creeps anyway."

"Maybe if those guys broke in they're just being held until the police can come and get them." said Molly, hoping this could be true but realising that if it wasn't her situation was more dangerous than she'd imagined.

"Maybe." said Dawn. "But you stay away from that Clayton guy anyway, skinny guy with round glasses, he's bad news."

60

James Carver could feel a familiar tension behind his eyes. It wasn't from reading the report in front of him or the excessive amount of screen time he had been spending recently. He could remember feeling something similar before, more than once. Usually this was when he needed to make a decision that he knew would involve the taking of human life. As Home Secretary, he had thought that his remoteness from any actual violence and his conviction that sometimes such steps were necessary for the greater good would ameliorate his natural feelings. Three years in office had shown him differently. In the same way that junior doctors have to learn to handle bad outcomes and sometimes death, so it is for fledgling Home Secretaries. Military men had sometimes confided with him that his uncertainties were natural. Members of the clandestine organisations had also helped him to understand the realities. He could barely imagine the thoughts of those tasked to find and kill an enemy of the state who might be at home with his family. As he reached for his glass of single malt, he told himself that this situation was different.

The Church of the Reclamation bore all the hallmarks of a religious cult and its leader, the Rev. Ethan Daniels, did not seem to be the wholesome, all-American that his media profile would have you believe. According to the MI6 report in his hand, Daniels had a chequered past and of particular interest was his fixer, Wallace Clayton. It seemed incongruous that a man of the cloth would need a right-hand man with several run-ins with the law, usually involving violence. None of these charges had stuck but the conclusion reached by MI6 was that Clayton was quite good at what he did. The unproven allegations made by the journalist, Gatts, that Daniels had gained his political foothold through deceit and coercion, possibly including murder, was given backing in the report. It also mentioned that the authorities in the US, the CIA and FBI, also had files on Clayton and Daniels but were being prevented from investigating due to political pressure.

Under normal circumstances, the fact that an apparently extremist right wing, religious con-man was running for the Whitehouse would have been cause for concern and probably many shared jokes at cocktail parties. Politics across the globe was becoming less predictable in the age of social media and with the inherent difficulties in sorting fact from manufactured fiction. From a government perspective there was no reason to expect a radical change in the UK's relationship with the US even if the unthinkable happened and this religious zealot achieved election. That was Carver with his Home Secretary's hat on. The reality was that he knew some things that even MI6 had not yet learned. He knew that the CoR had acquired a former US military base and had begun building a machine unlike anything known to humanity. The purpose for this machine was still unclear but he had to give credence to the possibility that it was related to the conspiracy theory that he had become a part of. There was no denying the apparent effects of the device, even though it appeared to be unfinished. What was a 'church' doing building such a thing in the first place? The fact that the two ex-special forces men that had reported on the secret base had not returned was further cause for concern.

Finally, the most recent addition to the MI6 report concerned the results of various opinion polls across the US in advance of the selection of candidates for the Presidential election. These made dismal reading. Rev. Daniels was more than eight points clear of his nearest rival, who was also a more extreme candidate and whose supporters would likely join the Daniels camp if their man was eliminated. This suggested that Rev. Daniels was virtually assured of the nomination.

Carver laid the report down on his desk and took up his glass again. He turned his chair and looked out of his window across the London skyline. He picked up the smaller of his two mobile phones and pressed a speed dial. Sir Alastair Kenwright answered almost immediately.

"You've seen the report?" asked Carver.

"Yes." replied Kenwright. "I see no alternative."

The call ended. Carver performed the sim-card ritual to protect the communication channel. He then called a different number.

"Cantrell."

"Faith." said Carver. "I'm sorry to call at this time."

"What is it James?"

"Have you seen the latest polls?" said Carver.

"Yes." said Cantrell.

"We need to stop this going too far."

"Agreed."

"Is this something you can handle?" asked Carver.

"It's complicated." began Cantrell. "To remove a candidate for the Presidency of the United States is treason in anyone's language."

"How do you want to play it?"

"Smear campaign, some sort of scandal, I have people looking into it already. The business in Florida stinks but evidence is sparse. We may need to get creative."

"Are we too late for a smear campaign?" asked Carver. "I mean it might have been straightforward in the Primaries but now Daniels represents the whole party. Won't people still vote for him?"

For a telling moment Cantrell was silent. With the two-party system in the US most adults of voting age were already firmly aligned with one or the other and would likely vote along party lines almost regardless of the candidate.

"We have to try this first James." said Cantrell at last. "Despite recent history we're not a banana republic."

"OK, what about the device?"

"Maybe cutting off the head of the snake will solve both our problems."

"So we wait?" asked Carver.

"Yes, but prepare, I have people on it this side. We'll

be ready if the time comes."

"I'll be in touch."

"Thank you James."

Carver switched sims and drained his glass then dialed another of his speed dial numbers.

61

Zach felt himself being slapped quite hard on the face. As he opened his eyes, he could see CJ staring down at him and it looked as if she was about to hit him again.

"What the hell." exclaimed Zach. "What are you doing?"

"Shit." said CJ. "You had us worried."

"We couldn't wake you." said Angie, who was the other side of the table gripping Zach's arm.

Zach made to sit up and CJ and Angie helped him into a sitting position.

"That was amazing." said Zach. "A bit scary but amazing."

The two girls looked across at each other and then back to Zach.

"We're listening." said CJ.

Zach started to describe what he had felt while he'd been lying on the table as CJ's program tried to find the frequency that would trigger his implant. He was surprised how well he could remember what had happened. He even remembered about the old man that had directed him to The Drowning Swan. As he got to this point CJ interrupted.

"You were hallucinating?" she asked.

"I'm not sure, maybe, but it seemed very real." continued Zach.

He went on to describe meeting the woman called Diana, that he remembered from a previous experience. Then he described the most fantastic and unbelievable parts. He described the city and what Diana had told him about how it came to be and who the inhabitants were.

"That's some crazy shit." said CJ. "So you think these other people are in your dream? Sharing what you see?"

"That's what Diana said." answered Zach.

As he continued describing what Diana had told him Zach realised two things, first that he seemed to have remembered just about every detail of his strange experience. Second, that this must be connected to the implant as he had never had any dreams like this before.

As Zach finished his story CJ grabbed her laptop from the bench and flipped it open on her knee.

"I think we've nailed the frequency." she began. "Could this thing really have caused what you saw?"

"Yes." said Zach. "It seems to be what the project I was on was trying to build. But it's so much more than just some way to communicate with people. It's like a whole other world and there were hundreds, thousands of people there. I've got to go back."

"It could be dangerous." said Angie. "We have no idea what that thing is really doing to your brain. We need to be careful."

CJ nodded in agreement.

"Angie's right, this thing could fry your brain so we need to do some tests to check its power spectrum." she said, moving back to her bench and sliding onto a stool. "I can rig something up but we should do that tomorrow, you need to rest. Listen, I can knock up a filter to block the frequency of that thing and we can go out if you like. There's a great Greek place not far from here, we can you know, talk things through a bit?"

"Sounds great." said Angie.

Zach nodded.

At the restaurant, although they tried to talk about inconsequential things the conversation inevitably returned to Zach's experience. They agreed that the stimulation of the device by a particular frequency clearly caused Zach's visions to begin. If this was a different world or reality then the device was enabling Zach to enter it.

CJ was toying with her kofta, wondering how to phrase her question.

"You say you were part of some project to look at 'non-verbal communication' at a distance?" she asked.

"Yes." said Zach, with a mouthful of moussaka. "But this changes everything. If there's a whole other place, a community, then this is huge."

"How can we know for sure." began CJ. "That this woman you met was, you know, real? We need some sort of evidence."

"Yes, I want to try again, it seems as if I am aware when I'm in this state, so I should be able to direct myself when I'm there."

"You mean deliberately experience things?" asked Angie.

"I mean go there with a plan to check on stuff, try to find out details, talk to others that are there and see if I can get any proof that means something to us."

Zach finished the last of his beer.

"When we get back, I want to try again." he said.

Angie glanced at CJ, who looked from one to the other. "Okay." she said. "Let's do it."

62

Mason paced the old sailing ship's cabin while Bartholomew toyed with a gimballed ship's compass that sat on the desk.

"But what can they do?" asked Mason. "Gail is powerful in the Realm, she was able to overcome those occultists that attacked me."

"That is true." began Bartholomew. "But I talked to the hospital staff and the person that visited Gail sounds like the same one that followed you and Molly. I traced the tattoos he has on his neck and I think that indicates that he belongs to a dark magic group called the Order of the New Dawn or OND. They are an old and significant group whose history extends back more than two centuries and perhaps longer. They are adepts in ancient Egyptian ritual magic. We believe that this particular mythology, introduced by the Others to early Egyptian priests from the time of the pharaohs, has some rituals and techniques that are dangerous to us."

"But how? They're just crazies that love dressing up aren't they?" asked Mason.

"Crazies perhaps but their entire belief system was created, we think, by the Others and they have built into it aspects that can influence the Realm. The effects that Gail is feeling are almost certainly the result of something this group has done or are doing. In their mythology they probably regard Gail as some sort of creature of the astral plane that is working against them. They would feel compelled to try to destroy her, to prove their worth and advance to higher planes and achieve greater knowledge."

"Will they try something physical?" asked Mason. "I'm stuck half a world away, I can't do anything?"

"Of course, but it seems there is another, who may be like you." said Bartholomew. "He is a newcomer but seems to have your ability to move between consciousnesses with some ease. Perhaps he can be of some service."

"But what do we know about him? Can he be trusted?" said Mason. "Maybe I should come home?"

"No, stay for now, let us speak with this newcomer and see if he is able to help. You must be there to help Molly if she needs you."

Zach regained the physical world more calmly. CJ and Angie were sitting on the sofa, talking, relaxed enough not to even notice Zach was back with them until he spoke.

"Do you think it's safe to have a beer?" he asked as he rolled off the table and made for the fridge. "Anyone else?"

"I'm good." said Angie.

"I'll have one." said CJ. "So what happened?"

Zach explained that he had met a strange man this time, who wanted him to do something to help him, but in the physical world. He explained as best he could what he had been told.

"So this woman is in a coma, she's in some private hospital and some group of satanists mean to do something to her?" said Angie.

"That's what he said." said Zach. "She sounds a lot like the subjects from our research, so she's basically reliant on being kept alive with technology."

"Do you believe him?" said CJ.

"I don't know." began Zach. "But some of this stuff is starting to make a bit more sense. Will that filter you made mean I can't be tracked?"

"Yep." said CJ. "You're not thinking of going to see this woman?"

"I need to know what's really going on here and the way this guy tells it we may be the only thing standing between this helpless woman and ...something bad."

"Gotta admit I'm curious too." said CJ. "I need five minutes to grab some shit. I can drive you."

63

As the voice from the speaker read calmly through a checklist, Victor Sanchez was explaining to Molly the changes to the device from the first test.

"...and the space in the middle between the supercooling towers there." he pointed to an enclosed space large enough for two people in the centre of the machine, surrounded by brightly coloured orange, yellow and blue cables and pipes. "That is the focal point of the field. That is where the pathway should appear."

Molly didn't understand any of the description that Victor had tried to provide. To her the machine just looked like something from a Hollywood movie. What she assumed was water vapour was rising from the areas of the cooling towers and there was a greenish glow from some electronic devices that seemed to be connected around the base. She glanced around and there were now more than thirty people along with Molly and Victor huddled at one end of the chamber, behind a makeshift barrier of a rope tied loosely between two of the ventilation ducts.

"Pre-ignition checks complete." stated the voice from the speakers.

At that point a loud buzzer started sounding in short bursts. Three technicians that had been topping up the supercooling tanks and checking that all connections were secure now retreated to a corridor to one side of the chamber. The buzzer stopped. There was a rustling from the speakers then the voice of Rev. Daniels.

"Brothers and sisters, today is a truly wonderful day. Thanks to the diligence and dedication of you all we are finally ready to send our first pilgrims on their greatest ever journey."

At this a number of the people around Molly looked at each other and she could hear muffled whispers.

"Because of the work we still must complete, I have chosen a brother and a sister from amongst us to be the first to make this beautiful transition. They will show us the way and prove to our Lord that we are worthy and ready to join him in his paradise. One day soon we will all be able to follow them. Praise be to him."

Just before Rev. Daniels finished speaking, two people dressed in white robes emerged from the far end of the hall. They were escorted by two of the security guards who held cables and tubes to one side as the robed figures climbed into the centre of the machine. Molly thought the woman looked terrified, but the man had a serene expression and held the woman's hand tenderly, trying to comfort her. As the guards retreated a low hum began and the glow of green around the base of the machine began to pulse and seemed to circulate around the base. Molly could see Victor and Dawn staring intently at the machine and saw that where their hands touched, by their sides, they were intertwining their fingers.

The low hum was increasing in volume. Molly started to feel some pressure in her chest. This was alarming and she instinctively put a hand to her breastbone. She wanted to step back, further from the machine but there was nowhere to go in the crowded section.

"Phase 1 complete. Performance optimal." said the voice over the speakers.

Molly could feel the hairs all over her body seeming to prickle, she felt a pressure behind her eyes, like the beginnings of a migraine. She really wanted to get out of the room and looked around to find a way. All around her the group was transfixed on the device, which was now starting to glow orange in the middle section where the two robed figures stood.

"Ready for transition." said the voice from the speakers "three, two, one...ascend!"

Molly watched in disbelief as the centre of the device seemed to dissolve before her eyes. Where there had been a cocoon of wires and tubes winding around two robed figures there was now only a shimmering blackness. The shape was not circular but oval and the edges were indistinct. There was no colour to it, just a total absence. A deep black that seemed to make the whole room less bright. As Molly watched she thought she noticed the oval getting slightly larger, but she couldn't be sure. Her headache was worsening and she was starting to see flashes of light in her peripheral vision. She closed her eyes and rubbed them gently.

When she opened them the oval had definitely got bigger. The green lights around the base of the machine were whirling around like some demented disco light show.

"Containment failure, zone 4, initiating emergency shutdown!" came over the speakers.

There was a loud bang and then total silence. After a couple of seconds, there was a hissing noise from the vents of the supercooling towers.

Everyone was looking at the centre of the machine. The black shape had gone. The two robed figures had also gone. The other side of the room was now visible through the device. Everyone near Molly was looking around or talking about what they had just seen. Victor and Dawn were in conversation too. All physical effects seemed to have gone, no chest pain, no pressure behind the eyes or headache. Molly tried to process what she had seen but couldn't. She needed to tell Mason but she also wanted to get out. She liked Victor and Dawn but this place was crazy. Her thoughts kept coming back to the two figures. Either that was the best magic trick she'd ever seen or those two young people had just vanished. But where had they gone, what could possibly have done that....was it just some sort of illusion? Molly was actually starting to feel panic rising when she felt a touch on her arm, it was Victor.

"Dawn and I are just going for a drink, would you like to join us?" said Victor, smiling but with a serious look in his eyes.

Molly nodded and the three of them picked their way out of the still murmuring crowd and made their way towards the canteen. Molly couldn't help herself and looked back at the device which was still quietly hissing before they turned a corner and it was lost from view.

64

As Zach looked down at Gail Hartston, he knew he had to help her. He'd wondered for the last few weeks what he'd got himself into but seeing Gail and how helpless she looked settled his doubts. His work had always been interesting, and he'd done some strange things without giving much thought to the bigger picture. In these past few days, he'd been shot at, had electronics put in his head without his consent, evaded one of the most sophisticated surveillance states on the planet and been introduced to an entire other world. He thought he understood that life or society as we know it was under some sort of threat and that this woman was important in protecting it.

"How are we going to move her?" asked Zach. "She can't fit in the Land Rover like this."

"We'll need a van or minibus, they must have hire places round here." said CJ opening her phone.

"She looks like she's just asleep." said Angie.

"Yeah." replied Zach. "But a sleep that's lasted five years so far and she's never waking up from."

He glanced at Angie whose eyes betrayed sadness as she looked back at Gail.

"There's a hire place about twenty minutes drive from here." announced CJ.

"Okay, I'll come and drive it." said Zach. "Angie, can you stay and get the paperwork started?"

"Sure." said Angie.

Two hours later, Gail Hartston was laying on a camp bed in the rear of a van heading towards the Suffolk coast. Bartholomew had instructed Zach to use a false name and contact details when registering with the hospital in case the OND tried to follow them. CJ had a surprisingly comprehensive collection of fake IDs from which they chose one. CJ and Angie were still surprised that Zach was able to give them such complete directions. Zach surprised himself with the clarity that he recalled everything from his conversations in the Realm. He could only assume that the implant was boosting his recall as well as providing him with the means to access the Realm in the first place. He wondered, as he followed CJ through the Anglian countryside driving CJ's Land Rover, whether his former employers had any idea of the effectiveness of these chips. He presumed he had been a guinea pig but if they hadn't used any others, they might still not realise the breakthrough they had made. He also wondered just how much, if anything, they knew about the Realm. Were they aware of the struggle going on and the risks to humanity if it failed. He thought about trying to contact Meek but he couldn't think of a way to get through to him that wouldn't put him at risk. He wanted to tell more people about this.

As the convoy of two passed through small Suffolk towns he saw people going about their daily lives oblivious to the dangers. Unaware that an apparent alien entity meant them harm. Meant to drive them to extinction or annihilation in order to use this planet for themselves. Zach had an almost overwhelming urge to call a news organisation or just stop people in the street and try to shake them out of their ignorance. But he immediately realised that nobody would believe a thing he said. He started to feel anxious, unsure if this bunch of satanist nutters could follow them. Wondering if even this new location would be safe for the defenceless woman on the camp bed.

65

There was a small brown spider making its way determinedly across the rough-hewn ceiling in Molly's room. She lay on her cot watching as it negotiated the inverted mountain range. She had no idea where it was going but it was determined to get there. Molly felt like that herself at that moment. After witnessing what she had in the chamber, with two human beings vanishing before her eyes, she'd been going over what she was doing and why she was there.

She was suddenly scared. Those people had to be dead, there seemed no other explanation. Vaporised by some giant machine built by what appeared to be a religious nutcase. As Molly rolled onto her side and drew her knees up into a loose foetal position she could feel the hidden cellphone. She had to tell Mason. She hoped he or Bartholomew would know what to do. She wondered if she could get away by climbing down the side of the hill from the ventilation shaft. It had looked steep and treacherous. She just wanted to be home. Getting involved in this had seemed like fun at the start.

A bit of a mystery, some puzzles to solve and she had to admit she enjoyed Mason's company. It all started to get a bit too real when they were being followed by the creepy man with the tattoos. Now she was half a world away buried in a mountain with people whose motives became darker the more she learned about them.

Molly looked at her watch, it was nearly midnight. She rolled herself into a sitting position and smoothed back her hair. She had to get a message out to Mason. She sipped some water from a plastic cup and then splashed the rest on her face to wake herself up. As she opened her door and looked both ways she was thinking that there was probably no good reason for her to be out of her room at this time. So, she needed to make sure she didn't run into any of the guards that patrolled casually through the night.

The corridors were silent as she made her way carefully and slowly to the base of the ventilation shaft she had used before. It was still just held on by one clip so she lifted it quickly and slipped inside, carefully letting it back into place behind her. The climb seemed easier this time, she had a better idea of where the hand and footholds were. Pulling herself into the cave with the lumbering fan she squeezed past the bent wire mesh and timing her lunge, slipped between the fan blades and on to the night sky beyond.

She sent the message during the brief moments when she registered a single bar on her signal strength but then sat and looked at the starry vista. She was no astronomer but knew enough to appreciate that looking into the heavens is really looking into the past. The vastness of the cosmos means even the light from the very nearest stars takes a significant amount of time to reach us. The distances are beyond our human imagination, even for the professionals. Most often when she looked up at a night sky Molly just saw the beauty of the patterns of pinpricks on the velvet backdrop. Tonight she pondered on what might exist beyond our tiny corner of it all. Then images of the black void in the device intruded and she shuddered. A chill mountain breeze brushed round her as she ducked back into the cave and negotiated the fan blades.

By the time she was near the bottom of the shaft she felt warm again. The temperature in the base was remarkably constant. She listened and looked both ways before carefully slipping out into the corridor and letting the grill tip back into place. Just as she stood up to set off back to her room she felt a pinprick in her neck and a strong, wiry arm encircle her.

66

Grobus was relieved that the man, Plater, had flown off somewhere and that he no longer needed to watch his house. At least his studies were possible again. He still felt he was being followed when exploring the astral plane but could never see who was doing it. He recorded all this in his diary but had not mentioned it to Oculus or any of the Council. They were busy preparing a new ritual with the express objective of damaging this woman creature. The lock of hair Grobus had obtained would help in this.

At precisely 10 p.m. the heavy double doors to the sanctum swung inwards and the Council members filed in. The Seven arranged themselves around the engraved circles in the stone floor. In the flickering candlelight their hooded shadows swayed on the heavy velvet drapery that covered the walls. Oculus began the ceremony by sealing the circles within which the Council members stood. He chanted incantations and alternately held open his arms with his head tilted upwards or took his ritual dagger and pointed to the cardinal points or drew symbols of power in the air in front of him.

Grobus was fascinated as he had read some of the wording for this ritual but had never seen it or been a part of it. He was both excited and a little afraid. They were calling on powerful forces for assistance in their work and this held dangers for all involved. Time is a quicksilver concept when engaged in magical work, and Grobus had no idea how much had passed. At this point the preliminaries had been completed and Oculus and three others of the Council were now working together. In the centre, between them, was a small table draped with a dark cloth. On the table was a scrying globe or crystal ball and a crucible that Grobus knew contained the lock of hair he had obtained from the woman creature's earthly form. Having been chanting separate incantations the four adepts now began chanting in unison and Grobus knew that the ritual was reaching its climax. He began softly reciting his protection spells and preparing to transition to the astral plane where their true work would begin.

With a strong smell of the incense that had filled the sanctum, Grobus found himself on the astral plane, with the four members of the Council and Leona, a young student like himself. Oculus took the lead and began moving towards a glow in the distance. The ground beneath them seemed to be earth but hardly felt anything to the touch. Each member was still in their ceremonial robes, and they flowed and billowed as the party hurried on. As Grobus looked the glow seemed to distill into the lights of a town or city in the distance. As they got closer, they saw figures moving about but nobody seemed to pay them any attention. Powerful protection enchants had been created to hide their forms from the watchers who might try to prevent their work. They reached the very outskirts of the city, which now seemed to be full of life. They started to walk in single file, still following Oculus who seemed to know where he needed to reach.

Gail Hartston was once more passing time at the cafe on the square. She was thinking about the new young man that had somehow managed to suddenly discover an ability to switch between the physical world and the Realm with even more ease and skill than Mason. She liked him and thought she recognised a seriousness of purpose in him to compliment his obvious excitement at his new found skill. She needed to speak to Bartholomew or Mason as well to learn whether Molly was safe and if she had discovered the purpose of the device. Her thoughts were suddenly halted as she noticed five men and a woman approaching her. They were dressed strangely and she immediately recognised them as occultists. As they got closer they fanned out into a rough semi-circle still about ten yards from where she sat.

This was not the first time she had seen these people, she remembered them as the group that had tried to capture Mason. She stood up and caused the table she had been seated at to disappear. To the OND members she appeared to suddenly exude a glowing aura. Grobus would later record it as purple with orange symbols but he would be unable to remember the exact form of the symbols.

Oculus and the three other Council members stepped

forward and closed the space to Gail. Oculus was slightly in front and reaching into his robe drew a shining broad bladed sword, extending his arm forwards, pointing it straight at Gail's heart.

"In the name of the gods I banish you from this place." said Oculus.

Gail looked quizzically at him.

"I command you in the name of the gods to leave this realm and not return for a thousand years." said Oculus in a louder voice.

By this time a small crowd was gathering in the square to watch this strange scene play out. Grobus heard the other Council members begin chanting an unfamiliar incantation. As they did so he could make out a shadowy form taking shape just in front of them and to one side of Oculus. As they continued the shape became that of a large dog whose shoulders reached as high as Oculus' chest. Powerful legs rippled, a stubby tail stood rigidly upright and heavy-lidded eyes sat behind a squared snout and a snarling set of teeth.

Murmurings in the assembled crowd became louder and some looked around to see if anyone might help the woman. None of the bystanders seemed to want to get involved.

"I am going nowhere." said Gail and Grobus noticed the aura surrounding her got brighter.

"So be it." spat Oculus. "Rip ex gutture suo!"

On hearing the Latin command to rip her throat out the beast leapt towards Gail, eyes wide and long leathery tongue flapping to one side of its open jaws. In a smooth movement Gail pulled her right leg back and behind her, bending her left leg and crouching slightly into what looked like a martial arts stance. At the same time, she lifted her left arm with her palm flat and facing the on-rushing dog. Grobus remembered seeing nothing but hearing a sound like a thunderclap. Instantly the dog exploded into a million tiny fragments which floated slowly to the ground.

For a moment Oculus seemed confused, then his wits returned and he held his left hand aloft. Evidently, it was a signal and the other Council members all began chanting in unison. The words meant nothing to Gail or even Grobus for that matter. As the chanting reached the third repetition Oculus lunged forwards. Gail moved to one side and thrust her hand forwards as before but this time there was no sound. Oculus' lunge felt only slight resistance from Gails garments and he saw the sword penetrate her body. There was a look of surprise on her face as she sank to her knees and pitched forwards onto the cobbles.

At this moment a group of around ten figures dressed in various military uniforms barged through the watching crowd. Without a word the uniformed men rushed the occultists who scattered immediately. Oculus had dropped his sword and was running as fast as he could, pursued by the uniformed soldiers. One of the soldiers knelt beside Gail and managed to turn her over. The wound was not deep but was close to the heart. He quickly applied pressure to stop the bleeding.

The incessant beeping interrupted a conversation about whether cats or dogs made the best companions. Angie was a cat person while Zach and CJ were in the canine camp. Zach noticed the beeping first.

"Might be an issue with the software, let me check." he said, leaving the other two still arguing. He made his way into a back room where Gail Hartston now lay. On a table next to the single bed a laptop was plugged in and cables led to a couple of plastic boxes that contained the mix of medicines that Gail needed to maintain her vital organs and to provide nutrients on a regular cycle.

As Zach checked the alarm, he looked worried. Gail's vital signs were out of the normal range but as he checked all the drug delivery systems, the nutrient supply and the medical sensors he could not see any reason for it. He hoped it had been something he had done in the cobbled together set of programs he had fashioned to replace the hospital systems. The more he looked the more everything appeared normal. As he cycled through log files and ran various tests, he also noticed that the vital signs were coming back into line. He wasn't a doctor so he had no idea what had just happened, but he added more alarms into his code and ensured they would alert to his, CJ's and Angie's phone if something similar happened again.

67

News media online, on television, social media and print newspapers, not to mention the blogosphere were alight with not one but two scandals. One involved the Democratic nominee for the Presidency, Ronald Carlson. Photographs had been sent anonymously to a notorious right-wing blogger called CaptainUSA. They seemed to show Senator Carlson, a happily married man, enjoying the company of a barely clothed young woman on a hotel balcony. Along with the pictures was a short summary of the Senator's movements around that time, suggesting whoever sent the pictures had been tailing the Presidential hopeful.

It took less than four hours for the mainstream outlets to pounce on the story. As soon as they cross-checked the itinerary and found it matched and the photographs were checked by ex-NASA photo reconnaissance experts the story went global. The hunt began for the young woman in the photographs. Senator Carlson had to cancel three engagements to fight the growing fires lapping at his campaign.

Within twelve hours of this revelation another emerged. While Rev. Daniels was on the road in his armoured limousine between rallies in Texas and Oklahoma, two of his three mobile phones lit up with a string of texts, emails and missed calls. As the Rev. read through some of the texts he put down his chicken taco, licked the salsa from his thumb and concentrated on the worrying details.

It seemed that documents had been found that implicated Rev. Daniels in not one but two unsolved disappearances of members of the CoR. Not only that, but they also laid out in great detail, with a thorough timeline, financial records and surveillance photographs a plot for the Republican nominee to blackmail the former Texas Senator Rupert Vance. It described how Rev. Daniels had manipulated the former Senator after the Senator's son, Darrell Vance, had become a Church member. The claim was that members of the Church, rather than help Darrell with his existing drug habit, had actively facilitated it. There was surveillance footage showing Church members buying drugs from a notorious Florida dealer. Those same church members were later seen with Darrell Vance on several occasions indulging in the use of controlled substances. Later, it was claimed, Rev. Daniels approached Rupert Vance with evidence of his son's heavy drug use. Rupert Vance was a hardliner against drugs, advocating a one-strike-and-you're-out policy with long prison terms. It was claimed Rev. Daniels offered to take care of Darrell, including discreet addiction treatment at a Church facility, in return for the Senator stepping down and supporting Rev. Daniels as his replacement.

Rev. Daniels discarded the phone onto the seat next to him and took up the third phone.

"Yeah." said Wallace Clayton.

"You seen the news?" asked Rev. Daniels, pushing pieces of taco from between his teeth with his tongue. "Where'd they get this shit? You said you had that motherfucker Gatts' files and there were no loose ends."

"I got the files from his office, maybe he had copies."

"'Maybe he had copies' !? Damn right he had copies. Get ahold of Clem see if you can't put a lid on this thing."

Clement William Reaver III was a notorious attorney recognisable by his signature western dress and his gentle southern accent. Also known for his representation of certain business interests in Las Vegas and Atlantic city. Discretion and efficiency were the hallmarks of Clem Reaver and Rev. Daniels now needed him to start earning his $1 million annual retainer.

"Okay." said Clayton.

Rev. Daniels cut off the call then shoved a thick finger into his mouth to try and reach a particularly stubborn piece of chicken stuck between some back teeth. Almost at the same time, he swiped the remains of his boxed taco off the foldout table spraying salsa and chicken across the fine leather upholstery of the Maybach. Looking down he noticed a large patch of salsa was soaking into his crisp cream trousers.

"Shit." he snarled through grinding teeth.

"The timing could have been better." said Faith Cantrell.

"From what I'm hearing voters are viewing both candidates being hit with scandals as just dirty tricks by both sides and hardly paying either any attention." said James Carver, switching the phone to his other ear while he retrieved the toast from the toaster.

"Clearly Daniels had dirt on Carlson all along and was just waiting for the right moment."

"Doesn't help us though. Do we have anything else? Something tangible? Witnesses? People we can put up on the talk shows?" said Carver.

"No." said Cantrell.

"What if the mud won't stick?" asked Carver.

"Plan B." replied Cantrell.

"Which is?"

"I have no idea. Leave it with me."

Carver sipped his coffee and surveyed the Surrey countryside through his kitchen window. Even without the pressing need to derail the CoR and whatever it was doing in the old military base he couldn't imagine the most powerful nation on earth with Rev. Daniels as its Commander-in-Chief.

68

"But I thought you were safe?" said Mason.

"Zach and his friends have relocated Gail to my house in Aldeburgh, she'll be quite safe there. You definitely weren't followed?" said Bartholomew glancing at Zach, who was holding on tightly to a candleholder on the wall of the cabin as the old ship rolled gently.

"Definitely not." said Zach. He'd only just met Mason but he could tell there was more than friendly interest in Gail's safety.

"Raymond." said Gail, who was sitting in the Captain's chair but not looking fully recovered. "My worry is that this man was able to reach me at all, in the square. I felt weak. It took all I had to remove the hound."

"There may be something." said Bartholomew pausing, deep in thought.

"They were the same people that attacked me?" said Mason.

"Yes." said Gail. "An occult group, ancient according to Raymond. We had little trouble with them before. We need to know what is different."

"It could be." began Bartholomew. "That they did something when they visited your body in the private hospital."

"Did what?" asked Mason.

"I'm not sure." said Bartholomew. "Perhaps they took something personal of yours, a lock of hair or nails, something from your body."

"That's creepy." said Zach. "What for?"

"These people are believers in ritual magic. Through rituals they can gain power and exert power over other entities they encounter on the astral plane. I know of numerous rituals which could make use of hair or blood from the target. It's the only thing I can think of that would have caused Gail to be vulnerable."

Bartholomew looked from Gail to Mason to Zach, nobody spoke.

"Can't we shut this lot down in the real world?" asked Zach.

"Perhaps." said Bartholomew. "Although we've never seen the need before. They were just a bit of an amusing sideshow."

"Not so amusing now." said Mason. "Zach, I wanted to say how grateful I am that you've been able to help Gail. I've felt rather useless doing nothing over here."

"No problem, this is all a bit new to me still and I've got to say a bit weird. I mean I'm not like you guys, I have this thing in my head or else I wouldn't be here."

"From what Raymond has told us you're just like us. I'm not sure any of us would have chosen to be here." said Mason, then looked across at Gail. "Gail, I didn't mean…"

"You're absolutely right." said Gail. "None of you

really chose to be here, Raymond got lost in his younger years and came here in a similar way to those other occultists, you Mason fell into our world totally by chance and Zach, I'm afraid you were rather pushed. But we're all here now and we need to focus on how we're going to stop the Others from using that machine. Mason, or Raymond, have you heard from Molly?"

"It looks like they are almost ready with the device." said Mason. "Molly's last text said they had tested an updated version and that two of the CoR members had disappeared from the centre of the machine. Some void opened and when the machine was shut off the two people were gone. That was yesterday. I think we need to get Molly out of there. That machine sounds dangerous, they've already had one accident and it had to be shut down as an emergency this time too. With the energy that's involved we need to get Molly out of there and far away."

69

As Molly's vision slowly cleared, she instinctively went to rub her eyes. The cable ties around her wrists and the rail of the gurney she was laying on stopped her. At first, she didn't register what it meant and jerked her arm causing the rail to rattle and the ties to pinch the skin of her wrist. She was now completely awake and lifted her head and looked around. She seemed to be in some sort of storeroom. There were boxes and wooden crates piled high on two sides of a large room. Two bare bulbs were the only light and as she looked over to her left, she shuddered. Two men in military camouflage were tied to chairs and didn't seem to be conscious. There was a dark stain on the floor under one of the chairs.

"Hey!" said Molly in her best stage whisper voice. "Hey!" But neither man moved.

Molly turned her head and noted a single door in the far wall. There was a large metal table on her right side that had what seemed to be a lot of tools on it. She could make out saws, several knives, pliers and some boxes with electrical wires. She lay down again as she was starting to feel dizzy. The drugs were not completely out of her system and her eyes slowly closed.

The banging of the door brought Molly awake again. As she opened her eyes this time, she immediately saw a wiry man with round glasses looking down at her. She stiffened and pulled both her arms, causing the gurney rails to rattle loudly.

"What are you doing? Why am I tied up? Who are you? What's going on?" she screamed, very scared and trying hard not to let the tearful emotions she was feeling spill out.

"Miss…James is it?" asked Wallace Clayton, reaching down and carefully lifting some hair from Molly's face and arranging it to the correct side of her forehead. "I think you have something you want to tell me."

"What? Who are you? Why am I tied up?"

"Miss James, we could make this a whole lot quicker and easier if you'd just tell me who you really are and who you're working for."

Molly said nothing but her mind was desperately searching for something to say that would sound convincing, would not give her away and would give her time to think her situation through. As she was thinking she suddenly realised she could still feel the concealed phone. This was good, it meant that the only thing this man knew about her was she'd been sneaking around at night.

"I would seriously recommend you helping me out." said Clayton, turning away from the gurney and walking to the table "Although I detest inflicting pain, they do say that needs must when the devil drives."

Clayton had selected a multitool shaped like a thick pen. The attachment he fitted looked like a needle and was about 5 cm long.

"I don't understand." began Molly. "I don't work for anyone, I was on holiday with my husband and he left me, I'm here to help."

"I think we both know that isn't true." said Clayton eyeing the needle point suggestively "You may have fooled these local idiots, but I'm afraid we cannot have anyone interfering with the Lord's work."

Molly felt a firm hand clasp round her left index finger and seconds later felt a sudden stab of pain unlike anything she could remember. She screamed without even realising and as Clayton moved the needle beneath her fingernail, she soon passed out.

Braberson settled into the modern sofa in the corner of the Home Secretary's office. James Carver was on one of the telephones on his desk and had motioned Braberson to sit.

"Sorry about that Edwin." said Carver as he perched on the edge of the seat, opposite Braberson, elbows on his knees. "You have details of the surveillance of the book seller?"

"Raymond Bartholomew, yes." began Braberson. "Aside from his shop in Walberswick in Suffolk he has two other properties, a small flat in Battersea and a cottage in Aldeburgh, which is also in Suffolk. Through Sentinel and other sources we know that Bartholomew has been in contact with some others that seem to have moved the woman Hartston, from the private hospital to Bartholomew's cottage."

"Do we know who these 'others' are?" said Carver.

"Details are as yet unconfirmed, there are no electronic fingerprints for these people that we can discern. They are either Luddites, which seems unlikely or have very good opsec. One of them, the male, could even be Zachary Hamilton."

"Your guy?"

"Yes, although we have no useful visuals on him, he clearly knows our technology. The other two are not on our facial recognition databases and do not appear to use social media, which is of course odd, even suspicious nowadays."

"You think they may be hostiles?" asked Carver.

"No, but certainly very conscious of their digital footprint. We think it more likely they are low level hacktivists of some sort or simply highly tech savvy and have a desire for privacy."

"How are they communicating with Bartholomew?"

"We're not sure, sir." began Braberson. "There is an unregistered mobile that is the likely means. We don't think they have met in person so far."

"Your man, Hamilton is it? He has one of your chips implanted? Can that be used to monitor him in any way?"

"It seems he has developed a method of shielding from our signals or jamming perhaps. We cannot even detect his movements currently." admitted Braberson.

"Next steps?" asked Carver.

"I plan to visit them myself." said Braberson. "If it is Hamilton he'll be worried about repercussions, we can use that to get him onside. As for the two women we can positively ID them and verify they pose no threat."

"When?"

"Heading there immediately."

Carver stood and Braberson took his cue to leave.

"An update as soon as you have one please." said Carver to the retreating Braberson.

Dawn sat alone at the table, in the emptying cafeteria at Redemption, turning her grandmother's ring round her finger. Victor had eaten with her but needed to check on some details of a report he was writing. Oddly, Molly had been absent from dinner. Dawn liked Molly. She seemed happy and cheerful all the time. So many here at Redemption were very serious and shy. Some even appeared worried or frightened at being there.

She kept returning to what Molly had said about her mother and how she'd done her best. In those weeks and months after her father left it had been hard. Not just because there was less money coming in but also, Dawn now understood, because both her and her mother were grieving and angry in their own ways. As the last few people walked past her table, Dawn remembered conversations she'd had with her mother. What had seemed like efforts to control her life, she now recognised as her mother trying to stop her from going off the rails. Trying to draw her back to the important things in her young life, like school and thinking of her future. She guessed all parents must do that.

Molly said that she'd resisted her parents' attempts to get her to go to medical school and was always at loggerheads with her mother over boyfriends. That had struck a chord with Dawn. But Molly said she'd realised, after she'd gone to college, that her parents had only wanted the best for her. She told Dawn that she joked with college friends about how right her mother had been about a couple of her boyfriends too.

Dawn wondered what her mother was doing, at that moment she really wanted to speak to her. She wanted to listen and maybe say sorry. Her emotions were very confused. Whatever her life was to become she didn't think the CoR was the answer and she wondered how she could find a way to go home. She wanted some help and although Victor had been so kind to her she felt she needed to go to her mother. Before that she wanted to talk to Molly again. Molly seemed to be the first person that understood. Dawn resolved to go to Molly's room and see if she was there and would talk more with her.

70

Once again, the High Order convened. They believed they had successfully hurt or killed the woman creature but they now knew she still lived. Oculus saw this as a personal failure and vowed to conjure the mighty Aziel and with his help, finally remove the woman creature to enable their great work to proceed unopposed. At midnight the seven members of the High Order filed silently into the sanctum through the great oak doors, which closed behind them with a noise that echoed in the flickering light.

Only two other people were present, Grobus and the tall, willowy Leona. Oculus began to recite the summoning, in quiet but assertive tones, breaking only to cast powders into the brazier on the altar before him. Hissing and crackling sounds accompanied coloured flares of light and sparks. The ceremony continued, with occasional input from members of the High Order as they either joined Oculus in demanding the presence of Aziel or chanted protection spells. After almost two hours the ritual now approached its climax.

Oculus had been in what seemed a sort of trance for half an hour or more. Reciting from memory the ever more threatening demands that Aziel appear to the assembled company. Grobus could feel the hairs on his neck prickling as if in some powerful electric field. He was scared.

Oculus was now shouting his words and stood, arms outstretched near the North point of the circle. He seemed to focus his attention on a smaller triangular design also etched in the black floor, some eight feet outside the circle. This was where he intended to conjure Aziel and hold him, in magical bonds, while they questioned him about the woman creature.

As Oculus exhorted Aziel in thunderous tones to attend or be made to suffer, he gave a sign to the other members of the High Order and as one they began chanting in an ancient tongue. These words had special power and as the High Order chanted Grobus felt changes within himself. He began to feel a lightness and his vision seemed to sharpen, even in the gloom of the chamber. In the triangle beyond the circle, he thought he saw a shape. It was the shape of a huge dog-like creature, standing on its hind legs. As he looked upwards, he could just make out an angular head, with long snout and oversized canine teeth. Above the chanting of the High Order, he could hear the terrible snarling and whining of the creature. It was partly anger and partly pain, as the magical bonds strained to hold this creature from another world.

Oculus made several choreographed movements with his ceremonial dagger before plunging it into a vessel on the table in front of him. At that instant, the creature tipped its head back and released a terrible howl.

Grobus would recall that this was the point where he lost his hearing. It would be six hours before he was able to hear speech again. As was written in the ritual, he and the girl knelt and cast their eyes down, so as not to behold the full form of Aziel. Oculus then asked for the information he needed. The High Order chanted ancient words of defence and protection as the questioning proceeded. They did not dare behold the form of Aziel either. They held each other's gaze to increase the power of their protective chants.

For what seemed an age Grobus knelt, muttering his own feeble spells of protection. Too scared to look up or around. From the corner of his downcast eye, he suddenly saw the creature Aziel rise up and then cross the small gap between the conjuration triangle and the protected circle where Oculus stood. Oculus, wide-eyed in terror, seemed to stiffen then collapse to the ground like a slow-motion silent movie.

US politics, at the highest levels, can resemble a marathon, with its vast geographical footprint and relentless schedule of appearances and rallies. Some commentators would also say it bears similarities to the early days of cage fighting, before there became a need to introduce rules. To even contemplate joining this periodic slugfest requires not only an unshakable self-belief but the skin of a rhinoceros. A close cadre of technical and emotional supporters who need comparable levels of self-assurance and energy.

As Rev. Daniels prepared for his ninth rally in five days across seven states, he scrolled through his messages assessing the damage the recent revelations had brought. Clayton had people in Florida trying to paper over the cracks that the journalist, Gatts had uncovered but it could all be too late. The Democrat-leaning news media were having a field day painting Daniels as a fanatic, a hypocrite, even a gangster. In his defence the right-wing media, led as ever by Fox News, were describing an alternate reality with a succession of small-town preachers, housewives and mid-western businessmen all extolling the virtues of taking the US back to a more Christian way of living. They portrayed the smearing of Daniels as a left-wing conspiracy, born of a desire by the deep state to maintain the status quo. There was more than a hint of irony as the conspiracy theories hit full swing with groups in the Q Anon mould even floating ideas that the government had been usurped by lizard people that had come to earth millenia ago and remained hidden. Controlling humanity through small elites like the Bilderberg Group and even the Illuminati.

Rev. Daniels sipped from the whiskey glass and tapped his phone; the call was answered quickly.

"Yeah." said Clayton.

"What about the girl?" said Daniels.

"Nothin' yet." said Clayton. "She's got some balls."

"...and Reaver?"

"He says we can deal with most all the shit. Got friends on the TV and folks are just thinkin' it's mud slinging. He says there could be favours when it's all over though..."

"Just be sure he understands that if I don't get in it'll be the opposite of favours." Daniels sank the rest of his whiskey and closed the call with a stab from his huge thumb.

When Oculus regained consciousness, he felt a renewed purpose. Members of the Order had been concerned for his well-being after the sudden end to the ritual, but Oculus was able to reassure them that all was well, and he had never felt better. Grobus actually thought Oculus appeared younger. Despite many questions about what happened Oculus would not go into detail about what caused him to pass out.

When he left the sanctum, Oculus walked for hours in the London night. He felt an energy that he had not known he possessed. His vision seemed sharper; his hearing more acute. At one point he stopped suddenly to listen to the distant call of an owl.

Even when he had reached his house, he felt no need of sleep. Instead, he went straight to his study and began poring over old occult texts. It was beginning to get light when he finally closed the heavy bound book on his desk. He crossed to a cupboard door in one corner and inside the cupboard, he quickly turned the combination lock of his safe left and right before pulling open the door. He carefully drew out a monogrammed leather pouch. He laid the pouch on his desk and undid the brass buckles. Lifting the flap, he revealed the Smith and Wesson Model 10 revolver. The old service revolver had been his grandfather's and seen action in World War 2. It was in museum condition, cleaned and oiled regularly until his father's death twenty years ago when it had been passed to him.

Without really wondering how, he confidently turned

the weapon over in his hand. He drew back the hammer and opened the revolving cylinder. It was empty. Returning to the safe he took out a box of .38 calibre bullets and filled all six chambers with practiced ease before spinning the cylinder and snapping the gun closed with a flick of his wrist. It felt good in his hand, it had a reassuring weight. Although he had never fired a handgun in his life, he felt sure that he could do what needed to be done.

Angie was cooking a giant pot of chili, CJ was busy on her laptop replying to a new potential client and Zach was running a final checkout of updated software to control Gail's medicine supply and vital signs monitoring devices. The sun was shining on the small village of Aldeburgh and the local fish and chip shop had a queue of hopefuls running twenty yards down the pavement outside. From Bartholomew's cottage, it was possible to see the sea but only from one of the upstairs bedrooms and then only by standing on tiptoes in one corner of the room. The stony beach was still only thirty yards away across a cobbled lane.

Gail had been peaceful for two days now and the alarms had remained silent. Zach hadn't managed to tell what the problem had been, but he suspected that it had been caused by the attack on Gail in the Realm by the OND. Somehow, their actions in the Realm were having a real effect on Gail's physical body. With what little Zach knew of the Realm, he didn't understand how this could happen and wanted to talk more to Bartholomew in case there were steps they could take to protect Gail further. It was a little confusing for Zach as he had been told almost as soon as he got to the Realm that Gail was very powerful and appeared almost invulnerable. He had been told that people like Gail, as she wasn't the only one by any means, were known as The Present. He took this to mean that they were always 'present' in the Realm. Unlike he and people like Mason or Bartholomew who moved between the Realm and the physical world Gail was only really 'present' in the Realm. He assumed these were also unfortunate people that were in some sort of coma or distorted form of consciousness. Perhaps some with multiple personalities or other serious mental conditions that would cause them to function poorly in the physical world but which enabled some of them to exist and even flourish in the Realm.

The knock on the front door caused CJ to immediately stop typing an email. She slid the laptop off her knees and crossed to the small window looking out onto the street. The lace curtains masked her from the outside and she could see three men at the front door. Zach appeared and asked who it was.

"Three guys." said CJ. "Not dressed for a day on the beach,"

"Shit." muttered Zach.

"Who's that?" asked Angie from the doorway.

"I'll get it." said CJ and walked slowly to the front door and undid the latch.

"Good afternoon, may I speak to Zachary Hamilton please ?" asked Braberson.

Zach immediately recognised the voice. How did they find me, he thought. No point trying to run, there'll be people at the back. Zach walked across until he was beside CJ. Braberson smiled.

"Hello Zach." he said. "May we come in?"

71

The black Range Rover pulled smoothly away from the secluded cottage. Braberson was already on his phone in the backseat.

"I'll be right outside, sir." said the young man in the dark suit to Zach as he opened the front door and stepped out. Zach couldn't recall ever being addressed as 'sir' before. For a moment he just stared after the man.

"Ohh-kaaay." said Angie. "I wasn't expecting that."

"Practical." said CJ. "These people tend to be practical."

The deal that Braberson had laid out was simple. Either the three of them agreed to sign the Official Secrets Act (turned out only Angie was not already a signatory) and to involve his department in their future actions or they would likely spend a good portion of their lives in a government facility that was not to be found on Google Maps. One of the security services men, Patterson, had remained behind to provide some protection.

"This is all getting a bit too real." said Zach. "I'm going to check on Gail."

Angie and CJ sat in silence for a few moments.

"I'm going to make some coffee." said CJ, Angie just nodded silently, still processing their discussion with Braberson. She hadn't realised exactly how secret Zach's work had been. She also got the impression that Braberson's department wasn't particularly mainstream.

CJ assembled the components of a fresh pot of coffee. The boiling kettle clicked off and CJ poured the water over the grounds. As she replaced the kettle she remembered the canister of mace that was in her rucksack pocket. She'd bought it years ago, just in case. She hoped it would still fire if needed.

Angie glanced up as Zach came back in.

"All good." he said.

CJ put the tray of coffees on the table between them.

"Do you think we should tell Raymond about our new deal?" asked Angie.

Zach pulled out his burner phone and dialed Raymond's number.

Bartholomew was relieved in many ways that this Braberson had located Gail and Zach. He was sure that they would need real world protection as the attentions of the OND were becoming more violent. He wasn't sure what this meant for the continued work that he and Gail needed to do in the Realm, but it could solve the problem of how to alert society at large about the threats they faced. He put the phone down on the small table in the back room of his shop and relaxed back into his armchair. After the latest attack it seemed that Gail would need protection in the Realm as well as the real world. She was the most powerful person he had seen or heard of in the Realm but her inability to fight off the occultists in their last attack worried him. He got up and searched a pile of books tucked right in the corner of the small room. He drew out two of them, both with luxurious leather binding. Both had fine paper pages, covered in small print and occasional full-page diagrams. Somehow Gail had been attacked using ancient magic so perhaps, despite Bartholomew's distrust of its methods and knowledge of its likely origins, as part of the entity's way of perverting human society, it might also hold the secret of a way to protect her.

After two hours and two pots of tea, Bartholomew had made nearly three pages of notes. He thought he had found the ritual the OND had used to gain the power to attack Gail. Now he needed to understand how to counter it. As he pinched the bridge of his nose and squinted at the clock on the mantlepiece he thought he heard a car revving up outside. Unusual for people to be out and about around here at this hour, he thought, but resumed his research.

Oculus consulted his notes from the automatic writing session following the Third Eye ritual. The small antiquarian bookshop opposite was definitely one of the addresses he had seen while looking through the eyes of Mason Plater. They had lost track of the woman creature, so they needed to go back and check other possibilities. Oculus got out of the car. He closed the heavy door quietly, conscious of the virtual silence around him. A gentle breeze rustled some trees nearby and there was a distant quiet noise of traffic on the main road. He looked around and could see no-one. The streetlighting was not bright and many deep shadows formed pools along the road. He crossed and looked in the window of Bartholomew's shop. It was dark within, what little light there was only helped to show the few books in the window. Looking around again Oculus searched for a way to the back of the row of small shops. He found an alley barely wide enough for a small car. The backs of the shops all had small patches of ground behind them. Peering over the fences of varying heights, Oculus noted that most were used for storage, one had been made into a small garden. This was at the back of the bookshop he calculated. There was a light behind the curtained window so someone was inside. He carefully lifted the metal latch on a small gate and entered the garden. The curtain in the window covered almost all of it but a small sliver at one corner allowed him to peek into the room. Bartholomew was still studying one of the old books intently; carefully turning the old pages and occasionally noting something in a small black book.

As Oculus stood up and moved back from the window, he knocked against a garden fork that had been propped on the wall. He lunged for it but missed and the handle crashed against a zinc bucket beside the back door. Bartholomew jumped at the sudden sound. He crossed to the window and pulled the curtain aside. Peering through the window, shading his eyes from the light in the room, he could see nothing amiss in his tiny garden. Probably Mr. Simkins he thought. Mr. Simkins was the black and white cat owned by Mrs. Winter who ran a sewing and crafts shop two doors down. Sometimes he would nuzzle Bartholomew's legs if he was in the garden hoping for a saucer of milk.

Oculus pressed himself against the wall by the window and waited. Bartholomew decided to check on the noise as it was unusual for Mr. Simkins to be out this late. Picking up a torch from the kitchen worktop, he undid the back door and stepped into the garden. The tight beam of the torch played on the floor as he scanned for the source of the noise. Oculus hit him once but quite hard on the side of the head with the butt of his service revolver. Bartholomew crumpled to the ground, the torch bouncing and rolling away.

72

The sleeping arrangements at Bartholomew's cottage weren't ideal. There were only two bedrooms upstairs and Gail was in the smaller one, alongside her life-giving equipment. There was only enough room left for someone to enter the room and squeeze around the bed. The other room was larger and had a double bed. CJ and Angie used this room and were asleep, back-to-back. It was a full moon so the room was lit with a silvery light. Downstairs, Zach was on the larger of two sofas in the sitting room. It still wasn't quite long enough for him to stretch out so one leg hung off and extended out of the blankets.

Patterson was not sleeping but circling the building doing his hourly check. There were no other houses close by. The nearest was a similar small cottage about two hundred yards away South and the start of the main village of Aldeburgh about three hundred yards North. The road was very quiet, and Patterson hadn't seen a car for at least a couple of hours. The garden around the cottage was well cared for and there was a mature wisteria that gracefully sprawled across the front wall and surrounded the front door. As he rounded the corner at the front of the house, he thought he caught some movement in his peripheral vision. His training kicked in immediately and he crouched and drew his weapon. The movement had been down the far side of the house, so Patterson cautiously and quietly crossed the front until he reached the corner. Pausing for a moment he then carefully peered around the side. In the moonlight all he saw was the manicured lawn, the well-tended shrubs and the shadows of the rear fence. He started to relax and with his gun still drawn he continued down the side of the cottage to the rear corner. Pausing again he then cautiously looked round the back. Tall shrubs lined the back of the cottage and some fruit trees cast moonlit shadows. He began to move along the back wall, scanning the garden where some woodland began just beyond the ramshackle fence.

It had probably just been a fox, or maybe a badger, as they were in the country. Patterson straightened and holstered his gun. As he turned to retrace his steps round to his chosen watching position his world suddenly ended. A hand covered his mouth and nose, so quickly that he found himself already fighting for breath. His right hand instinctively grasped the hand over his mouth but before he could apply any real force, he felt something sharp slide rapidly across his throat. His body seemed to lose all motor control and he pitched forwards onto the damp grass. His mind knew what had happened but refused to believe it. He rolled to his left until he was on his back, his hands clutching at his throat. Dark wetness was everywhere, his hands sliding through it as he tried to push the fluids exiting his body back in. As he lay facing upwards beneath the moonlit Suffolk sky a face appeared.

Oculus looked quizzically at the dying man. At another time he would have been curious to observe the moment of death. The instant that life was extinguished. It used to be said that the eyes of the dead retained the last image they saw. The last image was of Oculus wiping his ceremonial dagger clean of the dark fluid on the dying man's jacket.

As he stood and sheathed the knife, etched with magical symbols, Oculus felt a sudden rush of emotion. Feeling as if he was an observer, he saw himself thrust his arms wide and face the moon, bathing in its glow. For an instant, he felt as if he wasn't alone. He could feel the presence of someone, something, seemingly in his thoughts, as if he was not totally in control. Images of a desert stormed his consciousness, a wind whipping the sand into careening, whirling shapes. He seemed to be standing amongst the raging wind. He thought he felt the sting of the sand on his cheeks. He held his arm up to shield his face. As he did so, he saw his arms were covered in tattoos, symbols of power, ancient emblems of Egyptian magic. Even down to the backs of his hands, the symbols and hieroglyphs extended. Intricately drawn and vibrant in their colours. Then the winds abated, and he lowered his arms. The breeze from the North Sea ruffled his hair and he looked down again at his arms and hands. They were inside the sleeves of his jacket. He stood over the dead man in the cottage garden. The duality in his mind was quieted. What did the mighty Aziel require of him now? he wondered. He did not need to wonder twice. His mind was not his own once more. He felt the presence and the command was clear. Oculus moved quietly towards the front door, the keys from Patterson's pocket glinting in the light.

Angie woke up. She had never been one for seafood. Why she had let the others talk her into trying shellfish she didn't know. It was fine at first but she'd felt funny all evening after that and now she felt her body finally rebelling. She sleepily rolled out of bed and padded to the tiny bathroom. She knew what she had to do and knelt before the porcelain bowl waiting for the inevitable. Just as the first surge hit her she thought she heard someone moving about downstairs. As she paused to catch her breath she thought that it must have been Patterson, the spook, or maybe Zach couldn't sleep either. Angie clutched the toilet gratefully as her body began to relax from the spasms. She pushed herself up and scooped some cold water from the tap into her mouth. She definitely heard a noise from downstairs so she decided that maybe a cup of something to take the taste away would be good.

She padded towards the narrow stairs. As she got to the top, she thought it was odd that there wasn't a light on downstairs. Whoever it was was moving about in the dark. Maybe spooks can do that she thought. But she couldn't so she flicked on the lights at the top of the stairs. The figure she saw at the bottom of the stairs wasn't Patterson. It wasn't Zach either. As she turned the light on the figure spun towards it. It was a long, angular face and as it looked up at Angie the mouth seemed to draw out and back into something like a snarl. Without even realising she had done it, she screamed. A completely reflex action born of sudden and all enveloping terror. As she was expelling the piercing sound she saw the gun in the figure's hand. He turned towards her and the gun was moving up to face her as she lurched away and ran towards her room. A loud bang was followed by an almost imperceptible puncturing sound as the bullet ripped through the old lathe and plaster ceiling of the landing. As Angie reached the door to the bedroom CJ was already out of bed and tearing at her rucksack. Below in the living room, Zach had been wrenched from a restful, dreamless sleep by the pandemonium. It took him a second or two to realise that there was a man standing in the hall that wasn't Patterson. As he registered this the man headed up the stairs. Zach threw off the blankets and looked around in a panic for some sort of weapon. He settled on the first thing that came to hand from the fireside tools and headed to the hall and the stairs.

Angie charged into the bedroom and spun around shutting the door and leaning on it.

"There's someone out there!" she shouted. "And they've got a gun!"

CJ had found the can of mace and was joining Angie by the door as the door itself moved inwards before pushing back with Angie's weight. CJ joined her and leant her weight to the door. They both listened intently. After a second they heard a creak from the landing. The intruder was moving away from their door. They both had the same thought, but CJ was the first to vocalise.

"Gail!" she blurted and they both stepped back from the door and flung it open.

As they crashed out of the door onto the landing, they saw Oculus standing outside the room where Gail's body lay in its protective but delicate cocoon. As they looked, they saw Zach reach the top of the stairs beyond Oculus, brandishing a metal bar with a wicked looking curved hook and spike on one end. For an instant time stood still. Angie and CJ locked eyes with Oculus and Zach took in the scene before him. Then Oculus raised his gun towards the two women but CJ was already taking a stride towards him and unloading a torrent of mace directly into his hollow eyes. The jet from the canister seemed almost to push Oculus backwards but it would be the sudden excruciating pain that did that. He uttered a horrendous cry that was part animal and dropped the gun to bring both hands to his burning eyes. Zach took a huge swing with the poker and the glancing blow caught the very side of Oculus' head and bounced off his shoulder. Turning towards Zach, Oculus charged him and catching him mid-chest knocked him backwards. Zach's foot missed the top stair and his weight crashed against the wall as he bounced back across and hit the banister. His flailing hands caught the banister and helped slow his fall, but he still toppled backwards and thumped down the stairs until he reached bottom, on his back and temporarily winded.

CJ continued to empty the can of mace towards Oculus who cried out again and began to wildly strike out with his hands, unable to see through the pain.

Angie was riveted to the spot and frozen completely by fear. She had realised that Zach had been knocked down the stairs but she also knew that this man, if he was a man, was still there and seemed more dangerous than ever. She wanted to go to Zach, to help him, but her muscles wouldn't respond. As she watched the appalling scene before her, CJ had finally emptied her mace and cast the canister aside. Within a split second, she took a step towards Oculus and aimed a passable karate sidekick, using all the force she could muster, into his stomach. Oculus bent double under the attack and staggered backwards. CJ followed up with another kick, this one less cultured but effective enough to send Oculus beyond the top of the stairs. Grasping at thin air, Oculus resembled, for an instant, those cartoon characters caught with no support before they plunge. Oculus plunged, legs and arms windmilling to arrest the fall but failing. He struck the stairs halfway down and slid the rest of the way, his shoes thudding as they slipped from stair to stair.

Zach had pulled himself up and was standing close to the foot of the stairs as Oculus crashed to the bottom. Zach had dropped the poker as he fell and couldn't see it. He watched in surprise and horror as Oculus raised himself from the floor and turned his twisted face towards him. Streaks of mace fell from his sunken eyes and down his cheeks, giving him the appearance of a demonic clown. As Zach watched, Oculus drew his knife from its sheath. The engraved blade glinted in the moonlit hall. Before Zach had a chance to move, Oculus had sprung towards him. Zachs' only instinct was to stop the hand with the blade. Both his hands shot to

Oculus' right hand that held the knife. One of Zach's hands grasped the wrist but the other had landed on the blade. The pain Zach felt was instant but somehow subdued. He knew he needed to stop this man and if he relented at all, he was going to die. Oculus' forward motion caused them both to coalesce and fall backwards onto the hall floor. Oculus' left arm was reaching for Zach's face, the bony fingers clawing for a hold. Zach was bracing his bare feet on the wood floor and trying to lift Oculus and roll over. Over Oculus' shoulder Zach thought he saw CJ coming down the stairs, but his only thought was to stop the broad bladed knife from finding a way into his body. Zach felt Oculus' breath on his face as they rolled but as Zach emerged from under the other's weight, he felt the knife shift position; glancing down he suddenly kicked his legs out from under himself and leaned down with all his weight.

When he thought about it later, he couldn't recall if he had felt the knife sink into Oculus' abdomen. He just remembered that the pressure on him eased, his assailant's body seemed to suddenly relax and he rolled off him onto the cool woodblock floor of the cottage hallway. Again, he couldn't remember closing his eyes but the next thing he recalled was CJ shaking him and shouting. As he opened his eyes, he just saw CJ descend on him and clutch him to her, pressing a teary cheek against his.

73

Braberson checked his phone but there was no waiting message.

"And you have no idea how this man found you?" he asked Zach, CJ and Angie, who were sat side by side on the long sofa in Bartholomew's living room.

"None." said Zach, as he looked down while Angie carefully tied off the bandage around his cut hand.

"You think this man could be part of a secret society that is active in this 'Realm'?" said Braberson.

"Yes." said Zach. "Raymond told me that they had been having issues with them. One of them had been following him. Knew where his bookshop was as well."

Braberson motioned for one of the two young men in suits, standing near the hall doorway to come over. He whispered something and the man left.

"Why do you think that man was here?" asked Braberson.

"Raymond was sure that these occultists meant harm to Gail...Ms Hartston." replied Zach.

"The woman upstairs, that you moved here and that

was removed from Lievesham?"

"Yeah."

Braberson was really not on top of the situation. He had no idea what the significance of this woman was. He knew she had been a candidate for their experimental program. but his knowledge of the technical details was sketchy at best. In his mind they had been trying to establish if there was a way to communicate over long distances and if so, to synthesise the mechanism so that it could be implanted. Now he seemed to be faced with the prospect of some sort of parallel world and by chance their technology seemed to enable moving between them. He needed to inform Carver of the latest developments. His team could finish the cleanup here.

"What's going to happen to us now?" asked CJ. "Is it safe to stay here?"

"We will take steps to relocate Ms. Hartston to a secure facility." said Braberson. "But we have no way to be sure if this man acted alone."

"He looked like he was on something." said Zach. "Maybe crystal meth or something, he's only skinny but he was very strong. There was something about his eyes and his face. He didn't look normal."

"That'll come out in the postmortem." said Braberson. "You have somewhere safe you can go?"

"Sure." said CJ, unwilling to volunteer anything further.

Braberson's phone emitted a sharp metallic jingle. He answered it. He said nothing then stabbed the end call icon.

"Looks as if your visitor made another call earlier

tonight." began Braberson. "Bartholomew was assaulted at his bookshop."

"Is he okay?" asked Zach.

"He'll have a sore head for a few days but other than that yes. That's probably how this character found you."

"Where are you taking Ms Hartston?" asked Zach.

"She'll be quite safe Zach, we'll put her in the facility you absconded from initially." Braberson smiled at Zach, who didn't look particularly reassured.

"Just for her safety." said Zach. "Nothing else?"

"She seems to be a valuable individual." said Braberson. "I have no intention of interfering. We will keep her safe and well."

Zach looked at Braberson but couldn't tell if he should trust his former boss or not. He had little choice in the matter.

"Zach, please take this." said Braberson, drawing a new phone from his coat pocket and offering it to Zach. "It's a direct line to me."

Zach took the phone, aware that it was a means to track him but also aware that he knew several ways to avoid that. It could mean they could summon the cavalry if things got hairy again. It also seemed that Braberson wasn't going to take him into custody. He thought it best to play along.

74

The old ship was rolling gently on the calm sea. In the rear cabin there was a lull in the conversation. Puffy white clouds glided silently past the small windows with the sun glinting off the gentle, rolling wake to stern.

"You're sure this Braberson can be trusted?" asked Plater.

"I think so." began Zach. "He knows Gail is important."

"He seems to have acted reasonably so far." said Bartholomew. "I think right now I am more concerned that we haven't had more communication from Molly."

"Yes, the test of that machine has happened now." said Gail.

There was another pause while everyone considered why Molly hadn't sent another message.

"Maybe she hasn't been able to find a chance to get outside." said Plater.

"If the device is ready for whatever it is they intend it's getting more dangerous to be there." said Zach.

"Unfortunately, our communication is one way." mused Bartholomew.

"I can try to get in there." said Plater. "We have to do something, we can't just leave her."

"Can't the authorities do something?" asked Zach. "Braberson knows about this stuff right?" He looked across at Bartholomew.

Batholomew nodded. "Yes, they are aware of the device but that is here in the UK. Perhaps the US don't know about it."

"So much for the special relationship." muttered Zach.

"Exactly how much does this Braberson know about the CoR, Daniels and the device?" asked Gail.

"Well I can't be sure." said Bartholomew. "But he was extremely interested in the device and he must be aware of Daniels, with the profile he has now."

"But does he know they are all connected? Does he know about the mountain base?" said Gail.

"I don't know, do you think we should tell him?" said Bartholomew. "I'm not sure what he could do."

"He could get the cousins involved for a start." said Zach. "You'd think the CoR would be on the alphabet organisations' radar anyway but they might be missing some pieces. They could probably bust the whole place."

"They might just bomb it if they think it is really dangerous." said Plater. "It wouldn't matter that Molly was in there."

There was another tense silence.

"Let me explain to Braberson what we think's going on." said Zach. "Like it or not he could be our best way to help Molly."

"Be sure to stress that we have someone on the inside." said Plater, feeling he needed to get across the risk in involving the authorities at this stage. "Molly could provide vital information. She's an asset, in their vocabulary. Make sure they know."

Zach nodded.

Plater desperately wanted to suggest an alternative, do something himself to help but he had to admit to himself that involving Braberson, the UK authorities and then the US authorities was probably Molly's best chance. He felt helpless then angry then returned to being worried.

"Alright." said Gail. "Unless anyone has any better ideas?"

Nobody did.

75

It was nighttime in Washington DC and the bustling seat of government was in a quieter period. It never stopped entirely, of course and across the city office lights burned. In one office, with an antique desk light the only illumination, Faith Cantrell was replaying the video call she had just completed with James Carver and his man, Braberson. It seemed that she and they were behind in their understanding of the significance of the device and its purpose. Beyond a strange group of people relying on what used to be thought of as the supernatural or magic and unfortunate souls too ill to live a normal life.

Her worst fears were seemingly confirmed that some outside or alien force really did exist and mean humanity harm. Despite her involvement for more than twenty years, Faith Cantrell had always harboured doubts, wishes even, that the theories put forward weren't right. The theories that formed the basis of the secret organisation she belonged to. The theories that proposed that much of humanity's spiritual side had become the tool of this alien intelligence intent on the destruction of humanity. If this device in the mountains really was some sort of bridge that might allow these aliens to travel to earth, it could be the end.

Her thoughts wandered to her daughter, living in Seattle, and her two grandchildren, Mark, aged four, and Eleanor just turning eight. What if there was no world for them to grow up in? What if some malevolent race exterminated them before they had the chance to grow up and fall in love, see some of the beauties of this planet and maybe have families of their own?

She knew what she had to do. The mountain base must be destroyed, the device must be destroyed. The woman Molly was brave. She'd done a great job but like all agents, she couldn't take precedence. Sure, she wasn't a professional as Cantrell was more used to dealing with, but individuals in these equations rarely tipped the balance. The needs of the many had to be the priority.

She was happy with her decision. She had been clear to Carver. "...we'll do all we can to get the woman out of there." As she'd said it, she'd meant it too, when she'd said it. Her finger paused, just for a second, over the phone keypad before dropping onto the numbers and quickly dialing.

"Richards."

"Sleeping Beauty." said Cantrell in a hoarse whisper.

"At once ma'am." said Richards.

The sun had dipped below the horizon but the glow had yet to fade from the Western sky. Nighttime creatures of the hills were stirring and preparing their never ending search for food. High above, a United Airlines jet left a faint trail in the darkening blue. To the East, about thirty klicks from the main entrance to Redemption, two Little Bird: MH-6 helicopters lifted into the air and began heading west flying low.

"Sleeping Beauty en route." said the lead pilot into his comms.

Inside each helicopter were fourteen canisters with hazard warning labels and six men wearing blackened faces and mission-specific kit. The aircraft were low enough to kick up dust from the ground but also very hard to spot, even from an elevated vantage point, with the natural undulations of the terrain.

As the helicopters approached two klicks from Redemption they split to circle the base of the hill within which the alien machine lay dormant. Within two minutes of each other both craft landed, disgorged their cargo and left the way they had come. The two teams of men ran through another comms and equipment check before separating into pairs and collecting canisters. Each pair then moved off to locate the rough-hewn ventilation shafts casually disguised on the slopes above.

76

The slight figure closed the door quietly. Nothing moved in the room, least of all the figure bound to the gurney in the centre. After a moment's thought, the figure picked up a medium scalpel from an array of bladed instruments arranged in neat rows on a neighbouring trolley and stood, looking down at Molly James. The figure leaned forwards and placed one hand over Molly's mouth. Almost immediately Molly convulsed and was awake. Wide eyes stared up at the figure who held a single finger to their lips. Slowly Molly relaxed and the tension slipped from her body. Dawn Moran quickly cut the cable ties that held Molly to the gurney and helped her into a sitting position.

"Dawn!" hissed Molly.

"We must be quick." said Dawn, dropping the scalpel and supporting Molly under her arms as she tried to stand. Her legs didn't want to work at first and the pain from her hands was intruding. Both hands were bloodstained and there were several fingernails missing. Dark stains were on Molly's shirt and jeans. As she finally felt her legs again and could stand by herself Molly noticed that the two chairs where the men in camouflage had been slumped were empty. She couldn't help thinking the worst after what she had endured in that room.

Dawn was urging Molly towards the door and motioning for quiet again she opened the door and quickly checked the corridor. Tugging Molly forwards, they both left the storeroom and moved silently along the corridor, staying tight against one wall. It must have been nighttime, Molly thought, because nobody seemed to be about. Her head was still a bit foggy as they stopped outside a door and Dawn tapped gently on it. Opening a crack, she could see one eye looking cautiously out, then the door swung open and Victor motioned them quickly inside.

They seemed to be in another storeroom and not one Molly recognised. Dawn sat her down on some boxes and whispered some words to Victor that Molly couldn't make out. Victor turned around and began checking some boxes before coming back with what looked like packing tape and some cloths. Working quickly, Dawn ripped some of the rags into makeshift bandages and wrapped Molly's hands, cocooning them in packing tape halfway up her forearms.

"What's going on?" asked Molly as Dawn tore the final piece of packing tape with her teeth and smoothed the end down.

"We need to get out of here." said Dawn. "There's something bad going on. Did you see those men in the room where you were?"

"Yes." replied Molly.

"Well they're dead." said Dawn. "I saw them being moved yesterday by that creep Clayton"

"Who were they?" asked Molly.

"We don't know." said Victor. "But why would they be killed?"

"How can we get out?" asked Molly.

"There's a tunnel that is used to bring in equipment and to remove trash." said Dawn. "I've seen stuff arrive through it, it must lead to the surface."

"But they'll stop us leaving." said Molly.

"We must try." said Victor. "I don't think what is being done here is the Lord's work."

Dawn looked at him and nodded slightly in agreement.

"But it'll be dangerous." said Molly.

"Staying here will be dangerous." said Victor. "You've seen that machine, it's not safe, it could take out the whole mountain with the energy it produces. No, we must leave and warn people about this. It's wrong."

Molly could see the conflict on Victor's face. She knew him well enough to know he was devout in his beliefs and a sincere member of the CoR. His eyes betrayed the fear and panic he was feeling, and it was overcoming his faith.

One hundred and fifty feet above Molly, Dawn and Victor, the six pairs of ex-special forces men picked their way carefully over the hillside in search of the ventilation tunnels. It was a clear and chilly night with a beautiful carpet of stars. The mission leader had a small device strapped to his left forearm. Occasionally a short message would scroll across the small screen. It was other pairs reporting when they had deployed their canisters and the remote-control devices. After forty minutes, all pairs had placed their canisters inside the ventilation tunnels, as close to the large-bladed fans as possible to avoid leakage of the deadly contents to the night outside. A second scrolling message informed the mission leader that satellites had observed no unusual movements around the base, so it was likely that their presence had not been detected. Not yet at least.

The men then descended and quickly covered the two klicks to the pickup point, where within ten minutes they were collected by helicopter and whisked away into the night.

Faith Cantrell's mobile buzzed and danced on her desk. The message read:

'Sleeping Beauty deployed'. Having spent a lifetime in public service, when she had been approached as others before her, and been indoctrinated into the knowledge about the threat from the entity, she had almost felt honoured. It had terrified her that so much of human society was apparently being influenced and that this entity clearly wished harm to humanity. She had felt that she could really make a difference. That her life would really mean something. But she had to accept, along with all those that work in secret, that her efforts could never be acknowledged. There had been times, of course, when decisions she had made caused lives to be lost. In all positions of real power this is an inevitability, but choices like the one before her now were hard to reconcile. With her knowledge she had to believe that the vast majority of members of the CoR were ordinary people. Like so many other Americans that put religion in a place of special significance in their lives. She knew that Rev. Daniels was an unstable, deluded and possibly evil man. The people in the mountain base were doing what they were doing for some misguided belief but that didn't make it any less dangerous. The whole reason the organisation she had become a part of existed was because it was quickly realised that they could not trust the changing winds of politics to maintain focus. Apart from the risk of widespread and uncontrollable panic amongst society, if the truth was revealed there was the very real likelihood that successive governments could mishandle, play down or even choose to ignore the situation if political expediency dictated. Unidentified Aerial Phenomena (UAP) were another class of events that, although known to the public and governments, were paid little attention. Evidence for the entity was less concrete than that for UAP and it was in this way that the entity had been able to operate unchallenged for centuries.

Cantrell sipped her coffee, but it was cold. Time was standing still for her, yet she also knew it was racing ahead and that she had to act to prevent a possible catastrophe of literally global proportions. Her mind had gone over the information more than once. A device that can distort spacetime and perhaps form one end of a bridge to a distant place. It could be another part of our galaxy or even in another galaxy entirely. She could barely comprehend what had been suggested. As her mind wrestled with what she had to choose she also wondered if somehow, they might have got it all wrong. Perhaps the entity was not malevolent at all but trying to help humanity. She remembered that this proposition had been put forward many times over the years by prominent academics enrolled in the organisation. History reminded her that when a group is faced with such options when judging another group's intentions, the cautious approach, which may then become defensive and finally aggressive, is often considered the most prudent.

Cantrell picked up her phone and pressed a speed dial.

"Ma'am?"

"Execute." said Cantrell, a tear was forming in the corner of her left eye.

In six separate rocky tunnels in the side of the same mountain a screen flickered into life. A countdown began from ten. As the number reached zero a soft click and whirring began, followed closely by loud hissing. The blades of the large fans slowly circled in their cages, drawing the lethal chemical deep into the mountain.

Molly, Dawn and Victor were moving in single file along corridors heading roughly east. Dawn was in front as she thought she remembered the way to the supply tunnel. They passed the hall with the device, its huge bulk almost filling the entire chamber now. Moving further they had to stop suddenly as a guard walked across their path about thirty feet ahead but seemed to be heading somewhere and not patrolling, thus paying little attention. At the next junction they paused as there was a group of four guards talking in a corridor they needed to cross. They were about fifteen yards away but would probably notice any movement if Molly, Dawn and Victor tried to cross. Dawn looked back at Victor and Molly, her brows knitted in a frown, and she nodded her head in the direction of the guards.

"What now?" she whispered.

Molly edged forwards and peered carefully around the corner at the guards.

One of the guards was walking down the corridor away from them.

"Do you hear that?" he said. "Sounds like a sort of hiss, maybe a leak somewhere."

The other three glanced his way then resumed their conversation. Molly watched. The first guard was now about ten yards further down the corridor when he bent to look at one of the air circulation vents. As he bent down, he suddenly seemed to lose motor control and his arms went limp, he sank to his knees then fell forwards crashing against the vent. The other guards turned.

"Chuck, don't fuck around." said one, as he walked towards his colleague. When he got within six feet of the fallen guard he too seemed to go limp and sank to the floor.

"What the fuck!" said one of the two remaining guards.

"Gas!" said the other and they turned and ran. They ran straight through the junction where Molly was watching without noticing her presence.

The effects of nerve agents are similar. Able to enter the body either by inhalation or absorbed through the skin early signs are chest tightening and difficulty in breathing. Other symptoms include vomiting and incontinence. Usually, victims die from asphyxiation or cardiac arrest.

"We need to move!" said Molly. "There's some sort of gas."

"This way" said Victor and they followed him back the way they had come. Turning right, then left, he stopped outside a door before pushing it open. Inside hanging on a rail to one side were two full Hazardous Material (HazMat) suits. The same suits that the technicians used when preparing the machine for its tests.

"Quickly." said Victor. "Climb inside."

Molly stepped into the bulky suit through the long slit down the back. She ducked into the helmet and Victor carefully zipped up the back. He then helped Dawn into the other suit.

"What about you?" asked Molly from behind the face mask in muffled urgency.

"There are only two here." said Victor. "You must go, now! I'll find another."

"We can't leave you." said Dawn but Victor was guiding her by the arm and opening the door.

"You must." he said, looking quickly up and down the corridor "Go quickly."

Dawn and Molly exchanged a glance, but Victor was insistent and pushed Dawn through the door. Molly quickly hugged Victor, pain shooting up her arms from her damaged hands.

"Thank you." she mouthed through the foggy glass of the HazMat helmet.

Dawn was running as best she could in the clumsy

suit with Molly behind. As they rounded one corner, a small woman collapsed against Dawn and clawed at her arms to stop herself falling. Her eyes were wide as she fought for breath. Dawn could do little but watch the life drain from the woman's face and let her gently slide to the floor. Dawn turned to Molly with a look of fear and despair. Molly touched Dawn's arm and encouraged her to keep going.

At first, Dawn and Molly could hear shouting, then screaming but now there was silence. They reached a locked door and Dawn picked a card from a fallen guard and held it to the lock. A heavy metallic clunk and they were through. Another similar door waited for them at the end of that corridor until they found themselves in the long tunnel used by the delivery trucks. They began to jog along the tunnel but soon slowed to a walk, breathing heavily in the hot suits. After what seemed a long time, they could see shapes ahead that looked like an opening. As they got closer, they could see the night sky. Molly could feel some of the tension dropping away. Dawn turned to look at Molly and Molly smiled, Dawn smiled back, tears running down both cheeks.

77

Molly and Dawn scrambled down the unmade road leading away from Redemption. It was slightly downhill and allowed them to take bigger strides as they tried to put enough distance between them and whatever it was that had been killing everyone inside. At about a hundred yards from the entrance they stopped, breathing heavily and Dawn helped Molly out of her suit. With her bandaged hands, Molly took longer to release Dawn but they were soon sitting together on a rock getting their breath back after their narrow escape.

"What happened in there?" Dawn asked at last.

"I don't know, some sort of toxic gas or something. Maybe a leak?" said Molly.

"I don't see anyone else, do you think they got out?"

Molly looked back up the slope to the hidden entrance. There was no noise and certainly no people. She looked back at Dawn but said nothing.

"Victor, do you think Victor's ok?" asked Dawn.

"He could be." said Molly. "He knew where these suits

were, maybe he knew about others."

Dawn began to cry quietly, hanging her head. Molly moved closer and put an arm around Dawn's shoulder.

"He was so kind to me." said Dawn.

Molly was breathing normally now and realised that she should get a message to Mason as soon as possible. She realised that she would need help as she felt her hands throbbing beneath the bandages.

"Dawn." said Molly. "We have to get away from here. I have friends that can come and get us but I need your help."

Dawn sat up and drew her sleeve across her eyes, taking away most of the tears.

"I have a phone." began Molly. "But it's hidden and I need you to get it."

"Okay."

Molly opened her legs and pointed with a bandaged hand to her crotch. Dawn looked at Molly as it sank in where Molly had hidden the phone.

"Really?" said Dawn "Here let me..."

Dawn undid Molly's jeans and slipped them down to her ankles, gently moving aside her underwear. Dawn carefully retrieved the phone in its prophylactic sleeve and passed it to Molly. Molly shrugged and held out her hands.

"You'll need to do it." she said.

Dawn dialed the one speed dial number in the phone. It rang but the signal was inconsistent. It was answered and Dawn passed the phone to Molly who cradled it as best she could in her hands and held it to her ear.

"Mason!" she said. "Is that you?"

"Molly, what's happened? Are you okay?" said Plater.

Molly was close to tears as she managed to reply: "Yes, I'm okay. Can you come and get me?"

"Yes, where are you?" asked Plater.

Molly thought for a moment and glanced around, remembering the direction of the sun when she had made her surface excursions to send the messages.

"I think we're on the East side of the mountain. There's a rough road, with a shack and an old rusty truck."

"Okay." said Plater. "You said 'we'?"

"Yes, I have Dawn Moran with me."

"Moran? Dawn Moran? Is it Kathleen's daughter?" said Plater.

"I think so, yes." said Molly. "But I'm not sure."

"Okay, you stay put, we'll be there as fast as we can." said Plater.

Molly looked over at Dawn, who was looking out across the valley. The cool air was starting to turn colder.

"My friends are coming." said Molly. "Maybe we should walk down the road, I'm sure they'll come that way."

Dawn seemed shaken out of a dream.

"Yes, yes, right" she said. "All those people, there must have been hundreds."

They started down the rough road in silence, both trying in their own ways to understand what had just happened and wondering why.

It was more than three hours later and the sun had risen over the peaceful landscape as Dawn and Molly first saw the dust clouds in the distance. Two vehicles were approaching, moving quite fast considering the terrain. It was a while before Molly could make out the shapes and confirm that it was Mason and Erik. She put her arm around Dawn as if to reassure her that they were about to be rescued.

As the 4x4 made short work of the slope just in front, it slid to a gravelly stop and both front doors opened at once. Erik got out one side and Kathleen Moran the other. They both began to run towards Dawn and Molly. Kathleen suddenly stopped and stared.

"Dawn!" she cried "Dawn! Is that you?"

Dawn Moran was shocked to see her mother on the dusty unmade road ahead of her. Without warning strong emotions of relief, gratitude and joy overwhelmed her and she dashed to her mother's open arms and clutched her as the tears flooded.

Erik reached Molly and at once checked her bandaged hands.

"What happened? Are you okay?" he asked as he put an arm around Molly and scanned the hillside for any movement. He saw none.

"Molly!" cried Plater as he joined them "I'm so glad you're safe."

Erik stepped back and Plater hugged Molly so tightly she could hardly breathe.

"What happened? You're hurt..." said Plater as he let her go.

"I'm okay, really." said Molly. "I'd like to sit down."

Plater helped Molly to his car and Kathleen helped Dawn to the 4x4 unwilling to let her go for a second. They drove in virtual silence back to the makeshift camp about five kilometers away. Erik made some coffee while Plater carefully undid the bandages on Molly's hands.

"Who did this?" he said.

"They said his name was Clayton." replied Molly, feeling the pain in her hands again as the bandages came off.

"What sort of a man does this." muttered Plater as he gently dabbed the wounds with antiseptic before carefully re-wrapping the hands in fresh bandages.

"They killed two men." said Molly. "I saw their bodies; they were dressed like soldiers."

"Could you tell if they were Americans ?" asked Erik as he placed two steaming cups of coffee on the ground beside them.

"Not really." said Molly. "They just had camouflage jackets and trousers on."

"Guess Uncle Sam wouldn't be too pleased to find one of his old bases being used for this stuff." said Erik as he moved away to give coffees to Dawn and Kathleen.

"How did you get out?" asked Plater.

"Dawn found me and helped me escape and..." she paused. "...Victor."

"Victor?" said Plater.

"Yes, another man I met in there. He was kind. He found us the suits so the gas wouldn't get us."

"Gas?"

"Yes, something strong, people just collapsed and then...died." Molly was looking into space, her thoughts back in the tunnels of the mountain base, watching people topple over and draw their last breaths on the ground.

"Some sort of accident?" asked Plater.

"I don't know, I didn't see anything there that could have caused this kind of reaction or this quickly."

Plater smoothed the last piece of tape to hold the new bandages and Molly moved beside him and rested her head on his shoulder.

Kathleen eventually let go of Dawn and they sat side by side cupping the coffee in their hands.

"I'm sorry." said Dawn at last.

"What for?" asked Kathleen.

Dawn started to cry again.

"For all this." she said. "For the trouble I've caused you, and Erik." she added, glancing at Erik who was busy by the tents.

"It's okay." began Kathleen. "I'm just so glad you're safe and well."

They sat in silence for a few seconds then Dawn said:

"You were right, the Church is not what I thought it was. I thought they were doing so much good, helping so many people. But I saw dead people. They killed people. And what they did to Molly..."

Kathleen reached out a hand and put it on Dawn's leg.

"You're safe now. We won't let anyone harm you. We'll go far away from here, somewhere they'll never find you."

Dawn smiled but it was a tired smile. The stress of the past days with first the accident at the machine test, then her discovery of the two dead men, then seeing Molly be put in the same place as the dead men, then the rescue and their narrow escape had left her drained. Kathleen could see this and took her to her tent to sleep.

"Do you think what happened up there was an accident?" asked Erik.

He, Plater, Molly and Kathleen were sat together outside Plater's tent.

"No." said Molly.

"So, someone knows about the base, about the CoR and what they were doing." said Plater.

"...and didn't like it much." finished Erik, throwing the dregs of his coffee behind him.

"The Church must have made plenty of enemies." said Kathleen. "But to be able to get right out here and do whatever they did takes planning and money and people."

"We have some contacts that might have some ideas." said Plater, realising he should probably try to communicate what was happening back to Bartholomew, Zach and Gail.

"Yes, we should probably get back to England." said Molly.

"Sure." said Erik. "I reckon we can get you to an airport tomorrow, but Dawn needs rest and you too Molly. That was quite something you went through in there. A few hours won't make no difference."

78

Rev. Daniels had been asleep in his hotel room in Seattle when Clayton's call had come through. Another rally in the morning, then back to his home state of Texas for a number of interviews, some for print and some for broadcast media.

At first he couldn't process what Clayton was saying. Redemption had been destroyed. Well not literally destroyed, but everyone dead. Clayton had discovered this as he returned from checking on leads about the woman, Molly, and her background. It seems she had no background at all. She was a plant, but by whom? Clayton described the scene at Redemption with panicked piles of dead people by exits and others half in and half out of their beds. Whatever had killed them had done so quickly. Clayton had to leave himself as three helicopters approached. He said they looked military but with no markings.

Daniels drummed his fingers on his favourite, leather bound bible, an ever-present prop at his public appearances. The device, their pathway to the Lord, was now out of reach. This was the work of the devil. Who could be their agents of evil on earth? He needed to find them and stop them.

News on the latest opinion polls was more to his liking. Since the stories about each candidate had broken across the media outlets and the wilds of the internet his popularity had only grown. He was now a solid twenty-seven points ahead of his rival and with only days to go to the election he could taste victory. This was the power of the Lord. To place his loyal servant in such a position of eminence, the better to perform his works. Once he was President he could build a new device, bigger and able to transport more followers at once. Heck, he could devote most of the resources of the US to preparing for the Lord's arrival.

Clayton would continue to search for the agents of the devil and destroy them wherever they might be. Daniels flung open the curtains to his suite, opened the sliding doors and stepped onto the large balcony. The fresh morning air washed over him, carried on the stiff breeze from the sea. There was a slight salty smell and Daniels took several big breaths, inflating his huge lungs in his fifty-inch chest. Grasping the handrail he surveyed the city, just starting to wake to a new day. Thoughts turned to the rally and the expectation of another large crowd baying for the candidate that promised so much change. Righteous change and righteous fury for those that refused to follow the will of the people, and the will of the Lord.

"It had to be done, James." said Cantrell in a voice James Carver considered preternaturally calm under the circumstances. The circumstances of having just ordered the certain death of hundreds of people. People that in Carver's mind and on his ethical scale were probably 'innocent'.

"Did you manage to retrieve the device?" he asked.

"Yes, a crew dismantled it and it has been transported to our facility in New Mexico."

"Was anyone left alive?"

"Nobody was found alive." said Cantrell. "But no positive ID on Clayton so he's still out there and of course Rev. Daniels still graces our TVs every night."

Carver had not been considering Rev. Daniels' Presidential bid for the past few days as he'd been preoccupied with the device and how it could be stopped. Now that he thought about it, the prospect of Rev. Daniels actually winning was just as bad or perhaps worse. As President he would have the ability to pursue creating another device. He could deploy top scientists in a black project. US taxpayers would never know what their President was up to in their name. Carver shuddered at the thought.

"What about media? Locals? Whoever supplies the place will realise something has happened." he said.

"Being handled, James, suppliers will be told operations have shutdown, accounts will be settled. The remains will be removed and properly interred. We have a satellite monitored five-mile exclusion zone around the property to catch any nosy locals. The final act will be to collapse the entrances and make it impossible to tell this Redemption had ever existed."

"And the relatives? What are they going to do?" asked Carver.

"Their connection is to the Church, it will be for the Church to handle. They're not about to go public about what they were up to. The families, I'm sure, will be told a load of hogwash to keep them quiet."

"What can we do about Daniels?" he asked.

"There's only a few days until the election, we don't have time for soft techniques." began Cantrell. "Maybe we hold off, and in the worst case we convene a full meeting of the society?"

Carver was secretly relieved that Cantrell, a hawk by nature, was prepared to be more considered in any actions against Daniels.

"Agreed." he said.

79

The usual competition between the broadcast media stations to be the first to call the election was won by Fox News. The sun was barely sinking below the Californian horizon when their lead Election Night anchor was confidently predicting a landslide victory for Rev. Ethan Daniels. On a day that had seen a larger than average voter turnout, he had carried many of the swing states and with significant margins too.

By 1 a.m. Pacific Time the following day Daniels' opponent conceded with a sombre speech that included the perfunctory 'thank you's' to his loyal campaigners and supporters but ended with a plea that sanity prevail in his country as the new administration took control. He described the vitriolic tone of the later campaign and called for citizens to come together to heal wounds and rebuild a country torn by ideological and political strife as had never been seen before.

In a bar in downtown Fort Worth, Erik Nordstrom was in disbelief at what was unfolding on the small screen. How could this happen? How could a country as diverse as the United States elect this man to lead them. They didn't know him. They had been fed a stream of lies, half-truths and faith-based rhetoric until they must have believed they had woken into a nightmare that only Rev. Daniels could lead them out of. In truth it seemed to Erik that the nightmare was likely just beginning. He was glad Kathleen and Dawn were safe at home, living as a proper family again and with a deeper bond as a result of Dawn's trauma. He wished they could have been spared the pain of seeing and knowing that the man responsible for their pain was now their President.

He cocked his hand at the barman and got another beer. He couldn't deal with this now, he'd let the beer temporarily wash away thoughts of the future and deal with tomorrow when it came.

Although thousands of miles away James Carver was no less interested in the outcome of the US election. His laptop was streaming a US network's election coverage while a European 24-hour news channel was on his wall mounted TV. It had been pretty clear for many hours now that Rev. Daniels would be the next President of the United States of America. He had already spoken to several of his political colleagues in the UK, who were almost universal in their bewilderment and uncertainty as to what this may mean for the future.

Carver had poured himself a generous whiskey some hour and a half ago but soon realised he needed a clear head for the inevitable chaos that was about to follow. It stood barely touched on his desk. His Government issue mobile had already received more than 60 texts and emails in the past two hours. He knew he needed to speak with Faith Cantrell, but he honestly had no idea what to say. He needed to come up with some sort of strategy to handle what had become the archetypal worst-case scenario. There was now a man in the White House who had been developing, in secret, a device which would likely have opened a bridge to an alien species that seemed to want nothing less than the destruction of humanity. This man now had at his disposal the full resources of the only real superpower on Earth. Carver knew full well that the US maintained a so-called Black Budget larger than most countries' GDP which could be used without Congressional or Senate oversight. It was surely only a matter of time, and probably not much time, before development of a replacement device to the one seized from Redemption would begin. He knew that Faith Cantrell would favour a hard-line approach to this problem and he could think of no alternative to propose. This would certainly mean assembling the entire organisation to decide on a strategy. His own UK government would likely convene to discuss how this new resident of Pennsylvania Avenue should be handled.

Mason Plater woke up on the morning of Rev. Daniels' ascendancy to high office in his own bed. It was the best night's sleep he had had for weeks. Rolling onto his back, he saw that the bed was empty on the other side. He heard the faint sound of the kettle from the kitchen and rolled out of bed.

Molly was struggling to get a coffee mug off a hook,

needing to use both bandaged hands.

"Hey." said Plater. "You're up early. Let me…"

He went to help unhook the mug but Molly managed.

"I'm okay, you want one?" she said.

He nodded. "Thanks."

"Have you heard?" said Molly. "About the election?"

"What?" said Plater, already investigating the refrigerator for breakfast.

"The election, for President…that bastard's got in."

"What Daniels?" said Plater. "How?"

"Easily. They're calling it the biggest winning margin in thirty years."

"But he's a fake." said Plater. "A charlatan. Thank god we're back home."

"But he can do anything now…he can build another of those things…nobody can stop him now."

As Plater stood up from the fridge, Molly came over and wrapped her bandaged hands round him, burying her head in his shoulder.

80

Carver had managed to clear his calendar for the emergency meeting but not without raising a few eyebrows. His mention of a domestic security alert and a need to confer with security services was flimsy but he needed to be on this call.

The giant screen in his office started to fill up with windows as participants joined. Casting his eyes over each, he knew some, as he'd met them personally, and others by sight while others only by their name and reputation. When Faith Cantrell finally called the gathering to order there were twenty-three attendees from all corners of the globe. Each was a person of either great power and influence, extreme wealth or technical brilliance.

"I would draw the Council's attention to item 1 from the package." began Cantrell. It was video shot from a bodycam of one of the team that attacked Redemption followed by more footage from the clean-up crew.

"You will notice." she went on. "That the nerve agent was 100% effective. The latter part of the video shows the device. As you can see it is very large and requires extensive support systems. Significant components need to operate at supercooled temperatures."

"Where is the device now?" asked a representative from China who Carver didn't recognise but knew was a theoretical physicist of some renown.

"It has been dismantled and transported to New Mexico, to Installation 7. Technicians are analysing it and processing what data files we were able to extract from their computers. There were other files and data on their database that will require careful study but are not germane to our topic today."

Cantrell paused, briefly then continued.

"Item 2 in the package is a report of the smear campaign mounted against Rev. Ethan Daniels the new President of the United States. Although not 100% true there is enough verifiable evidence to determine that Rev. Daniels is running a Church that is little more than a cult. Members have disappeared, presumed murdered by the man in Item 3, Wallace Clayton. Since the device was ready for use, we have every reason to believe that Daniels will waste no time recreating it. The principal difference being that his budget will likely be greater by a factor of 100 and we may not be able to easily track it. It will likely operate as a Black Project. I need hardly emphasise the critical importance of neutralising this device and Daniels himself."

"Do you have a recommendation?" asked Francois DeGrange, the French industrialist and owner of the largest transport company in Europe.

"I would like to first throw the question open to the Council. In a matter of such importance all voices should be heard." said Cantrell. As she finished speaking Carver noticed many of the attendees switch their session to mute and fall into conversation at their end. Nobody spoke for a very long two minutes.

"Does anyone have a proposal?" asked Cantrell.

A dark skinned South American delegate spoke:

"If he were anyone else our direction would be clear." he began, his broad-shouldered torso filling the screen. "But we cannot assassinate a serving head of state let alone the President of the United States. We would risk almost certain exposure as a result."

"Yes Miguel." said Cantrell. "Yet we cannot take no action either. It took Daniels' cobbled together team only nine months to create the device. With the resources of the US we would have to assume he could halve that time at least."

"Is there a way to disrupt acquisition of materials?" said Vittorio Cannelli, the Italian Defence Minister. "I believe even the Americans do not keep supplies of all these items."

A number of the delegates nodded silently behind their muted sessions.

"I agree Vittorio, we will work towards this, but that can only be a delaying tactic. We have also looked at the possibility of sabotaging components during procurement, but this would also only cause a modest interruption. Ultimately, we must still confront the inevitable. We must somehow remove Daniels from the field."

Carver noted another prolonged silence, although some frantic discussion was also enacted in silence on the muted sessions.

"But he has just won a crushing election." said Cannelli. "Even in the US a President gets a, how do you say it...honeymoon period, no?"

Carver could hardly believe what he was about to say but he appreciated the situation so he said it.

"Presumably, the President will make at least one foreign trip before the device can be operational?" he paused and noted the nodding. "So we could look at the possibility of an accident or unnamed terrorist incident involving the President." He expected to be shouted down and even started to blush as he suggested assassinating the head of the world's only military superpower.

"A bomb?" queried DeGrange.

"I thought perhaps some chemical agent." said Carver. "Reduce collateral damage as much as possible."

"Do you have a scapegoat?" asked Cannelli.

"There are more than thirty terrorist groups throughout the world that have the resources to attempt this." said Carver. "All hate America and some have a strong desire for publicity. There are even factions within established groups that would potentially be interested in claiming responsibility to gain favour."

There seemed to be a mix of reaction to this. Some delegates were nodding while others were shaking their heads and still others having renewed discussions at their end of the virtual meeting. Carver's phone vibrated, there was a message from Cantrell.

'And you thought I was a hawk!' it read.

"I would propose that we adjourn unless anyone has any alternative ideas at this point." said Cantrell. "We will form small teams to work on each aspect, disruption, sabotage and elimination. I recommend we reconvene in 72 hours."

All delegates nodded their approval and windows began to go black as they disconnected. Carver stayed staring at the huge black monitor wondering what they were about to set in motion.

81

It is not uncommon for new Presidents to announce their intentions in office with some early, eye-catching executive orders. Rev. Ethan Daniels was no exception. With moving vans still coming and going, depositing equipment and belongings into the White House Daniels was already executing the first part of his grand plan. The very first executive order signed by Rev. Daniels on his third day in office imposed a punitive tax on all income to the previously exempt TV evangelist churches. He had made an impassioned speech, broadcast on national television. In it he decried the greed of the televangelists and promised to investigate their institutions with a view to criminal charges on tax evasion and money laundering with likely imprisonment for the most egregious offenders.

Happy with his day's work, Daniels was asleep soon after midnight. His dreams were becoming more vivid. He was a great leader and his people loved him. However, he knew that there was an evil he must confront. He preached about the evils facing his congregation and the need to face this threat and to defeat it. He spoke before huge crowds that cheered and cried out encouragements. He recalled that they seemed to be dressed strangely but he was focused on the words and the expressions of love and faith that emanated from the assembled masses.

As he woke the next morning, he felt slightly less alert than normal. He needed a coffee to feel ready for the day's busy schedule. It was as if his vivid dreams were taking some of his energy. But that would be ridiculous. He was just tired with the heavy responsibilities he now enjoyed. Having drunk his coffee Rev. Daniels felt ready to take on the world once more.

"That guy was one of the spies you told me about before?" asked Zach.

"Yes, and he seemed quite specific." said Bartholomew. "A large army."

"It's been a long time." said Gail. "I hoped we would not see this again."

"Could you explain a bit." said Plater. "What army?"

The old sailing ship was rolling gently, with an occasional sound of a wave knocking on the wooden hull. The gathering in the captain's cabin had been mostly cordial and lighthearted until Bartholomew had arrived bringing news from the city.

"As you know there has been unusual activity in the Valley for some time." began Bartholomew. "According to Malik, the man who returned last night, they have assembled a huge army. It seems they plan to march on the city."

"Can they do that?" asked Zach. "Do you have

defences?"

"Of course." said Bartholomew. "We have guards and even an army but from what we know now we may need to reinforce them. Malik reported that the Valley have gathered behind a new leader, a messianic figure, a giant of a man, that has them eager for war."

"A war? In the Realm?" said Plater.

"There have been many before." said Gail. "There are books written in the library. From the earliest times. They won't rest until we're gone."

"Okay, so how do we win?" asked Zach. "I haven't seen much military equipment around."

"The Realm is simpler in some ways." said Bartholomew. "We don't have modern military equipment. Although a lucky few can exert special power here." he glanced at Gail. "Most of us fight with more traditional personal weapons." he walked to the side of the cabin and took down a cutlass from the wall. He dropped it noisily onto the table.

"You have to be kidding." said Zach. "Swords?"

"Spears, bows and arrows, cavalry." said Bartholomew. "For reasons we don't understand we cannot seem to develop modern weapons here. But a sword will kill you just as well as a bullet."

"How does that work?" asked Zach. "So we're fighting here with those...people from the Valley...what if I get killed?"

There was a pause and Zach looked from Bartholomew to Plater to Gail.

"Injuries sustained in the Realm do not translate directly to the real world." began Bartholomew. "But..."

"Why is there always a 'but'." said Zach.

"But if you suffer traumatic injuries then it can affect your physical self." said Bartholomew.

"I could die?" said Zach.

"In extreme circumstances, yes." said Bartholomew. "But it is very rare. Most of the people in the city are not really aware of where they are. They are just living, literally, in their 'dream world'. For those people we believe that they will not suffer serious issues when they suffer injuries or even death in the Realm. They probably just experience a bad dream or nightmare. But for those of us that are sentient in the realm the rules appear to be different."

"We think it has to do with the fact that different parts of our brain must be active for us to be sentient here." said Gail. "This means that traumatic damage here translates to traumatic damage in the real world, but of a psychological or mental nature. We think this can also affect physical processes, like the natural biorhythms of the body and the autonomic systems like breathing and heart rate."

"There have been cases where people just don't wake up." said Bartholomew.

Zach looked at each of them again, but no words came.

82

The London cabbie had barely understood the lanky American when he had settled into his cab at Heathrow. On the third attempt, he registered the address and with a practised flick set the meter running.

Clayton tipped the cab driver, checked in to his hotel, showered and changed before ordering his rental car to be delivered to his hotel. As he waited, he scrolled through some details on his phone; locations, addresses and telephone numbers.

It was late morning when he stopped in front of King George Place, an imposing block of mansion flats, built around the start of the twentieth century. Stylistically Victorian but with a reduction in size and grandeur more in keeping with the new century. Clayton checked the address again with the one in his phone. Satisfied, he loitered close to the entrance until a man in a black anorak mounted the steps, with his small dog in tow, and opened the door with his key. Clayton quickly approached.

"Thank you." he said, in as neutral an accent as he

could manage. The dog walker barely gave him a second look and disappeared into a ground floor flat.

Clayton took the stairs to the third floor and found 317. The door lock was a fairly ordinary five pin Yale lock and Clayton had picked it within two minutes. Molly's flat was her pride and joy. She had got a small inheritance from an aunt she had barely known and it had just enabled her to sell her studio flat in Battersea that she'd had since college and get this two-bedroom mansion flat. She'd hardly spent any time in it since that fateful day when Mason Plater had asked to see her and explained about his weird experiences at Lievesham. Indeed, there was some food in the refrigerator that would not warrant close inspection, having been in there well beyond its useful life.

Clayton saw no reason to hide his presence, so cast drawers aside once he'd opened and rifled them. He was methodical in his approach and moved around the living room first before choosing the obvious master bedroom. He pulled clothes from the hanging rail in the wardrobe and dropped them to the floor. A small desk in the bedroom had a laptop on it. Clayton flipped it open and powered it on. He only knew two ways to break into computers but fortunately one of them worked on the old Windows laptop. Within a few minutes he had addresses and contact details downloaded to his phone along with email conversations that he could read and digest later.

He checked out the kitchen and did make the mistake of opening the refrigerator but quickly closed it again as the smell of ancient food made him nauseous. Before he left, he sat on the sofa in the living room and composed quite a long text to Rev. Daniels. He was moving on from the girl to her known associates.

Plater was relieved. Despite the talk of some sort of war in the Realm, Molly had seemed eager for normality and an Italian restaurant seemed a good bet. It was the first time he had seen Molly laugh since they'd returned from America. He hadn't thought his remark that funny, but he was extraordinarily pleased that Molly had.

"So." said Plater. "Dessert?"

Molly snatched up the menu.

"Of course." she said.

A tiramisu of truly epic proportions duly arrived in front of Molly. She began to attack it with enthusiasm. Plater's espresso arrived and he took a small sip from the accompanying glass of water.

"What did the doctor say about your hands?" asked Plater.

Molly grimaced.

"The nails'll grow back in time, but it'll hurt when they do." she replied.

Plater took another sip from his espresso and Molly sank her spoon into the tiramisu then stopped. She'd glanced out of the restaurant window into the street. Her expression changed and fear filled her eyes.

"What is it?" said Plater. "What's wrong?" he reached across the table and laid his hand over Molly's, at the same time trying to follow her gaze into the street outside.

"It was him!" said Molly, dropping her spoon and sitting back in her chair. "He's here."

Plater looked out of the window but saw only people

passing both ways as they went about their daily lives.

"Who?" he asked.

"Clayton!"

Plater stiffened and looked again out of the window, but he didn't know what he was looking for.

"You sure?" he asked.

"It was him." said Molly. "I'd know that face..."

Plater waved for the bill.

"We need to get home." he said. "We need to check with the others, we need to make sure you're safe."

Plater didn't know what to do. How had this Clayton found them back in England? They thought they had left the Church of the Reclamation and all its evil back in America. Molly could have imagined seeing this man. Plater wasn't about to suggest this, but it could be true. She had been under a lot of pressure in the past few weeks. The mind can play tricks when under stress. Molly certainly looked worried and that was enough to worry Plater. As they walked back to his house Plater kept a careful watch to be sure nobody was following them.

The private ambulance had collected Gail to transport her to the laboratory in the Suffolk countryside. A doctor and nurse were present to ensure all the equipment was properly set up and that Gail was fit enough for the short journey. Angie and CJ had slight misgivings about releasing Gail to Braberson's people, but Zach reassured them that the facilities were as good as any hospital. He also suggested that Gail was too important for Braberson to let anything happen to her. She would certainly be better protected than they could hope to manage on their own.

They agreed to return to London. CJ had a new client but insisted that Angie and Zach stay with her at least until the whole situation with the device and this 'war', or whatever was sorted out. She pointed out that she was best able to manage the stimulation of Zach's implant and to handle any issues if it misbehaved. Zach was quite happy with the arrangement as the net connection from CJ's ramshackle warehouse was truly impressive.

On the way down to London Zach felt the phone Braberson had given him in his pocket. He was less concerned than before about being tracked but nevertheless it went against his natural instincts to be constantly monitored. He knew CJ would always be suspicious about Braberson's motives in all this and deep down Zach was too. He wasn't stupid and he knew that Braberson's loyalties were to King and country well before Zach Hamilton. He pulled the phone out of his pocket and looked at it in his palm. Then he unzipped his rucksack, fished around in it and drew out what looked like something wrapped in carpet tape. It was a homemade Faraday pouch made with layers of tin foil and wire mesh covered in black carpet tape. It didn't look great but was effective. He slipped the phone inside and folded the flaps carefully to seal it completely. He felt quite safe at CJ's and he knew where the phone was if he needed it. As he settled back into the back seat of CJ's car his mind returned to the prospect of fighting battles with swords in his dreams. Angie and CJ had both been silent when he'd told them. He wondered sometimes how much about the Realm they actually believed. If he was in their place he wondered how much he'd believe. As it was he certainly believed what he had experienced. If anything, he had felt more alive in the Realm than in the real world. Whenever he was there it was as if he could feel all the parts of his body at once. Bartholomew had suggested he speak to a man called Silas next time he was in the city. Silas had been there a long time and was an expert in the weapons they would need to use if it came down to fighting. Zach wasn't convinced he'd make much of a fighter. He certainly wasn't one in the real world. He was pretty handy in World of Warcraft, but he doubted that those skills would be much help against an alien entity bent on destroying humanity.

Once back to the warehouse it was getting late but Zach fired up his laptop and sent a message to Meek. He guessed it would be okay to contact him again now that he was back 'on-side' with Braberson. Angie turned in almost as soon as they were back. CJ checked her emails and after making a large pot of coffee settled in for a long session combing through technical details for her new project. Zach watched CJ work for a while. She seemed pretty cool, he had to admit. After the long drive she'd changed into some frayed denim cut-offs and a baggy vest with 'Deny Everything' printed in red on the front. Zach was tired and decided to turn in. As he glanced up at CJ to say goodnight he caught a tantalising glimpse of her body under the loose vest. He couldn't really let those thoughts in right now. There was too much else going on.

"I should probably check-in, you know." said Zach.

CJ looked up.

"Right, yes, of course." she said and reached for the laptop that controlled the signal generator which could activate Zach's implant. "Dream on."

"Goodnight." said Zach, CJ smiled and then returned to reading the screen. Zach looked again at the fascinating contours of CJ's vest. As the frequency began sleep enveloped him quickly and he decided to find Silas.

83

Grobus stood for some time in front of the cracked mirror on the back of his front door. The new robe was much more luxurious than his old one, with more intricate embroidery of the subtle magical symbols around the cuffs and down one side at the front. This was what he, Grobus, deserved. His hard work had finally been recognised. Regardless of the fact that it had taken the mysterious death of Oculus for Nefer-Ra to invite him to join the High Order he felt that it had been inevitable. His chin began to rise almost imperceptibly as he stared at himself. He gradually assumed a more assured and powerful stance as the realisation that he was to be invited to learn the secrets of the Order crept over him.

But he needed to study, perhaps even more now than before. He slipped out of the robe and settled at his cramped desk. The old desk light weakly illuminated the ancient book he was now reading. Given to him by Nefer-Ra, this single volume contained the details of the high rituals but also other secrets of the higher realms of the astral plane. Grobus felt nothing as he avidly turned the pages, knowing that this very copy had belonged to Oculus. A section of the book told of a great war on the astral plane. There were illustrations showing great armies of light and dark doing battle. Between the rearing horses and swirling lances and swords, strange creatures could be seen. While he recognised some, he needed to refer to his manuals of demonology to identify them all. One image, taken from an engraving in a satanic temple from the thirteenth century showed a big man, perhaps a giant. This man wore armour that was covered in symbols of power and protection. Grobus assumed that this was The Great One, reputed to have been the founder of their Order and the greatest astral warrior ever to take up arms for the Dark Lord. As he studied the picture Grobus traced his fingers lightly over the body and face of the figure. Surely just a coincidence, but the features seemed very similar. No, it couldn't be, he thought. He pulled out his phone and searched online. There it was. There really was no doubt. Grobus lifted his hand to his mouth and could feel his heart begin to beat faster. He felt that he was now witnessing something he had not dared to dream of. He slowly placed his phone down next to the picture from the grimoire. The faces were identical in features and expression. Even the pose of the figures was similar. A commanding stance, observed from a slightly lower angle, adding to the stature of the figure. Grobus needed to tell the others in the High Order if they were not already aware. This changed everything. The Great One addressing his army before the great astral war and the new President of the

United States addressing a crowd of supporters after declaring victory in the election.

"I just never saw you as a fighter." said Angie as she retrieved a coke from the fridge.

Zach was only briefly knocked by the gentle dig.

"No, it's just that over there I'm not like I am here." said Zach. "I was with this guy, Silas, who trains people to use swords and I just felt, I don't know, stronger."

"Go on." said Angie settling next to Zach on the sofa.

"So, like I said, they don't have modern weapons over there, so we have to learn how to use what they do have. Honestly it was just like WoW. Just like you see on the movies. But I just seem to be stronger over there. I was using a katana and it felt as light as a feather."

Zach was lost in his recollections of his first lessons with Silas. Angie took a sip of her coke and dug him in the ribs.

"So, what happens next?" she asked.

"More training." replied Zach. "It seems the Others have some new leader that is intent on war and we have to try and stop him. At least be ready to defend ourselves."

"You said that fighting over there can be dangerous, for you I mean?"

Zach didn't answer immediately as he recalled his discussion with Bartholomew.

"Why can't you leave this 'war' to the others?" said Angie. "How much help can you really be? You'll be no good to them if you're...." Angie left the sentence hanging and looked away as Zach looked at her.

"I have to try and help." he said. "We'll be prepared.

They'll need everyone they can find. If they lose, then I don't know what will happen. The Others will be able to cause their havoc without anyone able to stop them."

Angie could see the logic but still couldn't shake the other worldliness of the whole situation. It all seemed so remote to her. She was sure it was real to Zach and even the Government were taking it seriously, but she just couldn't believe this was really happening. She especially couldn't believe that one of her oldest friends was seemingly about to enter some conflict, while he was asleep. A sleep he may not wake from.

CJ swept into the room and slipped her work laptop onto the worktop.

"Okay, my knight in shining armour, I'm off the job so I can send you over if you like?" she said.

"Right." said Zach switching to lay down on the longer sofa "Ready when you are."

Angie looked at each of them but couldn't find the words to express how she was feeling. She watched CJ open her other laptop and open the trigger program. She looked over to where Zach was plumping a cushion under his head before slipping across to continue his martial training. It just seemed mad. Angie stood up suddenly and left the room. She needed some air and was soon stood on the roof of the warehouse watching a boat slowly heading up the Thames in the distance.

Carver's screen flipped from the crest of the United States of America to the grim face of Faith Cantrell.

"What have you got James?" she asked.

"We have a proposal for removing our obstacle." began Carver in a halting voice. He didn't like what he was about to propose any more than Cantrell would like hearing it. "We have a substance, we call it 'velox mors', it is a special formula, which is designed to be absorbed through the skin. It is odourless and colourless and is deployed via a dropper. It is non-reactive to latex and can therefore be safely handled. We recommend application to the target's cutlery. Target is scheduled to stay at three locations at which we have personnel that could affect application of the agent. The effects on the target begin within one hour. Various peripheral systems begin to breakdown. There is internal bleeding and total organ failure within two to four hours depending on the target's constitution. Symptoms appear conflicting and likely first response treatments will probably exacerbate the situation, assisting spread of the toxins and hastening death. Such is the decay profile of the agent that it should be 97% undetectable within six hours from application. As far as we are aware it is unknown to science, or other nations."

There was a pause as Cantrell considered what she had heard.

"There are times" she said. "that I am seriously glad we're on the same side. We'll need the full council's agreement but for now make all necessary preparations. You have potential scapegoats?"

Carver nodded.

"We are ensuring that at each location we can place members of known terrorist organisations within reach and fabricate necessary surveillance data."

"Alright. The meeting is in six hours. Thank you James."

The crest of the US reappeared on Carver's laptop; he closed the lid. He needed some sleep before the full council meeting, where they would decide the fate of the most powerful man on earth.

84

A long line was forming outside a nondescript building near the large square towards the centre of The city. People were filing in through one door and re-emerging later from a door on the other side. As they left, they carried swords, bows and quivers full of arrows, pikes, crossbows and battle axes. Some had weapons that looked as if they belonged more to the screens of Hollywood than to ancient battlefields, but the countenance of those carrying them all portrayed a seriousness of purpose. Even children came out grasping either small bows or short swords.

Gail Hartston watched in silence from the balcony of a building on one side of the square. Plater stood beside her.

"How will it start?" he asked.

Gail turned slightly to look at Plater then resumed watching the crowd.

"The very first time we know this happened." she began. "The Others just ran, like some screaming mob across the Great Plain and threw themselves against the defences. It was before, many years, lifetimes ago. Those in The city beat them back. They didn't try again for a long time. When they did, they had learned some tactics and laid siege with flying creatures that dropped burning bundles and archers firing arrows from distance. They did this for days before finally charging the gates like before."

Plater turned to look at Gail, who continued watching the lines below.

"Those in the city." she went on. "Had also learned. They were ready and dropped rocks and burning bundles of their own on those below. It was a long and terrible struggle but once more The Others retreated to their holes. The last time was not so long ago."

"Were you there?" said Plater.

"Yes, we decided this time to face them on the field. We noticed that they did not have any horses or other land animals with them. By this time, we found out that some people in the city had some military knowledge and we chose to use cavalry. It worked better than we could have hoped. They were clearly surprised when we opened the gates, and they rushed forwards. Our cavalry poured out and trampled most of them while the rest just scattered and ran. We were sure they would attack again, we kept double the guard for a long time afterwards, but that was the last time."

"They will expect the cavalry now." said Plater.

Gail just nodded.

"Did they have a leader before?"

"It was not recorded for the earlier battles, and I don't remember them being very organised even for the last one." said Gail looking round at Plater. "But it seems they do this time."

The mobile slid off the bedside table and bounced silently on the thick carpet. The huge hand that had caused it to fall made more noise as it collided with the heavy brass lamp on the same bedside table. Rev. Daniels crashed into wakefulness, lurching halfway to a sitting position in the huge bed. It took him a few moments to understand, then he leaned out of the bed and retrieved the still beeping phone.

"Do you know what fucking time it is?" he growled.

"You wanted updates soon as." said Clayton, who was fully aware of the five-hour time difference between the UK and DC.

"What have you got?"

"The woman, I have located her. Living with a man. Setting up a tap on her cell."

"Who's she working for?" asked Rev. Daniels, impatience evident in his voice.

"That's the strange part." began Clayton. "She seems to be working for a film company, just some intern."

"She's no intern, what the hell would she be doin' pokin' around our place if she's some intern?" he almost spat the last words. "Find out her story and don't call me again until you've got somethin'!"

Rev. Daniels jabbed a thick finger to cut the call off and cast the phone aside, hearing it thud to the floor. He slumped back into bed and stared at the ceiling. What was an intern at a film company doing nosing around Redemption? Did she have something to do with what happened there? It was too much of a coincidence. As he stared at the ceiling, he remembered the dream he'd been having when the call came. It was like the others, only if anything, more vivid. He'd been addressing a crowd, like a rally, but he couldn't recall what he'd been saying. He couldn't tell if the crowd were happy or angry. He thought they were waving things at one point, but he couldn't remember clearly. He knew he was tired and really needed to go back to sleep. He had a string of meetings coming that morning. The CIA Director was first at 0800 with his daily briefing. This to be followed by a brief for his first foreign trip, to the G7 Conference in Paris. Then he had arranged to speak with Jordan Blake. It seemed Blake had as many resources at his disposal as a medium sized country. Blake managed the Black Budget of ultra secret projects. He held no official position in the US Government, but everyone knew to take his calls. If anyone could rebuild the Tower of Babel, it was Jordan Blake. A smile began to edge onto Rev. Daniels face even as he slipped back into an animated sleep, his eyeballs moving under closed lids as he began to dream again.

Molly was finding it hard to get a good night's sleep. She couldn't help worrying about the man she'd seen outside the restaurant. She didn't want to bring it up again with Plater as she knew he had enough to worry about himself with some sort of war brewing in the Realm. She always checked the locks on the doors and windows at Plater's house before going to bed. She still lay awake for ages playing over scenarios of intruders and planning what she might do. She had placed a thick bladed chef's knife under her side of the bed and would often slide her hand down to check it was still there.

Her hands were a lot better, but it was still uncomfortable to grip too tightly, the skin on her fingers pulling tight and stretching the wounds around her newly growing nails. Often, she would lay next to a sleeping Plater and wonder if it would be better to face dangers in the Realm or the real world. It seemed there were very real dangers in both. She slowly eased herself up in the bed and picked up her phone. She tried to take her mind off her problems by doom scrolling through Facebook for a few minutes. As she did so an email arrived. Without thinking she tapped and opened it. As she did so the screen refreshed, almost as if her fingers had brushed the screen, which they hadn't. The email body had some offer for 2 for 1 cinema tickets for trying an app that rated new film releases. She hit delete and it slid off her screen. But not before it had delivered the Mikado malware to her phone. Even before she had slid her phone back onto the bedside table and resolved to try to get to sleep again, the malware had established full control of her phone and reported back to a command-and-control server in the cloud. Twelve seconds later Clayton's mobile received confirmation that the trojan was installed and working on Molly's phone. With the phone able to not only record all Molly's communications but also act as a personal tracking device, Clayton decided to return to his hotel room and grab some much needed sleep.

Grobus always felt uneasy when on the astral plane. He was adept at entering and exiting the plane but while there, he always felt some fear. It was a very different place, at times, from the books he had read. There was a category of magical operations that his Order performed where the plane and the creatures on it appeared almost exactly as they did in the magical books. Yet at other times, they seemed to be not in some mystical space where mythical creatures lived but a rather dark and dystopian version of the human world. It was this place that worried Grobus. Never one to mix easily socially, he found this human-like dark world even harder to tolerate than reality. Figures would approach him, sometimes male, sometimes female but always with something different or disturbing about them. Perhaps a deformity, a grotesque injury or simply an expression that unsettled him.

As the newest member of the High Order, he found himself more often in this disturbing place than the familiarity of the lower planes. It seemed they needed to work with other forces to further their search for The Book but also to help with a coming battle. Grobus flinched unintentionally as a black clad woman with hair to her waist stopped beside him and he felt a hand slip under his robe and grasp him between his legs. A perfect smile, but for one black tooth, crossed the woman's face. She had dark eyes and dark lips, but Grobus could feel his body responding to the woman's touch. In his surprise and uncertainty, he brushed her hand away. The woman tipped her head to one side and slid a long, pointed, tongue along her lower lip before sliding her hand from beneath the robe and turning away. He had not expected the higher planes to be like this at all. Moments later he saw Nefer-Ra, who beckoned him to follow and they made their way through a crowd towards a clamour in the distance. As they got closer Grobus could see a platform and on the platform the giant from the grimoire. He was already speaking and the crowd was already excited. Grobus could sense the energy and power flowing through the assembly. As he listened, he heard the giant speak of the coming great war. The war to end wars, the war to finally eradicate those who would interfere with the work of the Dark Lord. As the giant spoke Grobus felt his uncertainties and fears begin to ebb away. At some point he shouted agreement along with the crowd and brandished his ceremonial dagger above his head. As the oration went on Grobus felt a warmth flooding his body. He felt strong. A confidence that bordered on euphoria broke over him. As he glanced to his right, he saw the woman again. She stood no more than six feet from him. Without realising what he was doing Grobus pushed aside the figures next to him and waded towards the woman. As he arrived next to her, she looked around and smiled again. Without a word Grobus grasped the woman's breast and kissed her forcefully. In moments they had fallen to the ground in a tangle of limbs and robes. Around them others were doing the same and rapidly the crowd of onlookers became no more than a mass of copulating bodies. The giant looked on from his platform, satisfied that the energy necessary to mount the first attack was building in his writhing horde.

85

The assault began without warning. Bartholomew was standing with Gail Hartston atop the Tower of Hope surveying what they believed would become the battlefield, outside the city walls, when the first winged creatures from the Valley swooped down and careened across the city. Bartholomew recognised two distinct types of creature. Most of them resembled the Harpy, said by Greek mythology to be the hybrid of vultures and ugly hags. Behind these Bartholomew thought he could make out a few, much larger, creatures. As they came closer, he thought they must be Nue, creatures from Japanese folklore believed to be the bearers of misfortune and disease. These were much larger than the Harpies and seemed to be circling higher while the Harpies began swooping low over the city streets.

Sounds of horns bellowed from points around the city and the streets began to fill with figures, many knocking arrows to bows and selecting targets. Gail closed her eyes and lifted her hands until they were chest high. Her eyes opened and quickly fixed on a

Harpy that was arcing across her field of view. She thrust her hands out in front of her body and Bartholomew thought he saw a ripple, that distorted his view, explode from her hands and strike the Harpy. The screeching creature immediately rolled out of control and plummeted to the ground.

One of the Nue began a slow curve and then dropped into a steep dive. It had the head of a monkey, the feet of a tiger and the tail of a snake. Its vast wings held wide the huge creature looked set to dive into a row of buildings. As it seemed it must crash it suddenly flared its wings and thrust forward its huge, clawed feet. The feet crashed through the walls of the first building sending masonry tumbling to the streets below. As its momentum carried it parallel to the ground it carved out a huge gouge across the entire row of buildings before one huge beat of the giant wings caused it to gain height and disappear into the gloom.

A hail of arrows rose into the night sky. The Harpies dodged and rolled but some arrows found their mark. As Bartholomew watched, he saw three of the winged monsters fall. He also saw more of the winged beasts swoop and tear into the bowmen on the ground, knocking some aside and even carrying some off in their talons, dropping them to their deaths as they soared away.

Zach had been in the middle of a lesson with Silas when the horns had blasted. He rushed outside but was almost immediately pushed back by one of the guards. Only the archers were now in the streets and most of them had found places with limited cover to make it harder for the Harpies. He leaned out from behind a sturdy doorpost to watch the diving, swooping creatures trying to pluck more archers while avoiding the swarms of arrows. Occasionally Zach would sense rather than see one of the Nue as they circled overhead. At one point, he heard the terrible crashing and rending of timbers as a Nue lunged into the domed roof of the main council assembly building only two streets from where he stood.

Within a few minutes of the attack beginning loud cracks could be heard. These were the firing of large crossbows mounted on carriages that fired bolts longer than a man. It took several attempts but eventually one found its mark and a Nue made a sound unlike anything heard before and glided away into the gloom, the long bolt shaft trailing from its abdomen.

As Bartholomew watched from the tower, he could see that a second wave of Harpies were approaching, clutching burning bales in their claws. As he watched, the first few crossed the city boundary and released their payload. Most bales fell harmlessly into the streets, causing the bowmen to scatter but one or two fell on the roofs of buildings, starting fires. Bartholomew saw the frantic efforts to quench the flames. Chains of people passing buckets to stop the spread as the flames licked at neighbouring rooftops.

Gail had dropped more than five Harpies but now realised that her talents were needed elsewhere and reached across to grip Bartholomew's wrist. When he turned to look at her, she nodded almost imperceptibly and began to rise slowly into the air. As he watched she floated towards the worst of the fires and as she approached, she tilted her head back and assumed a pose reminiscent of the crucifixion. After a second or two she brought her hands together and then swept them apart again. As she did so, the flames about to engulf the building beneath her splayed out and flickered, gradually dying. There was an audible cheer from the human water chain below as the fire ebbed away.

Bartholomew was elated at the sight of Gail hovering like some god above the city. He knew he was witnessing something very special, but he also knew that Gail alone could not protect the city from oblivion. It was then that he noticed the dark shadow on the horizon towards the Valley. It hadn't been there when he and Gail had first surveyed the likely battlefield but there was now a dark patch. He peered through the wisps of smoke from the fires and stayed watching. As he did so he could see the patch was moving. It was the Others. It had to be. An army larger than he could remember and larger than he had read about. He watched on in fascination as the horde moved closer. He needed to warn someone, but at the same time, was gripped by a fear he had not felt before.

"How exactly are you going to help?" asked Molly.

"I don't know." began Plater. "But I have to do something."

Molly was laying on the long sofa in Plater's house with her feet on his lap.

"If there's a real chance you could be hurt or even..." Molly choked off the end of the sentence. "I just don't see how you can help, there are hundreds, thousands of people that can fight this war. They can't do what you can. You need to be careful."

Plater tipped his bottle of beer and took a healthy slug.

"I can't just do nothing." he said. "Even Zach is fighting."

"What about Clayton? He's a threat in this world."

Plater knew she was right. He had to believe that if Clayton had managed to follow Molly as far as the UK and was outside the restaurant they'd been in then he probably knew where Plater lived as well. Even with all the curtains closed, the doors and windows locked, he didn't feel entirely safe.

"I can talk to Bartholomew, get this Braberson involved. He's something in the government, he can provide protection." said Plater.

Molly was silent. She reached to the floor and picked up her beer.

"Okay." she said, taking a drink. "But I'm scared when you're, you know, 'not here'."

"We have to sleep." began Plater. "I can't control whether I enter the Realm or not, maybe that's a thing but I can't do it. Once I fall asleep, I'm there. I'm really tired now. I don't know how long I'll be able to stay awake."

"Can you at least be sure to talk to Raymond so we can get help from Braberson. I can't stand that that guy is out there."

They retired to the bedroom and Molly sat up on her side of the bed, unable to sleep, while Plater dozed, knowing he needed to speak to Bartholomew to get protection in this world while wondering how he could help the effort in the other world.

* * *

Zach watched from the ramparts of the city as the dark horde advanced. The Harpies and the Nues had gone and while some fires still burned across the city, he thought that it could have been much worse. The group he had been assigned to were atop the main rampart above the city gates. There were some thirty archers and forty men-at-arms with anything from broadswords to battle axes to samurai swords to warhammers. Zach had chosen a samurai sword, the katana, as he had found this to be well suited to his build and fighting style. He'd come to this conclusion along with Silas who had tried him out with most of the martial weapons available.

There was a reason that Zach was not part of the cavalry. He had managed to unintentionally dismount from his horse on every single training exercise. He could feel every bump and graze obtained during his horsemanship training. By the end of the second session, it was clear to everyone that Zach's undoubted skills with a blade would be best exploited on foot.

Turning around Zach could see the cavalry massing in the city square. More than six hundred strong they were split into sections of around fifty horsemen each. They would hope to rout the advancing horde as they had done in legends of battles long since fought. Turning back to face the plains he could not begin to estimate the strength of the enemy advancing slowly across the open plain. The longer he looked the more he worried that six hundred cavalry might not be enough.

* * *

"I've been looking for you all over." said Plater as he stepped out onto the parapet of the Tower of Hope alongside Bartholomew. "Is there a way to reach that Braberson? Molly is in danger from Daniels' hitman."

Bartholomew was watching the continuing efforts to quench the fires across the city.

"I can reach him." he said finally. "A welcome relief from watching this. I'll return when it's done. Gail is with the Council."

Bartholomew bowed slightly to Plater and made his way down the stairs to find a quiet place so he could re-enter the real world without distraction.

Plater followed a few minutes later and headed for the Council Building. When he got there, he noticed the damage to the roof where one of the Nue had caved in large parts of it. He found Gail talking with other Council members among the rubble.

"Mason." said Gail as she noticed him. "Good to see you. We need your help to the east wall. The main assault is coming. Are you ready?"

"I'll do what I can but I'm not skilled, I can't do what you do."

"I know. Just try some of the things we practised. It will help us greatly." said Gail, clasping Plater's arm and squeezing gently.

Plater tried to smile but failed. He nodded slightly and as he turned away Gail pulled him back and planted a kiss full onto his lips. They parted and Gail held Plater's gaze until finally resuming her conversation with the Council members. Plater turned and headed for the east wall. He just hoped he remembered what he'd been taught.

* * *

Molly could tell that Plater was in a deep sleep. His breathing was shallow but utterly regular. He had not changed position for at least an hour. She shuffled from cheek to cheek and bent and stretched her legs to get some blood flowing. She wanted to get a drink. She slid off the bed as carefully as she could, and Plater's breathing maintained its rhythm.

The clock on the cooker showed 1 a.m. Molly poured herself a shot of brandy, not something she would usually drink and winced slightly at the first mouthful. She appreciated the warmth as she swallowed and sat on one of the stools in the kitchen and sighed.

At first, she wasn't even sure she'd heard it. A very faint click, like pressing the button on a ballpoint pen. She put the brandy down and slid off the stool. She turned her head slowly to see if she could pick up any other noises. There was another click, this time louder and from the direction of the front door. Molly looked quickly around the kitchen and grabbed a slender carving knife from the knife block on the counter. She stepped slowly towards the kitchen door into the hall. Peering around to look at the front door, she could make out a shape through the frosted glass panels. She gripped the handle of the knife tightly and felt the needles of pain from her injured fingers.

There was another soft click and then a faint scraping sound as the front door gave inwards a couple of inches. A dark gloved hand grasped the edge and slowly opened it admitting a figure of average build and a few inches taller than Molly. The figure slid one hand into a pocket to deposit the lockpicks and emerged holding what looked to Molly like a gun with an unusually long barrel in the dim light.

She wanted to run upstairs and wake Plater, but she feared that she'd only alert the intruder to her position and put Plater in danger too. She could feel her muscles tightening, from her toes that seemed to be gripping the kitchen floor to her teeth that were clenched and she could feel every breath as she tried to stay quiet and calm.

Clayton took a few steps down the hall and turned into the living room. With his eyes used to the low light and the limited glow from the distant streetlights Clayton could make out the main contours of the room without a torch. He moved to the coffee table, checked along a bookcase and turned around to check doorways out of the room. He wasn't sure what he was looking for, but he needed to know who this woman Molly James really was and who she was working for and what their interest in the CoR was.

Molly edged out from her spot in the kitchen, deciding to take up a position near the stairs. With Plater asleep Clayton couldn't be allowed upstairs. She tried to remember where her phone was. It was on a side table in the living room. The house phone was also in the living room, in the far corner and well beyond reach. She saw a shape enter the kitchen through the door to the living room. She flattened herself against the hall wall next to the stairs and in shadow from the kitchen door. Her breathing was edging out of control as the adrenalin took over. Her arms were starting to quiver. Molly took a deep breath. The dark shape emerged from the kitchen on its way to the foot of the stairs. Molly exhaled sharply and lunged forwards with all her strength and felt the carving knife stab something.

By the time Plater had reached the east wall, it was a hive of activity. People running along the wall in both directions either taking up positions or distributing ammunition. This was either arrows or baskets of rocks.

Looking outwards, Plater could now make out individual figures in the dark mass that was advancing across the plain. Out front were large men wearing armour that seemed more like some sort of insect carapace. Between them scuttled creatures he couldn't identify but seemed to be moving like small monkeys, on knuckles and hind legs. As his eyes adjusted, he could make out larger shapes beyond. They could have been elephants or some other large creature but had platforms on their backs which carried two or more smaller creatures. As he noted this, he heard and then saw more of the Harpies swooping and diving across the plain in front of the advancing army.

"You can do magic right?" said a young man who seemed to be in command.

Plater took a moment to realise the man was speaking to him.

"Er, yes." he said, totally uneasy with the term magic.

"You need to be over here sir, where we can protect you." said the commander.

Plater walked across to a small group of archers and swordsmen that were forming a cordon around a platform. He saw them step aside and climbed the three steps onto the plinth. Looking out he now had an uninterrupted view of the entire plain as it faced the city. At first he felt hopelessly self-conscious and then desperately tried to remember all that he had practised with Gail.

Rev. Daniels slept soundly in his bed at Le Grand Controle hotel in Versaille. The G7 would begin the next day and he hadn't needed any nightcap to calm him down from another hectic day as leader of the free world. In fact, he had been only too glad to see the back of his assistant whom he had to force out of his rooms while still describing his busy timetable for tomorrow. He had barely pulled off his trademark crocodile skin cowboy boots and cast aside his suit before he was sound asleep. But he was afforded little rest. He now found himself at the head of an army. An army bent on doing the Lord's work. Every way he looked he saw a mass of bodies some human, some not. Without needing to think he knew what had to be done. Raising his right hand high above his head, holding a huge combination battle axe and warhammer he thrust his arm forwards and saw the assembled horde begin to rush towards what looked like a walled city in the distance.

The force of the thrust stopped the dark figure in its tracks. Molly pulled the knife free and stabbed again. This time, her knife glanced off an arm and she was pushed back herself as the dark figure fell forwards. She heard a sound like a loud cough and a loud crack like a spoon tapping on a saucepan come from the kitchen. The silenced .22 bullet had dented the stainless-steel wok hanging on a rack in the kitchen before burrowing into the wall. Molly didn't realise what the sound was and stepped back to let the dark shape fall. As she did so a hand grasped her arm and she lost her balance. As she toppled the carving knife dropped from her hand and fell silently on the hall carpet. Clayton let go of Molly and clutched his side as the pain from the wound hit home. Molly scrambled backwards away from him and tried to get to her feet. Clayton pulled the gun around and tried to find Molly in the gloom. Molly saw a faint glint of metal and dodged into the living room. Another loud cough and splinters exploded from the doorway to the living room.

Molly looked desperately around for another weapon. She grabbed a heavy ashtray from a side table and hurled it pointlessly towards the doorway. It crashed off the doorpost and thudded harmlessly onto the hall floor. She scuttled backwards until she was behind a large armchair and watched the doorway. Clayton came in, hunched over and favouring his left side. She couldn't see any other likely weapons within reach and hoped that Clayton would step far enough into the room to let her reach the doorway and back to the kitchen. She tried hard to slow her breathing which was coming in huge gulps. She tensed her muscles in an attempt to be silent. Clayton disappeared from view as he walked further into the room. Molly risked peering round the chair and saw Clayton, still hunched, crossing towards the door to the garden. Seeing her chance, she got up and made for the door. Clayton heard movement, swung round and another cough produced another hole in the wall on the opposite side of the hall from the doorway. Molly pulled open drawers haphazardly trying to find something to use. Her left hand brushed the handle of a cast iron frying pan. She grasped it and felt the pleasing weight in her hand. She ducked down behind the island in the middle of the kitchen and strained to hear any movement. As Clayton crossed from the carpeted hall to the tiled kitchen, there was a faint rubbing sound from his left shoe which was sliding along the floor. His leg was largely numb at this point and good only for stopping him falling over. The pain in his side was starting to spread to the left side of his chest and breathing was becoming uncomfortable. He needed to get this done before he had to stop moving.

Zach could feel a strange sensation and he couldn't tell if it was abject fear or something else. The dark horde were now clearly visible and no more than half a mile from the walls. He could hear the commanders of the cavalry shouting their final orders; then the cry to open the gates went up. It took six men to pull open the huge gates. Once open the cavalry cantered out in two columns and turned right and left, moving along parallel to the city walls. Almost as soon as the cavalry exited the city the hail of arrows began. The first wave fell mostly short of the walls. The second wave was a little closer but still well short. Within minutes the third wave began to rain down on the ramparts. Zach and the others ducked beneath the makeshift wooden roof that covered about half of the parapet area they protected. A few poor souls were not so lucky and were caught. Some fell immediately dead, others moaned in pain as they tried to find cover, black barbed arrows embedded in their bodies.

Zach's mind retreated to memories of his lessons. Silas had been clear in his instructions. Zach's strengths were not in melee combat but one-on-one. He was to try to isolate an opponent and fight that way. He grasped the handle of his katana, at once impatient to draw it and at the same time wishing he didn't have to. Peering through the slits in the wooden shelter, he could see the horde approach. They were now no more than a hundred yards from the walls. Soon they would try to climb them. He would be ready.

Gail Hartston was sitting, as if sleeping, in a room just off the parapet of the Tower of Hope. She was not sleeping. Her consciousness had been shifted to a small bird. The bird resembled a swift. Small, delicate and a master of flight. Bartholomew watched as Gail's body seemed to relax and the bird suddenly became more animated. It hopped urgently to one side then the other before taking flight and speeding out of the window and across the plain. Bartholomew watched it go. Such a frail thing, heading towards a seething mass of violence, hatred and evil.

Zach heard the cry from the group commander. All those sheltering emerged and took their places at the ramparts. The sight that met them was of a scrambling, roiling mass of dark figures pushing up ladders and beginning to scurry up them. Zach hurled rocks down on the climbing creatures as fast as he could. Some bounced harmlessly off the ladders, but one caught a climber square on the head, and he fell back into the morass of bodies below. To his right Zach could see one creature had reached the top and had sunk their teeth into the neck of a defender. Zach immediately drew his sword and without thinking, brought the blade down hard on the creature's head. The cranium split almost completely in two and dark liquid splashed in all directions, some landing on Zach's boots. The creature fell back off the wall and managed to take the next climber with him to the foot of the wall.

Zach turned back to find a creature at the top of the ladder by his side. He swung his blade but it was blocked by a dark sword. He stepped back and regained his balance. The creature jumped down onto the rampart looking left and right, waving his sword aimlessly. Zach stepped forwards and struck downwards, the creature parried but not accurately and the blades slid against one another. Zach's sword skated up the creature's blade and skipped onto his arm slicing it close to the shoulder. The creature cried out and Zach spun quickly and brought the fine Japanese blade in a murderous arc and took the head of the creature off in one stroke. Adrenalin rushing through his every fibre Zach was elated but soon reminded of his situation as a warhammer crashed against his shoulder and spun him to the floor. He rolled quickly to one side and the hammer crashed down on the spot he'd vacated. Scrambling to his feet he faced his new foe. It was a creature, larger than the first, with shoulders wider than any Zach had seen. He stepped back while he assessed how to approach this opponent. As he did so an arrow hissed past his ear and buried itself deep in the chest of the creature. Zach glanced round and saw one of the archers smile and nod at him. Turning back, the creature was on one knee but clearly not done. Zach stepped forwards and slashed at the bowed head. The blow hit home but the creature continued to stand. Dark fluids ran down his head and body, but he raised the warhammer again. Zach lunged forwards again, but this time went low and slid slightly past the creature's legs and slashed across the backs of both achilles. The creature howled and began to turn but his legs failed to support him, and he toppled into the city.

The little bird sped across the battlefield. Scarcely noticing the heaving masses below, she sought only one thing. The leader of this dark horde.

The further she plunged into the cloudy, dusty mass of the dark army the stronger was the feeling that the leader was close by. Then she caught sight of a small group set apart from the masses. Several unusually tall, yet thin, figures surrounded a large man. At least two metres tall the figure was imposing, wearing ornate armour that glistened like obsidian. As the little bird circled, she could see him give orders and one by one the tall slim figures bent to listen then slipped away to convey those orders to the creatures. Having seen enough the bird circled away and headed back towards the city. Just as she lined up with the city a screeching wail pierced the air and a Harpy flashed past the bird catching her with a talon and causing the bird to flap in panic and lose height. Feathers floated away from the wound in the little bird's side, but the tiny wings kept working. Her head twitched side to side to find the Harpy and be ready for a second attack. It came almost immediately but this time the little bird was ready and easily avoided the Harpy's swipe. The little bird decided to try and lose the Harpy in the chaos of the battle and dived down towards the seething masses below. Seconds later the Harpy tried again and this time getting in front of the little bird and trying to corral it with its large wings. The little bird ducked and swooped below the Harpy's huge wings and easily skirted the grasping talons. By the time the Harpy had regained flight and turned around the little bird had vanished.

Plater watched in horror as the dark hordes scaled the walls of the city. The men and women on the ramparts defended bravely as the first wave of creatures stormed up the ladders. It was Plater's job to deal with the second wave, the human wave.

Below, he could see that the scaly creatures that had first climbed the ladders were replaced by the bulk of the dark army. These were humans. Masses and masses of humans were jostling for position to climb the siege ladders. Plater began his ritual. It involved attempting to relax and release his mind from immediate thoughts. This would prove almost impossible in the middle of a battle, but he had to try. Then he needed to visualise a sequence of images and memories that were designed to bring his consciousness to a particular state. Gail hadn't been able to explain it, but she had been able to describe how to do it. Images were forced into Plater's mind in a pre-arranged order. Starting with the birth of his first son, then images of a lightning storm, then explosions from a war film or blasting at a quarry, and finally a symbol that Gail had shown Plater for the first time only weeks before. He had no idea what it represented but it seemed to trigger something within him and that is exactly what happened. His body made a violent and almost involuntary movement like vomiting. He had his hands extended in front of him and his fingers and thumbs formed a circle. Through this circle appeared what could be described as a bolt or a ball of energy which hurtled to the ground before exploding in a mass of yellow, orange and red flames. Such was the force of the blast that perhaps a hundred souls from the dark army were scattered, lifeless, leaving a large crater in their place.

A loud cheer went up from the guards on the ramparts. Plater was almost oblivious to it all. Throughout his practice with Gail, he had only ever used a portion of the sequence and concentrated most on aiming his energy where he wanted it. The sheer power of what he had just done overwhelmed him and he felt drained of all energy. One of the guards jumped onto the platform and grabbed his arms.

"Are you alright?" he shouted.

At first Plater wasn't aware of anything then his present came into focus.

"Yes, yes, I'm Okay." he said.

The guard smiled, clapped him on the arm and turned to rejoin the fight.

Molly knew she had to protect Plater. She hatched a plan and quietly opened one of the kitchen cupboards. Removing some of the contents, she put the cast iron frying pan down, took up several saucepans and threw them to the far side of the kitchen. Immediately she scooped up the frying pan and dashed for the door into the living room. She gambled that Clayton would have to follow the noise and that would allow her to get to the stairs and up to where Plater was sleeping. As she ran on her toes out of the kitchen she heard the tell-tale cough and saw a dark shape disappear into the kitchen from the hall. She was up the stairs before the last saucepan had rolled to a stop and the house fell silent again.

Bartholomew watched anxiously for the return of the little bird. He watched it streak into the tower room with relief. As soon as the bird settled on a chair, Gail's body moved. It took her a few moments to adjust but then she urged Bartholomew to unfurl the map of the plains. After getting her bearings on the map, she pointed to a place perhaps half a mile north and west of the city gate. It was obscured from the city by a slight hill which came in front of a slight dip in the terrain beyond it. This meant that the position could not be seen from the city.

"He's smart." said Gail. "I'll give him that much."

"Can we get to him there?" asked Bartholomew.

"Not yet, he has reserves that are close by. This one knows some military strategy. It's as well we are better prepared."

"Will the plan still work?"

"Perhaps with some minor alterations, yes, I think so. We need to speak to the General." said Gail.

* * *

The British Airways flight was on time to Paris. The passenger from seat 2A made his way smoothly through immigration. After collecting his bags, he passed through customs, having displayed his Diplomatic passport, without inspection. Inside forty-five minutes, he was at his hotel and having showered and changed, he opened the seven-digit combination on his steel-reinforced attache case and took out the small bottle of aftershave. It was still in the retail box showing it to be a high-end brand. The man slipped it into his pocket and left the hotel.

A short taxi ride later he was in a down market club drinking what he knew to be watered down Jamesons and checking his watch. Ten minutes late, at 2210, a couple approached his table and asked if they might join him. After a carefully worded exchange involving the price of the drinks, they established trust.

The man took the small box from his pocket and passed it to the male half of the couple below the table. They chatted and enjoyed a drink before they all three left and parted company. The man breathed a sigh of relief. He hated handling such lethal materials and even though he had followed all protocols to the letter, he had a twenty-minute shower when he returned to his hotel. He would be on the first plane in the morning back to London.

86

Before Zach had even had time to realise he had just defeated a giant creature intent on separating his head from his body, more of the dark horde clambered over the walls. The advice of his swordmaster came back to his mind: 'Avoid melee combat, you are best one-on-one.' As Zach glanced around, he saw that the horde were overwhelming his group on the battlements. Looking down into the city he could see dark figures had already reached the ground and were engaged in combat with guards. He decided to join the guards on the ground where he could select his opponents and had more room. He quickly slid down one of the internal ladders and paused only to slash at the back of a creature locked in combat with a guard on the platform. The figure slumped to the ground and the guard quickly acknowledged Zach's help before turning to engage another dark form.

As he reached the ground Zach looked round. The guards were still fighting where they stood and were not being pushed back. It was chaotic with groups of the guards in formation and the dark creatures darting in all directions with no attempt to work together. He saw a tall, slender figure twirling a double ended lance or spear move easily past a guard and spinning rapidly sliced the guard across the back, dropping him to the ground. Zach ran towards the figure, who saw him approach. The figure stood tall and bared its teeth, twirling the long lance above its head. Zach twirled his katana by rotating his wrist in an almost mocking gesture and the creature brought the lance down and lunged. Zach easily dodged and brought his sword down onto the lance. Sparks sprayed from the contact and Zach allowed the taller creature's momentum to take him past. He tried a strike to the legs of the creature as he passed but missed.

The creature spun the lance again, this time behind his back and around his waist in a move Zach may have found impressive under different circumstances. He was focused on his lessons and ways to attack. He feinted to strike, and the creature reacted swiftly to block but Zach was already altering his swing to glide past the lance and slash at one of the arms holding it. Dark fluids leapt from the gash and the creature recoiled, emitting a screeching wail as it did so. Within moments it regained its stance, lance pointing forwards and circled Zach. Knowing it would expect something similar, Zach knew he needed a different attack next. Before he could choose the creature lunged again and this time, although Zach ducked and dodged to one side part of the many bladed lance knicked the side of his head. Quickly lifting his left hand to his head he could feel the blood running down past his ear. Fully focused again the two combatants circled. Emboldened by seeing the blood, the tall creature attacked once more. This time a slashing attack at the end of a twirl of his lance above his head. Zach knew what he should do. He crouched without moving to the side and this gave him the balance and closer distance to bring his katana down in a rapid arc and cleanly sever the creatures hand that brought the lance down towards him. Immediately the creature wailed, and the lance was now out of control and stuck into the ground. Seeing his chance Zach brought the katana up in a return arc from the initial strike and cut across the creature's exposed throat. As he felt the blade meet resistance, Zach knew the fight was over. As he completed the movement, a shower of dark fluids cascaded from the gaping wound and the creature toppled silently to the ground.

Looking around again, Zach could see that the walls were now a sea of black creatures and some humanoid Others. Remembering the briefing, he knew that at this stage they were to withdraw to reform further into the city. He clapped other fighters on the shoulders and nodded his head towards the assembly point and the other guards nodded and moved away with him. Slowly the guards from the ramparts were also falling back as the dark horde continued to swarm over the battlements. As they ran to the assembly point, they could hear the screeches and wails of the Harpies circling above.

Plater found his newly acquired skill tiring. He seemed only able to generate a fireball every few minutes and he had to watch as the dark horde streamed towards and over the walls of the city. He managed three explosions of power before one of the guards grabbed his arm and shouted at him to retreat to the assembly point. Still exhausted from the last fireball, Plater stared back dumbly at the guard, who then hauled him from the platform and dragged him down the stairs, around the chaos that was playing out at the foot of the walls. Slowly Plater regained his senses and was soon running alongside the guard back to the assembly point, deep in the city.

The house had fallen eerily quiet. Molly was crouched on the landing watching the foot of the stairs and the shadowy hallway, straining to hear any sound from below. All she could hear was her own accelerated breathing and the dull beat of her racing heart. She gripped the heavy frying pan as if her life depended on it, the pain from her wounded fingers overridden by her very real fears of death. She wondered if she should try to barricade herself in the bedroom with Plater. Her mind racing to work out how she might do it. Without her phone, she couldn't call for help so any plan needed to realise that. It was just her and Clayton.

She knew he was hurt, but how badly? He had a gun. She'd seen enough movies to know it was silenced so probably not making enough noise to attract any help from outside. These and other thoughts raced and tumbled through her head as she strained for any indication of where Clayton was. Then she saw a faint shadow emerging from the living room door into the hall. He was moving in the same slightly awkward fashion as before; she must have hurt him she thought.

She decided to move back from the top of the stairs in case she could be seen from below but as she transferred her weight to her back leg, the landing floorboards creaked. She looked down. Clayton looked up. Molly knew he'd seen her so now only one plan remained. She ran the few steps to the bedroom door and once inside jammed a chair under the handle as she'd seen done countless times in films. Looking round she saw Plater, lying as he had been when she'd left the room. He looked peaceful, she thought. Then she heard the noise of the stairs and flattened herself against the wall to one side of the door. Moments later there was a loud bang and the bedroom door jumped and the chair under the handle scraped on the floor. But the door held. Another bang, Clayton was either shouldering or kicking the door, but the makeshift wedge still held. A moment later there were two staccato coughs and splinters burst from the door around the handle. This was followed by another bang and the door started to split open close to the handle. Two more coughs and another bang and the door handle broke off, the chair that was wedged under it careened away and crashed to the bedroom floor. Simultaneously the bedroom door pushed open and Clayton lurched into the room. Molly swung the frying pan with all her strength and it slammed into Clayton's shoulder. She couldn't know it, but the blow had broken the scapula in three places. Clayton screamed in pain and sank to his knees. Molly raised the pan for another blow, but Clayton turned and rammed the hand holding the gun into her stomach, knocking all the wind from her and making her crumple to the floor. Through eyes blurred by involuntary tears

Molly could see Clayton struggle to his feet. She saw him look down and see that she was incapacitated. He staggered a step to his right and felt his shattered shoulder with his gun hand. He grunted and moaned. Then he straightened and looked again at Molly. He moved his dragging leg around so he faced her and lifted the silenced Glock G19.

The assembly point for the defenders of the city was a square about a mile from the centre. As Gail and Bartholomew arrived, they could see that the General was already there speaking animatedly with a group of officers. As they made their way towards them, they could also see more and more fighters arriving, from all directions. A sign that the battle was not going well and that the dark horde had breached the city walls.

"General, I have located the command location." said Gail.

A stocky man of no great height, wearing a plain uniform with one purple badge on it turned to her.

"That is good, can you show me?"

Gail pointed to the location on the map spread out on the folding table.

"Alright." he said. "When was he seen there?"

"No more than fifteen minutes ago." said Gail. "I saw him myself."

"Good, good." said the General. "Are you able to help the other Present?"

"Of course General."

With that the General turned back to his commanders around the map and Gail and Bartholomew headed for one of the taller buildings in a neighbouring street to the square. In preparation for the attack the city had been divided into sections, A to H and Gail had been allocated section C to help with defence. Those others like her, the Present, were each given responsibilities to help a different sector. Their abilities, which varied wildly and rarely as effective or powerful as Gail's, would nonetheless greatly help the defenders.

By the time Gail had taken up her position atop the Court building the surrounding streets were already a battleground. She immediately set about taking out Harpies as they harassed the defenders on the ground. Bartholomew was unable to help but watched as Gail was able to generate ripples of energy that either caused the Harpies to fall from the sky or sometimes blew a wing off, or a head. Unlike Plater, this level of exertion seemed almost effortless.

To her right, there was a man standing on a building three or four streets away. He was also one of the Present, but his powers were not as refined as Gail's. He could produce fire but could not aim very well nor control intensity. Knowing this, he restricted his powers to blocking streets with fire and effectively funneling the invaders down narrow alleys to give the defenders on the ground a better chance to hold.

The woman who had met her contact the previous evening and collected the package arrived for work at the Chateau de Rambouillet, location of the G7 conference. Security was tight, with metal detectors and body searches at the staff entrances.

The guard asked about the expensive aftershave in her bag, but she smiled and explained it was a gift for her fiance. The guard thought for a moment then handed the bag back. The woman smiled and headed for the kitchens.

Antoine was always concerned about his appearance. He found the gay stereotype of men obsessed with their looks to be largely inaccurate, at least in his experience. He on the other hand was always proud to look his best. As he strode down the long carpeted corridor, he adjusted his tie such that it was properly central in his collar and shot his French cuffs to just the correct amount of sleeve showing beneath his Armani suit jacket. Just because he was a humble Hotel employee was no reason not to exude refinement, particularly at Le Grand Controle.

As he rounded the corner, he saw two large men in poorly fitting suits standing either side of the doors to the Necker Suite. One of them stepped into the centre of the corridor as he approached.

"Does the President require breakfast in his suite this morning." began Antoine. "As we have no order?"

The large man didn't know what to say and spoke quietly, behind his hand, so that the microphone could pick it up but the small man in front of him could not. A moment later he lowered his hand.

"An order will be made." said the big man. "Thank you."

Antoine turned on his heel and headed back to the kitchen. It seemed the President of the United States was sleeping in today.

Zach was starting to feel very dizzy. As he jogged

through the streets of the city, heading for the assembly point, he suddenly knew he needed to rest. He slowed and stopped by a half open door. He slipped inside and saw it was a shop that was empty. He sat down on the floor, leaned against the shop counter and felt the side of his head again. The blood was still oozing from the gash. He looked around and grabbed a garment that was for sale in the shop. He ripped strips from it and tied them around his head. The exertion proved enough for him to slip quietly into unconsciousness.

Grobus was afraid. This had already been his longest experience on the astral plane and it was all becoming overwhelming. The High Order were being kept together. They had been told they would serve a special purpose but what this was to be they did not know. They were escorted by several Others, who were humanoid and heavily armed. As the battle had commenced, they were close to the rear of the horde. They could see the leader, standing on a slight hill to the east, surveying the battlefield. As the swarm mounted the walls, they began to move forwards and by the time they reached the city walls the huge gates were open and they passed directly through.

All around Grobus could see bodies. Above his head the Harpies swooped and circled. He glanced at Nefer-Ra and was satisfied to see that the old man seemed equally scared. Their escort guided them to a wide street that seemed to run all the way to the very centre of the city, where the tallest tower stood. There they were told to wait. After some minutes, Nefer-Ra indicated for the members of the Order to come closer, and he spoke:

"Brothers we have been given a great honour. We are to kill the greatest champion of the enemies of our Lord. It is the woman creature we have been seeking. She is known to be on top of that building." he pointed at the city's Court building. "She is engaged in killing our Lord's servants as we speak. But we have the power, we have the connection, we can use the ritual of Memeth to bring down this creature and help the Dark Lord to victory."

Grobus felt proud. Was it not he that had managed to obtain a lock of the woman creature's hair? Such a powerful and personal connection would surely enable success and victory over the demon.

Their escort humanoids formed a protective cordon around the High Order although there were few city defenders left where they were. The members began to construct the circle on the ground and began the chanting as set out in the ritual of Memeth. To an uninformed ear, they sounded as if they were uttering gibberish, but it was an old, extinct language. Indeed, it was only known how the words were spoken through tribal memory, passed down through generations of members of the Order, by word of mouth alone.

The General was pleased. According to his commanders, the huge, wheeled crossbows had managed to shoot down three of the Nue. They had only seen four, so only one remained. The Harpies were still a danger, but their numbers had been severely reduced, mainly through Gail's energy pulses. The archers were effective against the Harpies too, although it usually took many arrows to bring one down. With the help of the Present, they were holding the Others to a frontline several streets away from the central square. By funneling the attackers into the narrower streets and alleyways they were reducing the number of attackers faster than they were losing defenders. They had no real idea of the number in the horde, so the General was maintaining focus and not yet becoming optimistic about the outcome.

Gail was beginning to feel elated as she blasted another Harpie from the sky. This time one wing of the grotesque creature had caught fire and it had fallen into a grisly death spiral right in front of the Court building and crashed in a shower of cinders in the square below. Then Gail caught sight of a Nue. The huge, winged monster was gliding silently, high up in the dark sky. She hadn't seen one for some time and she had thought that the crossbows had shot them all down. Unchecked a single Nue could lay waste to the entire city so it needed to be destroyed. She determined to use her most powerful weapon against it, but for that she needed to bring it closer. For all her confidence and elation, she knew that this creature was inhumanly strong and although she had heard tell of these things, she had never faced one before. She glanced at Bartholomew but he had found a bow and was trying as hard as he could to help with the defence. His aim was not the best. His council and wisdom were more effective weapons in this struggle, she thought. Looking up once more she located the Nue, still gliding menacingly high above the burning city. Gail closed her eyes and summoned up a small fireball that she then launched with all her will towards the distant Nue. As she watched, the fireball struck the Nue without seemingly affecting it at all. Except the giant creature seemed to adjust its glide path and now seemed to be circling lower, as if looking for the source of the irritation. Gail began to prepare. The Nue fell into tighter circles and came lower and lower.

Gail began to feel strange. She was going through the usual mental processes needed to generate her power but there was a fogginess in her mind. She didn't seem able to clearly align her thoughts. She looked around, unsure of what was happening. She had felt this once before, when the occultists attacked her. She had been unable to marshal her consciousness and direct her energies. She looked up and saw the enormous shape of the Nue grow larger as it descended.

Grobus was struggling to recall all the words of the Memeth ritual, and he was grateful that the other members seemed to know it well enough. Nefer-Ra was leading the chanting and mixing substances in a deep earthenware bowl that sat above a fire. Strange smelling smoke wafted round the group and as the chanting continued, Grobus began to see flashes of colour in his eyes. The sounds of battle and the crackling of fires sank into the background as strange music floated to the fore. He thought he recognised Pan pipes along with a relentless drumming that seemed to synchronise with the pulse he felt in his ears and through his body.

Zach opened his eyes and for a moment didn't know

where he was. Then the cacophony of noise from outside brought him to his senses. He felt his head. The makeshift bandage was working, and his face was dry. He turned himself into a squatting position and peered over the counter and out of the shop doorway. All he could see was a number of humanoids standing swords drawn, and they seemed to be surrounding others in robes. He crept out from behind the counter, staying crouched and listened at the doorway. Alongside the clash of steel, the shouting and the noise of fires consuming the city, Zach could hear what sounded like people speaking nonsense. Peering around the corner he could see it was the robed figures, chanting. The words of Silas popped into his head again but this time he chose to ignore them and sprinted out of the shop doorway to engage the nearest humanoid. So quick was he that he managed to sever its head immediately. The other humanoids saw and moved to engage. Grobus saw as well, and he stopped chanting in fear. The robed figure next to him jabbed him with his elbow to urge him to focus on the work. Reluctantly Grobus resumed reading the words of the ritual but found it hard to concentrate.

Bartholomew was finding his attempts to help the defenders frustrating. He saw arrow after arrow miss its target and fall harmlessly. As he lined up his next target, he glimpsed Gail. She was looking unsteady on her feet, almost as if about to faint. Bartholomew cast aside the bow and began to approach Gail across the rooftop. It was then he saw the massive shape loom out of the smoke and darkness. The final Nue was now at rooftop height and fast approaching, skimming buildings a dozen streets away and catching chimneys and buttresses with its huge claws scattering rubble and debris in all directions. Bartholomew screamed at Gail in warning, still rushing towards her. The Nue was now over the square and the defenders below cowered as the huge beast suddenly appeared fifty feet above their heads. Bartholomew realised he was not going to reach Gail in time and launched himself towards her in a desperate dive. He smashed into Gail and they both fell to the floor as the giant winged abomination struck the Court rooftop with huge force. Its giant talons carved huge gouges through the roof and walls pushing masonry, timbers and slates aside and showering them to the square below. Gail and Bartholomew found themselves falling through the shattered roof and Bartholomew lost his grasp on Gail's waist as they fell. Gail found herself caught between a roof beam and a supporting strut and as the structure ruptured, she fell some six feet to the next floor. Masonry fell and rolled around her, but none struck as she lay in the dust filled silence.

"Raymond!" she called. "Raymond!"

Pushing herself up she managed to stand although she had a splitting headache and her entire body seemed to ache. Her vision seemed impaired, and she needed to support herself on one of the fractured beams as she looked around for Raymond.

Zach was encircled by four humanoids. He was adopting the classic pose of crouching with the katana curving above his head. Turning slowly to check on his opponents, he tried to remember tactics for melees involving multiple opponents. The four humanoids seemed unsure how to proceed themselves. Eventually the largest of them stepped towards Zach and swung a warhammer. Zach easily dodged the cumbersome weapon and quickly slashed at the leading arm of his opponent. He caught the arm and the large humanoid wheeled away in pain and dropped the hammer. Two more then attacked but both from Zach's eyeline, and he avoided their lunges with swords and rapped both their blades with one swipe of his. Turning to face them Zach circled his blade in an exercise pattern before stopping in a ready stance. The two seemed tentative and as Zach took a sudden step towards them they both dropped their weapons and ran.

As he turned quickly to where he remembered the last guard had been he just avoided a downwards strike from an axe. Such was the effort of the attempted blow that the humanoid was off balance because he missed. Zach was able to lift his blade in an upward curve, almost like a backhand shot in tennis and carve a gaping slit in the humanoid's throat. The robed occultists continued their chanting but one or two of them had realised their predicament. Nefer-Ra saw Zach drop the last guard and their eyes met. The flickering firelight glinted off the curved katana and what remained of Nefer-Ra's courage left him at that moment. He turned and ran. Grobus was not quick enough, however, and Zach cut off his escape. Not knowing what to do Grobus pulled out his ceremonial dagger and lunged unconvincingly at Zach. With a half step to the side Zach brought the katana down viciously and severed Grobus arm at the elbow. Immediately the katana began another upward curve and slashed Grobus' neck and carotid artery. He was dead before his body had hit the ground.

At moments of great stress, it is said that time can seem to pass more slowly. As Molly stared down the silenced barrel of the semi-automatic her only thought was that time was about to end. At that instant she heard two more coughs. That's it she thought, but then wondered how she could hear the shots that would kill her and then wondered how she could still be wondering how she could have heard the shots. Before she could make sense of it all the lifeless body of Wallace Clayton thudded to the floor in front of her.

"Miss James?" said a tall figure, bending to offer a hand. "I'm Paul, from the Home Office." He helped her to her feet and then pulled out a nondescript card displaying the Home Office emblem and some words Molly was in no state to try and read.

"Let me get you some water, or perhaps something stronger?" said Paul. "Are you hurt?"

Molly looked at Paul, then across as Plater, still peacefully asleep, despite all this. She almost wanted to laugh and instead dissolved into tears of relief, burying her head in Paul's shoulder. Paul gently laid a hand on her back.

It took Gail some time to find a safe way down to the ground in the shattered Court building. As she walked out into the square she looked around for Bartholomew and then suddenly remembered the Nue and urgently scanned the sky. As she turned around, she saw the Nue. Its giant form was bridged with one huge wing opened against the front of a row of buildings while the huge head and body lay in the street below. There were three large crossbow bolts buried in its body, looking as if they had come from three different directions. Gail felt huge relief but now needed to find Bartholomew. She turned back towards the Court building and began to climb over the chunks of masonry. After a few minutes she found Bartholomew. A single arm protruded from beneath a fallen, sculptured stone panel. The antique signet ring was unmistakable. Gail sat down and cried.

87

The three blasts on the horn meant that the final phase had been reached. Plater was becoming more adept at creating his fireballs and it seemed to him that each one was taking less out of him. The defenders of the city also seemed to be pushing the horde back. The fighters in Plater's area had advanced hundreds of yards since he'd arrived to bombard the horde with his fireballs. Even though, he still only managed one about every five minutes.

He knew he must find the General; the final phase would need all the unconventional weapons at the city's disposal. Plater told the guard commander he needed to leave and began jogging back to the square. As he arrived he thought he saw Gail but she didn't seem herself. Plater ran over.

"Gail, are you alright?" he asked.

"Raymond is dead." said Gail.

"Dead?"

"He died saving me." she said, tears welling up once more.

Plater put his arms around Gail and held her. Moments later she pulled away.

"It's not over." she said. "If we don't end it then Raymond will have died for nothing."

Plater's eyes met hers and he could see the old fire was back.

The General explained that the leader of the horde was seen approaching the city, evidently confident that victory was at hand. He was accompanied by his reserves, a modest force of mainly humanoid Others with a few Harpies. The General planned to confront him just outside the gates, but with only a few men, making it appear a last desperate stand. It was vital that the leader not escape back to the Valley so some sacrifices may need to be made. Those listening looked at each other, uncertain what the General meant. With that he began to move off accompanied by about ten others on horseback and around fifty men at arms. Of the rest of the assembly, the Present, including Gail and for this exercise Plater, moved off in a different direction.

As the General approached the inside of the city gates, he started to appreciate the extent of the devastation. Hardly a building within direct eyeline of the gates was not ablaze or in ruins. He kicked his horse into a canter and passed out through the gates into the plain. In the distance he could make out some dust. That should be the horde leader. He looked over his shoulder and saw the horn carrier two riders back.

It did not take long for one of the Harpies to report back to the horde leader that a small force had left the city and was heading their way. Yes, the city was still burning; yes, the horde forces were still advancing towards the centre. The leader considered the situation. This had to be a last stand, or perhaps an attempt to surrender. Either way they would destroy them. He gunned his horse on, raising his arm aloft and waving his forces forwards.

The General had drawn his forces up around five hundred yards from the city walls. He could see the dust cloud getting closer and soon could make out the movement of the dark mass of the Others. Almost immediately, the Harpies began swooping from the sky. The few archers with them began to fire but many of the Harpies found targets on the ground. Men at arms swung their swords as the grotesques tried to slash and grab with their talons. After some time, the Harpies withdrew, and the General looked around. He saw more fallen men along with three Harpies. He needed the plan to work.

The advancing Others were now clearly visible and the city guard stood ready, forming as best they could a wall of shields. The General's horse tossed its head from side to side as if eager for the battle to commence. As the first humanoid Others got within a hundred yards of the shield wall the General gave his signal. The horn carrier blew as hard as he could, and the horn's insistent note rang out across the plain. As it did so the horde leader looked around warily, then began to mutter chants in an increasingly loud voice.

A new sound could be heard alongside the clang of steel as the foot soldiers clashed across the shield wall. A low rumble, slowly growing louder until it was unmistakably the sound of horses, many, many horses.

At that moment the city's cavalry converged on the horde reserves from both flanks. The crashing, crunching and screaming was raucous as the cavalry charge decimated the horde foot soldiers.

Just as the battle seemed over a huge bolt of lightning crashed to the ground in the midst of the city cavalry's First Unit, those that had come from the east. Such was the blast from the release of energy that dozens of riders and horses were flung outwards, in some cases their bones broken even before they landed. Almost at once another lightning shaft hit amongst the Second Unit of cavalry, those coming from the west, with similar carnage. The horde leader's obsidian armour was now glowing with an iridescent hue of many colours while his eyes were completely devoid of anything, just deep pools of black. Those guards closest to him had stepped back in fear for their lives.

As the battle continued seventeen more horses drew up on a slight hill to the west. It was the Present and Plater. Gail surveyed the battlefield and noted that the horde army was routed but her gaze was drawn to the intense glow which she realised was the horde leader. Before she could say or do anything, there was a huge eruption of energy from the horde leader which illuminated the whole plain for a second. Its focus was the remaining cavalry from the city and the General's entourage. As Gail and the others watched, a black void began to form between the horde leader and the city army. There was a crackling in the air and a massive wave of heat as the dark void grew. It reached the foremost horsemen and their screams added to the cacophony as they were swallowed by the darkness. As the cavalrymen saw what was happening, they tried to run but the void enveloped them all. The General, regal on his fine mount was swallowed where he stood.

Gail dropped to the ground from her horse and the rest followed. They gathered into a makeshift circle and immediately fell into deep concentration. Plater only knew part of what they intended but joined in as best he could. As he glanced up at the plain, Plater saw the dark void billow and then rapidly draw back towards the horde leader, now standing virtually alone. It was a surreal sight with the empty plain reappearing as the hideous void shrank. As he watched the void eventually seemed to reenter the horde leader's body. It was as if he had absorbed the city army into himself.

At a signal from Gail all of the Present placed their hands on the ground, their fingers and thumbs touching each other's to form a circle. Only Gail was not a part of this circle and she then touched one of the circle's heads with her left hand. She turned to face the horde leader and held her right hand out towards him. There must have been half a mile between the Present and the horde leader. As Gail held out her hand, threads began to emerge through her fingertips. Plater couldn't describe them later when he tried. These threads seemed to be displacing the reality of the Realm. Like rubbing out parts of a drawing and leaving a white line across the paper. The threads were erasing this reality. They snaked quickly from Gail's hand and sped across the plain towards the horde leader. After a few moments he must have seen what was happening as he spread his arms wide and the void began to grow once again from his body, this time spreading towards where the Present and Plater were gathered. Plater began to recoil at the advancing nothingness but could not take his eyes off the spectacle. The threads were multiplying as they spread from Gail's hand and resembled a badly made spiderweb as they came into contact with the growing void.

As Plater watched he had no idea what he was seeing but it seemed to him that the threads were erasing the void as they encountered it. More and more of the void was being absorbed by the growing web of threads and as Plater looked, he thought he could make out shapes beyond the web, shapes that weren't the plain, but something else. The web now covered around a quarter of his field of view and he thought he could detect a landscape through it. He certainly couldn't see the horde leader anymore as that area of his view was completely covered by the threads. At that moment all the members of the Present threw their arms above their heads and shouted together. Plater had no idea what they said but his vision was suddenly overloaded, and he had to close his eyes from the brightness. He'd brought his hands up to shield his eyes and as he cautiously peered through his fingers he could see the plain once more.

This time it was totally empty. No General, no city army, no horde army and no horde leader. He looked at the Present. Some were standing, most were sitting and one was lying flat on her back. Gail was standing, looking out over the plain, in the direction of the horde leader.

"It's finished" she said.

88

"Hey sleepy head, you've been out ages." said Angie as Zach sat up on the sofa and rubbed his eyes.

"What time is it?" asked Zach.

"You mean what day is it." said CJ looking up from her laptop smiling "You've been out for thirty hours."

"Yeah, if it wasn't for that thing in your head monitoring vital signs we'd have called an ambulance by now." said Angie.

Zach looked at CJ then Angie, his eyes were still quite glassy.

"A lot's happened." he said standing up and then thinking better of it. "Could I get a coke or something please?"

"So what happened?" asked CJ moving from her bench to sit beside Zach on the sofa.

"Yeah spill 'em." said Angie handing Zach a coke and sitting the other side of him.

"You're not going to believe it." said Zach still a little drowsily. "I could be a ninja."

* * *

Antoine pushed the silver plated trolley along the corridor and turned towards the Necker Suite but stopped dead in his tracks. There was a crowd of people by the double doors including what looked like paramedics with a gurney. One of the two men in suits saw Antoine and gestured for him to leave.

By the time Antoine had reached the kitchens and placed the trolley back in the rack someone, probably from the hotel staff, had posted anonymously online that the President of the United States had been found dead in his bed in a luxury hotel in France.

Carver's screen filled with Faith Cantrell's office and she turned to the screen.

"I assume you've heard?" she began. "Was that us?"

Carver allowed himself a smile.

"Actually no, it wasn't." he said. "Natural causes from what has been released so far. I had to call off our little intervention but this of course is even better."

"Damn right." said Cantrell. "Mind you I'm not too sure the VP is a massive improvement but at least he isn't the head of a cult with a messiah complex."

"Can we assume the black project will be canned?" asked Carver.

"Can't assume but it's more than likely. We'll monitor the situation our end, I have some contacts that can keep us updated."

"We do have very good news on our little research project. It seems we have made a significant step forward and the technology is even better than we hoped."

"Thank you James, I look forward to your next update

for the council. You have a nice day now."

"I think I will." said Carver and closed his laptop.

Plater lay on his bed looking at the ceiling. He had no idea what he thought he had just witnessed. He really wanted to hold Molly and stay in this world for a while. His view of the Realm had changed a lot. He'd thought of it as a kind of dreamworld where everything was fine and sure some weird stuff happened sometimes but otherwise it was benign. Well, that misconception had been well and truly dispelled. Suddenly, reality reminded him of the threat to Molly from Clayton. All at once, Plater's body stiffened and he pulled up into a sitting position on the bed. The sudden move alerted Molly, who was sitting at the foot of the bed and she turned.

"Good morning." she said.

Then Plater saw the body lying on the floor, it was the man Clayton. Then another man came into the bedroom, Plater had never seen him before. The man stepped casually over the lifeless form of Clayton.

"Ah, Mr Plater, you're awake. I've just made a pot of tea would you like some?"

Plater was confused. He looked at Molly who was smiling, which then became a laugh and then Plater started to laugh as well.

Braberson stepped into the empty lift and as the doors closed, he chose a key from his keyring. Pressing a floor button on the panel he also inserted the key in a slot below the floor buttons and turned a quarter turn to the right.

The lift slid silently down past -4 then -5 then -6, at which point the display above the door went blank. With a quiet whisper, the doors opened on the unnamed floor and Braberson stepped out into darkness. As he began to walk down the corridor lights came on automatically. He passed four featureless doors and stopped outside the fifth. A card reader and palm print reader granted him entry.

The small room inside came into view as a light automatically came on. Opposite the door was a window, beyond it more darkness. Braberson crossed to the window and more lights came on. In the bare room was a single bed, surrounded by medical equipment. In the bed Gail Hartston lay, motionless, on her back, eyes closed.

Braberson stood still, watching for a few minutes. He thought that this woman was now the most closely guarded secret in the UK. So secret in fact that apart from Carver no members of the government or military knew of her existence, including the Prime Minister. As he turned away and left the small room the lights inside turned off again within ten seconds. The only sound in the room was the quiet hum of the medical equipment keeping this most secret of weapons alive.